THE LAST SUNRISE

THE LAST SUNRISE

Robert Ryan

headline
review

First published in Great Britain in 2006 by HEADLINE REVIEW

An imprint of HEADLINE BOOK PUBLISHING

1

Cataloguing in Publication Data is available from the British Library

ISBN 0 7553 2188 X (hardback)
ISBN 0 7553 2189 8 (trade paperback)

Typeset in Janson Text by
Palimpsest Book Production Limited, Polmont, Stirlingshire

Printed and bound in Great Britain by Clays Ltd, St Ives plc

Headline's policy is to use papers that are natural, renewable and
recyclable products and made from wood grown in sustainable forests.
The logging and manufacturing processes are expected to conform
to the environmental regulations of the country of origin.

HEADLINE BOOK PUBLISHING
A division of Hodder Headline
338 Euston Road
London NW1 3BH

www.reviewbooks.co.uk
www.hodderheadline.com

This book is dedicated to Lorna MacAlister and John Debenham–Taylor, formerly of the Special Operations Executive, and to all those who, as crew or passengers, flew The Hump.

'The night sky is a celestial river; every man must find the one true star that will guide him along it.'

From 'A Meeting at the Summer Palace' by Yi Ping

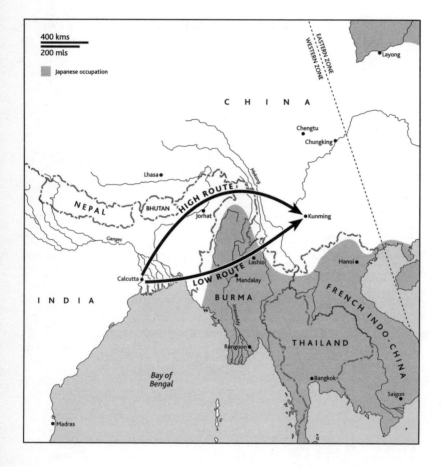

Part One

Elsa

One

Singapore, 1948

Three years after the city's liberation and they still hadn't fixed
the holes in Bras Basah Road. The four of us waited until the
stream of American cars, bullock-carts and rickshaws thinned, then
walked briskly across to Raffles, dodging the water-filled potholes
as we went. We skirted the corner onto Beach Road and turned
into the familiar palm-lined driveway. As we passed the Sikh *jagger*
he hesitated, looked us up and down like the RSM he probably
once was, then gave us the benefit of the doubt and saluted. It
was more than I got the last time I was in the place, seven years
ago, a boy with a fighter-pilot's swagger I had yet to earn. Then
the turbaned doorman had done his best to keep me and my rowdy
companions out.

   This time I had come to tie one on with Henri Raquil, a fellow
pilot and transport officer for Indo-Air, my Australian co-pilot
Mosh and Derek Jordan, the local agent for the airline, if you
could call it that. I had just announced to them that I was doing
the unthinkable: leaving the East. Jordan had insisted on a drink
to celebrate and, he claimed, to recover from the shock.

   We strode through the lobby and across to the Long Bar. Like

3

the rest of the hotel – like all of Singapore – it was looking tired and scuffed. The place had yet to recover from its time as a transit camp for the dispossessed at the end of the war. Still, I could smell fresh paint in the air and a poster announced the triumphant return of the Ray Macrae Orchestra every Saturday. Maybe things were looking up for the old girl. We parked ourselves by one of the frosted-glass screens, right under a fan which wobbled alarmingly on its thin spindle, as if it might fly off at any moment. I ordered bourbon, the others went for Singapore Slings. I'd never got my tastebuds round that particular cocktail. Now it seemed unlikely I ever would.

'Where to then?' asked Jordan. 'Back to Virginia?'

'Eventually,' I said. I unfolded the telex from my pocket and pushed it across the glass top of the rattan table. It was from Robertson, my skipper from the days of the American Volunteer Group, the AVG, when we flew over China in shark-faced P-40s. His telegram was terse and to the point: *Come Rhein-Main Air Force Base Frankfurt stop we need pilots stop planes stop good money stop great broads stop come soonest stop all forgiven stop bring soap stop*

'All forgiven?' queried Jordan.

'Private joke,' I said, ducking the issue.

'Soap?' asked Henri.

The table boy arrived with the drinks and I took a hit of bourbon. 'In very short supply. Like gold dust. I thought if you could get me a consignment en route . . .'

'Of course,' said Henri with a grin. I could see his brain working behind those crinkled eyes. Although he wasn't what you might call a handsome guy – he rarely shaved, had crooked teeth and a nose you could open a bottle with – there was something winning about that smile. I guess he had character instead of looks. He had come out East in 1946, after flying with the Free French in the war and then finding himself disgusted at the hypocrisy of his homeland when he got back to discover that every man, it seemed, had been a Resistance hero. He was also the best pilot in the airline, bar none. I'd seen him land C-47s on jungle clearings I swear were no bigger than a decent-sized pair of bloomers.

'I can give you that machine-parts lift to Calcutta, rice and tea from there to Athens, and a good chance of picking up soap in Greece.'

'Thanks.'

He lowered his voice. 'And if you don't mind using that little customs-avoidance bay we put in . . .'

'No,' I said firmly. Like every outfit in the Far East, Indo-Air thought the import and export rules were flexible enough to be bent double if possible. 'Legit only, Henri.'

Jordan, pretending not to hear, frowned and pointed at the piece of paper before him. 'It doesn't say what you'll be doing.'

I tapped my pocket where the second half of the telex was sitting. 'Does here. Flying into Berlin. The airlift.'

They all nodded. They knew there was trouble with Uncle Joe over there, that decent pilots with their own plane – and I almost owned a C-47 – could make good money.

'*Kan bei*,' said Henri.

It means 'empty glass' or 'cheers', and I replied with the expected toast: 'May all your landings be happy.'

'How do you feel?' asked Jordan.

'About leaving?' I asked and he nodded. 'I had to, some time or other.'

'Yes, I thought that once. I only lasted six months back in London. Not the same.'

'You get changed. And spoiled,' said Henri. 'You forget what it is like not to be an overclass.'

Jordan laughed. 'I'd keep your voice down, old boy. Communists everywhere these days. I think they are beheading the overclass up the road.' He inclined his head north towards the jungles of Malaya, where a Communist insurrection was brewing nicely. I scanned the bar for reds, but there were only two old guys at the bar in sweat-stained cream suits, a man and his wife sitting in frosty silence and a quartet of tipsy tin miners from up-country. None looked like rabid socialists to me.

'I shall miss you,' said Henri, raising his glass. '*Kan bei*. Good flying. You, too, Mosh.'

'I ain't goin' to Berlin,' he said quietly. I'd offered for him to come along for the ride. Mosh was my second best-ever co-pilot; I sometimes wondered what had happened to Cowboy, who still held onto the top spot, despite everything. Anyway, Mosh had said he'd think about it. I guess he had.

'Sorry, Mosh,' I began.

'Nah, no worries. Time for me to bale out, too. I'll ride with you as far as Dum-Dum.'

'I hear Berlin is a bit rough,' added Jordan. 'In terms of living conditions.'

'So was Rangoon when I got there,' I remembered. 'The rooms were just bug parties. They had this hotel-cum-restaurant-cum-whorehouse, where you could get a good meal in the booth, ask for a girl, have the screens pulled across . . .'

I let the words drift away and the trio looked at me, waiting for the punchline. There was no punchline. When sober, I'd been too scared, too indoctrinated by US Army Air Force doctors on the various ways my dick could drop off, to avail myself of the services at the Silver Grill. And when drunk . . . well, I hadn't learned to take my drink back then.

Yet that wasn't the reason why I had shut up. I was staring at the bar, at the woman in the black pencil skirt and white blouse, her head a cascade of red curls, her mouth as big and scarlet as I remembered it.

When I had first arrived in China, someone had told me that Elsa, who was married to one of the AVG admin officers, was the kind of woman who would make a dog strain at the leash. It was still true, and I found myself standing and taking a step forward, even though a more sensible reaction would have been to run screaming from the place. She had just collected a martini from the bar when she turned and saw me, no doubt gaping at her. But then, so was every other guy in the bar.

'Elsa?' my mouth said without being told.

As she came over, I realised I'd forgotten just how tall she was, nearly at eye-level with me. I felt a crackle of envy from my companions. That was when the martini hit me in the face, the spirit stinging my eyes, the vodka fumes filling my nose and causing me to splutter.

She was just turning on her heels when I licked my lips and said: 'You know, Elsa, I always had you down as a gin kind of girl.'

It was then she hit me. Not a girlie kind of slap, but a full-bore fist that sent me sprawling over a rattan chair. I bet it hurt her hand, because it sure as hell made my chin smart.

Without a word she went back to the bar for a refill, and I was aware of the stares as I pulled myself up. Henri had a bemused grin on his face; Jordan had the decency to look embarrassed and furiously stirred his Singapore Sling. Mosh just furrowed his brow, unsure of what he had just witnessed.

I pulled my damp shirt away from my body. 'That's a first.'

'And a fist.' Henri winked at me. 'Maybe it is just as well you are leaving the East, eh?'

I looked over but Elsa had gone. I wondered if she was staying at the hotel, if I could make some kind of peace, but I decided she had put her side of the story more eloquently than I ever could.

'What on earth did you do to deserve that?' asked Jordan, overcoming his chagrin at being party to a brawl, no matter how short-lived.

'I chose badly,' I replied.

'When? And what was on the menu?' asked Mosh.

I ignored him. 'I've got to change.'

'We can get a drink at the Swimming Club afterwards,' said Jordan eagerly. He was a member and so could sign drink chits for the likes of us. 'If you wish.'

I called for the tab. 'I'm done,' I said firmly. 'I'll catch up with you tomorrow.'

'But tell me this now,' said Henri impatiently. 'Is that the woman you are always asking around about?'

'No,' I replied. 'That's Kitten. She did hit me once, but she never tried to blow me up, far as I can recall.'

'Who tried to blow you up?' asked Mosh, baffled.

I thought that would have been obvious, but I still said: 'Elsa.'

Two

Following my ignominious slugging in the Long Bar, I spent the next day putting my affairs in order, getting ready to ship out of Singapore one last time. I also spent a lot of it trying not to think about what it meant that Elsa was alive. I honestly thought I had signed her particular death-warrant four years earlier. And if she was still walking this earth in one piece, maybe Cowboy, my old co-pilot, was too. I suppose I should have been glad rather than sad that I wasn't guilty of murder – no, make that manslaughter, Y'Honour – after all, but, given they might have a score to settle, it was a close-run thing.

I paid my bill and gave away my Zenith radio to the desk clerk of Dexter House, the favoured Indo-Air hostel that I called home when in Singapore. Raffles it wasn't, but I got a decent-sized room, two electric rings if ever I decided that cooking was a good idea – which hadn't happened yet – and somewhere to hang my meagre collection of clothes.

Indo-Air was the usual postwar South-East Asian hotchpotch. There were former Air Transport Command – ATC – flyers like me, a couple of ex-Marine boys, a few RAF and RAAF graduates, Mosh, who was an outback flyer originally, and Henri, the best natural aeronaut among us, all piloting a collection of demobilised transports such as the C-46 and my C-47, which the Brits called the Dakota and we Americans the Gooney Bird. I had scraped up the deposit to buy my plane at Calcutta's Dum-Dum airport in 1945. Now I leased it to Indo-Air, and paid off as much of the loan as I could each month.

We flew stuff around for the Chinese Nationalists for a while, mostly peasants going back to the provinces they had fled when the Japanese had invaded, and the odd missionary, dropping them into some steamy backwater where they would try to plant the Good Lord's seed.

The previous year, we'd done a roaring, if fraught, trade during the Indian partition, getting Muslims out of Hindu areas and vice versa. For those four or five months I always made my repayments for the Gooney on time. It also gained a couple of rifle-fire holes as well as a cramped smuggling compartment in the rear for really hot items – usually humans.

Meanwhile, my six months had become three years. Some day, real governments and proper airlines would come in and blow us all away, but for the moment it was a living. And there was always the chance I would find the woman I'd been looking for, for nigh on six years. Dead or alive, I just wanted to know what had happened to Kitten.

That reminded me. My room also boasted a loose floorboard where I could stash my old service .45. It was something else I had had trouble consigning to history, along with, it now appeared, dear old Elsa. For the first time in an age I took out the Colt and checked the action. It was still sweet.

Henri, scenting a juicy tale like sharks smell blood, came to circle me at around seven in the evening, still hoping to get the skinny on Elsa. I agreed to a beer and we walked through the streets in silence, our passage lit by the sulphurous glow of Singapore's aged streetlamps, to Lower Orchard Road. We crossed into the quieter side roads, where children played and adults gambled under the covered five foot ways. Every city has its characteristic smell, and that of Singapore wafted around us – a mixture of hot coconut oil, fried meat, incense and sweat, sometimes cut by the scent of frangipani. I knew where Henri was taking me. The Tashi, at the edge of Emerald Hill.

The Tashi-Delat, to give it its full name, was a long, low, single-storey house in a neglected garden, surrounded by ill-kempt palm trees with more than their fair share of brown, sagging fronds. It was colonised by those who had been blackballed from the likes of the Swimming or the Island clubs, with a large smattering of Australians, Kiwis and Rhodesians who didn't want to belong to such places to begin with. There was even the odd Yank: me.

The main room was divided into two by a waist-high carved teak screen; one half was a restaurant, which served a mixture of Malay and South Indian dishes and the kind of food the British liked – lots of duffs, puddings and watery curried soups. There was no polite term for it. The other half of the Tashi was a clubby bar, with secondhand padded chairs and sofas that gave it a sense of shabbiness and history that a three-year-old club didn't really deserve.

We sat ourselves on a button-backed leather couch, opposite a wall which was covered with racks of week-old British newspapers and dog-eared magazines such as *Horse & Hound*, *Punch* and the *Illustrated London News*.

A dozen people were at the bar, their conversation punctuated by over-raucous laughter at familiar jokes.

'I hear,' said one plummy voice, 'that there are entire islands in the Canaries where people are abnormal.'

'Abnormal?' asked his colleague.

'Yes.'

'Do you mean deformed in some way?' piped up a third.

'Good God, you know what I mean. *Abnormal*.'

'Sexually abnormal?'

'Queer, yes. Abnormal. Whole bloody island,' insisted the first speaker. 'Lanzarote, I think it is called.'

'Maybe we should send Boo out there.'

Boo, the Peranakan barman – half-Malay, half-Chinese – managed a thin-lipped smile which suggested he had fantasies about mass murder. There was a pause as two strapping Western girls came in, looked around, and left. Dancers, in all probability, at the Chinese clubs that paid top Straits dollars for well-boned 'big noses'.

'You want drink?' Boo shouted after them, but it was too late. Those girls could get a chit signed in any club in town, or at least any that welcomed women. Why would they bother with the Tashi?

I ordered an Anchor from the table boy and when our drinks arrived, Henri raised the subject that had been stuck in his throat ever since Raffles: 'Want to tell me about the girl last night?'

I rubbed my chin. 'Don't get on the wrong side of her.'

'I figured that much out for myself, my friend. Old lover? Wife? Someone else's wife perhaps.'

'You French. It has to be sex, doesn't it?'

'It is always about sex, Lee. You know that.'

No, sometimes it was about money, I thought, but I just nodded. 'I was—'

'Henri!' a voice barked and we both turned to look at the stooped figure hovering over us. 'How are you?'

'Fine. Bill Clarke, Lee Crane.'

We shook hands. He was in his fifties, wiry with muscular, knotted arms and sad, rheumy eyes. He sat without asking and indicated the bar. 'Those damn fools are driving me mad. Lanza-bloody-rote indeed. I'm going to move back to the Corrie.' He meant the Foreign Correspondents' Club on Orchard Road.

'Bill's a newsman. *Straits Times*. Been here since 1925,' explained Henri.

'The whole time?'

12

He nodded. Now I knew why his eyes looked like that. 'Right through Syonan-to.' It meant Light of the South: it was what the Japanese had renamed the city when they had captured it.

'Changi?' I asked tentatively.

'Changi.'

There, the invaders had held 30,000 people in a prison designed for about 6000. I took a hit of my drink, hoping I wasn't in for a long prison memoir. I'd heard a lot of them from men, women, priests, doctors, Brits, Aussies, Kiwis. None put you in a party mood.

'What about you?' he asked.

'The Hump,' I said.

'Lee,' spluttered Henri at my reticence. 'Not just The Hump. He was with the American Volunteer Group at first.'

Bill's reaction summed up why I didn't mention the AVG too often: legend had overtaken truth. He smiled and I thought his tightened skin was going to split. 'The Flying Tigers? I see. Regular John Wayne, eh?'

'I never saw the movie,' I said truthfully. I was searching for a trace of resentment in his voice. I knew what some of the British thought of the AVG. 'But I hear they got a lot of it wrong.'

'What did you make of your chap Chennault? I heard he was a glory-seeking son of a bitch who would roger anything that moved.'

'Yeah. I heard that too. You hear he saved the RAF's sorry ass in Burma?'

'Maybe,' said Bill, giving up on trying to provoke me. 'Maybe.' Just then, the table boy came over and went to fetch us refills and some spring rolls. Bill looked at Henri and pointed a bony finger in my direction. 'He a good pilot?'

'Almost as good as me,' Henri replied. It was a rare compliment.

Bill made a noise which suggested this was a satisfactory answer.

13

'A bite to eat?' he asked, gently prodding us away from confrontation.

'Here?' I asked suspiciously.

'Why not?'

'Don't get me started,' I said.

'Where did you have in mind?'

'Laozhiqing. The Dai place,' I said. The Dais had been a
minority in the Kunming area of China. Ethnically related to some
of Thailand's hilltribes, their cooking was a fusion of Yunnan and
more fiery Thai influence. I'd grown addicted to it while I was
with the AVG at Kunming.

Bill considered for a moment and said: 'Or we could pop along
to Anson Road later. Get a devil curry.' Anson Road was a collection of bars like the Gold Anchor and Captain's Table – the
sort of places where a European could pick up a cheap, clean girl.
A devil curry was a Eurasian dish of limed chicken with Coleman's
mustard: it was also a euphemism for a mixed-race woman. I
looked at his face, but was fairly sure his mind was only on food.

'I've got my tastebuds set on a Dai,' I insisted, just in case.
'Maybe see you later?'

Henri nodded. Bill held out his hand and I took it. 'Nice to
meet you, Mr Crane.'

The Dai restaurant was to the south of the river in Chinatown.
When I left the Tashi, I considered taking a trishaw, but my head
was buzzing slightly, and although the dense soup I was breathing
hardly counted as fresh air, I elected to walk. That was dumb.

Reaching the restaurant meant crossing the river, running the
gauntlet of the hawkers hoping for a final sale, all yelling at me in
Malay, the *lingua franca* of the street-traders. The vendors fell away
as I entered the dark alleys known as The Backs. These were short-
cuts between the streets of three- and four-storey shop-houses, each
one of which contained dozens of families and artisans living cheek-

by-jowl in tiny cubicles, all sharing one kitchen and a water closet.

These passageways amplified the sound from within the buildings, upping the volume of the gramophones playing crackly recordings of Fei-Fan He, the Cantonese opera star who was suddenly ubiquitous, the clack of mah-jong tiles, the heated family arguments, the crying of children and the hacking of tubercular lungs. I caught the soft smell of opium, briefly, and it was gone. If I strained my ears I could discern other sounds, the *pipa* song-girls trilling on the roof of the Great Southern Hotel, the wailing and drum-banging of professional mourners down on Sago Lane, the street where the old and feeble went to die, the vendors yelling prices at People's Park Market and the clack of clogs on cobbles. It was the soundtrack of everyday life in Chinatown's slums.

The first of The Backs gave way onto a gaudily lit street and I skirted past Frankie Lo's dancehall, with its enervated doll-faced taxi-girls peering from the doorways. Frankie was on the verandah as usual, in his luminescent Hawaiian shirt. 'Lee!' he shouted. 'You want dance?'

'Not tonight, Frankie.'

'Two for one.'

'Frankie, I can barely manage the one at my age.'

He laughed and showed his gold teeth. It was a ritual exchange. It had been a long time since I had sought the company of a taxi-girl.

I dipped down another section of The Backs, smoking a rare cigarette as I walked to help kill the smell of rotting garbage that accumulated in these passageways between the coolie quarters, where the feline-sized Straits rats chomped on the waste, hardly bothering to twitch a whisker at my passage.

I would miss this. Singapore might be a confused mess, but it was my mess. It spoke to me. So, in quieter voices, did Hong Kong, Malacca, KL, Saigon and various sodden corners of Laos, Burma and China. Going back wouldn't expunge them from my

15

soul. After all, back in the States, where was I going to get decent Across the Bridge noodles?

Then again, was the America I thought I was going back to still there? I always pictured Main Street with late-1930s model DeSotos and Dodges trundling down it, swerving to avoid horse-drawn carts. In my mind, Harry Manne was still serving sodas at Kranzi's to the same kids from my High School. I could taste milk still warm from the cow and smell cinnamon wafting from Schenk's bakery. My America was frozen in bright pastel colours and wide, welcoming smiles like Mrs Schenk's, but it must have been darkened by war in some way, just as I had been.

By now I had entered the final alley, the one that would bring me out onto Ambrose Street, where the Dai and a few other eateries were located. I was aware of the shuffle behind and to my left, and I tensed instinctively, but still I was unprepared for the sudden darkness, the feel of rough material on my face, the burlap pressing against my mouth and nostrils. I felt a cord tighten round my neck and panic welled inside me.

I leaned forward and kicked back, hitting air. I could hear only muffled sounds. I flailed once more, connected with something, then staggered, and felt myself fall into one of the carved security screens of the grander houses. It rattled and squeaked, but held. I spun around, rolling until my back was against solid brick and reached up to pull off the hood.

Something hit my hand with the dead weight of lead, cracking into the knuckles, and after the sharp stab of pain my fingers went numb. I was hit again, on the temple, and now all I could do was hold my hands up to protect my face. Metal smacked my left shin, and that leg buckled in agony. I started to pitch forward, and they got the money blow in right behind my ear. I hit the slime of the alley floor, a useless sack of Jello, my vision bursting with stars and lights that reminded me of the flash of tracer bullets across the night sky.

Three

'Get him in a trishaw. For God's sake, man, look lively. Over here. *Here*. Hey, you. Yes – here.' There followed a stream of fast pidgin I couldn't catch and some grunts. I felt hands under my arms and tried to stand, but it was as if someone had filleted my spine. My head was flopping backwards and forwards, and my feet were dragging. The voices receded again and I was hoisted into a vehicle. The sack was pulled from my head and I fell sideways in a heap, my temples pounding. I could feel something soft against my face and I let myself drift off again.

By the time the trishaw stopped and they lifted me out, I was aware that I had two companions, Henri and Bill. But hadn't I been alone when I was jumped? I stood leaning on Henri while Bill paid off the driver, and they heaved me towards a wide arched entrance, decorated with chinese characters and azuelos tiles.

'Where am I?' I slurred.

'Kampong Serani,' said Henri, but I was none the wiser. The name told me it was a traditional housing compound, but not one I was familiar with. 'Bill knows a doctor here who works late. If we are lucky.'

'I don't need a doctor . . .' I managed a couple of steps, and then let my weight hang on their shoulders, wondering where my muscles had gone. They took me across the courtyard, where lights burned in many of the low wooden houses. The tamarind trees in the centre of the compound were hung with lanterns, and a gaggle of young boys caught the hapless moths that fluttered around them.

'I don't need a doctor,' I repeated and managed to stagger upright and take a wobbly few paces away from them.

The boys stopped their sport to stare at the bizarre trio of whites arguing. I was aware of a swirling array of cooking aromas I hadn't noticed before – fenugreek and lemon, coriander and nutmeg.

'Christ,' I said. 'I'm starved.'

'You sure you are all right?' asked Bill.

'I need meat,' I said, shaking the fuzziness from my brain. 'Then I'll be good to go.'

'It's your head,' said Henri with a fatalistic shrug.

'Doctor de Souza—' Bill began.

Dr de Souza probably meant a police report, which could tie me up in knots I didn't want. 'A good steak,' I said. 'Cures most things.'

We stepped outside the kampong and looked in vain for a rickshaw or trishaw, so began to walk along Haig Road towards the taxi-cab rank. 'What happened back there?' I asked.

'After you'd gone, we saw what the Tashi had left on the menu and thought the Dai sounded like a good idea,' said Henri. 'Also, I realised you'd got away without telling me about Elsa. So we came after you. We saw them on you. Four of them.'

'What nationality?'

'Chinese, I think. Hard to tell in the dark. Bill waded in . . .'

'As best a man my age can,' Bill added. 'I think the police whistle helped.' He fished out a long silver cylinder and put it to his lips, but only mimed blowing.

'Well, thanks, guys. Dinner is on me.'

We made it to the taxi rank and Henri gave the driver the address of Moran's Steakhouse. As he climbed in, Henri said, 'They were probably a bunch of *tu fei* out to roll a lost sailor and you came along instead.'

'Yeah,' I agreed. 'Bandits.' Which shows you just how much of an idiot Lee Crane can be after a blow to the head.

I got back to the Dexter just after midnight, walking like someone with two wooden legs. I had stiffened up badly. I stood under the dribble of water that passed for a shower and stared down at myself. I looked like the foxing on old books, all yellow and brown splodges. I had decided to desert Asia, and she had reacted like a woman scorned by having me beaten up.

Well, she had convinced me I had made the right decision. It was time to jack it all in, to let the memory of Kitten go. If I could just earn enough money in Berlin to pay off the plane, then head back to the USA, I would pick up the pieces there. I just hoped I wasn't like some of those drinkers at the Tashi – stuck forever in limbo, not really belonging in any place.

I lay on the bed and a feeling of foreboding settled on me like a shroud. I tried to tell myself it was the coshing I had received, or bad memories brought on by seeing Elsa the night before, but nothing would lift it. The sense of dread in the pit of my stomach deepened by the minute. Asia hadn't finished with making me suffer yet, it seemed to be telling me. What else could go wrong, though?

The realisation was like the sting of smelling salts. Painfully, I heaved myself off the mattress and pulled on my pants. There was only one thing it could be.

Singapore's main commercial airport in 1948 was to the east, across the river at Kallang, close to the city centre. However, Indo-Air and a few other cheapskate outfits rented hangars out at Changi. The airstrip had been built by forced labour – much of it from the prison of the same name – as a fighter and bomber base by the Japanese. There were rumours that the city's flight operation might be moved there one day and Kallang transformed into housing and offices, but for the moment Changi was reserved for the ass-end of operations. Which was us.

The cab driver took the coast road, past the dairy farms and the seaside village of Bedok, with its black and white bungalows and their little piers jutting out into the sea. Oily shark-protection poles jutted above the waves some way off. The beaches here had been the venue for the *Sook Ching*, the Japanese purification of Western influences and those who supported China in the war. In all, around 50,000 males were purified in the early days. Most were buried in the hills that backed the area, but hundreds were also dumped at sea. That is why swimmers needed the poles – sharks with long memories still came back to see if the good times had returned.

I got the cabbie past the Malay security guard by slipping him ten dollars – the security rules said he should have dropped me at the gate – and made him drive his Austin around the perimeter to the Indo-Air complex. There was zero activity anywhere on the field; even the coffee shop was closed.

In the weak sodium lamps that were strung around the hangars I could see the familiar shape of my plane, *Myra Belle Starr II*. I told the driver to swing round in front of it. I was out before he had stopped and ran across towards her. There was no sign of Tommy Kwik, the chief mechanic, or any other personnel. A dog yapped and snarled from within one of the open sheds, but I knew it was chained up.

I was immediately aware that something was amiss from the way *Myra* was sitting, sort of hunkered down, rather than in the haughty, can-do, nose-up attitude I was so used to.

20

I knew why when I walked under the wing. My C-47 had slumped down on her undercarriage spars to the concrete, the big balloon tyres spread out beneath them. Somebody had slashed my Goodriches, but good. I knew a couple of things for sure now. That tussle in Chinatown had been no bandit attack: I had been their intended target. Somebody didn't want me leaving Singapore in a hurry. Someone, I suspected, from my chequered past who had finally caught up with me.

Part Two

Kitten

Four

Burma, 1941

Mingaladon airfield, just outside Rangoon, reeked of sweat, sewage and aviation fuel. The odour made AVG Wingman Lee Nathan Bedford Forrest Crane nauseous. His head hurt so bad he could barely squint, his face itched from bugbites and his intestines were rumbling like a storm drain. Drinking at the Silver Grill had been a mistake; topping it up with hooch of unknown origin back at the AVG hostel had been something close to suicide.

The previous night was coming in jerky flashback. He'd woken up alone on his cot, the mosquito net in disarray, which helped explain the red weals on his neck and ankles. His room-mate Lance Harper, a young God-fearing Georgia boy, had been snoring the sleep of the innocent, his net neatly tucked in at all sides. Lucky stiff.

Still, he'd done it. That was all that counted, even if it was with a *bo-kadaw*. Another landmark in his life had passed. A virgin no more.

He could do with going back to bed, allowing himself half a day to shake off such a humdinger of a hangover. Instead, he had to fly a P-40 – sometimes known as the Tomahawk – for only the fifth time and make it look good for his new Wing Leader.

Crane, Parkes, Wright and Harper – the AVG's latest recruits – were crouched outside the hangar of the Flight Test Area while Carl Robertson gave them a briefing. Robertson was a man with enviable combat experience, blooded in Spain fighting for the Republicans, but he was considered too old to be a fighter pilot by the regular USAAF. Which is how the craggy veteran with the steel-grey buzzcut ended up as a wing leader for the AVG, fighting for the Chinese.

'OK, listen up,' said Robertson. 'Eventually, as you know, we'll be grouping at Kunming in China. First, we're going to fly these Tomahawks to a base called Kyedaw, near Toungoo. It's still in Burma, about one-seventy miles north of here.'

'Toung-who?' asked Parkes.

'Toungoo. You'll get used to the names. They get worse in China.'

'Is it better than this place?' chipped in Wright.

'Can't be hard,' added Crane.

Robertson took off his Ray-Bans and pinched his nose. 'I wouldn't bet on that. It's hot, it's got bugs the size of your thumb and there is no ice-making machine for a hundred miles in any direction. And it's crawling with stiff-ass Brits.'

'Shoot,' said Harper, using his most aggressive profanity.

'It's a timber town. There are six bars and one decent restaurant that's always full of limey jungle wallahs or RAF officers. Unless you can find yourself a nice Burmese girl who'll marry your sorry ass for the duration, the best bet for food is to throw yourself on the mercy of the American or Italian missionaries.' He looked at Harper. 'I think that's your department, son.'

'Yessir.' Harper had been born in Shanghai to missionaries who had taken him back to the US when he was four; he had been hankering, so he said, to see the country ever since he could remember. The chance to do that and stop the ungodly hordes of the Japanese destroying all the work the Christians had performed had been irresistible. Harper had already said that he would donate any five hundred bucks he earned from shooting down planes to the Christian China Mission, the foundation for which his parents had worked.

'Which reminds me. You just all been docked twenty bucks gold for bringing women into the hostel last night.' Gold meant it was US dollars, not 'mex', as they called any Asian currency.

Harper looked aggrieved. 'I didn't!'

'Across the board, son – even if you did not avail yourself of the facility. Understood?'

Robertson had to raise his voice as behind him a portly RAF Buffalo taxied into the heat haze, its prop wash snatching at his words.

'Not my decision. But you knew the rules, didn't you?'

They nodded glumly.

'Thing is, you're gonna have trouble flying when you got bad guts, and you will get bad guts, boys, believe you me. But flyin' with a sore pecker as well?' He raised his eyebrows and they laughed self-consciously. 'Just be careful. At least till the prophylactics arrive. OK, Wright?'

Wright smirked. 'Sure, Skip.' He was from Idaho, a raffishly handsome boy with a pencil moustache who had done a spell as a Navy dive bomber and had been recruited by Colonel Chennault's semi-official agents at Norfolk, Virginia.

'OK, we'll be flying following the railroad. You recall that in this neck of the woods IFR doesn't mean Instrument Flying Rules, it stands for I Follow Rivers and Rail tracks?' They'd heard it a dozen times already. 'There are no beacons, and the mountains mess up the radios. And anyway, you had RAF sets in there, which were pulled out so we can replace them with our own. Trouble is, the sets got sent to Toungoo ahead of us. So this is also a case of YFM – You Follow Me flying. Got that? OK. Let's go then.'

'Is there anything good about this Toungoo?' Crane asked.

Robertson hesitated. 'Yeah. Man called Ron Cross up there has got a wife that would make a dog strain at the leash. A word of warning. Don't bother. She'll bite it off. Right, let's see what you can do. But let me remind you: one week ago these planes were in boxes, and a week before that, they were on the high seas. I suggest you don't stint on the visual checks, gentlemen.'

'What about guns?' asked Harper. 'Can we test those on the way?'

'No,' Robertson said, a hint of derision in his voice. He hooked a thumb over his shoulder, pointing at the row of parked British Blenheim bombers. The twin-engined planes looked ugly, vulnerable and outmoded. 'Our fearsome allies are frightened the Japs might hear and come runnin'.'

'Bring them on,' said Parkes softly.

Robertson caught it and allowed himself a smile. No good denying what they were all here for. 'Yeah, son, bring 'em on.'

As they walked towards the planes, Crane said to Harper: 'I'm sorry you got hit with the fine.'

Harper shrugged.

'I mean, it's not like you had any of the fun.'

'Nor you,' he replied.

'What?' Crane bristled. 'Felt like fun to me.'

'You came in and fell into bed. Ripping the net. You didn't have no girl with you. Didn't look like much fun to me.'

Crane heard Parkes behind him, chuckling.

'No, no. I had . . . I was with . . .' He tried to remember.

'You were by yourself. It's the gospel truth.'

'Gospel?'

'Absolute gospel.'

Crane reached his Tomahawk and touched the wing, burning his fingertips. It was that kind of day: a hangover and nothing to show for it but twenty bucks lighter. It was then that he noticed Parkes's little dance. The former flying-boat pilot was scratching himself as he went, pulling away his flight suit from the crotch region and bouncing from foot to foot. Well, perhaps twenty dollars gold was a small price to pay. Hell, he couldn't even recall what any of the women he had danced with in the rec room looked like. It would be a good idea to be able to remember the face of your first girl, he figured, even if she was a *bo-kadaw*.

He walked over to where Harper was performing his visual on the P-40 and waved two tens at him.

'What's that for?' Harper asked.

'I been thinkin'. You shouldn't have to pay,' said Crane.

'I told you, you didn't—'

'I know, Gospel. You said.' Crane grinned and pushed the money into the newly christened 'Gospel' Harper's hand with a force that suggested there would be no argument. 'But I would have.'

The five P-40s warmed up on the apron, each with their own newly painted fuselage number over the RAF 'sand and spinach' camouflage – a reminder that these planes were originally meant for the North African desert. Chennault's horse-trading in Washington had secured them for his American Volunteer Group, but nobody had told the paintshop.

Once airborne, they did two circuits above the patchwork of fields surrounding the aerodrome, before Robertson waggled his wings and headed off south, over the rectilinear pattern of crowded, garbage-strewn streets, across the giant gilded pagoda that was the city's landmark. The ragged formation looped back over the limpid brown river, the murky waters crowded with sampans and lighters, its banks lined with the various installations of the Burmah Oil Company.

Another turn, nosing the Tomahawks north once more and they

could see the dark ribbon of the railway line, heading off past Mingaladon and Haiwgo Lake. They moved into tighter formation, single file, climbing slowly but steadily, passing over the Up Mail train, which was belching a plume of smoke so thick it hid the loco and coaches beneath it. Crane checked his altimeter; they were at 5000 feet, just below the grey lid the sky had sealed over them.

Crane watched the cultivated fields slowly disappear under the march of creepers, climbers and bushes. This quickly gave way to the forest proper, a densely woven mat of green, interrupted only by the unnaturally straight scars of logging roads and the bald, blighted patches where trees had been freshly felled. In the far distance he could see a wall of ground mist, hiding the curves and jagged edges of the Karen Hills.

Ahead of him the four other planes mostly kept a level course, only occasionally swooping out of line, as if pilots and machine were eager to discover what they could do.

How different would it be when they went into combat? The bravado he had felt back in the USA, even as recently as Singapore, had slowly evaporated in the tropical heat. At home, the American Volunteer Group had been sold as an unofficial branch of the USAAF, a secret guerrilla force of the air. It was a daring and romantic concept. On the ground, it was clear that everything was seat-of-the-pants – accommodation, planes, spares, staff, food: all had to be cobbled together as best they could. There were times when six hundred bucks a month – plus combat bonuses – barely seemed worth it.

The thought had only just lodged in his mind when he saw Wright's Tomahawk dip to the right and start to roll. Crane quickly scanned the sky, his neck twisting this way and that, his helmet banging against the Perspex, the straps biting into him as he tried to move his bulk in the seat. What had spooked Wright? It could only be Japs.

Robertson hadn't seen the manoeuvre, and was flying on straight and even, with Parkes glued to his tail. Gospel had dropped perhaps 300 feet, but Wright was into a genuine evasive dive, as if he was going to seek cover in the tree canopy.

Crane began to weave frantically, hoping to throw off whatever was hunting them, and was relieved to see Gospel do the same. It slowed them, though, and Robertson's Tomahawk was shrinking, powering on towards a destination that was only fifteen minutes away.

Crane dropped a wing and saw clearly what happened next. Wright's Tomahawk began to turn, slowly at first, then with one quick, final flip she was on her back. The dive was shallow now, but the airspeed was still high, and when it went into the trees the explosion billowed red and black. Instinct made him want to swoop down and look. Commonsense told him to pick up the railway tracks and continue. A knot of twisted black smoke punched its way into the sky. There was nothing he could do for Wright now.

'And he just dived down?'

'Yes, Skip,' Crane insisted.

'Son of a bitch. Like he was spooked?'

Crane nodded, biting his lip to keep his composure, although he really wanted to cry. He had never seen a human being snuffed out like that before. It seemed so arbitrary and wasteful – not an enemy in sight, and still a man manages to die.

Robertson cursed under his breath. They were on the ground now at Toungoo, standing next to the planes that had made it, surrounded by the tick-tick of cooling engines, sweating in super-heated air that was heavy with moisture. There had been two good landings – Robertson's and Gospel's – plus one that was jittery but OK – Crane's – but the fourth involved a burst tyre, a torn wing and a bent prop. Parkes had forgotten he wasn't in a flying boat and tried to touch down fifteen feet too high. That plane now sat forlornly on the edge of the field, tangled in a stand of palm trees, wallowing at strange angles like drunken feather dusters. A few dazed jungle fowl had emerged from cover and were pecking around the twisted P-40.

'One plane, one pilot lost, another almost scrap,' Robertson said. 'The Old Man's gonna love this. Go on, go and report in. Tell Ops to get a ground search organised, see if they can find anything to bury.' He indicated a collection of teak and bamboo lean-tos near the centre of the X that made up the runways. Robertson whistled to one of the mechanics and had him walk over with him to inspect the wreck. He seemed more concerned about the damaged Tomahawk than he did about Wright, thought Crane. *See if they can find anything to bury.* Shit, would he be dismissed that lightly if he went into the jungle? Probably, he realised.

Parkes threw down his helmet and stomped on it in frustration. They waited until he stopped and looked up, panting. 'It was when I realised we were a man down,' he explained. 'I just . . . it shook me. I forgot about the height.'

Gospel said: 'Shook us all, don't worry about it.'

'What do you think is going to happen to me now?'

'You'll get a new plane,' said Crane flatly. 'Easier to get a P-40 than a pilot out here.'

'He's right,' said Gospel.

'What the hell do you think happened to Wright?' asked Parkes, picking up his helmet, re-shaping it and dusting it off. 'I mean, there were no other planes, were there?'

Crane shook his head. 'Maybe he just thought he'd see what she could do and she bit him back.'

Just as he said it, they came upon a Tomahawk on a crushed-stone taxiway being repainted. Outlined on the nose in chalk, partially filled in with red and white, was a fearsome mouth full of triangular teeth and, positioned to the front of the exhaust, an eye. The artist stepped off his homemade teak steps to admire it. He saw the three newcomers staring and asked: 'What do you think?'

'Very nice,' said Crane.

'What is it?' asked Gospel. 'A dragon?'

'A tiger, you klutz. One of the guys saw it in *Life* magazine. The British do it to their P-40s in the desert – to scare the Eyeties.' He indicated their planes behind them. 'Hey, for twenty bucks gold I'll do yours.'

They stayed silent. Crane batted away the flies that had arrived to suck on his sweat.

The painter wiped his hands and came across. 'Wingman John Sloebuck. People call me Bucky.'

They introduced themselves and Bucky pointed at Parkes and then the P-40 in the shrubbery. 'You the one that—'

'Yeah, that was me.'

'Don't worry about it. Probably get docked some pay, and if Chennault comes, he'll chew your ass off real good. But it happens. Shit, up in China we've lost more aircraft to each other than the enemy so far. So what about it?' He waved a hand at his half-finished snarl. 'The teeth? OK, ten gold, how's that?'

Crane nodded. 'Sure. Why not?'

'OK. Welcome to the Flying Tigers, boy.'

Toungoo was just as bad as Robertson had suggested. It was a town built of teak in all senses – the houses and its fortune, such as it was. The air was clammy and choking. There was dust and grit from the ragtag army of trucks that ground wearily through the centre towards Lashio and the main Burma Road into China, and thick black smoke from the trains that pulled into the rail terminus. Every surface was covered by brown powder from soft coal cooking fires and a fine sawdust that swirled from the giant sawmills that ringed the town.

The newcomers dumped their stuff in the AVG billet, a low wooden hut on the airstrip side of town. Despite the whir of ceiling fans, it seemed even hotter inside. Crane could just catch the smell of the latrines out back and the air was full of circling flies. They asked some of the AVG 'vets' – people who had been in the outfit all of several weeks and who were sitting in their shorts playing cards on a spare cot – where Parkes could tie one on. He wanted to drown the sorrow of totalling a new P-40.

'Mess'll be finished in a week, if you can wait that long.'

'What about the Gymkhana Club?' said one man, his mouth full of imaginary marbles as he feigned an English accent. 'For a nice chitchat and chinwag.'

'Or there is the hotel,' smirked another pilot, trying to hit some of the marauding flies with a Flit spray.

'Where's that?' asked Crane.

'On the main drag just up from the railway station. Two-storey bamboo building. Can't miss it.'

'I'd try and miss it, though,' said one of the more thoughtful-looking guys, who removed a pipe from his mouth as he spoke. 'It serves whisky, beer, gin, crabs and clap. Not always in that order.'

Gospel spoke quietly into Crane's ear. 'I think I'll check out the missions, see what is happening there—'

The new voice made them all spin. 'Is my useless husband in here?'

She was standing in the doorway, mote-laden sunlight streaming through her red hair, hands on hips that were wrapped in tight white jodhpurs. She looked the three newcomers up and down and dismissed them with a flick of her head and turned back to the card players. She pointed to the one who was sucking on his pipe.

'Monty, you seen Ron?'

'He's at the field.'

'He's not at the friggin' field. If he's under one of these cots . . .'

'Nope,' said Monty. 'Not here.'

She took a deep breath.

'He might be with that Colonel of the First Burmas. Something about airport perimeter defence . . .' suggested another pilot, but the bamboo door was already swinging shut with a hollow clack.

'Who was that?' asked Crane.

'That, gentlemen, was Elsa Cross,' said Monty. 'And as you might have guessed, no matter how much you want to see what's in those pants, you don't want to be in Mr Cross's shoes.' They were still laughing at this when the newcomers left to find something to eat and drink.

Crane, Gospel and Parkes picked their way down the hill towards the railway station, trying to avoid the rivulets of foamy, yellowish water issuing from the tightly packed thatched-roofed houses. Dogs snuffled around in the mud like filter-feeders, snapping at the chickens that competed for the best spots.

From doorways and verandahs the locals stared at them, mostly full of curiosity, some with obvious hostility. They had just reached the junction with a larger street, where the various effluent streams pooled and drained sluggishly away, when they heard the woman's voice behind them.

'Hey, boys. Wait up!' They turned to see her walking briskly down towards them. 'Hi, guys. Elsa Cross. Welcome to Toungoo. Just got in?' The voice was no longer the slash-and-burn weapon she had wielded moments before, but soft and smoky. 'Well, listen, the thing is this. How are your manners?'

'Just fine, ma'am,' said Gospel.

'Your table manners?'

'We don't slurp soup or nothin',' said Crane, cranking up his Virginia accent. 'And as long as we got a spittoon nearby, we're real happy.'

'Oh, stop it. Sorry, didn't mean to sound . . .' She waved it

35

away. 'I have a dinner with the British to attend and my damn husband has forgotten. I need a companion.' She indicated up the hill with her thumb. 'Someone who won't make us all look like hicks, like some of your pals up there.'

'Sure,' they all said at the same time.

'Oh well – uh, you go, Gospel,' said Crane.

'Hey, now wait a minute,' said Parkes. 'I'd quite like a decent dinner. Just 'cause he's a Bible booster, doesn't mean he gets first peck. We should toss, or draw straws or something.'

Elsa put her hands on her hips and frowned. 'You aren't arguing over who gets the prize sow. It's not like it's a date or nothing, boys. Oh hell, why don't you all come? You can get cleaned up at my place.' All three looked down at themselves, unaware that they needed cleaning up. 'I'll send a runner over to Kitten to tell her that there'll be extra places.'

'Kitten?' asked Crane.

'Kitten Mahindra. She's . . . well, you'll see. She's *sui generis* Kitten. This way.'

The trio exchanged glances. What did she mean, she was *so generous*? Still, they needed little encouragement to follow the swaying cotton-clad backside down the street, through the filthy clouds churned by the overloaded trucks en route to China.

At Elsa and Ron's bungalow on the fringes of town, she let them 'freshen up'. Crane shaved with Ron's razor while she explained to them the difficulty of getting Elizabeth Arden products in the jungle. There was Yardley for the Memsahibs, and Coty or Chanel for the Frenchies, but American cosmetics were rarer than ice in these parts. And ice was impossible to get, unless you nipped up to the American Club at Lashio.

While she kept up a torrent of talk from various rooms, the newly scrubbed AVG pilots sat in the living room on tatty furniture, letting Elsa's Number One Boy ply them with warm Mandalay Pale Ale. They waited, and when she emerged they leaped to their feet as one. She had reapplied her lipstick into a colour that seemed to flame across the room, her hair was tied back, and she had on a full-skirted sleeveless floral dress and a shawl round her shoulders.

'Here,' she said. 'Rub some of this on.'

Elsa threw a screw-capped container, which Crane caught. The Arden label was faded and torn.

'Don't worry, it's nothing sissy. My *pani wallah* makes it up for me. Keeps off the bugs.'

Crane unscrewed the lid and sniffed. He caught the faint aroma of decay beneath the sharp scent. 'What is it?'

Elsa shrugged. 'I asked her,' she indicated the doorway to the rear porch, where the Indian maid sat sewing, 'but it was all double Dutch to me. Plant extracts, I think. Forget it if you want, but Kitten's place is right next to a stream and pond . . . if you get my drift.'

They smeared the cream on their faces and necks and Elsa fussed, making sure it was rubbed into their skin. 'So,' she said, 'tell me your names again.' They did. 'OK. Forgive me if I forget them. Ron says I shouldn't get too fond of you boys, that you're all going to die soon anyway. Drink up and follow me.'

She swept out of the room, barely leaving them time to absorb what she had just said.

Five

'OK, Gospel, I expect you to remember this,' whispered Crane. 'Any time we are offered sherry from now on, claim we're tee-total.'

Gospel nodded his agreement, but Parkes knocked back the sticky brown liquid in one and grimaced. 'Oh, I don't know. I'm going to get a refill.'

Kitten Mahindra's house was much like Elsa's but four times as large, with six times the servants. The whole rear opened out to a vista of well-kept lawns and shrubs that must have taken a legion of gardeners to keep so fastidiously trimmed in a climate where, by all accounts, a walking stick would sprout shoots within two days.

They were in the lounge, the shutters open so they could see the light-show as the sun dropped behind the trees. It also gave the mosquitoes easy access. Crane was glad of Elsa's strange cream.

As well as the three pilots and Elsa, there was an English nurse in her thirties who was something called a 'matron'; a British Colonel and his willowy wife; two civilian Limeys in full evening dress, who worked for the McGregor Timber Company; Sandra, a lovely girl in her late teens with high cheekbones, and a planter's wife at her side who acted as chaperone; a Burmese policeman called U Ba San, who said little but nodded furiously and smiled a lot, and Kitten Mahindra.

Elsa had briefed them about Kitten on the way over. The local Indians, she explained, were a wealthy, entrepreneurial group, resented by the Burmese, who thought they were stealing the country from under them. Kitten was the half-caste wife of an Indian teak exporter, a man very well thought of in the business, who had suddenly died of a heart attack. There were those in his community who thought Kitten should have committed *sati*. However, when it came to self-immolation, the English part of her make-up was somewhat stronger than the Hindu component and she continued to run the business with the help of her husband's English partner, whose Anglo-Indian daughter was the one with the razor-sharp cheekbones.

Normally, Elsa had explained, there would not be an 'all mixed-up' dinner party like this – it took a moment before they realised she meant a cross-section of race and social class – but Kitten was funding the refurbished hospital which would be staffed by mostly American nurses and used by both British and the AVG. So it would be rude to refuse her invitation.

'Sholto Snelling. McGregor Timber.' The bow-tied Englishman with the swept-back dirty-blond hair held out his hand and Crane took it. 'Here to save us from the Japanese?'

'Do you need saving from the Japanese?' asked Parkes.

Snelling shrugged. 'Well, we are squarely in the frame here. Right on the Burma Road.'

U Ba San nodded once more, but his smile had faded.

'They'll have to get past us first, sir,' said Gospel.

'That's the spirit,' said Snelling, with a tone to his voice Crane didn't much care for. 'How many planes do you have?'

Crane shook his head. Two less than they did yesterday, that was for sure. 'Can't say.'

'Twenty or so, I hear.' The 'or so' made Crane think of Wright and his suicidal dive, and he felt something unpleasant rise in his throat. The chaplain had told them that if the search teams recovered the body there would be a funeral tomorrow, but that there were no caskets to be had unless they made their own or had them shipped up from Rangoon. Burial wasn't the Burmese way. 'Plus our Brewster Buffaloes and the Blenheims.' He paused and sipped his sherry. 'Not a lot, eh? I hear the Japanese have several *sentai* in Indo-China already.'

The use of the term for a group of three squadrons suddenly smelled peculiar, even to a newcomer like Crane. Would a teak exec know about *sentai*? Crane himself had only heard the word a week or so before. 'You're in the timber business are you, Mr Snelling?' he asked pointedly.

'Yes. In the business of protecting the interests of the timber business anyhow.' The Burmese policeman was chortling now, as if sharing a joke with himself.

Elsa was across the room on the far side of a low, intricately carved table, talking to Sandra and her fearsome chaperone. She caught Crane's eye and smiled at full wattage. He reminded himself not to get too dazzled; Elsa was another man's wife.

Kitten appeared behind Snelling. 'Shall we go through, gentlemen?' Snelling turned to offer his arm, but Kitten stepped forward, held out her crooked elbow and smiled. 'Captain Crane, isn't it?'

Parkes snorted, and Crane realised the guy was well on the way to being drunk. 'Wingman,' he corrected.

'Wingman?' asked Snelling. 'What kind of rank is that?'

'The kind that's gonna save you from the Japs,' slurred Parkes, and emptied his fourth glass of sherry.

Kitten gently pulled Crane free of the group and he inhaled her spicy perfume as they walked towards the dining room, where white-jacketed boys stood around the table, towels over their arms, and a dazzling array of silverware gleamed at each place setting. Crane felt hot under the collar when he remembered the part about table manners. His probably only went up to Thanksgiving dinner standard, and this was much grander than that.

Kitten leaned over and he felt her hot breath in his ear. 'Don't worry about Mr Snelling. He's no *box wallah*. He's a spy.'

'A what?'

'Shush.' She quickly stepped ahead of him. Crane reckoned she was in her early thirties, although it was hard to tell with that fine skin and those unlined brown eyes. She quickly shuffled some place names on the table. 'Here, you sit next to me, Captain Crane. I know, I know. Wingman. Such an ugly word. Indulge me. I'm doubly damned, a widow and a wog – or half a wog at least – but it means I can do pretty much as I like.'

Crane screwed up his face at the word 'wog'. He'd heard the British use it time and time again, and although he had no idea where it came from, it was clearly not a term of endearment. He gazed down at the rows of polished flatware glinting back at him from the table and swallowed hard.

Kitten learned over: 'Outside in, Captain. Just follow my lead.' Her eyes sparkled in a way that illuminated her whole face. They were full of mischief and humour and something else he couldn't quite place.

'YFM,' he muttered to himself.

They sat, and he placed the napkin on his lap, just as his hostess directed.

'What Snelling finds it hard to admit about the current situation,' she said, 'is that the Burmese don't like the British. They don't much like Indians, come to that, but they loathe their European lords and masters. Can you blame them? They come and take their oil and their wood and treat them like dogs. Of course, people like myself and Sandra over there,' she pointed at the pretty girl, 'are wogs too, but with a touch of the home country.

41

Thus acceptable in some circumstances.' She flashed a wry smile. 'Especially if we are giving money. Still wogs, though. If I'd tried to hold this party in the Gymkhana Club, well . . .' She clicked her fingers at one of the boys, who disappeared into the kitchen. 'So, with a proportion of the Burmese proving to be unreliable allies, Mr Snelling is here to gee along the hill people, the Karen to the south, the Kachin to the north, the Shan to the east, to fight for King and Country. If the Japanese come, these people will be his – what's the word? – guerrillas.'

Her voice was still low while the others were busy introducing themselves to their neighbours. As she leaned forward, he willed himself not to follow the line of her neck down to the small valley that signalled the start of her breasts.

'Surely, ma'am—'

'Don't you dare!' Her raised voice caused a few concerned glances, but her grin reassured the guests. 'Kitten. Mrs Mahindra if you must.'

'Surely, Mrs Mahindra, the Burmese don't want the Japanese here.'

'Don't count on it. Better Asia for the Asians is the thinking behind it. And listen, the local troublemakers have difficulty telling apart Americans, British and Commonwealth servicemen. There have been . . . incidents. A few brawls and some machete wounds. Have you seen the *dahs*? – the long knives they carry? Very nasty. Do you pilots get issued guns?'

'Yeah, we have a .45 each.' He indicated it was back with his kit at the hostel. 'Never really fired it much.'

'Do yourself a favour, Captain Crane. Carry it at all times.' There was a flash of kohl-darkened eyelid that he assumed was a wink. 'Just in case. And get some practice in.'

An ornate silver tureen was placed on the table and the lid removed to reveal a dark, steaming soup. With food served, the round robin of dull conversation began and his moment of intimacy with the hostess was lost for the rest of the evening. Crane was surprised to find himself saddened.

After dinner, when the cigars and the brandies came out and the women retired, Crane wandered away from the fevered speculation about war and into the garden. It sloped down towards the stream Elsa had mentioned. He couldn't see it beyond the reach of the torches burning on the lawn, but he could hear the soft hiss of water over stones. The air was full of the sickly scent of night flowers, cut with the all-pervasive smell of decay. The whole country seemed to be rotting down into compost.

He felt a tickle on his cheek and slapped it. The magic bug potion was losing its powers. He checked his watch. It was gone midnight and the realisation made him yawn. What a day.

He thought once more about Wright, the ghost at the dinner table nobody wanted to confront. They had never really got to know him, and now they never would. Would that be Crane's fate? One day, an empty bunk, the next a fresh face taking his place? He shivered at the thought.

He heard the pad of small feet on the grass and turned. Kitten held out a coffee cup. 'I guessed. Black, no sugar.'

'Perfect,' he lied, taking the fine china from her.

'What brings you out here, Captain Crane?'

'Needed some air, ma'am.'

'Kitten. And I didn't mean out here to the garden and you know it.'

He grinned. 'To Asia? To fly without the red tape they wrap you up in at home. They think I am too tall for a P-40.'

'That simple? No noble passions about freeing an enslaved people? Saving China for the Chinese?'

'I'm a farm boy, ma'am.' He sipped his coffee, making sure not to wince at the bitter taste. Two sugars and it would be palatable. 'But when I was a kid my pa took me to see the barnstormers

43

every time they came to town. I saw Ivan Gates, Claude "Upside Down" Davis, Pancho Barnes, who was a woman, and Wiley Post. They banned the circuses eventually as too dangerous, but they'd done the trick on me. So when a few years back President Roosevelt started the Civilian Flying Program, I enrolled. I was good enough to get into the Army Air Force but, they decided, two inches too tall for fighters. Just then, a man from China came sayin' as long as they could close the canopy over your head, you could have a P-40. That's it. I leave the politics to men like that.' He nodded back towards the dining room, where they could hear Snelling's raised voice arguing a point.

Kitten laughed at the disdain in his voice. 'You know, soon the British Empire will be gone. What will they do then?'

'Treat people with more respect?' he ventured.

Those eyes twinkled once more. Sexy, Crane thought, that's the other quality he couldn't get. Her eyes had that smokiness he'd only ever seen in pin-ups before. Or perhaps he'd had more booze than he thought.

'Where are you from, Captain?' she asked next.

'Virginia.'

'I do believe Virginia has had some of its own issues about race.'

It was Crane's turn to laugh. 'Issues – yes. My grandfather fought for the Confederacy in the Civil War. Only died ten years ago. That's pretty amazing, isn't it? I knew someone who fought in a war where single-shot rifles were the normal Army issue. Here I am flying planes with machine guns and cannons.'

'He was an anti-Abolitionist?'

'No,' said Crane slowly. 'Just anti-Yankee. Not the same thing.'

'Lee?' It was Gospel, peering out into the garden from the house. 'Lee Crane? We gotta go, buddy.'

'Coming.' He swigged back the coffee. 'Thanks, ma'am. Kitten, excuse me.'

'How long will you be here?'

'In Burma? Till we get radios and guns fitted. Then, some combat training before we ship out to China.'

'I do tiffin at three-thirty every day. You'd be most welcome. And your friends, of course.' She reached up to shoo a mosquito away from his face.

'Thank you. I'd like that.'

'Lee? Elsa wants to go.'

'Hold your horses, Gospel, I said I was coming.'

'You'd better go. You'll very quickly find that whatever Elsa wants . . .' Kitten let the words fade into the perfumed night.

'Sure. I'll be back to see you.'

'LEE!' Parkes bellowed. 'We're going off to the hotel. Wanna come?' It was followed by a loud belch and a mumbled apology.

Kitten shook her head, as if warning Crane that the hotel wasn't a good idea. 'On second thoughts,' she said, 'come alone.'

Tiffin at Kitten's house consisted of two sets of pastries, one savoury, featuring minced meats with spices, the other astonishingly sweet. The house was quiet, altogether more sombre than it had been the other night, the windows shuttered against the heat and dark wood furniture lending it an oppressive air.

Dressed in a more casual *kameez* tunic and loose trousers, Kitten welcomed Crane into her sitting room, offered him a bewildering array of teas – including grilled leaves with salt and sugar, the hill-tribe method – and pumped him for further information about himself, his family and America. When she had refilled his cup the second time, she asked: 'Did you go to the hotel the other night?'

'No. I got the impression that . . . well, that it might . . .'

'End in tears,' she finished. 'And stinging. And lots of oint-ment.'

Crane reddened. 'Yes.'

'You think me rather forward, I suppose?'.

'I'm just a—'

'Farm boy. From Virginia. Here, try one of these.' She pushed a plate of marzipan parcels towards him. 'You can't hide behind that out here, you know. One day soon you will be fighting with people who don't care if you are a farm boy or a teak salesman. They will want to shoot you out of the sky.'

Crane swallowed the tiny cake whole before he spoke. 'That's some pep talk.' He licked his lips. 'And some fine pastry.'

'Good. I make them all myself. Not much else for me to do.'

'You have servants and cooks, though.'

'Not today. Vijay and the others have an afternoon free.'

Crane coughed. 'Excuse me.'

'Bad chest?'

'Sore throat.'

'It's the dust and damp. Be careful. The bronchitis is very bad hereabouts. I will give you something for it later.' She rose and moved over to sit beside him and he could smell her perfume, a different, lighter one than on the previous night. He shifted in his seat.

'Relax. I am not some sort of black widow, drawing you into my lair.'

'I didn't think you were.'

'Not unless you want me to be.'

Crane licked his dry lips. There wasn't much he could say to that. 'Ma'am?'

'These are strange times, Lee Crane. People do strange things. I surprise myself sometimes.' She leaned forward and, with a minimum of movement, her lips brushed his. She sat back, the better to examine what response this engendered.

Crane blushed harder and ran a finger under his collar. 'You know, I am learning things real fast, but sometimes I wish there was a book on women. Like the Pilot's Notes you get with each plane. I don't reckon there is a section on this in the family Bible. Not that Pa showed me, anyways.'

From the corner of his eye, he could see a trail of ants, their abdomens swollen like tiny grapes, organising the removal of the pastry crumbs.

'No, I think perhaps other religions cover this ground rather better than Christianity. There is really only one rule out here, Lee. Be true to yourself, to what you think is right. I suspect you have a strong sense of what is right and wrong.'

He swallowed hard and suppressed another cough. 'Maybe. I hope so.'

Her dark eyes sparkled as she said: 'Lee, you are free to go. I don't want to lead you into anything you will regret.'

Crane managed to keep his voice firm and strong. 'I'd like to think I'm not the regretting kind.'

Kitten laughed at this. 'No, that comes with time. But try not to regret this.'

She took him by the hand, rose and pulled him up, and led him, still blushing, towards the rear of the house.

Six

Crane's head was full of sleep when he stumbled into the teak lean-to next to the airfield's Ops room that doubled as a classroom. All around him men cursed and scratched and protested at the early hour. Crane coughed, feeling acid burn his throat. He took a swig of the oily liquid Kitten had given him to soothe the membranes.

It had still been dark when the houseboy shook him awake and shoved a cup of tepid coffee under his nose. Now, thirty minutes later, the sky had barely lightened, and the classroom was unexpectedly chilly. In the week he had been in Toungoo, he'd forgotten what shivering felt like.

On the blackboard at the front of the room was a series of diagrams that looked like football moves. There was but a single word, in letters six inches high, and it was underscored with a scribble of lines: TACTICS.

Crane did a headcount. There were nineteen men in this batch for induction. It should have been twenty, of course. They were one down after Wright's suicidal dive.

He shuffled up a place as Gospel sat down next to him, clasped his hands together and began to mumble.

'What you doing?'

'Praying,' said Gospel from the corner of his mouth.

Crane shifted uncomfortably in his seat. His father had a pragmatic approach to religion. You praised the Lord if the crops did well, cursed Him if they failed. He didn't hold with praying.

Gospel's 'Amen' echoed around the room and several of the trainees sniggered.

'A man who covers all the bases. I like that.' The voice from the doorway had a distinct Louisiana twang. 'If a pilot wants to make sure the Man Upstairs is on our side, it's fine by me. Should be with all of you too.'

So this was him, the Old Man. Colonel Claire Chennault, former barnstormer and Army Air Force legend, now the saviour of China. He was shorter than Crane had expected. Both of the men who entered the classroom with him – Wing Leader Robertson and Ron Cross, Elsa's husband – were taller, but they seemed like pale shadows next to the leathery Chennault. His face was like a record of his life: tanned, weathered, and scarred in places, it looked like the bark of a gnarled tree. And just as tough, Crane had no doubt.

Several pilots started to struggle to their feet, but he waved a hand. 'At ease, gentlemen. Welcome to the American Volunteer Group. I guess you know who I am.'

On the desk he laid a stack of booklets and papers. He indicated it. 'My homework. Everything we know about the Japanese. Planes, tactics, intentions. It'll be your homework too, soon. But first . . .' He parked one buttock on the table. 'Who knows where we are?'

'Burma, sir,' said a voice from the rear.

'And to our west is . . . ? Come on, what? China? India? Wisconsin?'

There came no guesses.

'To the east? No? It ain't New York. OK, let's aim low. What's the capital of Burma?'

As they had all shipped through there, it was a softball. 'Rangoon.'

'And of India?'

'Calcutta,' said Parkes.

'Once upon a time, son. Once upon a time. Now, I know you all want to get up to Kunming and start earning all those bonuses you've been promised, and start finding out who is ace material and who isn't. Hell, I want you to get up there. And believe you me, the Chinese want you up there, toot-sweet. The Japs are bombing the crap out of the towns. But there are two things. One, I want you to know where we are fighting. I want you to be able to tell Lashio from Lanzhou, Chungking from Kunming and Kweilin from Shaolin. Then, and only then . . .' He pointed at the board. 'Tactics. I know you think it's easy. You find a plane, you shoot it down. Not here. We don't fight like the Brits. Whatever you see them doing, ignore it. The Japanese— Yes? You have a question, son?'

All eyes swivelled to Hodson, the kid with his hand in the air and the red cheeks. 'The British saw off the Germans in 1940, didn't they, sir?'

'They did. In better planes than we have and against an enemy that fought differently from the Japanese. The boys you'll be facing are no rookies. They've bombed and strafed this country for almost ten years. They are trained in ways you wouldn't believe not to let their fellow pilots down. Better to die than be shamed, that's what they believe. It's strangely difficult to kill a man who doesn't mind dyin', son. No, forget what you know about gentlemen duelling in the skies over Europe. This is a down and dirty war.'

He helped himself to some water from the desk, held it up to the light then put it down, untouched. 'By the by, you will all get the shits at some point. Then get them again. There will be a hygiene lecture this afternoon. Don't even think about skipping it. So, the battle for Britain. There is one similarity between us and what happened over England. The British were helped because they were above home ground. They baled out, there would be friendly faces waiting on the ground for them. They had bases they could get back to when fuel and ammo were low. The Germans were operating over hostile territory, at the limit of their fuel range, having to watch their own backs and the bombers. We are not in that game. We never will be. We are fighters, gentlemen. We are here to defend China. I will not throw lives away on bomber escorts far from home. I will have bases all over our corner of China where you can refuel and rearm. We already have an early-warning system in place, with sky-watchers at strategic positions to radio in reports.' His voice swelled in volume, while staying deep and resolute. He clenched a fist as he spoke. 'We will meet the Japanese and we will grind them into dust until they think twice and then three times about taking on Americans.'

Crane looked around the room, and he could tell from the gleam in their eyes that every man present would happily jump into a P-40 there and then.

'But there is a downside. You have a sorry excuse for a plane. It dives well, it has big guns. That's it. In fact, it dives so well it is sometimes hard to pull up – as I think one of your colleagues recently discovered. So we have to play to our strengths. That's why we are here in this classroom, to learn what those strengths are. But first . . .' he signalled to Cross, who began to unfurl a large map of South-East Asia. 'Let me tell you about China . . .'

For the next few days, starting at six every morning, Chennault drummed tongue-twisting place names into their heads. He had them chanting the sequence of towns and villages strung along the rivers and railway lines that would be their navigation aids. Once they could parrot those back at him, they moved on to identifying the dispersal fields his 'army of ants' – the Chinese – were building to provide emergency fuel and ammunition. Then he moved onto fighting tactics and his two favourite words: *hit* and *run*. Always gain height. Never stay in what he called the squirrel cage, the firing zone. Dive, fire, carry on going. Don't mix it up with enemy fighters. Never lose speed. Don't try and out-turn the Jap planes. Don't try and outclimb them. You'll be outnumbered, but not outgunned. Watch out for your partner. *Hit* and *run*.

More pilots arrived and he started the lectures all over again, so Crane and the others got the geography twice. It helped. There were air-raid drills, hours spent with the crew chiefs going over the pros and cons of the plane. And, at last, flying practice, dog-fighting with each other, followed by mock attacks on the lumbering British bombers brought up from Rangoon.

The evenings were mostly free to play poker, acey-deucey or try and rustle up something else that qualified as entertainment. Crane wanted to visit Kitten, but she had been very firm about evenings. They were out of bounds: it was afternoon tea only. So once they were dismissed for the night, Crane either drank in the new pilots' mess or studied maps and the Pilot's Notes for the P-40 and wrote letters home. He had no need of whoring, he told himself. He had a lover.

The other trainees suspected Gospel had secretly converted him to a holy and wholesome way of life, but he let them laugh. With too much time on their hands, trouble had already started brewing among the AVG recruits. There were brawls, thefts from the RAF car pool, vociferous complaints about the food the British cooks dished up – which Chennault backed – and more about the heat, the bugs, the women, the commanders, the droning guest lecturers who managed to make the idea of shooting down a Zero boring. Not that they really were Zeros, but with names like Hayabusa and Nakajima it was a convenient shorthand for any Japanese fighter.

One weekend Parkes, the flying-boat man, organised a tiger

hunt. Ten pilots went along. They managed to shoot one of the Burmese beaters, for which they picked up a hundred bucks penalty each. The space for the tiger skin they had made on the mess wall remained empty until someone bagged a wild boar.

Crane bided his time, kept his nose clean. As Chennault had predicted, he spent a couple of days laid up with stomach cramps and worse. He drank plenty of boiled water with a pinch of salt and ate small spoonfuls of rice and it passed. With all this, it was two weeks since their last meeting before he could get an afternoon free to make the journey up the stony street to Kitten's house once more, the air full of dancing yellow butterflies that captured his mood perfectly.

The sparrow-like *amah* who answered the door to him looked alarmed. Crane checked his jacket was buttoned and straightened his shirt, making himself as presentable as possible, but still she stood open-mouthed.

'I am here to see Mrs Mahindra.'

The woman nodded and slammed the door.

Crane casually stepped back on the oiled-wood verandah and turned to survey the street. Only a mangy dog, its neck swollen by a goitre, was looking at him, a thin line of spittle hanging from its jaw. Some way down the unmade road was a British staff car, with a Gurkha driver polishing the bonnet, but he didn't look up from his work. Overhead a Tomahawk performed a slow barrel roll and waggled its wings. It was looking for a fight, the wagging a signal it was ready to duel. However, it looked like there were no takers up there and so it continued its lonely patrol.

The door opened once more and it was Vijay, Kitten's head-wallah, dressed, as always, in immaculate white cotton top and trousers.

'Captain Crane,' he said, giving the *namaste* of clasped hands with a small inclination of his head.

'Wingman.'

'Wingman Crane, I am afraid Shri Mahindra has company,' he said, using her Indian honorific.

The knot in Crane's stomach looped so tight he thought he was going to throw up. 'Company? What kind of company?'

'You should have sent a message, sir. Perhaps you would like to leave your card.'

'What card? I don't have a damned card.' Vijay raised an eyebrow in surprise. 'Are you saying I can't come in?' Crane went to push him aside but the little man wedged himself in the doorway.

'Perhaps tomorrow.'

'Tomorrow my ass,' Crane spat out. His pride told him to turn and walk away. Something else pushed him on towards making a further fool of himself. 'Will you please tell Mrs Mahindra that I would like to see her at once. If that is not possible, then I am prepared to wait. All day and night if need be.'

A look of irritation crossed Vijay's normally imperturbable features. He nodded and closed the door once more. The dog still drooled, the driver continued polishing but the Tomahawk had gone, although a red kite had struggled aloft in its place, its invisible controller making it sweep in ever-widening arcs.

Vijay reappeared and finally the door was opened wide. With relief Crane stepped into the hallway, relishing the breeze from the ceiling fan on his face. He handed his jacket to the *amah* and followed the chief servant through to the rear of the house, where Kitten was sitting with two men. One he recognised as Snelling, the timber-wallah-cum-spy; the second, older man, with his swept-back white hair and a bushy moustache, was unfamiliar. He was in uniform, with an impressive array of ribbons over the left breast, and it wasn't hard to spot that he, too, was a Brit, and to guess that the car and driver outside belonged to him

Kitten smiled at Crane, but there was little warmth in it.

'Captain. What an unexpected pleasure. Vijay, could you lay another place for tea?'

Crane sensed the enormity of what he had done, even if he wasn't sure what it was exactly. Somewhere around him, protocol lay shattered in pieces. He had no idea how to put it back together. Chennault had been teaching them the ways of the Chinese, not the subtleties of tea ceremonies with the British in Burma. 'No. I don't want to interrupt. I just—'

'Yes?' she asked in a way that conveyed perfectly her anger and disappointment. She was dressed in a tunic and long skirt, both in an iridescent green. Even when her face was set hard against him, he thought, she looked lovely.

'I just . . .' No more words came. He just what?

She put him out of his misery. 'You know Mr Snelling, don't you?'

'Yes.' They shook hands.

'And this is General Donald MacLean.'

'Sir.'

The older man struggled to his feet and enveloped Crane's fingers in a fleshy grip. 'Pleased to meet you. One of Chennault's people, are you? How d'you like Burma?'

'Haven't seen much of it on the ground, sir. Looks beautiful from the air.'

The General lowered his voice and tapped the side of his nose. 'One of my adjutants who came here from Hong Kong described it as like living inside a giant fart. You get used to the smell, don't worry.' He gave a guffaw and the ends of his moustache oscillated. 'Well, have my place, m'lad. Mrs Mahindra, I really must be going. Thank you for your hospitality. Snelling – good talking to you as always.' He winked. 'Haven't changed my mind, though.'

While Kitten escorted General MacLean to the door, Snelling took out a cigarette from a gold case, tapped it on the lid three times and then lit it, blowing a thin line of smoke into the room. 'Your timing could have been better there, Crane.'

'I'm sorry. What did I interrupt?'

Kitten returned and the two of them exchanged glances before Snelling answered. 'There has been an offer of several Chinese divisions to help bolster the defence of Burma. Under the table, through unofficial channels. General MacLean is the C-in-C of Burma forces. We wanted to sound him out, see what the response would be from the regular army.'

Crane waved away the tea when it arrived, but Snelling held out his cup for the *amah* to refill.

'And?'

'Didn't really get a chance to put the case properly. The General said no thanks, and that was it.'

'Why?'

Kitten rapped the teak of the chair as she sat. 'Burma is British. Its oil and its wood are British. They think if they let the Chinese get a foothold . . . Well, there isn't enough oil and teak to go around.'

'But if the Japanese . . .' Crane began.

Snelling laughed. 'I am afraid the General and most of his high command think the Japs have no interest in Burma.'

Crane thought the man seemed more troubled than he had at their previous meeting, less sure of himself. 'But you do?' he asked.

Snelling sipped his tea and grimaced, as if realising he had overstepped the mark, confiding in a mere pilot. 'I hope nothing we say here goes beyond these walls.'

'No, Mr Snelling. Of course not.'

'The Japanese want to strangle China. The Burma Road is its main artery at the moment. Cut that, you cripple the war effort there. But the General thinks with the large garrison and the navy at Singapore and Hong Kong, they wouldn't dare touch Burma. A few months ago I would have agreed with him.'

Crane risked a glance at Kitten, and the set of her jaw more than suggested she was still furious at him. 'Well, my apologies for having broken up the party. I'd better go.'

Neither of them tried to dissuade him, but Kitten followed him out into the hallway. He relished the swish of material on skin as she walked. He wondered what she had on underneath. It looked as if he wouldn't be finding out. 'Really, Lee,' she said in a low voice. 'Next time, listen to Vijay. What were you thinking?'

He shook his head. 'I wasn't thinking anything. I wasn't thinking, period. I'm sorry. I wanted to see you. It won't happen again. Anyway, why do they have to meet here? You're not . . .' he indicated Snelling '. . . one of them?'

'A spy? Goodness, no. I leave that to Sholto.' It took him a second to realise she meant Snelling. 'But my husband was very loyal to the Empire. It made him, after all. He used to do some favours in return and—'

'You carry on the family tradition?'

A silence stretched between them, threatening to snap.

'Things are sometimes best settled over tea and tiffin,' Kitten said eventually. She hit him lightly on the chest with a clenched fist. 'Oh, bother. How were you to know? Can you get away tonight?'

Her voice was softer, and he felt a crawling in the pit of his stomach. 'Tonight? We-ell, I promised Gospel I'd teach him peaknuckle, but if you insist . . .' He couldn't suppress the grin that split his face.

'Good. Around nine then.'

'Are you sure?'

Kitten yanked open the heavy front door and the *amah* handed him his jacket. 'I will see you then, Wingman Crane,' she said, awarding him his correct rank with a sly wink.

He stepped out into the clammy heat of the day once more and skipped back towards the AVG hostel, whistling loudly, ignoring the top-knotted children giggling under their dark fringes at the lunatic foreigner.

The AVG had been split into three squadrons, designed to turn an amorphous force into tighter sub-units who would live, train and eat together. Gospel and Crane were assigned to the 1st Squadron, and although their new hostel was just as hot and cramped and bug-ridden as the original, at least they got to sleep two to a room instead of ten. When he had arrived back from Kitten's, still floating a foot above the ground, Crane flung open the door, sending the wall lizards scattering for cover, to find Gospel pulling on his boots.

'Where are you off to?'

'Same place as you. Night flying.'

'What?' blurted Crane.

'We are down for night flying,' said Gospel. 'You, me, four others. All of Green Flight. It's pinned up in the hallway on the roster board. Didn't you see it?'

'I can't do it,' said Crane, chewing his lip.

'What do you mean?'

Crane kicked the cot in frustration. 'Can't. Unable to. Not possible. I'm busy.'

Gospel hooted. 'Yeah? Do you want to tell that to Chennault or shall I do it on your behalf? When do you think the next ship to the States leaves?'

'Jesus fuckin'—' he began.

'Lee,' admonished Gospel at the combined blasphemy and profanity, with a shake of his head at the sad sinner. 'Please.'

'Sorry. Night flying?'

'Yeah. But first we got fifty lamps waiting at the alert shack to fill with oil and trim, because there are no landing lights. Best get started.'

Crane sat on the bed and put his head in his hands, his mood deflated. A thought struck him and he looked up. 'You think maybe Parkes would do it in my place? Or Bucky or Monty? I'd pay them.'

'The order was, Green Flight to report for night flying. Chennault and Robertson expect Green Flight. Not whoever goes to the highest bidder.'

Crane punched his pillow. 'What's the point of being a volunteer if you still have to follow orders?'

Gospel slapped Crane on the back. 'I thought you couldn't wait to get in the air. You told me that the "classroom crap" – your words – was boring the pants off you. Cheer up.'

'Yeah, right. Rustle me up a houseboy, will you?'

'Why?'

Between gritted teeth, he said: 'I've got to send someone a note.'

Seven

As Lee Crane hoisted the tin-lined coffin onto his shoulder he felt the material under his arm rip. His last decent khaki shirt, he thought. He steadied the casket with one hand and, on the signal from the chaplain, the pallbearers began to walk steadily towards the little teak church that sat at the edge of the jungle.

It was the fourth funeral he had attended in as many weeks. Four pilots gone since he arrived, five if you counted Wright. One plane simply exploded at 5000 feet, another bellied into the jungle, a third crashed on a night-training exercise, killing a boy from Idaho who had been in the AVG for a whole week.

Inside the teak coffin with metal liner, which had been specially shipped up from Rangoon, was the latest victim: Jimmy Parkes, the PBY pilot turned tiger hunter turned, they all thought, a damned fine pilot. He had been slated to move to instructor, to help train the thirty new pilots who were somewhere on the high seas heading their way.

But two days previously he had challenged Bucky's P-40 to a dogfight, waggling his wings aggressively. The other plane had accepted and they had swooped and dived first over the aerodrome and then out above the jungle. It became a game of chicken as they tangled closer and closer, until Bucky's prop had sliced through

Parkes's tail, sending him spiralling to earth. They found him still strapped in his cockpit, the lower part of his body smashed from the impact, the upper spookily intact, a look of bemusement on his face. The other plane had landed safely, albeit with a traumatised Bucky; it could easily have been a double funeral.

The quartet of pallbearers entered the church to a low drone from the out-of-tune organ. The pews were full. General MacLean was there, two whole rows of British officers and Snelling with representatives of the McGregor Timber Company. Then there were pilots and mechanics of the AVG and, at the front, dressed sombrely in black, Elsa and Kitten.

The bearers lowered the casket onto the trestle, bowed their heads to the altar and took up their seats. The organ stopped and an expectant hush descended as they looked at the chaplain. However, it was Colonel Chennault who walked past the coffin, laid a wreath of white lilies upon it and strode to the lectern.

His eyes blazed as he surveyed the congregation, the only noise the rustle of makeshift fans as the assembly tried to cool themselves with the hymn-sheets. It was hard for the Old Man. He had lost five pilots, and almost twice as many planes, to accidents. Perhaps, thought Crane, he was beginning to believe in the Burmese *nats* that Kitten had told him about, the folk spirits who heap mischief upon those who don't placate them with offerings. There was a *nat* for everything including one for dysentery, which liked flower tributes.

Chennault cleared his throat and spoke, the voice familiar from hours of talks and discussions, but with a tremulous anger in it now. 'Make no mistake about it,' he began, surveying the upturned faces, as if daring them to contradict him. 'This American hero died in combat . . .'

The British donated a case of Haig whisky to the wake, which took place at the International, a recently opened bar close to the airfield. It had quickly established itself as the 3ʳᵈ Squadron's favoured drinking place and, like most of the bars, had a section out back where you could take the girl of your choice. In fact, choice was very limited at the best of times, especially since it was discovered that Lily, the closest thing to a beauty the place possessed, had leprosy. Business out back became slack after that.

As a mark of respect there were no girls at all that day, just twenty-odd pilots and as many technicians again, sitting in the gloomy half-light admitted by the shuttered windows, all ripping through the British Army's finest Scotch. Normally the AVG segregated naturally into pilots and ground crew, messing and drinking separately. On days like this, the barriers were forgotten.

Crane sat with Gospel and Schlummer, his crew chief, in charge of maintaining his P-40. Ernie 'Daddy' Schlummer was from Detroit and had worked on car assembly lines before moving into aviation. He was short, tough, nearly thirty, with a wife and four kids back home, and Crane was ever so slightly scared of him.

'Nice service,' the mechanic growled.

Crane and Gospel nodded. After Chennault's eulogy, there had been several readings, two hymns, and a Gurkha trumpeter had played 'Taps', the famous bugle call, as the coffin was lowered into what was fast becoming the American corner of the Christian cemetery.

As Crane reached for the bottle of whisky, he felt his shirt rip once more. 'Goddam. Sorry, Gospel, but look.' He showed them the new ventilation hole under his arm.

Schlummer shrugged and indicated a neatly sewn repair under his own arm. 'You noticed the oxygen masks yet?'

'Slimy,' said Gospel. 'Why is that?'

'They are rotting,' said Schlummer, 'and so is all the rubber on the plane – the tyres, the tubes, the gunbelt feeds. It's the humidity and the heat. Looks like we'll have to rebuild each plane every month or so. If we can get the spares.'

'Jesus,' Crane breathed.

Gospel made a small huffing sound of disapproval.

'Tell me,' said Schlummer, as he knocked back his drink and pointed a finger at Gospel. 'You are a God-fearing man. How do you, y'know, square that with being here to kill people?'

'People die in the Bible, people get killed, there are wars,' said Gospel. 'There are bloody battles. It's a matter of being on the right side.'

'The winning side,' said Crane, and Schlummer laughed with him.

'Gospel's gonna be an ace, aren't you?' said Crane.

Gospel flushed. 'More money for the missions if I am.'

'I hopes all of yous are gonna be aces,' said Schlummer. 'I got fifty gold, two to one on Monty.'

'What about me?' asked Crane indignantly.

Schlummer smirked. It was actually bad luck to bet on your own pilot, but he assumed the kid didn't know that. 'Well, maybe I'll risk a single.'

'Gee, thanks.'

'Don't mention it.'

'Japs! Japs!' Daylight streamed into the bar as one of the mechanics held open the door. Sobriety swept over them in an instant, and Crane was one of the first out of the door. They shaded their eyes as they scanned an unusually cloudless sky. A cruciform shape was circling high above the town, like a tiny metal vulture riding the thermals, the sound of its engines all but drowned by the noise of a working town.

'You sure it's a Jap?' asked Schlummer.

'Twin-engined job. Could be a C-47.'

'It's not a C-47,' someone said. 'It's a Sally. A Mitsubishi Sally. Weren't you at that Limey's lectures on identification?'

'Hey – what kind of eyes you got in that head?'

'Shouldn't we go up and take a look?' asked Gospel.

'Be night by the time you got a P-40 up there,' said Crane.

'I'm gonna get me a Jap!'

'Yeah!' A dozen men began a sprint down the dusty street towards the airfield, the pack jostling each other to be the first to get a P-40 airborne.

Crane went to follow and felt a hand grip his bicep. Schlummer let go and said, 'Don't be too eager. I think we should thank our lucky stars he'll be gone by the time they get up there.'

'Why?' the pilot asked.

'The Japs know what they are doing. None of you do.'

'Yet.'

'Yet,' Schlummer agreed. 'The trick is, live long enough to learn from your mistakes.'

'Will I?'

Schlummer looked back up at the enemy plane. 'You pick your time and place, son, you will. This isn't it, believe me.'

Crane felt another tug at his arm. It was a runner, one of the young kids who hung around the airfield and hostels to carry messages between the various AVG and RAF buildings. Crane unfolded the note, slipped the kid fifty cents' worth of rupees and read the single sentence: *Come now if you can.*

He watched the others disappear around the corner in a cloud of dust. 'I'll remember that, Chief.'

He turned and walked as nonchalantly as he could on legs that felt like they'd been deboned.

'You do that, son,' said Schlummer to his back, a smirk to his voice, almost as if he knew where he was going.

Eight

'Lee, what is an ace, exactly?'

Crane pulled himself from the edge of sleep. 'Sorry, what was that?'

Kitten rolled against him and her body heat felt like it could blister his skin. They were lying in her bedroom, the windows tightly closed, the fan on full. The air was rich with smoke from joss-sticks and her sandalwood perfume. Crane pulled back the cotton sheet that covered them and examined the creamy body with its mocha-coloured nipples. She pulled the sheet back up. 'Don't.'

'I like looking at you.'

'Don't. Please.'

'Why do you want to know what an ace is?'

'Every time one runs into a pilot – at least an American – that's all they talk about. Who is or might be an ace.'

'Five kills,' Crane replied, batting away a long-stinged hornet which floated by. 'You shoot down five enemy planes, and those are confirmed by a witness or wreckage, you are officially an ace.'

'And that's what you all want to be?'

He laughed, thinking of Gospel. 'Some more than others. It's just a number, after all.' But he didn't believe that. Chennault maintained it was the equivalent of college graduation and a bar mitzvah all in one: the point at which you were taken seriously.

It was five days since the Japanese over-fly; as Schlummer had suspected, by the time the P-40s got airborne, the intruder was long gone. Afterwards, the Chief had had a word with the Old Man and the next lecture had included a part about how being too keen to rack up the tally, or pad the coffers with combat bonuses, could be fatal. Greed made you careless, blinkered and prone to mistakes.

'Let me ask you a question,' Crane said.

'Please do.'

'Why me? Out of all the guys . . . why me?'

'You make it sound like a slave bazaar.' She took her voice down to a low growl. 'Have him washed and brought to me!'

'You could have any guy you want.'

'Well, leaving aside that dubious statement, I don't think you should analyse these things. It was impulse. It felt right.' She kissed him. 'Leave it at that.'

He beamed at her. 'I'm just glad you did, that was all.'

'What?'

'Choose me. We should go out.'

'I beg your pardon?' she replied.

'We should go out.'

She gave a soft laugh and pinched him.

'Ow. I'm serious. We should go out.'

She pushed herself up the bed, gathering the sheet around her. 'Why?'

'I don't want you to think I only come round for . . . We need some fresh air.'

She pulled his face round so she could look into his eyes. 'You want to show me off, don't you?'

'No. Yes. I mean . . . if I did, where is the harm in that?'

Kitten blew out her cheeks. 'You don't understand, do you?'

'Understand what?'

She slid off the bed and into a silk robe. She padded across to the window and opened one of the shutters to let in some of the grey, overcast light. Then she sat at the mirror and brushed her hair with a silver-backed combing set. He watched the long, languid strokes with fascination, until it became clear she wasn't going to answer him.

'Kitten? What's wrong? Come on. What harm can it do?' He pulled on his underwear and his pants.

'And where would we go, the brazen man-eating Hindi widow with the young American flyer?'

'The Gymkhana. Pilots have honorary membership as long as we promise not to play billiards again.' After the third repair to the baize, the committee had taken a dim view of allowing Americans near their table. 'We could play golf. Or bowls.'

'I am afraid I play neither.'

'Nor me. Aw, c'mon. Please?'

'No.'

Crane jutted out his lower lip as he finished buttoning up his shirt. In the mirror he looked like a boy whose birthday had been cancelled.

'I'll tell you what,' she said, 'the day after tomorrow is the festival of Zayat-gyi Pwe. It is celebrated at the full moon by the local Pa-O, Shan, Mon and Karen tribes. There will be a rattan football match, a lantern procession at dusk and a puppet show. And *nat-ka-daws*: the wives of the *nats*. They will prophesy your future. We can go to that.'

Crane didn't want anyone predicting his destiny but he said, 'Great.' He approached her but she warned him off with a hairbrush.

'Shoo. Now. Before I change my mind. The day after tomorrow.'

Unable to suppress his grin, he left the room to track down Vijay and see if he could hustle a cup of coffee before he left.

*

It rained for most of the next twenty-four hours, a vicious down-pour from a featureless gunmetal sky, wiping out flying and con-fining them to the inside of a classroom that reverberated under the downpour. Crane bided his time, trying to hold onto the finer points of deflections shooting, and comparing stall speeds and turning circles of various aircraft.

By mid-afternoon on the second day, the clouds had gone and the roads were steaming as the puddles evaporated under a scorching sun. Parasols quickly replaced umbrellas on the streets and the colours were bleached out of the village by the searing light. As the burning disc finally began to dip towards the jungle and shadows crept across the streets, Crane, having checked he was not on the training rota, sprinted from the airfield to the hostel. There he dressed in his best khakis, newly made by a Chinese tailor on base, and hurried to Kitten's.

The town was unusually silent as he threaded his way between the shacks, apart from the clang of ceremonial gongs and distant drumming. Because of the tribal holiday, the sawmills had declared a half-day and fallen quiet, and only a small number of trucks ground through the sunbaked mud that had hardened across the main street. He passed several timber elephants, newly washed, oiled and decorated by their mahouts with bright ribbons for the holiday.

The usual perpetual, if chaotic, motion of Toungoo had given way to a more pleasing sense of lassitude. For once, too, the smell of cooking masked the aroma of human squalor. Many of the locals had donned their best *longyi*, a sarong-like garment of richly woven or dyed textiles, often stiff Mandalay silk. Others had broken out their finest turbans and beads or appeared to be wearing even larger conical hats than usual.

There were dozens of cocky little kites dancing in the sky, some clearly doing battle, swooping, jabbing and feinting at each other. Here and there they were joined by makeshift paper hot-air balloons, carried aloft by candles. Every so often one of these caught and burned, plummeting to earth in multi-hued flames. Crane looked away as they did so.

The beggars were out in force, of all ages and disabilities. Clearly, giving alms at festival-time was expected, and Crane scattered some rupees as he went, careful not to be too generous. It wasn't difficult to trigger a feeding frenzy, especially if you distributed dollars gold rather than mex.

He knocked on Kitten's door and was led through to the drawing room by Vijay. Kitten was also decked out in her finery, a sari of shimmering gold and green, with delicate glistening threads dancing all over it. As she stood, he glimpsed an inch of dark flesh around her midriff and his throat constricted. 'You look swell,' he said.

She smiled and Vijay muttered something in Hindi, but she shook her head, and he bowed and retreated. 'Shall we?'

The day was rapidly sliding into a grainy dusk. The kites were sagging from the sky as the breeze dropped and the first of the lanterns were being lit and hung outside the ramshackle homes that made up most of the town. A group of girls, their faces whitened by *thanaka*, powdered tree bark, glided by. Burmese men, lounging in rattan chairs, the foot-long ceremonial cheroots that they smoked on holidays dangling from their mouths, admired the young women as they passed.

'Where to?' he asked.

'Beyond the pagoda, at the cricket pitch. It's actually the original common ground of the village. Two or three times a year, they claim it back from their betters.'

Something in her voice made him ask: 'Are you OK?'

She looked up at him and smiled. 'Yes.'

'What was Vijay saying?'

'Why?'

'Well, I don't speak the lingo, but he sounded concerned. Does he disapprove of me?'

Kitten gave a little giggle. 'It's not his position to disapprove or otherwise. He's a servant. He was asking if I wanted a parasol. He's afraid I will go dark.' She touched her cheek.

He pointed to the fading orange slash in the west. 'But there is no sun.'

'Can't be too careful. A woman's skin should be as smooth as ghee, as light as milk, that's what they say is ideal. I fear I might disappoint them. Sandra, however—'

'Whatever colour you are is just fine with me,' said Crane.

She ignored the remark. 'Now, there will be food. Mostly rice. I hope you are adept at eating with your fingers.'

'If it's something other than British bully beef, I'll gladly eat with my toes.'

She threw her head back to laugh when the teenage boy dashed in front of them. Crane only had an impression of jet-black hair and staring eyes, but he heard the hawking from the back of the throat and Kitten give a gasp of disgust as the phlegm struck her in the eye.

'Why, you little—' Crane snarled.

'Lee, don't,' said Kitten.

She grabbed Crane's sleeve, but he pulled away. The boy was disappearing between the wooden shacks and he took off after him. There was a jeer from onlookers as he ducked into the alley, careering off the walls and kicking up splashes of putrid liquid. The lad turned left and Crane skidded after him, just in time to see him swerve right. He was in a narrow maze now, the ground, untouched by the sun, sodden with rainwater and effluent.

He picked up the pace as the alley widened. He could still clearly see the boy's white shirt, flapping as he ran. Ahead of him, the way was blocked by a shoulder-height bamboo fence, but the fugitive scuttled over it like a spider. Crane kicked some startled chickens out of the way and launched himself at the barrier.

It collapsed with a loud snapping sound and he found himself face down, in a heap of garbage. He leaped to his feet and carried on. The light was fading fast and he feared he had lost the boy until he heard a cry from his right. The kid had bowled through a family trying to light their lanterns, knocking a young girl over. He was crossing one of the roads, heading for another group of hovels.

Crane kicked hard. He didn't know when it happened, but somehow he had his Colt auto in his right hand and was waving it in the sky, ready to fire warning shots. Which was ridiculous. He wasn't going to shoot a kid, was he? The lantern family saw him bearing down on them and quickly parted. The boy stopped, turned and made a gesture with his left hand, which Crane doubted was complimentary. Then he spun on his heels again and took flight.

Crane wondered whether he should loose off a couple of rounds into the air, but he still had some puff left in his burning lungs and running in his legs so he sprinted forward, yelling, 'Stay still, you little—'

Crane didn't see the pig until it was too late. He hit it broadside, the impact scything his legs from under him. He tried to twist and break his fall as he crashed onto the ground, and felt the slide of the pistol jam into his ribs and the breath of hot gas through his shirt. Only then did he hear the discharge, a loud crack that made his eardrums spasm.

As he struggled up, the boom of the gun was replaced by another, terrible sound. The pig was squealing. Over and over it yelped its piercing wail of pain. Crane stared at it. The entry hole from the bullet was small and neat, but the animal had flopped onto its side, and pinkish foam was forming around its lips. The big slug had obviously inflicted some terrible internal damage.

As the volume of its agony increased, so people began to appear from the shacks around him, some of them exclaiming angrily when they saw the suffering animal. Already the kid was lost to view, and Crane knew he would never find him now. The pig began to thrash its stubby legs and he did the only thing he could think of: he put two bullets into its skull until the screaming stopped.

This time the sound of the shots seem to echo throughout the whole town, growing as it went, bouncing off the trees of the forest. 'You rascal!' shouted someone in English, followed by curses he couldn't decipher. Spittle flecked the side of his face.

Crane turned to the crowd, their faces a jaundiced yellow in the light from the coconut-oil lamps, and they all began shouting at once. He made to leave as quickly as he could, when he realised he was surrounded. Someone punched him on the arm. They were yelling at full volume now, baring teeth blackened into stumps or stained with betel juice. Another punch was landed.

Crane brought up the gun and pushed it into the nearest face, and discovered he was shouting himself. The mob took a pace back, but he felt something dig him in the kidneys. It would take only one decisive action and, he knew, they would tear him limb from limb.

Then, a voice even louder and firmer than the others boomed above the hubbub. Kitten elbowed the men aside and took Crane's free hand. 'Put the gun away,' she hissed, and he did so. She continued to address the villagers in a voice that seemed to resonate from her abdomen, calm and assured now she had their attention. Crane had just relaxed when Kitten spun and slapped him across the face as hard as she could. His eyes began to water, and his cheek glowed red. The crowd sniggered at his discomfort and Kitten led him, like a naughty schoolboy, back down the alleys, occasionally yelling abuse at him, until they were away from the trouble.

'What did you say?' he asked her.

'That I would buy them a new pig. A sow. And they would have piglets. I also told them you were a stupid American.'

'Thanks. Look, that kid—'

'Oh, shush. It was my mistake. Vijay warned me.'

'Of what?'

'Of the consequences of being seen with you. You are just vis-iting my world, Lee. I have to live here. I have been foolish. Oh, my goodness.' She put her hand to her mouth.

'What?' he asked, but followed her eyes to his left bicep, where he had been punched. Except it wasn't a punch. As he pulled the material apart and saw the glistening red of flesh beneath, like a bloody grin, he realised he'd been chopped with a long-bladed *dah*.

'You up to date on your shots?' asked Elsa.

'Yeah.'

'Shame. I'd quite like to stick a needle in your ass. See if it can put any sense into you.'

'Why?'

They were in the infirmary of the hospital where Vijay had taken him by pedicab. Elsa had cut away the arm of his shirt, cleaned the wound, and was now preparing to stitch it. She laid out the needle and thread in a steel tray and washed her hands, for the third time, with a foul-smelling green soap.

'Why?' she repeated. 'Because of Kitten.'

'It's none of your business.'

'Well, everyone has made it their business now. I don't know what she was thinking of.'

'It was my fault. The pig.'

'Not the pig. The whole thing. She should know better. Stick with your own kind – it's a simple rule, remember it.'

'Not too many Virginians around here, Elsa.'

'You know what I mean, Lee. Jesus. Look, things aren't too great between the Burmese and the Brits – even you must have noticed that – and now we are getting caught up in it. Shooting their livestock doesn't help. Screwing Anglo-Indians and flaunting it doesn't either. I should never have introduced you two. I wouldn't have done, if I'd known you were going to start—'

'I love her.'

Elsa's cackle filled the room. 'Oh, please, Lee.'

'I do.'

She pinched his chin. 'You are barely shaving. Don't come over all puppy-eyed.'

'I've never met anyone like her before.'

For a second he thought Elsa was going to join in the local sport of slapping a flyer across the face. 'I might be wrong, but I'd also guess you haven't screwed anyone before. Nobody that didn't leave you a bill on the pillow, anyway. Jesus. You'll be thrilled to hear this might hurt. I know I am.'

'Don't you have anaesthetic?'

She smirked. 'Not for pig killers.'

Elsa pinched the lips of the wound together, just as the wall phone made a shrill ringing sound. She cursed and took the call. 'Yes. He's here right now. I'll tell him.' As she picked up the thread once more, she grimaced. 'Well, that should take your mind off the pain. Chennault wants to see you in his office first thing tomorrow.'

Nine

Lee Crane was up early, but whoever had painted the new additions to his plane had stolen a march on him. He touched the illustration with a forefinger and it left an imprint. It was still wet. The cartoon was a fat, smiling pig with a red line through it, just where the tally of downed enemy planes were meant to be recorded, under the cockpit. Furthermore, his P-40 now had a name: *Bringin' Home the Bacon*. It wasn't quite the one he would have chosen, but it still brought a smile to his face.

There was movement in the shadows of the hangar, and Crane shouted: 'Schlummer?' But it was Gospel who emerged. 'You do this?'

Gospel shook his head. 'No.' He stared at it. 'Nice pig.'

'Yeah.'

'You OK?'

Crane clutched his bicep. 'Arm's a bit stiff. Might be sore for a few days. I have to go. I gotta see the Old Man.'

'We heard.'

'OK.'

'Lee. Good luck.'

'Yeah.'

*

Chennault sat behind his desk, reading Crane's file, occasionally making small grunting noises. Crane couldn't tell whether they were of pleasure or displeasure, but he could guess.

Eventually he threw down the documents and fixed Crane with a stare that could melt steel. 'Why in the blazes didn't you just pay for it, son?'

'I—'

'Damn sight easier than getting romantically involved. Especially for a pilot. Robertson says you are a good flyer – '

'Thank you.'

' – but not a team player. Can't have that. Can't have a man thinking about where his dick is going next rather than what is happening to his Wingman. You understand that, don't you?'

'Sir.'

'Nor can we afford to have the locals up in arms about us. The beater was bad enough; apparently killing a pig is worse.'

'Colonel, Mrs Mahindra—'

'Is going to replace it. And so are you, son. The family will get two pigs. One from your handsome ladyfriend and the other from the AVG – via your CAMCO pay-packet. Understood?'

'Yes, sir.'

Chennault took a deep breath and then a sip of coffee. Crane, who was still standing, hadn't been offered one. 'How many hours on the P-40?'

'Fifteen, sir.'

'Fifteen? Well, you'll do. You're going to Kunming, son, with some of your compatriots. It's about time we showed the Japs that they can't have it all their own way.'

'Thank you, sir.' China meant combat at last, an end to the cycle of classroom and rehearsal. He felt a tingle of anticipation and apprehension.

'Well, it's not a favour. It's partly because we need to deploy there and partly to get you out of here. You'll need this.'

From the desk drawer he took a silk scarf and threw it at Crane. He caught it and spread it out. On it was a series of Chinese characters. 'What is it?'

'Your blood chit. It says, in several dialects, that you are basically one of the good guys. You end up baling out over China, show that to the locals before they string you up.'

'Sir.'

'How's the arm?'

Crane flexed it. 'I can fly.'

'Good. You leave at midday. Flight of eight. Which gives you a few hours to pack up and say your goodbyes. You won't be seeing Burma again, son.'

There was no reply when he hammered at Kitten's door. He tried to peer in through the shutters and latticework of the walls, but all seemed still within. No fans turned, there were no voices from the kitchen.

He sat on the verandah and watched the street dogs amble by, snapping at each other irritably as the oppressive heat built. The occasional local glanced at him, then turned away. He wondered if being a pig-killer was like being an outlaw.

He had two hours before he would have to start the pre-flight checks on *Bacon*. He shuffled into the cooler shadows and peeled himself a stick of gum. After thirty minutes, Vijay appeared, a straw bag of provisions over his shoulder. If he was displeased to see Crane, he didn't show it.

'Captain.'

Crane let the promotion pass this time. 'Vijay. Thanks for dropping me off at the hospital.'

'You were patched up all right?'

'Yeah. I think she made the stitches bigger than need be, but it'll heal.' He pointed his thumb over his shoulder. 'I'm looking for—'

'Shri Mahindra has gone away for a few days.'

'Where?'

He shrugged. 'With Sandra. The girl from—'

'The dinner party, yes. Where?'

Vijay did not reply but squirmed uncomfortably. He did not want to lie, clearly, nor refuse information.

'Did she say anything?'

'She left you a note. I shall fetch it.'

Crane stood and paced the verandah until Vijay returned with the single piece of folded onion-skin paper in an envelope with his name on it. The language was formal and flowery and it took a moment to translate it into plain English. It basically said: *So long, good luck. It was fun while it lasted.*

The flight to Kunming, over jungle and mountains, was 700 miles, around the limit of the P-40s' range, and they landed on fumes. Once they had reported to the Ops hut, Crane, Gospel and the others settled into a hostel that was more comfortable than the one in Toungoo. There was better food, a kinder climate, fewer bugs and an ice-making machine. Things were, on the whole, looking up. They were so busy with drill and welcoming the other pilots who were making the jump from Burma, that Crane managed to keep Kitten out of his mind until a week after arrival, when they were woken by the air-raid gong sounding.

As they ran out of the alert shack to collect their parachutes and helmets, they saw Branski, the flight controller, waving his arms, slowing them down. He pointed at the *jing bao* pole, which indicated the state of emergency by the number of fabric globes hung on it, one being 'get ready', three, 'take cover'. There were none. It was a false alarm. Then they saw the ashen pallor of his face and realised something was wrong.

'I just tuned into San Francisco KGEI,' he said in a voice he was struggling to keep level. 'Looks like the Imperial Navy have hit Hawaii. Pearl Harbor. Yesterday.' The international dateline meant it was 10 December in China. 'There are reports of bombing in Hong Kong, Batavia, Singapore and parts of Burma.' The last word caused Crane's heart to jitter. Kitten was in harm's way.

The AVG pilots stood rooted to the spot, their sleep-befuddled minds unable to fully comprehend the enormity of what they were hearing. One by one, it sank in. The US had been attacked. The Imperial Army had broken out across South-East Asia, spearheaded by the bombers of the Japanese air force and navy. The war they had all discussed for so long in abstract terms that it was beginning to feel like a parlour game had begun. The Japanese were coming; now they were all in harm's way.

Ten

China, 1942

Above 20,000 feet, the single supercharger of the P-40's Allison engine struggled to compress the thin air, making climbing slow. Crane was up at 24,000 feet, the last few thousand feet clawed painfully from the Chinese sky. He was crammed into the tiny cockpit, his helmet, as usual, wearing a hole in the Perspex, despite him having removed most of the padding from the seat. This plane was built for smaller men than him.

Crane flexed his left arm. It was still sore from the tattoo one of the ex-Navy mechanics had put across his bicep to hide Elsa's handiwork. Only after he had sobered up had he even thought about the risk of blood-poisoning, but he appeared to have got away with a slight muscle stiffness.

It was bone-chillingly cold at this height, and Crane felt his head swim. He sucked in more oxygen, reminding himself to breathe. To his right, far below, a dozen little pale-green crosses moved through the heavens in a tight V formation, oblivious to the eight shark-faced fighters lurking in the sun above them. The striving to gain height had been worth it.

Those twelve twin-engined bombers – Ki-21s, known as Sallys, easily identified by their huge rudders – represented a total of six thousand dollars to the Tigers. And maybe an easy six thou. In the past few months since Pearl Harbor, the AVG had christened the Mitsubishi bombers 'Flying Zippos': all you needed was one good burst and *ker-ching*! The cash register rang up another five hundred gold.

On the ground, beyond the intruders, he could see the enemy's destination – Chungking, China's capital since Nanjing had been pulverised and overrun. A dark walled city sitting on its hilltop, just where the silver strip of the Yangtze curved, it was wreathed in smoke, not from bombs but from the cooking fires of its grim mud-and-straw houses.

On the river were raffish junks, looking as if they had floated in from an illustrated fairytale. They also looked as if they would burn real good. However, as they droned over them, the Japanese attackers ignored the tempting target. They were clearly following their usual tactic of passing the city and then looping round for their bomb run, which meant they could then power on straight home. Not this time, boys, thought Crane.

His headphones crackled and he heard a voice full of impatience. Robertson, the Wing Leader, barked: 'What are we waiting for? Jones and Gospel – you're weaving.' That meant staying on the high perch to watch their backs. 'The rest of you . . . happy hunting.' It was time to earn those bonuses. And up the tally. Like Gospel, Crane was at three planes confirmed killed; two away from being an ace.

Once again, he felt his mouth fill with cottonwool and the fear crawl up his belly. At first, he thought it was cowardice, but after a while most of the pilots admitted to something similar. Whatever it was, it kept them sharp and alive.

'Holy shit!' someone shouted.

Crane's Tomahawk was buffeted as a plane flashed in front of him, filling the armoured screen with a pale grey underside, the wings sporting unmistakable bright red discs. Crane pushed the stick forward and scanned the sky. He could see Monty Hendricks below with a Japanese fighter on his tail. Not one of the slow fixed-gear Nates, either, but the sleeker, newer Hayabusas they had been warned about. The jumpers had been jumped.

This was it now, they were in the squirrel cage, a packed combat zone, a cube of sky within which planes were climbing, diving, firing and rolling, ripping across the sky, vectoring every which way. It wasn't like squirrels at all, thought Crane, but a swarm of angry, confused hornets. He saw one P-40 trailing a streamer of flame three times the length of the plane. The canopy was sliding back, and Crane just hoped the pilot could get free in time.

He felt his own aircraft twitch as it took hits and he instinctively threw *Bacon* into a half-roll and pushed the stick further forward and let her dive, the G-forces pinning him back. If the new enemy planes were like the old, their lightness – achieved by leaving out such sissy American devices as pilot armour and self-sealing fuel tanks – meant their dive rate was poor. He watched the altimeter spin anticlockwise as he took her down towards the bombers, his eyes aching as they deformed in their sockets. The airframe began to vibrate, tossing him around in the straps, blurring the world below.

Crane had lost 8000 feet before the bombers' gunners in their little greenhouses spotted him and the wobbly tracers arced up, slowly at first then zip, they were gone. The sky seemed to be ribboned with fire. He yanked on the t-grips to arm the wing guns, and the panel handles for the nose cannons, and turned on the optical sight. He waited until he was within range and squeezed the trigger on the stick, his retinas burning from the nose-gun's flashes, even in daylight. He saw a prop falter on one of the Sally's wings, and a puff of white from the huge radial engine, a spindrift of debris, and then he was beneath it. As he levelled out, Crane glimpsed a Hayabusa slotting onto his tail.

He banked into another tight turn to starboard. The P-40 was low now, running out of sky. The old Nates couldn't out-turn a P-40, but as a round skidded over the wing, sparking as it went, he realised this new crate could.

He tightened the arc, his vision darkening and tunnelling with the Gs, as he felt slugs punch into the armourplate behind his head. Something burned in his shoulder, shrapnel probably, brass and lead shards, but there was no real pain, not yet.

Crane pulled her level for a few seconds, then stood the plane on its wing, throwing the Tomahawk over to port. *Bacon* turned on a dime, and Crane felt the airframe deform in protest. The periphery of his world faded to black, shrinking to a long, dark tunnel, until he was out of the turn, hoping there would be an enemy plane somewhere in his sights. His vision snapped back in, even as a thudding started in one of his temples. His head flopped around as he scanned as much of the sky as he could, ignoring the chaffing of his straps. Nothing. It was empty. He could see some wisps of black smoke which suggested there had been action, but of his pursuer and his comrades, there was no sign.

Crane reached over and checked his shoulder. He could feel bumps in the armour behind it, but nothing had penetrated. There was no damage to his skin. Once he was certain the Hayabusa wasn't playing him for a sucker, he began to pull back some height.

As he passed through 9000 feet, small black spiders appeared on the windscreen. Oil. Something had been holed in the engine. It was still turning sweetly, but leaking oil was never good. Neither, he realised as he checked the gauge, was running low on fuel. He dipped one wing, searching for landmarks, a river or a railroad he could follow. The hills all looked unfamiliar, and there was no sign of the city. How long had he been blacked out in that turn? It had seemed like seconds, but must have been longer.

'Skip?' he tried over the radio. 'This is Green Three. Are you receiving? Over?'

There was only the lonely noise of static hissing into his ears. Damn, he said to himself. Then, loudly, he cursed Jesus.

'Is that you blaspheming?'

'Gospel?'

'Up above you, Lee. Nearer to heaven, as always.'

He looked up and saw the Tomahawk shadowing him. 'Does that make you my guardian angel?'

'Maybe it does. If I manage to save your soul, there'll be a feast in paradise.'

'Am I invited?'

'I wouldn't be in too much of a hurry to get to the entrées, Lee.'

The engine temperature needle gave a little jerk and began to rise. At the same time, Crane felt a change in tone from the power unit, a roughness at its heart. 'I'm leaking oil here. You know where we are?'

'Kinda. Look at one o'clock, on the ground.'

Crane peered through the darkening windscreen and, between the fine globules of spray, could just make out a light scar in the midst of the green quilt of paddy fields. Crushed stones. One of Chennault's makeshift dispersal fields, as promised, where there should be supplies and a skeleton ground crew who could make running repairs.

'That is Sang-Lu, I reckon. We get you refuelled, patched up, see if we can get you home to Daddy. Drinks on you at Kunming.'

'How come?'

'Number four. I saw the Sally you hit go down. Confirmed kill, Lee. One more, and you are an ace.'

It was late afternoon by the time *Bringin' Home the Bacon* was wheeled into the hangar at Kunming. Daddy Schlummer counted the bullet-holes with disgust. 'Thirty-one. Thirty-one holes. You shouldn't just sit there and let them take pot shots.'

Crane shrugged. One thing about the P-40, it could take punishment that would down any number of more thoroughbred marques. 'Can you fix her?'

'Look at this.'

Schlummer took Crane to the front of the plane and showed him the chunks missing from the prop blades. 'This was no Jap. This was you. The syncro is out on the nose guns. It'll need a new propeller, then we'll have to check the firing mechanism. Plus plug the oil leak properly, fill in the bullet-holes. That means two days, maybe three.'

'Shoot. If they send another big force over . . .'

'Yup. Fifty per cent of the planes are out. Nothing we can do. We need spares. And we might as well give *Bacon* a twenty-five-hour engine check.' He examined his clipboard. 'It's at twenty-three and a half anyways. So, looks like you're grounded.'

Meanwhile, thought Crane, legends were being created over Rangoon. The British had asked for help when the Japanese began bombing the Burmese capital, and Chennault had thrown more and more AVG pilots in. They were acquitting themselves well, outfighting the RAF and clocking up the aces down there all right. One pilot even managed all five kills in a single day. The Old Man refused to let Crane go down and join them, though; Chennault had made it clear, Burma was not his beat.

'OK, Chief, do your best,' he said and turned to leave.

'As always. And well done on number four.' He slapped the plane affectionately. 'I'll have it painted on.'

'Thanks.'

'Yeah. Shame the pig didn't count, eh?'

Crane flashed him the finger and he heard Daddy Schlummer laugh behind his back.

He spent two hours that afternoon composing the letter to Kitten. It wasn't until he sat down to write that he realised how tired he was. His eyes burned from shallow sleep, his head thumped with the cacophony of engines and weapons, and his mouth was soured with the permanent taste of metal. The tremor in his hand meant his writing was spidery; it looked as if it belonged to a very old or very crazy or very old, crazy person.

Slowly he forced himself to uncoil, to bring himself down from battle-ready to battle-weary. His writing improved, and the headache retreated to a soft drumming. He screwed up the fifth draft and began all over. He didn't want to gush or plead, and he had to make sure his feelings didn't drown out the main point: *Get out of there. Make sure you have an exit.* Although the Tigers were scoring victories over Rangoon, the Japanese were slowly squeezing them out by force of numbers. The RAF were on the run everywhere, their clumsy Brewster Buffaloes no match for the enemy. Then, at the end he put this: *Come to China. Be with me.*

He sealed it up in the thick-fibred envelope he had bought from the public letter-writers at the market and took a rickshaw from the hostel to the airfield, just as the day was slipping into evening.

Branski was duty officer at the Ops centre, a comic stub of an unlit cigar clamped between his teeth until he could score a fresh batch of stogies he could actually afford to light. He held forth behind a counter, organising a team of Chinese assistants in a combination of Brooklyn bark and pidgin English.

'Branski.'

'Crane.'

'The Beechcraft goin' to Toungoo?' This was the twin-prop transport plane the AVG had managed to scrounge from the US Navy.

'No, the Beechcraft is not going to Toungoo. The Beechcraft is in Chungking with the Old Man.'

'You got anything going down there?'

'There's a CNAC C-47 due in any time now on a return run. With movies on board. Andy Devine. And the second part of *Gone With the Wind*.'

'What happened to the first reel?'

'Gone. I guess we just got *The Wind*.' He took the stub from his mouth and chortled.

'What's its turnaround time?'

'Probably a couple of hours. And you ain't goin' back on it, before you ask.'

Crane nodded. Those lumbering Gooney Birds took four hours or more to reach Toungoo, slightly longer on the return thanks to the winds. Even with no serviceable plane for him to fly, skipping off base for that long would be a dereliction of duty.

He produced the letter. 'You think the crew will deliver this?'

'Ah, the girlfriend. My darling, my darling.' Branski snatched the hard-won missive and began to mock-kiss the envelope. Crane grabbed his arm and squeezed.

'Knock it off.'

'OK, OK.' He sniffed the paper. 'Not even any lousy cologne, ya cheapjack. Y'know, I haven't heard from my girl in three months. You're lucky to have one so close.' The lack of mail was one of the major gripes of the AVG. Crane didn't try and explain that having her so close was even more of an agony. 'I'll give it to them. Even so, I can't promise they'll deliver. They don't like being treated like US Mail.'

'I'll deliver it.'

Crane examined the man who had spoken from over his shoulder. He wore rimless glasses, had a dark buzzcut and thick eyebrows parked at different levels, which gave him a quizzical appearance.

'Hyram Nelson,' the man announced. 'I'm on that CNAC flight out of here.'

'Lee Crane.' They shook hands. 'I appreciate it, Mr Nelson.'

'Hyram. My pleasure. Anything I can do for the Flying Tigers.'

'Buy you a beer?'

'Sure, why not?'

The CNAC plane landed thirty minutes later. Crane and Nelson finished up their conversation – mostly about Chennault's tactics – and beer in the AVG mess and went to meet the incoming C-47. As the pilot swung it around in front of the Ops centre and cut the engines, the Chinese ground crew wheeled up the steps and yanked open the fuselage door. They stood back in amazement as a striking woman appeared, one hand holding onto her hat, long stockinged legs emerging from a tight skirt as she negotiated the steps down.

'Well, she'll have the guys baying at the moon,' said Crane as the sodium lights caught her pretty face.

Behind her, filling the doorway, came a man of enormous girth.

'Oh shit,' muttered Nelson.

'Who is that?' asked Crane, as the man tottered on the top step.

'Walter Gilbert. An Englishman, of sorts, who always turns up like a bad penny. What the hell is he doing here?'

The woman walked across the apron on wobbly legs. Nelson stepped forward and took her bag. 'Miss.'

'Thank you.'

Nelson looked beyond her at the figure waddling up to join them and shouted, 'Walter! Long time no see.'

'Hyram! Still pretending you work for Standard Oil?'

'Goodyear.'

'Splendid. This is Diana McGill, my assistant.'

Nelson nodded a hello to the woman but turned his attention back to the Englishman. Crane touched his forehead in greeting and she gave him a tired smile. 'Staying long, Walter?' Nelson asked.

'Just nosing around. Four or five days, perhaps.'

'It's not your turf, Walter.'

'Hyram. Hasn't anyone told you? The world is my oyster.' He turned to Crane and looked him up and down, as if trying to establish his place in the local pecking order. 'Do you think you could get our bags sent on, old chap? I have the address here.'

He thrust a piece of paper into Crane's hands, took Diana's case from Nelson and strode off with a cheery wave.

'Well, I'll be damned,' said Crane, staring at the address.

'Only if you stick around Walter.'

Crane watched the crew climb down from the plane, an American captain and Chinese co-pilot, tired and stiff after their hours in the lumbering C-47. Not for the first time, he thanked any lucky star that was up there that he flew fighters, not transport.

Eleven

There were fifty pissed-off pilots in the room at the American Club in Kunming. Some were recently returned from round-the-clock operations over Rangoon. Others, like Crane, had been pulled back from Kweilin, the AVG's forward base in China. It was a welcome break from the constant alerts and interceptions of probing bombers. The fifth kill, the one that would make him an ace, had proved elusive. For weeks now he had shot at and damaged dozens of planes, but not one had had the decency to explode or crash where he and his compatriots could see it.

Crane leaned back in his chair and closed his eyes for a second, concentrating on the words of the Army Air Force General who was standing next to the Old Man, addressing the group.

'As I said,' the General continued, 'America is proud of you. The world is proud of you. But your time is over. The AVG has to be integrated into an overall fighting strategy against the Japanese. Colonel Chennault has agreed that the pilots and technicians are to be inducted into the personnel of the USAAF at a convenient date to be advised.'

All eyes swivelled to Chennault, who in turn stared at the floor. He had been strangely quiet all through the meeting, as if he really wanted no part of it. Some kind of deal had been made, they all knew that, but what? Rumours had been flying around for weeks now that the Old Man was negotiating to bring the Tigers back to the fold, in exchange for his own reinstatement and promotion in the USAAF.

A hand went up. 'Will you honour our terms and conditions?'

'Those who choose induction will receive the difference between their Army pay and the balance for the year with the AVG. But we do not pay combat bonuses in the USAAF.'

A groan went through the group. Crane put up his own hand. 'Will the five-ten height restriction apply?'

The General shrugged. 'I can't say at this point. But all operational rulings will apply to the AVG, as it would any unit incorporated into the Army Air Force.'

'What rank do we have?' asked Gospel. 'Same as in the Tigers?'

'The appropriate and equivalent rank in the US Army Reserve.' There was a moment of uproar. The General's face soured. 'Which is the normal practice.'

'Why the Reserve? Why not a regular commission?' demanded Bucky.

'Yeah,' came a chorus.

The General waved an arm to silence them. He wasn't in the negotiating business, it seemed, because he said: 'Those of you who do not wish to join the USAAF will get five hundred dollars for travel home. When you disembark, believe me, there will be a draft board waiting to put you into the regular army. You can forget flying.'

The baying protest at this blackmail threatened to lift the tin roof off the building. Several pilots were on their feet. Chennault folded his arms and glowered at them until silence fell once more. 'Gentlemen, you are being offered the chance to—'

'Screw ourselves,' yelled Monty.

'You have no alternative.'

Crane raised his hand, unable to believe what he was hearing. To an outsider, the difference between Reserve and regular officers might seem trivial. Within the service, it was critical to a man's status. Six months ago, he would have kept quiet. Six months ago, though, he hadn't fought himself to the point of exhaustion. The thought of being tied up once more with USAAF red tape made him feel even more prickly. The contents of the belated reply from Kitten that was in his top pocket, saying she was sorry but she could not leave Toungoo, could not abandon her friends and her staff, had not helped his demeanour.

'Colonel Chennault, sir,' he said, 'I'd like to tender my resignation from the American Volunteer Group.'

Chennault's face clouded with fury as others yelled their support. 'Refused.' He pointed a bony finger at Crane. 'You have at least one more mission, Wingman.'

The General nodded. 'A flight of British Blenheim bombers will be landing here shortly to refuel. It will then fly on to Chiang Mai in Thailand to bomb the railyards there. The AVG is to fly escort—'

There was more bedlam, before Crane got himself heard. Outside he could hear a transport circling, so he kept the volume up, but he spoke as slowly and levelly as he could: 'Colonel Chennault. We will not be used as escorts. We will not fight at the limit of our range. We will not fight over hostile territory. Sound familiar? Is that what you are asking us to do?'

'And are you asking for a white feather?' the Old Man snarled. 'Because that is what it sounds like.'

Crane pointed at the patch sewn onto his jacket. 'It says *American Volunteer Group*. I'm withdrawing my volunteering.' A murmur of agreement came from the other pilots.

Chennault's mouth opened but he didn't get to speak. A young Chinese adjutant knocked at the door and entered. 'Sir,' he stuttered nervously, 'you asked to be told. The evacuees from Toungoo have just arrived from Lashio.'

*

Crane found Elsa at the alert shack, talking to her husband. Her face was streaked with dirt, and her clothes soiled with what looked like blood. 'Can I have a word with Elsa?' he asked Ron Cross, who nodded his agreement and kissed his wife on the cheek. His relief that she had got out safely was palpable.

'I'll just be a minute.' Crane took Elsa aside. 'How was the flight from Lashio?'

'Hairy,' she said. 'And overloaded.'

'You OK?' He looked at her eyes and thought she was going to cry.

'It's chaos. The British abandoned Toungoo without blowing the approach bridges, leaving it wide open. The Burmese are fighting each other, the pro-Japs against the others. It's horrible.'

'Where's Kitten?'

'Not here.'

'What?'

'She wasn't on the Lashio train. Look, Lee.' She grabbed his arm as if steadying him. 'The British were only letting whites on First Class, and that was the only place you could guarantee a place on the train. Even then, you needed a ticket.'

'Those fuckers,' he spat. 'Did she have a ticket?'

'I don't know, Lee. I had to set the charges to blow the hospital and get the patients out . . . I don't know. It was every man for himself.'

'And every woman?' he asked.

She shook her head. 'I'm sorry.'

'Sorry. Jesus. You sure she wasn't on the train?'

'She wasn't at Lashio when we arrived. I think I saw that young halfie-halfie girl? The one from the dinner – Sandra. She was light enough to pass as white. But they were beating people off with clubs and guns at Toungoo station. If you weren't in First Class . . . Lee, there was nothing I could do. You had to be there to believe it.'

'Yeah.'

He turned and walked away, striding across the crushed stone towards the hangars. A low buzzing in the sky told him the first of the Blenheims was about to land, but he didn't even look up. He yelled across at Schlummer, who was standing outside the stores, wiping his hands on a rag: 'How's *Bacon*?'

'Due for retirement.' Many of the pilots had switched to Kittyhawks, the newer model of the P-40, as the original batch of planes had worn out. Crane was reluctant to let his Tomahawk go. Superstition played a larger part in a pilot's life the longer he stayed alive. 'Apart from that, ready to roll. I heard about the meeting.' He wrinkled his nose in disgust. 'Chiang Mai?'

Crane spat on the ground, trying to shift the bitter taste from his mouth. He threw Daddy Schlummer the envelope that contained his scribbled resignation. 'Toungoo.'

There were two jagged bomb craters on the airstrip at Toungoo, but Crane managed to land his P-40 on a diagonal, missing the holes by several feet. He parked *Bacon* at the empty hangar and found a Chinese mechanic, who promised to refuel her after he slipped him twenty gold. There were precious few other aircraft. At the end of the strip, a Buffalo had been totalled on take-off, and a Blenheim without engines sat impatiently, waiting for repairs that would never come. The skeletons of some stripped Tomahawks completed the complement.

There were no cars or Jeeps available, so he walked, or rather ran, into town. There was smoke in the air, but not the usual cooking fires. He could smell charred wood and the stench of what he hoped was animal flesh. The locals glared at him, some shaking their fists. Many were too busy looting other people's homes to notice him. Within a few yards of entering the town he saw his first body, lying in one of the drainage streams, the head attached to the body by just a few sinews. Further on was a timber elephant, its great bulk strewn across the road, its blood almost black against the punctured hide. A human arm stuck out from beneath its belly, its fingers frozen clawing at the air, suggesting its mahout had died with his beast of burden.

There were sporadic gunshots ahead, so Crane threaded between the shacks, taking the route where he had chased the boy, just to stay off the main thoroughfares. The smell of burning became more intense, and as he emerged from one of the alleys he could see why. Half of Kitten's house was charred, the cracked and blackened teak still smouldering.

He swallowed back the bile that rose in his throat and, with his heart flapping wildly in his chest, he burst through the door into the house, picking his way between discarded cushions and pillows. Most of the furniture had been taken, as had the delicate carved screens. What hadn't been looted had been stomped on and splintered.

'Kitten?' His voice echoed through the hollow spaces. 'Vijay?'

The pungent smell led him to Vijay. He was in the kitchen, sitting with his back against the wall, a carving knife in one hand, his intestines in the other. One glimpse of the expression on his face was enough to tell me it hadn't been an easy death.

Crane pulled out his .45 and explored each room in turn, steeling himself for what he might find. The tiny *amah* lay spreadeagled across the bed, a few wisps of torn clothes covering her naked body. He took a sheet from one of the other bedrooms and laid it across her with a muttered prayer to a God they didn't share.

One of the boy-runners was in the garden, his body lacerated with *dah* strokes. Crane searched through the bushes, but there was no sign of Kitten. That came when he found her *kameez* in the drawing room, dirty and stained. He sniffed it, trying to ascertain if it was blood, but instead the smell of her body filled his head and he sank to his knees, the material pressed across his face.

*

More gunshots nearby eventually roused him and he discarded the tunic and left the house. Outside in the street, two grossly overloaded bullock-carts faced each other, both blocking the road. The terrified families were yelling abuse at one another and one of the patriarchs was waving a huge old British service revolver the size of a howitzer. Crane left them to it.

He ignored the glares and insults directed at him as he strode down to Toungoo's main drag. He kept the pistol good and visible. He'd be shooting more than pigs this time.

He found Snelling standing on the back of a flatbed truck, surrounded by a group of hill tribesmen, many of them heavily tattooed, others with intricate turbans and rows of polished beads hanging around their necks. For the first time Crane saw up close the apparently tumorous skin of those who had inserted subcutaneous precious stones and coins as talismen.

From a pile of weapons at his feet, the Englishman was selecting rifles and shotguns and handing them out to the eager crowd who surged forward, hands raised, as each weapon was produced.

'Snelling!'

'Crane? What in God's name are you doing here?'

With a smile and a bow, Crane carefully took one of the guns from a tribesperson and examined it. It was a double-barrelled twelve bore, with delicate filigreework and a plate that dated it to 1880, London. The man allowed him to handle it for no more than five seconds before he snatched the trophy back. 'What the hell they doing with these?'

'All we could get, old chap. From the finest hunting clubs of Rangoon and Calcutta. Army won't let us have weapons for what they call Irregulars.' The tone told Crane what he thought of the Army's policy.

Snelling brushed back his hair, leaving a smudge of grease on his forehead. He looked all in. 'I should get out of here if I were you.'

'Where's Kitten?'

'You are too late. She went on the train.'

'She didn't. I saw Elsa at Kunming. She never made it to Lashio. You bloody British made sure of that.'

Snelling looked perplexed. 'Are you certain?'

'Elsa was pretty damn certain. She got to Lashio and then flew out to Kunming. She didn't see her.'

'Crikey. You've been to the house?'

He nodded. 'All dead. No Kitten.'

The little fixed-wheel fighter plane came low over the jungle, the sound of its engine only reaching them seconds before it opened fire. Crane reached up and dragged Snelling down onto the ground, rolling them under the vehicle as the bullets thudded into the truck above their head, shattering the glass in the cab, pinging off the chassis. The river of lead carried on down the main street, slicing through human and animal. As the guns fell silent, Crane heard the pilot pull on the stick and give it throttle to climb.

A bullock started bellowing in agony, and he could hear several people – men or women, it was impossible to tell – wailing. Crane scrabbled out away from the truck, which now smelled strongly of gasoline. Snelling examined the fuel tank, which had three large punctures in it.

'Damn.'

'Just be thankful they weren't tracers. What will you do?'

Snelling pointed to the tribespeople picking themselves up from the dust. 'These splendid chaps are going to get me by truck to the Naga Hills, on the Indian border. Or at least, they were. Now I suppose I'll have to use shanks's pony.' He saw the look on Crane's face. 'On foot. Look, I'm sorry about Kitten.'

'Whites only, Elsa said,' he snapped angrily, turning on his heel. 'You were only letting whites on.'

Snelling shook his head. 'I don't—'

Crane strode away but Snelling caught up and grabbed his arm.

'I know she should have been on that train because I gave her my ticket. The railway police wouldn't have turned her away with that, no matter what her colour. What kind of people do you think we are?'

Before he could answer, Crane realised the Japanese plane had circled and was coming back. He thought of his P-40 sitting out in the open on the airfield, raised a hand to Snelling and shouted: 'Good luck!' as he ran back to the strip.

As he reached it, the little Nate was coming in low and he stopped, waiting for the bullets to shred the Tomahawk, to leave him trapped in Burma. He stood there while the engine noise grew and the plane got lower. He could imagine the glee of the pilot, having a Flying Tiger in his sights.

But no firing came. The plane flew over at around fifty feet and Crane instinctively loosed off two useless pistol shots at it, before it rose back into the sky. It must have been out of ammunition. The pilot had emptied the gunbelts on the strafe, which wasn't hard – 2000 rounds doesn't even give you a minute's firing time unless you are careful. He thanked the heavy thumb of the Jap flyer and sprinted across the field to check *Bacon* had been refuelled.

The twin-engined enemy plane he encountered on the way back to China stood no chance. He should perhaps have just kept going, not risked an engagement, but pure anger drove him on towards it. The rear gunner spotted him almost immediately and began firing. *Keep the prop disc between you and the gun*, he reminded himself. *It will protect you.* For once he thought of the human being within the aircraft as his cannon shells imploded the gunner's canopy, of the flesh and blood flying around the inside of the plane. His stream of fire moved to the cockpit, and as the shells punctured the pilot and smashed the controls to scrap, the plane tilted and began to dive.

He followed it down, still firing until the wing guns were empty and his cannons overheated and jammed. The bomber crumpled into a paddy field, its fuel spilling across the surface of the water, creating a circle of fire that poured black smoke towards him.

Crane flew through the oily debris from the pyre of kill number five and resumed the long haul back to China – an ace, albeit an unconfirmed one, at last.

Twelve

Singapore, 1948

There were probably lots of people who did self-pity better than me, but that day I was on championship form. I was leaning against a tow-truck, staring across at *Myra Belle Starr II*, willing the tyres to reinflate, but they stayed as flat as Olive Oyl's chest. It was getting towards midday, there was little shade, and I was stewing. I was keeping my body temperature at just below boiling point by drinking my way through half a case of American beer I'd bought off some China Airlines pilots.

I watched one of Changi's Chinese mechanics wander over and take down *Myra*'s serial number. He'd then use it in the *chap ji kee* lottery – the idea being that another's misfortune can be your salvation. I tossed a half-finished can at him, spraying him with foam and told him to *chu-la*: scram. He glared at me and I made the crooked-arm gesture that means you're welcome to have a go, if you think you're man enough. He cursed and shuffled off. He was lucky I was drinking from a can, rather than a bottle. I'd still have thrown it at him.

Henri emerged from the ramshackle Indo-Air office that clung onto the side of one of the hangars like a parasite, and walked across the apron towards me. His face was flushed with the heat and his jacket soiled with sweat stains. 'Can't we do this somewhere cooler?'

I tossed him a beer. He held it well away from himself as he opened it, letting the spray soak the concrete. The puddle was gone within thirty seconds. 'The price of DC-3 and C-47 tyres just trebled right across Singapore. Funny, that.'

'Absolutely hilarious,' I said. Indo-Air didn't keep spares for its planes, only buying on a need-to basis. Word got around aircraft chandlers and fitters so quickly when we required something urgently, I sometimes suspected telepathy.

'I got a contact who claims he has some coming up from KL tonight. Get them fitted by tomorrow . . .'

'In the meantime, I've got to check every last rivet,' I said gloomily.

Henri shrugged. 'Your cargo will be in tomorrow. I wouldn't hang around.'

'Would you fly her?'

'Yes, of course.' I didn't believe that for a minute. Pilots don't like strangers messing with their planes. In an ideal world the only people who touch them are you, your co-pilot, flight engineer and mechanics you know and trust. Preferably blood relatives. 'She's fine, Lee. I am certain.'

'Stop trying to make me feel better. I don't want to feel better. I want to feel like this till I meet the guy who did it. Can you get Mosh down here to help me do a full pre-flight?' His jaw worked, but before he could utter the words, I said, 'I'll pay his time.'

'Will it put you in a better mood?'

I drained the last of my beer, put the can on the floor and stomped on it like the whole business was its fault. 'No. But it might stop me getting in a worse one.'

Mosh came an hour later. We waited until the day began to cool, and went to work. We did the most thorough visual the old girl had ever had, using flashlights to look in every last crevice. I fished in the fuel tanks for foreign objects, while he siphoned some off and made certain that no water or sugar had been introduced, worked every control surface a dozen times, making sure there was nothing to snag or catch them. About three hours in, Mosh finally said: 'Gettin' hungry here, boss.'

He was sitting next to me in the scuffed and worn cockpit, clipboard in hand, ticking off the checklist as we went through the mechanical and electrical systems, working each pump and valve.

'Yeah.' I realised I hadn't eaten all day. No wonder I was feeling beat. 'Come on.' I clomped down the fuselage and walked out into the late afternoon. Instinct made me look up. Pilots always like to check the weather. The sun was low, and streaks of cloud were moving in on it, slicing through the disc.

I heard Mosh exit behind me. 'I'll buy you dinner at the Goodie. How's that?' I asked.

The Goodwood Park Hotel was, like Raffles, one of Singapore's institutions, now clawing its way back to normality after being used by the Japanese as an Intelligence HQ, and the British for war-crimes investigations and tribunals.

'Dinner's on me, old buddy.'

I spun round at the familiar drawl and saw him emerge out of the half-light, still in the ridiculous get-up of cowboy hat and hand-stitched boots. It had been four years, and he had hardly changed, apart from the swell of a nascent beer gut pushing into his polished belt buckle.

'Cowboy.' I tried to keep the shock out of my voice.

'Lee.'

'This here's Mosh.' Mosh stepped forward and offered Cowboy his hand.

'Good to meet you.' They pumped for what seemed like ten minutes, each trying to impress the other with his manly grip.

'I heard about you,' said Mosh.

Cowboy raised an eyebrow and pushed up the brim of his hat. 'That right?' He shot me a look that carried the weight of a punch.

'I heard you were dead.'

He winked at me. 'Yeah. I heard that, too.'

There was a silence and Mosh said, 'Look, you two want to talk old times, it's fine with me.'

'No—' I began.

'Yeah, we don't want to bore you,' interrupted Cowboy. 'Nothing worse than other people's war reminiscences.' He took out his wallet and passed a roll of notes to Mosh. 'It'll cover a cab back into town, few drinks. Hope that's OK.'

Mosh looked at the proffered money like it was a handful of excrement.

'Hold on,' I said, before Mosh took his offence and tried to shove it up Cowboy's ass. 'We still got work to do, me and Mosh. Someone's been screwing around with us.' I indicated the sad state of the undercarriage.

'OK. How about I wait over at the coffee shop? You fetch me when you're done.'

I nodded. I was just playing for time really, trying to get used to the idea that, like Elsa, he was still alive.

As he walked away, Cowboy slapped the fuselage with the flat of his hand. 'She's sound as a bell, Lee. Sound as a bell.'

'How would you—'

He winked at me and gave me a smug grin. 'It was only to get your attention, Lee.' It was at that moment I realised it was Cowboy who had slashed the tyres.

By the time we had finished up with *Myra* and were heading back into town, the dark clouds had bullied the last of the sun out of the sky, and rain was brooding. Cowboy had an ex-military Packard, which he steered around the potholes with ease. Roads were a low priority in Singapore that year. The death rate was twice what it had been in 1938, and there was a new programme of healthcare and slum clearance; subsidised restaurants had also been opened, to make sure cheap food was available to all. So when it came to fixing the legacy of Occupation, a few pits in the tarmac didn't matter too much.

Cowboy looped us away from the coast road, so we passed the pineapple-tinning plants, the sawmills, the street barbers and the now ubiquitous hoardings proclaiming Singapore's first skyscraper, for the Bank of China, due to break ground soon.

'Where we going?' I eventually asked.

'Thought I might buy my old partner a Tiger.' I assumed he meant a beer. 'Down on the waterfront, perhaps.'

We were past the small factories and the rubberworks and into rows of bungalows now, neatly kept, a displaced English suburbia. They were quickly lost as the road gave way to four-storey shop-houses and the trees disappeared from the sidewalks. The air became grittier, the smells both richer and sweeter. We were in Little India.

'Where have you been, Cowboy?'

'Me?' He negotiated a crowded bus, honking his horn like a native. 'Ceylon, Jakarta, Tasmania.'

'Flying?'

'Some.' I recognised where we were from the . . .VALTINE sign, the missing O something else waiting its turn in the long inventory of war damage to be repaired. A cop whistled at him from his traffic island and Cowboy waved and kept on going, as if a friend had just greeted him.

'Where are we going?' I asked again. 'Exactly?'

'Go-down night market.'

Something about the way he was sitting made me lean across and flip open his jacket. The pistol was in his belt, the handle digging into his gut. I let it flap shut. I didn't ask why he thought he might need a gun. I guessed he still bore me a grudge for trying to kill him a few years back.

Once we hit the water, we drove south. Most of the proud Victorian buildings that lined the frontage had survived the war intact, but like the rest of the city, they needed some serious care and attention. They were streaked with dirt and bird droppings and peppered with shrapnel, most of it of 1942 vintage.

Cowboy pulled the Packard into a space between the buildings, just where a run of scruffy warehouses ended and we could look right out over the murky Straits and its junks and sampans.

I stepped out of the car into the dusk. To the left, a line of coolies were working under floodlights, unloading coal from a battered-looking local veteran, the *Nellie Tan*, out of Penang. To my right was the market, quiet as yet, the first noodle stores just firing up, smoke curling upwards as oil burned off hot steel, the scene lit by gas and oil lamps.

The rain began to fall hot, like a spray of saliva. The stallholders ran to rig up awnings to keep the cooking area and the motley assortment of benches dry. Cowboy indicated we should walk through and I followed him past the hawkers, the sizzling suddenly reminding me I was hungry. A few shouted that we should try their oyster omelette, or crab and green onion but, much as it made my stomach rumble, that could wait. I didn't want to be distracted by food.

'You haven't asked me what happened when we left you, Lee,' he said in a tone that was almost truculent.

'Do I want to know?' In fact every nerve-ending in me was screaming to discover what had happened after we parted the last time. Some juvenile streak, though, was refusing to give him the satisfaction of knowing I even cared.

I saw something like pain flit over his features, the lines in his face deepened by the shadows thrown by the lamps. 'Probably not.'

'What are you doing here, Cowboy?'

'Trying to make up for lost time.'

I almost laughed. I had an inkling that, like me, Cowboy's last few years had been frittered away, gnawed at by what might have been. And there was no way either of us would ever be seeing those wasted minutes, hours and months again.

'Does that involve shooting me? Is that what this is about?'

Cowboy stopped and pushed up the brim of his hat, unlocking a stream of water that ran onto his shoulders. 'The gun's just a habit, Lee. I don't bear you any hard feelings.'

'Wish I could say the same.'

He punched me on the arm, right on the tattoo, as if that were a joke, and my bicep went numb. 'We're here to offer you a deal.'

'Like last time?'

'Only better,' he assured me.

'It couldn't be much worse.'

'Lee, for once, shut up and listen. Eh?'

I grabbed his arm and he swung to face me, as if ready to parry a blow. I raised my palms to show him I had no such thoughts. He had the gun, after all. 'I just wanted to say, I'm still pissed at you, but I'm glad you made it.'

His face creased into a lopsided smile. 'Me too. I mean, I'm happy you did. Especially now.'

'Why now?'

'You'll see.'

The trio he was looking for were waiting at the far end of the market, under a canvas cover, slurping their way through beef noodle soup and tugging on Tiger beers. One of them I didn't recognise. He was Chinese, probably around forty, dressed in a crisp white *tutup*, the long shirt with five buttons up to the neck. His hair was heavily oiled, and he had a look of one of the Internal

Security Force men that liked to hang around markets, listening out for murmurs of sedition and revolution. Or perhaps my paranoia gauge was in the red.

Next to him, her lips parted in a sardonic smile, was Elsa, a cigarette in an ivory holder held next to her cheek, still looking like she could make men howl at the moon.

But what really worried me was the third man. What the hell was Henri Raquil doing there?

Henri simply beamed at me and indicated the guy in the white shirt who I thought was an agent of misfortune. 'Good news, Lee. Mr Kip here can get us some tyres at a price that is almost a bargain.' I liked the 'almost'. Henri knew never to gloat about any deal with a local.

'Well, the Lord taketh away and the Lord giveth. Isn't that right, Elsa?'

'Hello, Lee,' she said, putting down her bowl of soup. 'How's the jaw?'

'That hurt. But the tyres . . . I didn't figure even a queen bitch like you would stoop so low.'

Henri looked puzzled, not understanding the sudden ionised crackle in the air, as if ball lightning were about to be generated. I laid it out for him: 'You got a good price from Mr Kip because it was these jokers who did the tyres in the first place.'

He frowned. 'I see. And why would they do that?'

'To keep me here. And I'm about to find out why.'

Elsa's expression didn't change much. She nodded at Kip and Henri. 'I think you two have some business to conclude. Cowboy, the *laksa* is very good.'

The three got the message, and when they had gone I sat down opposite her, studying her face. Once, I had thought her a remarkably beautiful woman, and I guessed she still was, but I could see the flinty hardness beneath shining through now.

'The Japanese really fucked this town,' she said.

107

'The Light of the South,' I said, using the occupiers' name for the city, 'was not somewhere to see out the war, no matter what nationality you were. It wasn't only the town that got fucked.'

'I was here in thirty-eight after the rubber price collapsed. It was bad enough then. It's a shithole now.'

'It's getting better. You should have been here last year,' I said. 'The riots were something to see.'

'Food?'

'Food and employment and a lot of Commie agitation.'

'You want something to eat?' she asked, switching tack.

'I'll have a beer.'

She clicked her fingers and the nearest *kway teow* man nearly eviscerated himself pulling a Tiger from the bucket of ice and getting it to our little corner of the market. The rain was easing now, the darkness solidifying. I could hear waves crashing against piles somewhere to our left. Singapore had shrunk to this wonky little table, where my distant past and immediate future were about to collide.

I wiped the bottle very carefully before I put it to my lips. 'What gives, Elsa?'

'Sorry about your tyres. Really. But it got your attention.'

'Seeing you got my attention. What are you doing in Singapore?'

'Until I ran into you, I was using Mr Kip to charter a plane and find us a good pilot. He really is in the aviation business. Well, he's moving into it. He was an old friend of Ron's.'

'Good for him. How is Ron?'

She waved her cigarette 'I haven't seen him in a while.'

Ah well, another man dumped on the way to wherever Elsa wanted to be. 'And Cowboy?'

'He's the same as me.' Not quite, I thought. Cowboy didn't have the horsepower under his hat that she could muster. 'It's an itch we have to scratch, Lee. No matter what it takes. You know that feeling? Unfinished business, the path not taken, all that bullshit.'

'You didn't get the gold out, did you?'

She blew smoke in my face, and the words betrayed the anger simmering inside her. 'You know we didn't.'

I shook my head. 'Never knew for sure, until now.'

She took another drag and exhaled. The smoke was sweet and scented, no American brand I knew of. 'Want a cigarette? French. I get them in Vientiane.'

'Elsa, let's stop this. It's like a bullfight. You are dancing round me, I'm dancing round you. At the moment I'm not sure who's the matador and who's the bull, but shall we move on? What do you want?'

'You. Your plane. Your flying ability. Your luck. Your pigheadedness. Not for free, this time, cash money.'

'To go where?'

'China.'

I laughed so loud, some of the noodlemen stopped and stared. I saw the shape of Cowboy shift in the lamplight, ready to come across if necessary. 'China and I are done. I have a job in Berlin. Then I sell *Myra* and take a Pan Am home and hang up my flying boots.'

Her turn to laugh, but it was softer and gentler and floated over me like the smoke from her cigarette. 'You'll never do that, Lee.'

'Which part?'

'Stop flying. Cowboy says you're the Man.'

I stood to go and she grabbed my wrist. 'Why haven't you asked what happened?'

'I don't want to hear the answer,' I said truthfully. 'Because I'll get angry. I'll slap you and go and try to punch the shit out of Cowboy, which isn't a good idea, even when he isn't armed.'

She pulled me back down onto the bench with a strength that surprised me. 'Yup, he can take care of himself.' Elsa reached over for my face with her free hand and I pulled back, but she was just moving some of my hair to see if a particular scar was still there.

It was, a little farther from the hairline than it had been, a jagged little reminder of how well Cowboy could take care of himself. 'I remember when you got that.'

'Me, too. The party at the Dragon House.'

'I fixed you up plenty, didn't I?'

'In more ways than one, Elsa.'

She tried to wrongfoot me by leaning close and saying, 'The gold is still there, Lee. Where we left it. Just waiting for us to go back.'

I'd guessed as much, so I wasn't surprised. She'd have to do better than that. Gold never sparkled that much in my eyes. 'There's a war on over there, Elsa. A nasty one. And I don't want your money.' Then I remembered, it wasn't even hers to begin with.

'We aren't offering money, Lee. Well, not just money. Itches and scratches, remember. We all have them.' She signalled to Cowboy who detached himself from the stall and ambled over with his bowl. He sat down next to me. 'Tell him,' Elsa instructed.

I should have left there and then, or clapped my hands over my ears, because I knew damn well what they were playing at. I'd made up my mind to leave, I had somewhere to go for once. It was time to bury China, Burma, India and all it entailed.

But maybe, as she said, we all wanted one last pick at our old scabs. Cowboy licked the chilli paste from his lips and smacked them appreciatively. 'Thing is, Lee, I know where she is. I know what happened after Toungoo. I can give Kitten back to you.'

Part Three

Laura

Thirteen

London, 1943

The minute hand on the elaborate clock above the empty Alvis showroom on Belgrave Square jerked closer to noon. Laura McGill glanced at it and picked up the pace as she hurried through the streets of Knightsbridge. There was barely a minute to spare before midday struck. Twelve o'clock sharp, she had impressed on Diana, only too aware that when her sister had left London, the rationing hadn't really bitten. Now, if they sat down for lunch any later than twelve-thirty, even at somewhere like the Berkeley, the list of 'offs' on the menu would outnumber the 'ons', and the chances were that the remaining 'ons' would be an appetite-crushing choice of fried snook, whale steak *bordelaise* or rook pie.

It had been two and half years since she had last seen Diana, and in all that time she had received just two cryptic postcards – from Cairo and Calcutta – whereas she had written reams of letters. It felt like a gushing one-sided conversation. Diana had always been the more restrained one, effortlessly cool and composed, whereas Laura surrendered all too easily to flustering and blustering.

Laura had put on her best dress and coat, with its fox-fur collar, but part of her was feeling guilty at agreeing to lunch at the Berkeley at all. If she ate in Town, it was usually at a 'British Restaurant', like the one in the drawing room of Gloucester House on Park Lane. The surroundings more than compensated for the basic food, and at least you did not suspect you were lining the pockets of black-market profiteers. Still, it was not every day the prodigal sister returned; so a fatted calf, semi-legal or not, was the order of the day.

Laura slowed her walk and took deep breaths as she approached the doorman of the hotel. It wouldn't do to appear hot and bothered. She hoped the powder was doing its work and stopping her cheeks from glowing. She smiled as the old soldier, the Mons and other medals displayed proudly on his overcoat, opened the door and she stepped inside.

She must have looked bewildered, because one of the managers approached and asked if he could help. She explained she was meeting her sister – Miss McGill – for lunch, and he told her 'they' were waiting in the bar. *They*? Who were *they*? Was Diana about to spring a fiancé, or perhaps even a husband, on her? And shouldn't she have come out to see Mother first?

She checked her coat, smoothed down the dress with its two pathetic, fabric-saving pleats and stepped into the permanent twilight of the bar. She saw Diana at once, seated in the far corner, her bright yellow blouse a bold statement slicing through the gloom. And next to her was the bulkiest man she had ever seen, with a second chin bigger than the first.

Diana waved as Laura approached and rushed around the table to hug her. She looked different. More blonde for a start, and her skin deeply tanned, both, Laura supposed, caused by the tropical sun. As they buried their heads in each other's shoulders she was aware of a grunting and scraping as the mountain of a man heaved himself to his feet.

'You look wonderful,' said Diana as she held her sister at arm's length.

'You too,' Laura came back quickly, although she thought she detected a slight sallowness to the skin close up.

114

'Laura, I'd like you to meet someone.'

Diana turned and indicated her companion, who was wheezing with the exertion of standing. Laura took the outstretched hand and felt her fingers engulfed in his great paw.

'Walter Gilbert,' he said in a strangely high voice. 'I am very pleased to meet you. Diana here has told me everything about you.'

Laura glanced at Diana, wondering how she could possibly know everything about her. Diana winked back in a rather shocking way.

'And I am very pleased to meet you, Mr Gilbert.'

Diana sat, Walter Gilbert slowly lowered himself back into his chair, and Laura, perplexed and confused, perched on the edge of her seat.

'Drink?' asked Diana.

Laura looked at those already on the table. Diana had a large glass of what looked to be gin, Gilbert a whisky of some sort. 'No Scotch,' he said glumly. 'Only whiskey with an "e". Irish muck.'

'Yes,' said Laura. 'I hear there's a shortage.'

Gilbert laughed. 'Only if you won't pay through the nose for it,' he said loudly and glared at the barman, who continued to polish his glasses.

'I'll have a sherry,' said Laura.

Gilbert signalled the barman and said: 'Sherry. Spanish, not South African – understand?' He turned to Laura. 'They charge you for Spanish, give you South African swill.'

'Not at the Berkeley, surely.'

Gilbert laughed again and his chins wobbled in a rather un-attractive way. 'Perhaps not.' He wore round tortoiseshell glasses, had erratically bushy eyebrows and a snub nose. No, this can't be the fiancé, Laura said to herself. Not Diana's.

'But the shortages are getting worse,' Laura said.

'Same everywhere, my dear,' the fat man said. 'A universal con-dition. And it'll carry on getting worse unless this war stops soon. Which is rather why we are here.'

'Shush, Walter, not yet. We have some catching up to do first.'

Diana quizzed her about their mother, about secretarial college, about her plans for the future, whether she had any admirers – as if, with most of the country's males away, and the rest despicable specimens – and how she thought the war was going. During all this Gilbert examined her intently, occasionally sipping from his whiskey. Laura hardly touched her sherry. She didn't like drinking at lunchtime.

'We should go through,' said Laura when she saw it was twenty to one by the dazzling wristwatch Diana was wearing. She assumed they were paste diamonds, because otherwise it would have cost a fortune, fifty pounds at least.

'I'll leave you two girls to it,' said Gilbert. 'I'm not coming through.' He pushed himself to his feet once more, and held out his enormous hand. 'I hope we meet again, Miss McGill.'

'Laura, please.'

'Diana. I shall see you later. At the Northumberland.'

Laura hoped he hadn't seen the jolt of shock. The Northumberland was a hotel near Trafalgar Square, which these days had become quite well-known for letting by the hour. Diana caught it though, because she giggled. 'Yes, Walter.'

The big man waddled off and Laura let her eyebrows hit her hairline. 'Di—'

'Oh, stop it. I know what you are thinking and I'm surprised my little sister can even harbour such thoughts. Come on – bring your drink. I'll tell you all about it.'

There was clear soup, grilled gammon with plums and stewed apples to follow, which constituted a feast. Laura finished her sherry and managed a glass of sweet wine while Diana regaled her with tales of places she could only imagine. She described dances at Shepherds Hotel in Cairo and then her time in Calcutta, a whirl of parties at the Saturday Club, tennis at the Swimming Club, bowls tournaments at the Tolly and racing and polo matches at the Turf Club.

It was a life vivid with heat and colour, not the drizzly dampness of poor battered, monochrome London.

She also told of the other side – bedbugs and dysentery, malaria and dengue fever, of the crushing sense of dislocation, so far away from home, friends and family, and of a life lived at a faster pace, yet oddly artificial, as if very little of what one did counted in the real world.

Even so, despite the downs, it sounded rather glamorous to a nineteen year old who was still trying to master shorthand and was waiting for her life to begin.

At one point, Diana leaned over and stroked Laura's face. 'Too much powder. Don't try and hide that beauty.'

'I'm not the one who is beautiful, Diana. You know that. Look at me. All skin and bone and gangly . . .'

'A clothes horse,' said Diana. 'See how that dress hangs.'

'A flat-chested nag, more like it. But look at you.'

'I look old. They say every year in the tropics ages you by two. No, really. I must look all of thirty.'

'Nonsense. I bet . . . I bet you have lots of chaps after you. Don't you?'

'Apart from Walter?'

'You mean . . . ?' Laura tried to stop her jaw dropping in horror at the thought.

'I'm teasing. Lots of chaps, yes, but they don't have much choice of white women out there. One mustn't let all the attention go to one's head.'

'And Walter?'

'Ah, Walter.' She spooned the last of the stewed apple into her mouth and grinned. 'I think I owe you an explanation.'

So over watery, chicory-infused coffee and cigarettes she outlined, in her lowest, softest voice, exactly who Walter Gilbert was, and what they wanted Laura to do and, although the details of the latter were sketchy in the extreme, the younger girl's heart

117

raced with excitement. It would mean undergoing training, at a large facility somewhere in the South of England, but she would actually be contributing to the war effort and, like her sister, she would see something of the world.

'So I will get to fly to the East? Will you be there as well? That would be fun, wouldn't it?'

Diana's mouth turned down. 'No, the thing is we need someone to run this end, the British end, of things. Sorry, I thought I'd made that clear.'

'No. You didn't.'

Laura's spirits plummeted. Not the excitement of travel, then, the dances and parties and swimming and tennis, but the mundaneness of running the office in dreary old England, of briefing what Diana called field agents: the ones who actually went on missions. The disappointment must have shown on her face because Diana produced a half-crown from her exquisite tooled-leather purse.

'What if we toss for it?' asked Diana.

'Toss for what, exactly?'

'Heads, I get to go back East, tails you do. Whoever wins, we swap after twelve months. Does that seem fair?'

'Well, yes. It is fair. But—'

Before she could finish her objection, Diana's thumb flipped upwards. The half-crown glinted as it spun in the air, hanging there for a second before dropping rapidly onto one edge. The coin bounced from the starched tablecloth onto the carpet. They almost upset the table in their haste to see the result, and giggled loudly as the coffee sloshed, attracting stares. It was heads, and again there was that sinking feeling in the pit of Laura's stomach.

Diana, a little flushed from alcohol, put her hand over her disappointed sister's and said: 'Tell you what: how about the best of three?'

'Very well.'

Laura would later reflect, long and bitterly, that it was at this moment that Diana effectively signed her own death warrant.

Fourteen

Calcutta, 1943

There were bodies along Old Court Street. Some of them lay sprawled in front of a tram which had stopped, the driver scratching his head, as if he were actually contemplating running them over. The Sikh chauffeur had to slow to swerve past a motionless child and Laura McGill felt a sickening bump as the car lurched into a pothole. Buzzards were perched on the spindly streetlamps, biding their time, their hard, featherless faces pitiless. They watched unblinking as a Brahmani cow stepped over the dead, carelessly crushing a limb every now and then.

'Almost there,' said Major Clutterbuck, patting her gently. 'That's the Great Eastern ahead. See the colonnade? Don't worry, there's plenty of *chokidars* there. Security, that is. All be safe again soon.'

'What's happened?' she asked. 'Was it a Japanese bombing raid?'

The Major looked glum. 'Food riot,' he said. 'Most of them were trampled underfoot. People in the countryside are starving, so they come to the city and we can't cope.' He pointed to a defaced cinema poster, advertising a film at the Metro, the actors' faces partly obscured by hastily daubed slogans. 'See the writing?

Give us *phaan*, it says. Starch.' He tapped on the glass partition with his swagger stick. 'Pull in here.' The driver swept in towards the kerbside, where a sea of pinched, eager brown faces waited. A clutch of babies was raised in the air in anticipation.

'Oh, for God's sake,' said the Major with real irritation. 'Let me assure you, it isn't normally like this.'

He opened the door and began to curse the hapless beggars in pidgin, using his stick liberally. There was a shrill whistle and a white police officer parted the crowd. 'This way, sir. Best get inside quickly.'

As Laura emerged from the rear of the car, she heard the roar of an aero engine and looked up. A British Hurricane came across the rooftops, its undercarriage lowering, the cartoon-ish bird painted on its nose clearly visible. 'My goodness, he's going to crash,' she said.

Clutterbuck grabbed her arm and shielded her as they pushed towards a formidably tall figure guarding the main entrance, his height exaggerated by a magnificent turban. 'No, he isn't,' the Major reassured her. 'Two boulevards have been taken over as emergency airstrips, with the Woodpeckers, as they style themselves, stationed there. Just in case.'

A young boy clumped up, worn wooden blocks strapped to his knees, the rest of the legs missing, a bowl clamped between his teeth, his brown eyes full of perpetual tears. Another street boy, this one impossibly handsome under the dust on his face, began to shout: 'No mamma! No pappa! No suppa!'

Laura felt her head swim with a combination of weariness, the claustrophobic closeness of the bodies and the after-effects of the armful of inoculations she had been given in Cairo. Her forehead burned like acid and she swooned forward, her vision clouding, the shriek of alarm from Major Clutterbuck a fading sound, like a distant train whistle.

*

Laura awoke with a rich, cloying scent in her nostrils, and she shook her head to dispel it. Her cheeks touched cool, soft cotton and she opened her eyes. She was lying on a bed, still fully clothed but with her shoes off. It was a largeish room, furnished with heavy dark pieces, most of them featureless rectangles in the half-light: the curtains had been pulled shut. A fan turned above her head with a faint squeak and she lay for a moment, enjoying the air on her face.

As she swung her feet from the bed she almost trod on the source of the overpowering odour. There was a stack of flowers, perhaps seven bouquets of them, a riot of colour even in the gloom, each with a small note attached. She yanked back the curtains and saw with relief that she was overlooking a small courtyard, rather than the hideous scene out on the main street.

There was a knock at the door and Major Clutterbuck poked his head in the room. 'You all right, Miss McGill?'

'Yes, sorry. How feeble of me to faint.'

'Not at all. May I come in?'

'Yes, please do.'

He entered but left the door ajar. She could just glimpse a figure crouched in the hallway. 'I've arranged for a *charpoy* to stay outside until all this fuss dies down. They are opening soup kitchens along the road, which should help calm the situation a little. How do you feel?'

Laura licked her lips. Her throat was dry. 'Rather thirsty.'

Clutterbuck pointed to a pitcher of water on a stand. It was covered by a piece of bead-weighted cloth. 'Boiled. Quite safe.'

She nodded. All the hygiene precautions had been drummed home to her in Cairo, and she had a list of must-buys from the Army & Navy stores that would, it was promised, make life bearable. 'All these lovely flowers. Who . . . ?'

'Word got out that Diana's sister was coming and . . . well, to tell you the truth, there aren't that many women here.' She raised an eyebrow and Clutterbuck coloured. 'That didn't come out terribly well, did it? What I mean is, you are an exotic species. A lot of the wives have shipped out, there are some FANYs, nurses, a few secretaries with your lot at the Oriental Mission, but that's it. You'll be very popular. We'll fix you up somewhere to live with the OM girls if you prefer. Till you move on.'

'I don't think I'll be here that long,' she replied, hoping it was the truth.

There was another soft tap and a second uniformed man, younger than the Major, appeared. Clutterbuck looked disgruntled. 'Ah, Snelling.'

'Sir.' The newcomer saluted then took off his hat.

Clutterbuck turned to Laura. 'Miss Laura McGill, Captain Sholto Snelling of the Oriental Mission.' The Oriental Mission was the cover name for what was really a branch of Special Operations Executive, known to those allowed clearance for such things as Force 136.

The Captain took two large strides towards her. 'How do you do?' he said, shaking hands vigorously. 'Welcome to Calcutta. Don't judge us by first impressions. It's not normally quite so chaotic.'

'So I gather.'

'Well, it's always chaotic, actually,' he admitted. 'Let's just say we usually manage the chaos a little better. Listen, I wondered when you would like a tour of the HQ and a chat about what you have let yourself in for. Tomorrow would be fine if you still feel . . .'

'No, no. Now would be perfect. I just need to get changed. Is that my luggage?'

'The maid unpacked it for you.'

'All of it?' gasped Laura.

'No, there was a leather bag she didn't have a key for. I said to leave it under the bed.'

She quickly checked the key was still on a chain round her neck. 'Fine.'

'Good,' said Clutterbuck. 'If there is anything you need?' He laid out his card on the water-stand.

'I'll see you downstairs in, what – an hour?' asked Snelling.

'Perfect,' she said.

The two men withdrew and Laura fetched the rather masculine valise and checked the lock was intact. She would have to find out if the Great Eastern had a nice big safe. People had apparently risked their lives to get the shipment this far; she wasn't going to let them down now.

By the end of the week, the food riots had subsided, although the streets, even on the fringes of the European quarter, were full of emaciated figures who seemed to be just two breaths away from death. As everyone had promised, Laura quickly adapted, until the mutilated beggars, the *bustee* hovels, the naked people washing at a stand-pipe, the packs of starved, mangy dogs, and the *punkah-wallahs* and the *charpoys* were hardly worth a second glance. She even gave up trying to kill the obscenely fat green flies that buzzed around in squadrons, bloated from gorging on the unburned corpses that were scattered across the city.

Snelling had given her a tour of the Force 136 set-up, explained how the Japanese were not having it all their own way, thanks to various anti-fascist groups, British 'stay-behinds' and the 'Invisibles': Chinese-Canadians who could blend in with the local populations. There was much he was proud of, but that didn't seem to include Walter Gilbert, whom he described as 'something of a rum character'.

Apparently it was little short of miraculous that Gilbert had managed to wangle space on one Dakota flight a month from the Americans, when the RAF were struggling to fulfil all their supply and parachute runs. Even 136 wasn't entirely sure what he was up to. Laura listened to this in silence over tiffin at the Tollygunge, one of Snelling's clubs, some way to the south of the city centre. She tried not to judge Gilbert on the raw facts; after all, her sister trusted the big man, and that should be good enough for her.

As she finished the last of her Darjeeling, Snelling shuffled in his armchair and leaned forward. 'It's the last Saturday of the month this weekend. That means a sunrise dance at the Morning Club – quite a big affair. There'll be dancing till dawn and we usually end up down at the Howth Bridge by the *ghats*. I wondered if you would like to go along,' he coughed nervously, 'with a chaperone, of course.'

Laura hid her smirk behind the rim of the teacup. Snelling must know that chaperones were ancient history back home. The thought that she would need a protector was ridiculous. 'Do I need a chaperone?' she asked. 'Is it a disreputable kind of club?'

'The Morning? Good God, no. And whites only, if that kind of thing worries you.'

'Should it?'

'It does some people,' he said noncommittally.

'Like Major Clutterbuck?'

He just smiled. Snelling must be about thirty-two or three, she guessed, and was quite dashing really. In normal circumstances he would have had his choice of girls, but as Clutterbuck had said, the pickings were really rather slim. After a moment's decorous hesitation, Laura said: 'I'd love to come along, Captain Snelling.'

On Saturday night, Snelling collected her in the Force 136 car, and presented her with a red hibiscus. He was in his best dress uniform; she was in a blue satin evening dress, the one she had almost not packed, because she could not foresee a need for party frocks.

As they drove past the 300 Club, one of the 'mixed' establishments, Snelling said: 'You know, some bloody maharajah rode his polo pony in there last week. Right into the bar.' He shook his head in disgust at such high jinks. 'Almost trampled one poor chap to death. Bloody irresponsible.'

'That's what you get when you let the locals in,' she baited him.

Snelling laughed. 'That's not what I meant. This might come as a surprise but some of the English chaps can behave quite badly, too.'

'At this club we are going to?'

'I should say not.'

The driver turned into the driveway of the Morning Club, which was visible beyond the row of tall palm trees ahead, standing proud like a gleaming white ocean liner, with sleek wraparound balconies at each end.

'Very nice,' said Laura.

'One of my favourites,' agreed Snelling. 'They have a pretty chiz band tonight – bunch of RAF chaps, do a very passable Glenn Miller.'

'Do you belong to every club?'

'Oh, just for the duration. So many people left town, they are glad of the custom, so we have "temporary special membership" privileges at most of them.'

They joined a queue of cars and rickshaws which had pulled up in the gravel semi-circle at the main entrance, disgorging guests, a great many of them uniformed officers, with only the odd wife or female companion. Some of the RAF chaps emerging from the big American car in front looked rather splendid, she thought, but didn't voice the opinion.

'I hope I can have the first dance,' said Snelling eagerly, and he touched her arm. 'Head of the queue and all that.'

As she stepped out into warm, scented dusk and felt dozens of male eyes rake her, Laura realised that, as far as her feet were concerned, it might be a long time till dawn.

*

The club was formed into a horseshoe shape around a lawn, used for croquet or bowls. One arm held the library and billiards room, the crosspiece housed the lobby and bar, and the eastern upright was home to a rather grand ballroom. At the far end a band played Joe Loss, Harry Roy, Glenn Miller and Benny Goodman, and some smoochie Ambrose for the slower numbers. Men outnumbered women, so swapping partners seemed to be the accepted protocol, and in four dances Laura was steered by Snelling, not a bad dancer, a pilot from the RAF 'Woodpecker' Squadron, slightly worse, Major Clutterbuck, rather good, and a New Zealand operative from Force 136, who was fast and fantastic.

Out of breath, she excused herself and headed for the powder room. It was lavishly appointed, with pin-backed brocaded chairs in front of a brace of mirrors, which were occupied by a couple of FANYs, who were discussing the available men in very frank terms as they reapplied their powder and lipstick. One of them turned to Laura and said: 'I saw you at Alam, didn't I?'

Alam Bazaar was a training camp on the River Hooghli, just outside the city. Officially, it was the School for Eastern Interpreters. In reality, it produced not linguists but agents trained in sabotage and subversion.

'Probably.'

'Are you the lucky thing who is going over The Hump?'

Laura looked taken aback and the other FANY said: 'She's Signals, dear. No secrets from her.'

'Yes, I am,' she confirmed.

'Been on the list for China for six months, I have.'

'She just wants to get her hands on some of those Yanks.'

They started giggling and Laura realised this was just empty boasting. They ceded their seats to her and as they left, one of them said: 'You're with Captain Snelling, aren't you?'

'Yes. Why?'

Another fit of giggles. 'Just remember – he's left-handed. You don't see it coming.'

Laura was about to protest, but in the end she joined in. It wouldn't do to be considered priggish. The girls then made some cutting remarks about a 'dusky' Major whom they thought shouldn't have been let into the club, and departed.

Outside she spotted Snelling drinking with an American. She could tell he was from the USA by his neat sand-coloured uniform, made of far better cloth than most British outfits and more flattering to the shape. The Captain was drinking with his right hand. The FANYs had been teasing her.

She took two steps forward, when there was a commotion to her left. Voices were raised and the dispute flared into violent cursing. A space appeared around the two protagonists, one a Major, who looked as if he was at least partly Indian, and a shorter, fatter man in evening dress. Looking on was a tall, dark-haired woman in a white silk dress, her hands held over her mouth in horror.

'You don't believe me?' yelled the Major. 'Then look at her damn knickers!'

The civilian lurched and swung a wild punch, which failed to connect. The Major produced a pistol, and a ripple of alarm shot through the crowd of onlookers.

'Go on – show him! Show him y'knickers!' yelled the Major, pointing the weapon at the woman who was the cause of the dispute. 'She writes the name of her lovers on her knickers! Mine is on there. Show him!'

'Hey, buddy.' It was the American who had been drinking with Snelling, breaking through the paralysis of the crowd. He grabbed the outstretched gun hand, bent it back sharply and twisted the pistol from the Major's grip. 'No gunplay. And no burlesque show.'

The Major turned, his face creased with rage. 'You bastard,' he snarled. While the American gripped his right wrist firmly, he attempted to land a blow with his left hand, but Snelling was there to intercept. He yanked the limb up the soldier's back, causing him to yelp.

The American could tell Snelling knew what he was doing so he stepped away from the mêlée and backed into Laura, treading on her foot.

'Sorry,' he said, turning. He paused and looked her up and down. 'You OK?'

'It's not the first time that has happened tonight. I'm fine. And well done,' she said. 'Disarming that chap.'

'Thanks.' They watched as Snelling escorted the wobbly-legged Major off the premises. The businessman and his wife were nowhere to be seen.

'Back in a jiffy,' shouted Snelling to Laura.

'I'm going to dump this,' said the American, holding up the revolver between thumb and forefinger. 'Will you still be here when I . . . ?'

'Yes.' She held out her hand. 'Laura McGill.'

'Right.' He took the hand. 'Hello there.' He flashed an infectious smile that crinkled his eyes. 'My name's Lee Crane.'

Fifteen

Calcutta, 1943

The sweat-drenched riggers, fitters, pilots, coolies, loaders and armourers at Dum-Dum airport all occasionally stopped what they were doing and examined the sky, waiting for the clouds that would signal the monsoon was on its way. It was rumoured to be the hottest Calcutta summer for eighty years, and all were feeling it; even the tar beneath their feet was bubbling and melting.

Lee Crane was also scanning the heavens, but not for portents of rain, which he knew was six days away. A dark swirl of crows was forming in the west, drawn by the garbage and the bodies that lay there. The buzzards, vultures and crows were having one long party this season and the massed carrion sometimes made for hazardous take-offs, which is why he watched the skies so intently.

Crane's twin-engined C-47 transport plane was normally based at Barrackpore, north of Calcutta, where he shared the ATC's *basha* with a dozen other crew. Today, though, was different and *Myra Belle Starr* was parked in one corner of Dum-Dum airfield, hemmed in by the Liberators of the RAF and the sleek silver bullets of the USAAF's B-17s.

Crane checked that his routing and flight-log were all in order. In contrast to the bomber guys, he had a simple dog-leg to fly: Dum-Dum to Chabua, a quick unload and passenger pick-up and then the 'Easy' route to Kunming, refuel, then another short hop to Chungking. Easy was the designation, of course, rather than any accurate description of the passage. In the topsy-turvy world of the CBI – China-Burma-India – theatre, Easy was the hardest route of all.

He watched the stick-thin porters heave the cargo on board his C-47. As Chennault used to say about the Chinese, they were like ants, lifting loads that seemed physically impossible, given their physique and meagre diets. He checked the manifesto: the British were transporting their usual rag-bag of documents, clothing, proprietary medicine and 'sundry items'. The last was probably that precious Bovril they liked to have with their biscuits, the meaty Wincarnis tonic they insisted was a 'pick-me-up' or the disgusting Horlicks they drank at bedtime.

The US component of his lift – by far the largest proportion – consisted of square steel containers, like ammo boxes, each stamped with their weight. They had arrived with an armed marine guard, two of whom would travel with the cargo, and they would be met by another escort at the other end in Chungking. Crane had to sign six forms before the impassive Marine Sergeant stood the majority of his men down. Even so, they stayed around the hangar until the plane took off.

As usual, his co-pilot Cowboy double-checked the manifests and weights while Crane did the visual check on their C-47. Cowboy looked and sounded like what was known as 'a hot dog' – cocky, swaggering know-it-alls who thought they all but wrote the book on flying in mountains. He wore non-regulation Olsen-Stelzer Western boots, a battered straw hat and even, when the mood took him, his monogrammed spurs. His face was craggy ahead of its time, his demeanour laconic, and when he walked he had a bandy, rolling gait that meant he could pass as a member of the Young Farmers of America. Crane suspected he came from Queens rather than Montana as he claimed.

The thing Crane knew about Cowboy was this: from his appearance and louche manner, everybody assumed he was one of those pilots shunted across to flying The Hump because he was dangerous in some way. The wild, the reckless, incompetent, drunk, disgraced: they had examples of all of them. Most flyers were good, that was expected, but nobody could deny The Hump was also a dumping ground for the troubled and the troublesome. Including ex-Flying Tigers with nowhere else to go.

Cowboy, though, was one of the best co-pilots Crane had ever had. Beyond the good-old-boy act, he was attentive, decisive and supportive in equal measure. Crane couldn't think of anyone he would rather have in the right-hand seat. Most pilots on The Hump had to put up with constant changes in co-pilots, as the juniors put in the hours and experience to get bumped to first pilots. Cowboy wasn't like that: he wanted to stay where he was. Crane knew that he was best suited to being number 2, a follower not a leader. If he had a fault, it was living in the moment, not planning ahead. That was just fine with Crane, because that was his speciality too.

Cowboy whistled across to him and he turned to see the British staff car sweep around one of the parked C-46s, and pull to a halt. In the rear was Laura with Major Clutterbuck. On the roof, a collection of new packing cases. She'd been shopping at the Army & Navy on Chowringhee Road, like all the Brits did. The Sikh driver yanked on the brake and leaped out smartly, opening the rear door with a salute. Laura emerged clutching a leather valise. Then he saw her face drop. At first, he thought she was displeased to see him, but when he spun around to see what had caused such obvious dismay, he realised he was standing under it. His plane.

He took a step back and looked at *Myra Belle* through Laura's eyes. The plane was a sludgy brown colour, faded and peeling from the effects of high-altitude weather. Her aluminium fuselage was dimpled in a few thousand places from hailstorms and ice-throws, and there was a slash of black across her tail where she had been struck by lightning. Even the image of a woman on horseback, rearing like Roy Rogers, although redone by Cowboy every few months, was scarred and lacerated. *Myra Belle Starr* had been through the wars all right, without a shot ever having been fired at her in anger. Her appearance wasn't helped by Crane's new addition – a large rearview mirror mounted on the pilot's side, which was bolted on by what looked like bits of scrap metal. Because that's what they were.

Laura was wearing a tailored cotton khaki safari-style suit, albeit one with a long skirt rather than trousers. She would be shocked in Kunming, where Elsa and the other Western women had abandoned skirts for all but special occasions, tired of bug-bitten legs.

As Laura approached, Crane stepped forward to take the valise but she swung it aside. 'I can manage. Hello, Captain. I didn't realise you were to be my pilot.'

Crane, of course, had known for a couple of days that he had been assigned a partial British upload to Kunming, and it wasn't hard to piece together who would be on it. His S section always got to run the spooks, and the young, fresh-faced Miss Laura McGill was certainly one of those. 'Hi. Welcome aboard the *Myra Belle Starr*.'

She looked at the name looped across the nose. 'Your mother?'

'Female Jesse James. Horse-thief, gambler, liar, and lover of Cole Younger. Not like my mom at all, really.'

'No, I should imagine not.' They had seen each other twice since the dance, when Crane had wangled a stopover, but it had been an hour or two only – a walk, a ferry-ride, tea. He had told her about his parents' small farm, his brother who was killed trying to break in a stallion, his love of airplanes. She'd told him pretty much zilch about herself or what she was doing in India or going to do in China. Which made her one of the Force 136 funny bunnies for sure.

Crane instructed some of the porters to fetch her luggage from the car. 'I'm going to need to weigh all that,' he said. 'And you.'

'Me?'

'And that bag.'

'Why?' she asked.

'Because these guys,' he pointed to the porters, 'are under orders to pack her to the gunwales. My job is to stop them.'

Major Clutterbuck, having satisfied himself that the loaders weren't going to steal his hubcaps, came up behind her and said solicitously, 'I'll see you to your seat, my dear.'

Crane almost laughed, but saw Pickle, his flight engineer, heading over from Ops and turned away to talk to him. Seat? he thought. Well, kind of. He should have told her to bring a cushion.

Chabua was a strip carved out of tea plantations, way to the north in Assam. While C-46s and C-47s roared in and out day and night, the traditional growing and picking of the plants continued all around. The crews based there permanently lived in large tents, and just about the only form of entertainment was the 'hide', a canvas shack which commanded a view across the fields where the beautiful young girls bent over to harvest the crop.

The weather en route was fine and Crane kept *Myra Belle* at around 10,000 feet for much of it, admiring the clear day and the gradual changing pattern of agriculture, from the parched fields, the wilting stands of mango, the dusty villages and dry rivers of Bengal to the increasingly dense, green covering of Assam as the land wrinkled and the region's trademark hills and terraces appeared. They circled the field, waiting for their turn to dodge the mountains and land. They touched down at one o'clock and, after taxiing onto the apron, Crane went back to ask Laura to stay on board. He would bring her a Spam lunch, perhaps a water buffalo pie that one of the British cooks knocked up as a speciality.

She opted for Spam and a banana. 'Captain? Why do I have to stay on board?' she asked, mopping her brow with a handkerchief.

Because there are a hundred guys here whose idea of a good time is waiting for an Indian girl's tits to fall out of her sari, was not an answer he wanted to give. 'Quarantine. There's a number of fever cases here. Best not take a chance. And there's snakes. Lots of snakes.' This last part, at least, was true.

'But it's roasting in here.'

'I'll get you a fan-boy.'

'And can you get a cushion of some sort? My . . . this bench is rather hard.'

'Well, *Myra Belle* was designed for paratroopers rather than Pan Am. But I'll see what I can do.'

A pillow landed at his feet and he looked down to see Cowboy's smiling face in the fuselage door. 'Direct from the PX, ma'am. Best duckdown. Chow's up, Lee.'

'I'll get you something to eat and we'll pick up our passenger and his gear and be gone. Next stop, Chung-kao: the Middle Kingdom.'

'Passenger?'

'Yup. You got more company,' he said, without adding: *a fellow spy*.

Hyram Nelson, the man who delivered his letter to Kitten, had become Crane's ringmaster: when he snapped his whip, Crane had to perform. He didn't like it, but he liked the idea of going home with a dishonourable discharge and then being drafted into the Army even less. Those had been the options when he had resigned from the Tigers: join the S section flying Gooney Birds or break his parents' hearts. Hyram, it transpired, was with the Office of Strategic Service, the OSS, and his job was . . . well, Crane still wasn't sure. 'Making Lee Crane's life miserable', it probably said somewhere.

Nelson had flown on *Myra Belle*, and dozens of other such crates, many times. After they had loaded on his designated 100 pounds of baggage, which included his personal parachute, the ultimate optimism, he inflated his rubber ring and sat down on it next to Laura, his eyes bright with the prospect of female company, and cinched his seat straps as tight as they would go. He'd been through turbulence before. Crane told Pickle, who in this C-47 configuration sat just aft of the cockpit bulkhead, to keep an eye on Mr Nelson while he went outside to do his visual.

After he had made sure that *Myra Belle* was still as fighting fit as she ever got and was filled with quality gas – a habit stemming from the fact that decent fuel wasn't always available back in his Tiger days – Crane stood in the shade of the nose looking towards the mountains and the first ridge. He'd got weather from the Ops hut and it didn't seem too grim. He'd checked with pilots just in from China on the Charley and Oboe – the more westerly – routes. Not bad, they said. Then again, on the return leg you were usually half-empty, with more room to manoeuvre if you needed to go around or above the weather.

Now he could see cumulus clouds forming over the Naga Hills and he squinted to try and see what was beyond them. It was pushing on to late afternoon. Would he get thunderheads? The 40,000-feet Himalayan monsters could flip your plane over and tear its wings off, like little boys playing with hapless moths.

Kunming – the first drop, with Chungking after that – was 561 miles away, well within range of the plane. Except that it wasn't normal flying, it was what one ATC planning officer called 'the Air Highway to Hell'.

Crane put on his old AVG Ray-Bans and looked at the hazy horizon once more. Something was happening; the sky seemed to be coalescing around the peaks, thickening into dense lumps. Ah well, it didn't matter really. There was a saying in the transport corps: *There is no weather on The Hump.* Because no matter what was up there, you had to get through it, so there was little point in worrying. He had a feeling that this particular aphorism didn't originate with the pilots.

There was one good side to any poor weather. It tended to keep the Japanese fighters, which operated out of the strips in Burma, down on the ground.

Crane glanced back up at the cockpit and got a thumbs-up from Cowboy. He checked he had enough gum for the trip – two packs – unwrapped one stick and climbed the ladder to inhale once more *Myra Belle*'s signature mix of gasoline, greased aluminium and ozone from the radio valves, and to fly his forty-third mission on The Hump.

Sixteen

The Hump, 1943

In the time it had taken to do an instrument check, the cloud cover had slid across above Chabua like a horizontal screen door. As it darkened, Cowboy had glanced at Crane, unbuckled his straps, and loped back across to Ops to try and get a weather update. When he came back he handed the sheet to Pickle and gave Crane a thin here-we-go smile before explaining that a C-46 from Paoshan was overdue and a B-24 had come in having been so badly shaken it had lost half its cargo of eggs.

Crane went back and warned his passengers that it might get a little bumpy, but not to worry, *Myra Belle* could take it, and that it was best if they could get some sleep. Nelson had snorted at the very thought of that. Crane then returned to the business of getting the ungrateful son of a bitch to Kunming in one piece.

Crane ran up the right engine, checked the mag drop, repeated the procedure with the left. Both Pratt & Whitneys sang their beautiful song to him.

'Call the tower,' he said to Cowboy.

'Victor Echo Zero One Two-Niner, ready for take-off. Over.'

'Victor Echo Zero One Two-Niner, you're cleared for take-off.

Circle to ten thousand before heading to LX, altimeter 2390, visibility two miles but dropping, ceiling five hundred. Give her the gas and God speed *Myra Belle Starr*. Over.'

A Jeep slid in front of them, its yellow FOLLOW ME sign illuminated, and Crane released the brakes and did as the wording instructed. *Myra Belle* trundled to the end of the runway, while Cowboy continued his singsong litany of the various engine functions. The jitters had gone now. Crane was committed. No turning back, that was the other rule, a matter of pride. At least, not while you had two functioning engines.

The tower came on again. 'Victor Echo Zero One Two-Niner, we have incoming traffic on a Priority One landing ten miles out. Please proceed as quickly as possible. Visibility now one mile, ceiling three hundred. Over.'

With the fuel mixture full rich and the props at high RPM, Crane pushed the throttles forward as soon as the Jeep swung out of the way. Cowboy put on his oxygen mask and got ready to grab the throttle and hold it steady. The routine dictated there was no locking down of the levers on take-off in case there was an abort.

The speed climbed slowly to 50 knots, then 60, the plane hopping over the bumps but staying true to the white line. A little more throttle and she was off, climbing reluctantly, airspeed up to 110, heading for the soup. The clouds reached out and grabbed them to their bosom, and the plane gave a cautious little judder. There were seven hours until touchdown and refuel at Kunming, and unless they could burst through the cloud cover, it was going to be entirely by the instruments.

The first ridge, the Naga Hills, poked into the sky at 12,500 feet, if they stayed on the Easy route. Stray to the north and there were 20,000-footers just waiting to welcome them in. 'Climb to ten,' said Crane, 'heading 214 to Moran. After Moran I want twenty thousand if I can get it. Pickle?'

'Skip.'

'They'll need oxygen back there. Can you tell them how to use it without getting high?'

'Will do, Skip.' Only the crew had a plumbed-in system; the passengers would take their supplementary oxygen from a bottle with a rubber mask attached. 'Listen, Skip, I just got the scuttle from a B-25. It's building over the Nagas. Building big.'

Crane looked ahead into a featureless dusk of rolling grey muck, and felt the plane ripple over unsettled air. What you prayed for were clear night skies and a big old moon, shining down to illuminate your path for you. He'd heard it even happened once or twice. 'I copy that, Pickle. Make sure they're strapped in tight.' He slipped on his own oxygen mask now as they passed 4000 feet. Couldn't be too careful.

The next fifteen minutes were spent maintaining a steady climb. Crane checked the instruments incessantly, and plotted their course on the 3-D topographical mental map he had created in his head. He knew where the treacherous peaks were, where the low-lying hidden valleys that would save your life lurked, and he knew every strip he might ever need in a diversion, from those carved into a plateau 8000 feet up a mountain, to one macheted and bulldozed from the Burmese jungle. The Hump was not going to have him without a fight.

They burst through the clouds at 8000 feet, into a clear sky, a beautiful deepening blue, the first stars just beginning to pulse. Cowboy took off his mask and whistled. He wasn't admiring the charms of the night sky. Ahead were the Nagas, and the clouds were broiling into one thick, towering wall of cumulo-nimbus blocking their way. Within it, Crane could see the faint spark of orange fire. 'Shit,' he said.

The glimpse of the heavens was shortlived, like a temptation dangled before condemned men, and the clouds enveloped them once more. The vibration became constant, chattering every loose surface, and Crane looked at the compass. It should have been on

210 for Moran, but was veering wildly. And this was just the first leg, before the real rockpile began.

Myra Belle began to buck, and Cowboy grabbed the controls with Crane, sensing what his first pilot was doing and quickly adding his strength, without fighting him. They could both feel the force pressing down on one wing, trying to flip them, and then it was gone and *Myra Belle* soared 400 feet into the air. Again, a downdraft, then its sudden release. No autopilot is going to work here, thought Crane; this was going to be manual all the way.

'Skip, we got vomit coming,' said Pickle in his ear, his teeth chattering from the vibration.

'Tell her there's bags behind her head.'

'Yeah, right. Oh – and Skip.'

'Yeah?'

'It's not her. It's one of the marines.'

'Right.'

The dark closed around them, cut only by subdued flashes of electricity, seen as if through thick muslin. The two of them fought in harmony to keep the plane level. They were over the nagas now, passing through 16,000 feet when they heard the first big thunk on the fuselage.

There was a second bang and a third. Crane thought for a second about the fear that must be gripping the passengers. They didn't know this noise was a good thing. Ice was forming on the props and being thrown off against the skin of the aircraft. It was when it wasn't thrown off that you were in trouble. He pressed the button that would feed alcohol to the propellers, which would help dislodge the frozen lumps.

'Ice building up,' said Cowboy.

'Yea—' The word didn't complete before the C-47 reared once more and Crane watched the altimeter spin as they were shunted upwards onto a flying carpet that was just as quickly pulled from under them. The nose swooped down and they were diving.

'Together. Together.' Cowboy and Crane worked the controls in unison, as smooth and unhurried as they could, and *Myra Belle* levelled out, the airspeed down to near stalling. Crane let it build up again. The compass was still oscillating, but he was pretty sure they were on the right heading. Not past the first ridge yet and he was already limp and sweating.

The airspeed dropped again. 'We haven't got the altitude,' said Cowboy. 'Your 'chute OK?'

Crane looked at him, but Cowboy slid his mask aside to show he was kidding. Baling out was not an option. Sure, their A2 flying jackets were lined with ideograms in various languages asking the finder to take the pilot to the nearest village for a great reward, but that wasn't much use on top of a Himalayan peak. It wasn't too much use in the Indo-Burmese jungle either, where some pilots swore the tribes were still cannibals and that tigers took those the headhunters didn't.

'We're going to have to de-ice,' said Crane.

'And lose some weight.'

'We'll see.'

Something was stopping them climbing, and they were burning up fuel at an unacceptable rate. The de-icing system was comprised of rubber 'boots' that could be inflated, cracking the surface of the ice, allowing the air steam to do the rest. That was the theory at least.

'I'm going to take a look.'

'OK.'

Crane took the flashlight and eased open the side window. Instantly the cockpit was full of a howling and swirling wind, as if a tornado had barged in through the gap. Tiny daggers smacked into his skin and Crane slammed the window shut again.

'Well?'

'Just do it, can't see a damned thing.' It was best if you could time it right, snap the ice at maximum build-up, which meant a

141

visual inspection. That was OK on clear days, but not on nights like this.

There was a series of thuds as more chunks flew from the props. They worked the boots and heard sections of ice break free and smack along the fuselage as they struggled through another 1000 feet. They were still 1000 feet shy of the safety zone.

'You have the aircraft?' Crane asked Cowboy.

The other man nodded. 'I have the aircraft.'

Crane let go, unstrapped himself and walked unsteadily back towards the rear of the plane. He smiled at Pickle who shook his head and said quietly: 'I just got three Maydays. One lost, one with an engine out, another icing up with boots that won't work.'

Crane squeezed his shoulder. There was nothing to say or do. You didn't want to be thinking about someone 'not sure of their position' – pilots never actually admitted to being lost – wandering around in the dark until the fuel ran out or the mountains claimed them, or trying to gain altitude while iced-up or with one feathered engine. All you could do was make sure you didn't join them.

The four passengers were all pale and grim-faced. Laura winced every time ice broke free and made its clapping sound on the aluminium, and he explained that it was nothing to worry about. One of the guards put his head between his knees and filled his third bag. The warm, pungent smell drifted up to him. Crane took a hit from Laura's oxygen bottle and said, 'We're going to have to dump some cargo.'

The guard snapped up, tried to say something, but thought better of it. His companion undid his sidearm.

'Not your stuff, pal. Not unless we have to. The rule is, personal belongings go first. Mail goes last of all.' He looked down at the valise case and Laura put her foot across it. 'No.'

'Yes. Or we don't clear the ridge into the high valleys. We've got about fifteen minutes.'

'You can toss all mine out,' said Nelson.

142

Crane nodded his thanks. The OSS man had been here before. He was on the legendary run when an engine went on a C-46 carrying a piano for the PX at Kunming. Somewhere on a Himalayan mountain were the shattered remains of a Bechstein, a broken symphony of polished wood, ivory and metal. 'And there are some fuel drums we can lose. But your cases . . .'

'Not this,' said Laura, reaching down and grabbing the leather bag. 'Everything else but this.'

'OK.' He braced himself as another shudder took the plane. 'Hyram, I can't stay off the flight deck. Can you give Pickle a hand? He knows the ropes. You must make sure you are tethered when you open the door. This slipstream catches you . . .' He indicated being sucked out into the night. Nelson nodded. 'Good. Do all the personal stuff first, and I'll let you know.'

Crane felt a flicker of dizziness, took some more oxygen, and swayed his way back up to the flight deck, listening to the splatter of ice on the fuselage. That was when the starboard engine misfired.

It was the usual weather trying to kill them, to make them follow their instincts rather than their instruments, to lure them to a lonely, forgotten death, just another plane never seen or heard from again. It was a combination of three air masses – lows moving west along the Himalayas, highs from the Bay of Bengal, and more lows from Siberia. Sometimes God stuck in an invisible spoon and stirred up all three at once, and the angry masses collided over The Hump.

'Nineteen thousand feet,' yelled Cowboy. Crane let out a sigh of relief. The combination of de-icing, dumping of cargo and the deploying of the carburettor heaters to stop the misfire had finally lifted *Myra Belle* to safety. Moran had steadied on the compass. Now they had to hope they could find the weak beacons out of Shingbwiyang and Tingkawksakan.

'You lost the mirror,' said Cowboy.

Crane looked to his left, where the stalk holding the convex glass disc had sheared, leaving torn metal spikes.

'Well, it was just a prototype. OK back there, Pickle?'

'So far.'

Crane reset the frequency to 1624 and began cranking the antenna, trying to locate Shingbwiyang. Static filled his headphones. Outside there were pellets of frozen rain hammering on *Myra Belle* and the windshield was icing up. The prop continued to shed clumps of it. Crane rotated some more, waiting for the signal to replace the crackle.

'Got her. At least I think I've got her. Shit.' It was in the wrong place, off the starboard wingtip. It should be over to port.

'Can't be,' said Cowboy, not believing his own ears. 'Can't be. Puts us fifty miles off course. To the north.'

To the north. Where there were peaks piercing the sky at 21,000 feet. And they were yo-yoing in turbulence between 18,000 and 20,000 feet. Cowboy looked at Crane, wondering what he was going to do. 'All we need is a decent star sighting.'

'Yeah,' Crane said. 'And sometimes, it's too much to ask for.'

'I guess.'

They both stared at the swirling mess outside, and knew the stars were a long way above them. 'I'm going to take us south,' Crane said levelly. 'Until I hit another beacon.'

'But—'

'I know I'm risking using too much fuel. But we can dog-leg it to Kunming. If we have to put down, there is an old AVG dispersal strip not far from Yunnanyi. It's got an emergency spares dump, including gas.'

'For us?' asked Cowboy, meaning ATC.

'For me. I stashed it there. It's an old Tiger tip I got from Chennault. But keep it under your hat. I don't want every Humpdog helping themselves.'

Crane didn't mention that the fuel, which had been decanted into suspiciously new-looking drums by the slug he purchased it from, might well be full of water and grit. Chinese fuel often was until the US had entered the war; there was still some of the gash stuff kicking around even then. *Myra Belle* could put up with a lot, but she hated water in the carbs at altitude. If they ever did land at Yunnanyi dispersal, they'd have to refuel, then let the stuff sit and then drain off the excess water and clean the filters. It would add hours to the trip.

'They still got the wires along the valleys there?'

Crane nodded. Early in the war, the Chinese had strung hawsers across certain approaches to airfields and cities to prevent Japanese low-level bombing attacks. There were some around Chungking, Yunnanyi, Paoshan and others. You just had to know where they were.

A voice crackled in his ear. 'Skip?'

'Yeah, Pickle.'

'Another Mayday. A C-46. Say they are showing position well north of the Shingbwiyang beacon. But they don't know how.'

Crane thought for a minute, desperately trying to compute their own location. Why would anyone end up north of that nav beacon? It was suicide up there. Unless . . .

'Tell them there's a side wind if you can raise them,' Crane said levelly. It was the only explanation. 'Everyone is being blown north and not realising it. They have to head south, they have to fight the winds.' South was Burmese jungle, and low hills. He'd rather run out of fuel there than risk making it between the more northerly peaks. 'OK?'

He waited for Cowboy to nod his agreement before he took a south-east heading, praying that he – and the instruments – were right. A few minutes later Pickle came back on.

'Skip. Can't raise that C-46. They've stopped transmitting.'

They flew on in silence, deeper into the unsettled night.

*

'Kunming Tower, this is Victor Echo Zero One Two-Niner. Request urgent priority approach. Not enough fuel to go around or stack. Do you read me? Over.'

After Crane made his correction and flew the dog-leg, which took them away from the most lethal peaks, but meant they were fighting a headwind for 200 miles, there was precious little fuel in the tanks. The weather at Yunnanyi had been so foul that they had been advised not to put down. Two planes had been totalled that night already. Now the Pratt & Whitneys were running on dregs, and he was hoping they wouldn't be told to stack over Kunming. He was letting her lose altitude through the clouds, following the beacon. The terrain down there was better than the Himalayas but Kunming sat on a plateau at 6000 feet, with a ring of mountains on three sides. You really, really wanted to come in on the correct approach.

'Kunming Tower—'

'Zero One Two-Niner, this is Kunming Tower,' said a welcome American voice. 'Glad to hear from you. You are free for a direct approach. Ceiling at two hundred. Watch for our flares.' Damn, they were using Very pistols to guide in lost planes, for those pilots tired, disoriented and confused. 'You're number two in.'

'Pickle?'

'Skip.'

'Tell the passengers they can stop praying now.'

'Me, too?'

'On your mark.'

'Yes, sir.' It wasn't until then that Crane realised how frightened his radio operator had been, and how tired his own jaw was from all the chewing. He checked his gum. Every last stick had gone.

As they broke though the muck and saw the runway lights on the far side of the dark waters of Lake Dian, and those of the chaotic town to one side, the sad arc of a flare calling home its wayward sons streaked into the sky in front of them. Crane checked landing gear, flaps, and began to drop the airspeed further.

Below them, reflecting the phosphor streaks of the flare, he could see the skein of canals that covered the plateau, and the dim oil lamps on the sampans that plied them, day and night, it seemed. *Myra* was past the mountains now, just the little matter of getting her in clean.

Crane broke out the flare pistol from the seat pocket and loaded a yellow cartridge. He slid open the window and fired, filling the cockpit with acrid smoke, and watched it arc away into the night. It meant, not enough fuel for a come-around, so stay clear.

The thin air of Kunming made for fast landings, but with nary a wobble, the bruised *Myra Belle* bounced just twice onto the crushed-stone surface and taxied past a line of Tomahawks and Kittyhawks. C-47s were notoriously difficult to land because the plane liked to fly, and touched down only reluctantly. Crane guessed that, this time, *Myra* was glad to be home, too.

A FOLLOW ME jeep swung in front and led them onto the grass, where the Gooney Bird rolled to a halt near the Ops building and its welcoming mess. Bacon, eggs and ham awaited them in there.

Cowboy undid his straps, held out his hand and said quietly: 'Nice flying with you, Captain.'

'You too, Cowboy,' said Crane, taking the hand. 'You too.'

Seventeen

Kunming, China, 1943

Laura McGill undid her straps and slumped forward on the bench seat. Her new suit was wrinkled beyond redemption, stained with sweat, splashed with vomit from the Marine Corporal and blood from the flight engineer, who had cut his fingers when he was dumping cargo. He had shaken his hand and flicked it everywhere. It must be in her hair, she realised. She felt like crying.

'Laura?'

She looked up and the weak interior lights had been blotted out. She blinked and saw a pale moon face looking down at her. 'Laura? It's me, Walter Gilbert. Are you all right?'

She had forgotten just how huge he was, almost filling the inside of the aircraft. She got to her unsteady feet, pitched forward, and he caught her. 'There, there. Come on, let's get you off this crate. May I?' He indicated the valise and she nodded. He swept it up with a small expectant smile.

Gilbert led her gently down the fuselage, supporting her all the way, and virtually lifted her out of the plane. As her feet touched solid earth and cooler mountain air caressed her cheek, she swivelled, ducked under the plane and was violently sick. 'Oh, dear

God, I'm so sorr—' Her insides heaved again and she doubled up once more, the sound of her stomach contents splattering on the cinder surface loud on the chill night air.

'I like a girl who waits till we're on the deck,' said a passing voice. Cowboy, the co-pilot.

Gilbert handed her his handkerchief and she dabbed her mouth. 'I'm sorry. What a mess. I—'

'The dogs'll eat it, don't you worry,' he laughed, and put a chubby arm round her. 'It was a rough trip, I hear. Don't worry, you'll get used to it.'

'Used to it?' she said, unable to keep the horror from her voice. 'I don't want to get used to *that*.'

From the Operations room came the sound of an argument, angry voices raised, the sound swelling as the door opened and slammed. Striding towards them was a tall, vivacious woman with a mane of hair trailing behind her. 'Oh God, save me from posturing pilots and thick-necked marines.' She wrinkled her nose. 'Hi, honey, just got in on the chuck-up express?'

'Ah, introductions,' muttered Gilbert. 'This is . . .'

'Elsa Cross. Pleased to meet you.' She looked around for signs of luggage. 'Travellin' light or did they ditch all your stuff?'

'They needed to lose weight.'

Elsa shook her head in sympathy. 'Everything?'

'Just that bag left. And it's not got anything of mine in it.'

'OK, come with me, you can borrow some bits and pieces till you can get to Fifth Avenue tomorrow.'

'Fifth Avenue?'

'You guys call it Bond Street.' She smacked at a bug on her neck and quickly lit a cigarette. 'Do you smoke?'

'Not really.'

'Then start. Keeps the damned mosquitoes away. Not so much malaria at this altitude but the little bastards still bite, just to stay in practice.' She offered a cigarette to Laura, who took it, accepted the light, and then held it around her head, taking the occasional puff, trying not to choke. 'Where you billeted?'

'I—' She looked pleadingly at Gilbert.

'Sandringham,' he said.

Elsa shook her head. 'Sandringham, huh? Look, ask them to show you the garden route into town, not over the sewers, OK? You dip a foot in one of those you better get your butt filled with jabs. But first, come to my place. I have clothes, I have Elizabeth Arden, and I have food.' She grabbed Laura by the arm and turned to Gilbert, who stood, still clutching the valise, looking flustered. 'I'll have her back before midnight. OK, pumpkin?'

Inside the Ops hut, the Marine First Sergeant began to fiddle with his carbine, not liking the direction the conversation was taking. 'My orders are to proceed directly to Chungking with our cargo,' he insisted.

The room was crowded with bodies and both the temperature and tempers were slowly rising.

'Listen,' said Branski, the duty controller, from his desk. 'We all have our orders.' He pointed at Crane. 'This man is within his rights to request a Form One.' This was a notification of a plane with technical problems. *Myra*'s port engine had stuttered a couple of times on the last leg.

'He can do that at Chungking,' said the Sergeant. 'Or you can give us another C-47.'

'There is no free plane. The others are scheduled to return to India with cargo.'

A groan went around the room. Those who had just come across had no desire to go back. Those who hadn't had no desire to discover why they were so reluctant. Crane finally spoke. 'Close The Hump.'

'The Hump never closes.'

'Do as he says. The marines can sleep in the plane. Close The

Hump,' snapped a voice like a whiplash over their heads. 'On my authority.' Hyram Nelson pushed his way to the front and handed Branski a piece of paper, which he unfolded, read and handed back.

'Hump's closed,' he said, resignation in his voice. 'Just till dawn.'

There was a sigh of relief all round and then a babble of conversation, as people tried to find somewhere to bed down for the night. Kunming was full to overflowing, thanks to the thousands of refugees who had come here for sanctuary from the Japanese. As he was meant to move on to Chungking that night, there was no space for Crane in the ATC *basho*.

Crane felt a hand on his shoulder and turned.

'Hello, Lee.'

'Gospel.' He took his old friend's hand and squeezed it. The fighter pilot did the same and smiled that big innocent aw-shucks grin of his. 'How are you? What you doing in Ops?' Crane asked.

'I just got in from a night instrument flying exercise on the Tommy. Rougher than I thought it was going to be up there, eh? Maybe you saw my pupil?'

Crane looked around. One of the elderly Tomahawks had been converted to a dual control two-seater for training local pilots. He couldn't see any of them in the room, though. He raised an eyebrow. 'Who?'

'Elsa.'

'Elsa? Christ, does her old man know?'

'Her old man is in Chungking badgering Generalissimo Chiang Kai-Shek on Chennault's behalf.'

Crane noticed the little gleam in Gospel's eye. A mite unChristian gleam, at that. He was sure there was a Commandment to cover such things, but said nothing. He hadn't seen Gospel in a while – he had made the transition to the 23rd, when Crane had walked out from the unit.

'Why does she want to fly?'

'Toungoo,' he said. 'Next time, she doesn't want to rely on the

British giving her a train ticket. She wants to fly.'

Crane said: 'The Japanese aren't going to make it this far.'

'Maybe not. I indulged her. Colonel Chennault said it would be OK.'

'Do you check her hands before flights?'

'Why?'

'In case she still has Chennault wrapped around her little finger.'

Gospel slapped him on the back. 'Where you staying?'

'I dunno. *Basho*'s full.'

'I'd invite you up, but . . .'

'Thanks.' Crane was banned from the 23rd Pursuit Group hostel, by personal order of Chennault – just in case he fomented more trouble with the pilots. Cowboy was welcome, of course, but not him.

'Sorry, I couldn't help overhearing. You need a billet, Captain?' It was Gilbert, still clutching Laura's valise.

'Yeah. If that's OK.'

'Oh, no problem, old chap. Anything for a bit of peace and quiet, eh? Look, we have a spare bed, if you don't mind a British breakfast.'

'Great. Much obliged. I've got to fill out a Form One saying the plane needs a look at and I've an A-bag with my gear in the plane, if the Sergeant will let me in to collect it. Where we headed?'

'Oh, nothing but the best for Hump pilots. How does Windsor Castle sound?'

Sandringham and Windsor Castle were two of the merchants' houses on the outskirts of the main town that had been taken over by the British as part of their Oriental Mission. One was for women – of whom there were half a dozen, mostly secretaries and signallers – one for men, around ten, and a third did duty as an office. The duo walked up the hill at a leisurely pace dictated by Gilbert's breathlessness, although the chill air meant Crane would have liked to kick up the speed a couple of notches.

'How much do you think it is worth?' asked Crane.

Gilbert turned and looked at him. He knew what the pilot meant. Nobody really talked about what got the marines so excited, but they were all aware of what it had to be.

'How much does it weigh?' asked Gilbert.

'On the loading manifest, a shade under two tons. Four thousand pounds, give or take.'

'Ah. In that quantity, it's probably in four hundred troy ounce bars. Well, as you know, the value of gold varies enormously. India, Bangkok, Macau . . . Premium prices paid. Either because of scarcity value – traditionally India can never get enough for its jewellery trade, or in the case of Macau, because it is shipped back to Portugal and sold at an inflated price to the Nazis.'

Gilbert paused to lean against the shutters of one of the street's shophouses. It was in these makeshift stores that much of the black market was conducted. All The Hump pilots knew that a fair sample of their cargo was skimmed off and sold on the streets. There was even evidence of quinine with US markings turning up on captured Japanese. To some people, the war was one big bazaar. Gilbert wheezed a little and moved off again. 'Should have got a ride on a Jeep. Sorry. Only a few hundred yards more.'

'Chelseas! Chelseas!' hissed a young voice from a narrow gap between the stores. He was after some of the cheap cigarettes that came with C-rations. If Americans had better smokes, they often gave the inferior ones away. Crane, who rarely indulged, just shook his head, but Gilbert snarled: '*Chu-la*.' The boy faded away as instructed.

'You want me to carry that?' Crane pointed to the case. Gilbert hesitated, then nodded and handed it over. They trudged on, stepping gingerly over crude cobbles slick with brown water.

'Let us say that a five-pound bar is worth one thousand five hundred dollars. Approximately. It's a conservative estimate, but it will do. It means that your four thousand pounds works out at—'

'One point two million dollars,' said Crane.

They passed one of Kunming's mosques, this one missing part of its dome from a bombing raid. It looked like a cracked eggshell against the night sky.

'Yes, very good.'

'What's it for, do you reckon?' asked Crane. 'Why are they wasting cargo space on that?'

'The gold? To keep Chiang Kai-Shek in the game, old boy. This whole theatre of war is about one thing – keeping the Japanese busy. Tying up divisions, planes. The Generalissimo isn't going to win the war for us, you know that. But while the Imperial Nippon army and air force are distracted here, and in Burma, your boys can chivvy away at them across the Pacific.'

Crane jumped over one of the streams of filthy water cascading towards him. 'That's a rather cynical view.'

'Left here. Perhaps. I've been out here, off and on, since 1932. I think it makes you cynical, old chap. For instance, I for one believe that the Generalissimo would seriously consider surrendering part of China to the Japanese, if they would help him fight the Communists. He hates them worse than the Japs. So, the gold makes sure that he and his cronies keep their eye on the main prize and come to no such accommodations.'

'And do you think you British will get your empire back?'

Gilbert smiled and raised an eyebrow, as if this were the dumbest question he had ever heard. 'Here we are.'

It was a three-storey white stucco house, set back in its own gardens, mostly European in style but with a number of Chinese architectural features bolted on. 'If I may . . .'

Gilbert took the valise and Crane found himself wondering what a cynical old China hand carried in his leather case. He dismissed the speculation. Sleep was what he needed now, if he was to do Chungking, back, and then The Hump again the next day.

*

Myra Belle Starr got a clean bill of health at 6 a.m.; by 7 a.m. Crane was down at Ops filing a flight plan and being told what he had to bring back from Chungking. The two marines were lurking around inside the C-47 in case anyone went for their $1.2 million. Crane was about to do an exterior visual check with Cowboy when he heard someone calling his name. It was Nelson.

'Captain. Have breakfast with me.'

'I've had breakfast.'

'Coffee, then.'

They walked over to the chow-shack next to the Ops room where the cook-boy dished out a vague approximation of American food, and excellent Across the Bridge noodles. Nelson fetched him a coffee and a *tuocha* green tea for himself and they sat on the packing crates that doubled as chairs. The angry weather had gone, the sky was dotted with inoffensive white clouds, and a weak sun was shining. The previous night, anyone would have laughed at the usual description of Kunming as the 'city of eternal spring'. That morning, it seemed nicely appropriate.

'Quite a flight, in,' Nelson remarked.

'One in three,' said Crane. 'You can reckon on getting shook up on a third of all flights on Easy.'

'I spoke to Miss McGill on the flight – when we could make ourselves heard. You saw her in Calcutta.'

'I met her at a dance. Told her I had also met her sister, briefly. We saw each other a couple of times. End of story.'

'She likes you.'

'People tend to like any pilot who gets them here in one piece.'

Cowboy waved him over but Crane held up five fingers and counted down to one to indicate he would be as quick as he could.

Nelson asked: 'You stayed with Gilbert?'

'In the British mission, yes.'

'What do you know about Walter Gilbert?'

'He's big and he's English.'

155

'No. He's Austrian.'

'What?'

'Walter Guber is his real name. Oh, he's naturalised now.'

'Austrian? Aren't they meant to be on the Germans' side?'

'Not this one, apparently.'

Crane took two quick mouthfuls of his coffee.

'You should switch to tea. It's very good.'

'I know. I just can't get the taste. My body seems to think bad coffee better than good tea. Look, I gotta Marine Sergeant who's going to get carbine fever again soon.'

'I know. Did you see what was in the bag?'

'The valise? No. It isn't gold bullion.'

'No, not heavy enough.'

'Why are you interested?'

'I want to know what that fat fuck is up to,' Nelson said with surprising venom. 'That time we saw him land, before the Japanese had even made their moves on Singapore and Hong Kong, he was sniffing around Kunming, setting up this "mission" of his. This is our back yard, now, not the Brits'. They can have Burma again once this is all over. China is ours. They know that. They are not allowed to run subversive ops within its borders. Yet somehow, Gilbert has managed to get an operation here, answerable to no one—'

'How?'

'I wish I knew. You know, the first thing the Brits sent him here to do was to deny rubber to the Japs. Tried to buy it all up.'

'And?'

'You notice any Japanese planes without tyres? The man's a fantasist, I think. Full of stupid schemes. But I need to know what the plan is now. Oh, the British mission here is supposed to be looking after the welfare of any POWs in China, helping those who managed to get out of Hong Kong. There are certainly some of those, but . . . no, he's up to something else. On my beat, Crane. And Uncle Sam's. I'm worried what, exactly.'

Crane pointed to his plane. 'That's all I'm worried about. *Myra Belle* is my concern, period. Look, Nelson . . .'

The OSS man peered back over the rim of his cup. 'I need you to get close to the girl.'

'What?' Crane spluttered.

'Find out what they are doing up there.'

'Close to her? That's very quaint. Spy on her, you mean?'

'Don't curl your lip when you say that. Surveillance, if you will.'

'Why me? There's dozens of guys round here who'd—'

'I don't control dozens of guys. I control you. You owe me, remember? You are still flying a plane rather than a foxhole because of me.'

It was true that Nelson had found him a job over Chennault's head. 'So, time to cash in your IOU?'

'Yeah, if you want to look at it that way.'

Crane watched two figures walking across towards the line of shark-faced Tomahawks beyond *Myra Belle*. Gospel and Elsa, off for another lesson. Elsewhere three Kittyhawks, the improved version of the P-40, were taxiing into position for a patrol. He felt a pang of envy, but couldn't decide if it was for the fighter pilots and their sleek monoplanes or Gospel's dalliance with Elsa. The former, he reckoned.

Cowboy ambled over towards them and Nelson said quickly: 'I can make sure you come to Kunming, get stop-overs, be the one to do the Calcutta runs. You know what that means?'

Crane nodded. Calcutta to Kunming on the low route. Over peaks that were more hills than mountains, and lots of jungle. Hugging Burma airspace, the trip could be undertaken without refueling at Assam, but there was an increased risk of fighter interception and flying over the ack-ack guns that the Japanese mounted on flatbed trucks.

'And you'll have to put up with the jumpy marines once a month maybe.'

Cowboy reached them, spat out his gum and held his arms wide in appeal, and Crane said, 'Just comin'. Mr Nelson here wants us to switch to the Calcutta run permanently. The low routes.'

Cowboy grinned. 'After last night, I'll drink to that. Now move your ass, Captain. That cargo isn't gettin' any lighter and if the sun gets any hotter we'll start bleeding gas into thin air.'

Crane looked up as the Kittyhawks circled back over the field, slotted into a 'V' formation and headed off into the sun, looking hungry and eager for action. The pang came back and didn't go away. Cowboy walked back to the C-47, shaking his head impatiently.

'Is that a yes?' asked Nelson, as Crane pushed himself off the crate and flung away the bitter dregs of the coffee.

'I'm not that welcome in parts of Kunming these days.'

'Are you talking about that pumped-up son of a bitch Chennault? He messes with us and I'll have him eating those phoney General stars with milk for breakfast.' There was a look on Nelson's face that suggested he could do it, too. 'Don't worry about him. His stock is falling. What about it? Did I mention the OSS field allowance? Three hundred a month on top of ATC pay. Shit, boy, I've made worse offers in my time.'

'I'll bet.' Why not? He didn't have to tell Nelson anything he didn't want to. And he'd had less pleasant assignments from on high than hanging out with a pretty girl whenever he got the chance. And compared with the Easy route, the southerly flight from Calcutta was a milk run. 'Yeah, OK,' said Crane eventually. 'It's a deal.'

'Flares,' said Cowboy, reading from the checklist.

Crane checked the pack at the side of his seat. 'Orange, red, green . . . shit, I never replaced that yellow.'

'We'll do it at Calcutta.'

'Right. OK, let's get them turning.' As they ran through the

Before Engine Start procedure, Cowboy mumbled something that Crane didn't catch.

'Say again,' he said.

'Girls.'

'Girls?'

'We can make a fortune if we can just get two girls in from India on each flight. Christ, the whole Twenty-Third are looking for a little action. Most of the women here are either out of bounds or you wouldn't want them anyway.'

'Cowboy?'

'Captain.'

'No girls, OK? We've got OSS breathing down our necks now. No girls.' He didn't tell him about the deal with Nelson, but he made a mental note to split the OSS bonus with him. He didn't want Cowboy looking for other means to top up his pay.

'But—'

'I know. Everyone is at it. Jeez, I'm not blind. But not us, OK?'

Cowboy pursed his lips for a moment, then grinned to show there were no hard feelings. 'Magneto master button?'

'In. Left and right switches off.'

'Check. And . . . clear!' Crane positioned his hand into the classic three-finger chord for the C-47 controls. Middle finger on the crank engine switch, ring finger on booster ignition switch, index on primer switch.

At that moment Crane saw a figure run across the front of the plane and duck under the wing. 'Watch for prop-jumpers when we start up. Ramis got one last week,' Crane said.

Some superstitious Chinese liked to run in front of the plane's propellers, believing it would chase away evil spirits. Crane had never hit one yet, but he'd seen the mess left by those pilots who had. Didn't do the props much good, either.

'Clear!' he said once more, and *Myra* spluttered into life.

Eighteen

Bond Street's real name was Shuncheng Jie, and it was a dusty strip of shophouses with pull-down fronts, onto which the articles for sale were spread. Sometimes it was trussed chickens, at other times it was ancient bicycle inner-tubes, mostly perished, followed by bunches of dried herbs, fly-infested animal parts, or racks of bizarre-shaped fungi. The proprietors of most stalls had yet to learn the art of the hard-sell; they simply stared at the two women who examined their goods, indifferent to whether they purchased or not.

The air was gritty with the ash from cooking fires, and the smell of effluent arose from the trickles of water that criss-crossed the street like a pungent capillary bed. Laura stepped carefully between them. Elsa seemed to have a built-in radar: despite strolling back and forth, mooching at each shop, her white tennis shoes remained unsullied. Laura's footwear, however, was soggy after five minutes.

Chickens pecked in the dust before them, and raggedy children stood and stared with baleful eyes and chanted: '*Tang*?'

Laura looked quizzically at Elsa. 'Candy,' she explained. 'But don't give it, at least not till you are ready to hightail it home. You'll get mobbed.'

Elsa dropped other nuggets of advice every few yards as they picked their way down the street. 'Watch the water melon,' she said. 'It's sold by *catty*, by weight. So some farmers inject them with water from the paddy fields. Suck on that and you'll get to know your local latrine real well.'

She indicated a bubbling pot of broth: 'And I'd go easy on the soups and stews till you know your way around. First time a whole frog floats to the surface is a test of nerve. But you know, with the canals and the lake, turtles and frogs and fish heads end up in lots of things. So if an unknown soup is offered, just say *sui bien*. It's a polite decline.'

Laura found what she was looking for on a particularly sparse counter, which mostly consisted of rusted machine parts. She snatched it up, removed the lid and rotated the base, watching with glee as almost an inch of bright red slid out. 'Elsa! Look.'

From across the street, Elsa tutted at her, narrowing her eyes. 'Price just went up, darlin'. Put it down. You look too keen. Come here.' She clicked her fingers and Laura placed the lipstick back among the gaskets and wandered across to where Elsa was taking an inordinate interest in a couple of sad strips of pork belly.

'Sorry. It's Rimmel lipstick. Pretty much unused, by the look of it.'

After watching the public letter-writers at work and examining the display at a lantern shop, a well-stocked and colourful emporium for once, Elsa finally said: 'OK, let's take a look at this Rimmel.'

They crossed over to the pile of metal and, after handling several spark plugs as if she really did have a use for them, Elsa picked up the lipstick.

'How did a Rimmel lipstick get out here?' asked Laura.

'Salvage, maybe from cargo dumped over the mountains, or loot from an abandoned missionary station. Not usually lipstick from the Bible folk, I'll grant you. A lot of Western stuff came across from Hong Kong and Shanghai, although that's pretty much dried up now.' She looked at the shopkeeper, an old woman who was tugging at her earlobe enthusiastically. 'That means we've made an excellent choice,' said Elsa. *'Ni goh geih doh chin a?'*

'Five dollah,' came the reply from the woman.

Elsa dropped the lipstick as if she had been scalded. *'No Mei Kuo Ren. Ying,'* she barked at the woman, pointing at Laura. 'It means you're British. They know you guys aren't as loaded as us.'

Laura hesitated, then opened her bag.

'What are you doing?'

'Giving the lady five dollars,' said Laura.

'Aw, c'mon—'

'Look, my lunchtime is nearly up, I can't play these games.'

'Games? This isn't a game,' snapped Elsa. 'This is how things are done.'

Laura thrust the notes into the shopkeeper's hand and pocketed the gilt cylinder. 'There. Wasn't too painful.'

'How much would that have been back home?'

'Two and six. About fifty cents. But we're not back home.'

'This is your home now.'

Laura shrugged. 'Sorry.'

'You'll learn.' Elsa looked at her watch. 'You want something to eat? We could go sit at the back of Billie's. Or they do a good *qiguoji* at that—' She stopped even as she pointed to the food stall at the end of the street, next to the bamboo and tin shack that passed for the local post office and telex centre. 'Looks like someone beat us to it.'

Standing at the stall, one elbow on the counter, enthusiastically pushing lumps of the stewed chicken from an earthenware pot into his mouth, was Lee Crane.

On the way to the lake the following Sunday, a scarf wrapped across her mouth to keep out the worst of the dust from the unmetalled roads, Laura wondered how a hurried conversation over a hastily consumed plate of fried noodles had turned into what she supposed was a kind of a date. It must be, because she had used some of her precious Rimmel on it.

Somehow, Lee Crane had managed to get her to agree to a picnic out in the country. Elsa, smirking, had claimed she would be too busy with Ron, her husband, to join them.

Crane was at the wheel of the Jeep he had borrowed, dressed in a checked shirt and khaki pants, a battered baseball cap wedged down on his head. It was a clear, crisp day, like a fresh shot of spring, with just a few ragged strips of clouds drifting over the Sleeping Beauty Hills to their right.

Lake Dian stretched south of town for about eight miles, and the road took them along its western shore, through the rice paddies and the poppy fields that provided the opium that was sold openly on street corners throughout Kunming. There were small fishing junks out on the water, their bamboo-battened sails taut in the breeze, and small clusters of houses on the banks every half-mile or so. Gilded temples winked at them in the sunlight, rich and opulent compared to the fishermen's shanties, including one near a summit in the hills. Crane saw her staring and said: 'That was a merchant's villa for a while, then it got religion. There's also a whole series of caves, sculptures and grottoes up there. Dragon Gate. It was dug by Taoist monks in the late eighteenth century. Quite something, although you need a head for heights.'

'After flying The Hump, big drops don't scare me. Just the thought of doing it again the other way.'

He smiled at her. 'Once you know *Myra*'s wings are going to stay where they've been put, it gets easier.'

She examined his face. He was probably in his early twenties, but the fine network of lines around his eyes aged him. She guessed it was from squinting into the sky, looking for stalking Zeros or looming mountains. 'Is that true?'

'Kinda. Wings are bolted on real good.'

'That's not what I meant.'

'Does it get easier?'

He pulled the Jeep offroad, heading down a rutted track towards the lake itself. His voice quavered as the vehicle bounced and jolted over the rocks that littered the path. 'You never can tell. Every trip is different. Still, you're here now. As you say, you only have to do it when you go back. If we haven't won by then.'

She didn't reply, and he swept the Jeep off the track over an area of tough grass and pulled up. The lake was lapping at a shingle beach. Two piers had been constructed from wood, about 200 yards apart, and they ran parallel out into the water. He pointed to them and explained: 'You seed the water with bait. Then, one man on each walkway, net in between them, walk out. Five minutes later, you got a meal – perch, crayfish, whatever.' He hopped out and grabbed the basket of food from the rear. 'Or, you can bring a picnic.' Something made him stop.

'You OK?'

She patted her stomach. 'Attack of the butterflies. Walter told me I may have to go back to Calcutta more than once. In fact, every six weeks, perhaps.'

He helped her out of the Jeep, walking down the grass slope with her towards the piers. 'It'll be OK. Sometimes you do a day flight over the mountains, and they are so beautiful, it makes your insides ache. You can see vast fields of snow, hidden valleys thousands of feet deep, knife-edged ridges that run for hundreds of miles, and wave after wave of these incredible peaks that seem like they go on for ever, then as you come down, lose altitude on the far side, there are eagles soaring over the meadows below, sometimes mountain sheep looking up at you, elephants, too, lots of ibex, musk deer. Some pilots say . . .' He stopped, as if the sudden attack of lyricism embarrassed him.

'What?'

'They say that there are times up there, mostly on full moons, when you can see tigers, sitting in the snow, not scared, just watching you. That's what they say.'

'You don't believe it?'

'You'd need good eyes, even lumbering along at a hundred knots. Also, moonlight plays tricks on you. It looks as bright as daylight, but it isn't, and that throws your senses. It's hard to judge distances, figure out what's a shadow and what isn't. You have to be careful.'

'So you've never seen one? A tiger?'

Crane shook his head. 'I've seen tracks, though, in the snow on plateaux, and I've wondered what made them, so high and lonely. But I'm no expert. Could be goats, for all I know. Anyway, it'll be fine. The Hump is mostly a walk in the park.'

On uneventful days over The Hump, they listened to the propaganda of sultry-voiced Tokyo Rose on the radio. She had taken to reading out lists of aircraft lost or missing in the mountains and jungles of the CBI, and the names of their crews. It was scary that she knew so much, even more worrying just how long that list was getting. Crane decided not to share any of this. All he said was: 'Trust me, I've done it a couple of times now.'

'That's what I was thinking. Can I fly with you when I have to go?'

'Well, it doesn't work like that. There's a rota.' Which Nelson could play with any time he wanted, of course. Those kind of people always could.

'Please?'

'Yeah, sure,' he said after a minute's thought. 'Why not?'

They sat on a blanket spread on the rough planks of the northernmost wooden walkway, watching the fishing junks make lazy turns as they trawled the lake. There was *baba* bread, goat's cheese, fat slices of ham from the PX, fruit and a delicious local rice dish laced with a sauce that made her lips glow.

Crane asked her about herself, and she told him more about Diana, her sister, and how she had recruited her to work for Walter, and about the tossing of the coin, and how she expected to swap jobs with her in a year or so. He was a good listener, only interrupting to offer her more food or a drink of what he called soda, but was actually lemonade.

'I don't really know what you do, up there at Windsor Castle and Sandringham,' he said eventually.

'Oh, we mostly keep an eye on British interests,' she said glibly.

'I didn't think you guys had any interests. I thought this was Uncle Sam's backyard.'

'Oh, it is. But a few little corners used to be ours. We'd quite like them back one day.'

'Hong Kong?' he suggested.

'Exactly.'

'It's eight hundred miles to Hong Kong,' he said.

'Well, yes. We'd be nearer but I do believe there are some Japanese in the way.'

He laughed and let it drop. There was plenty of time to fulfil Nelson's brief. He was having too good a time to pursue it now, the sun on his face, a pretty girl, a full stomach and, waiting at the bottom of the basket, two beers, which might still be cold.

'I've been invited to a party,' she said.

'Oh yeah? Whose?'

'The American pilots. Up at the villa in the hills.'

'Dragon House?'

'Yes.'

'You drink beer?' She shook her head and pulled a face. 'Mind if I do?' Another shake and he dug out a bottle and flipped off the cap with the opener in his pocket-knife. He took a swig. 'If

166

you don't drink beer at that party, they'll offer you gin, maybe in a cocktail. Don't drink it.'

'Why?'

'It's brewed somewhere up there.' He pointed to the Sleeping Beauty range. 'And it's got nothing to do with juniper berries. One is OK. The second one, you start seeing colours and shapes and patterns. The third . . .' Crane drank some more.

'What happens on the third?'

'Well, you won't remember the third. But you'll know you had it because you'll wake up in some very strange place with a drill trapped in your head, trying to get out through your eyeballs. Just a friendly warning.'

'Thank you.'

'And like Calcutta, you'll be outnumbered.'

'Are you fretting about my honour, Mr Crane?'

He took another sip of beer. He looked at her, enjoying the way the wind whipped the hair across her face, and how she reached up and tucked it back behind her ear, a gesture repeated every few minutes. 'I guess I am. Thing is, there were rules and conventions over there. This side of The Hump, anything goes.'

'I'll remember that. Will you be there?'

He shook his head. 'Not invited.'

'You know, Elsa said something funny about you.'

'Yeah, Elsa has something funny to say about everyone.'

'She's nice.'

Crane shook his head from side to side, as if weighing this up. 'She's a character, all right.'

A junk heaved close to shore, the crack of its heavily-patched sails like a gunshot as the wind filled them. The crew shouted something across to them. Crane cupped an ear to show he couldn't hear. After a while he shook his head.

'I think they're offering a cruise.'

'Shall we go?'

Crane smiled. 'Cost us twenty bucks gold to get on. Twice that to get off.' He smiled and waved at the cluster of men staring across at them, but they remained impassive. '*Sui bien*,' he yelled. 'No thanks.' The boned sails billowed once more, the junk gathered speed and began to tack.

'You know, in Burma fishermen are despised because they kill things, which is not the Buddhist way. The fishermen always say they don't kill the fish – they just put them out to dry.'

She laughed. 'And here?'

'Well, there's not so many Buddhists, so being a fisherman is a decent occupation.'

'We don't really know them, do we?'

'Who?'

'The locals. The Chinese. We let them cook and shine our shoes, but they are just like ghosts drifting through our lives. I tried to speak to our *amah* about her life, but I got nothing . . .'

Crane recalled some of the details of Chennault's early lectures. 'There are twenty-five different ethnic groups hereabouts, so I'm told. It'd take a lifetime to know all there is to know. That's assuming they want to tell a Big Nose – no offence – all their business. That's not why we're here. We're here to throw out the Japs, and let the Chinese get on with their lives.'

'And will we?'

'Let them get on with their lives?' He laughed and shook his head. He thought of Nelson, already obsessed with postwar boundaries, treaties and spheres of influence. 'Somehow I doubt it.'

She threw him a fast, low curve ball. 'Elsa also told me that you haven't got a heart.'

He thumped his chest. 'Well, something's driving the blood round.'

'You know what I mean. She said it belonged to someone else.'

Crane stood and brushed crumbs off himself. From the basket he fetched a canvas pouch containing lead weights, a fishing line and hook, and impaled a piece of bread on the barb. He dangled his legs over the side of the pier and cast the line out into the water.

'Well?'

'She's full of . . .' He took a breath. 'Elsa thinks I was in love with someone once.'

She shuffled over to the edge of the blanket to be nearer. 'Was?'

'It was a while ago now.' He pulled the line in and threw it further into the lake, watching the hook sink below the ripples. 'As time goes on, it kind of fades. Some days, it's like trying to wrestle smoke. Others . . .'

'Want to tell me about her?'

'Don't want to ruin a good day, Laura. If you don't mind. Some other time.'

'Did you love her?'

He tried not to wince as his stomach cramped. 'Some other time, eh?'

The guiding rule at Bille's on Dashea Lu Street was simple: the further back you sat, the better the service and food. Like every other US pilot, Crane favoured the rear wall, where he was eating a steak when Nelson came in. The OSS man ordered the chicken and a green tea. Outside, a squall of icy rain drummed on the tin roofs, sending the letter-writers scurrying for cover clutching their pens, ink and paper.

'Well?' he asked.

'Well what?' replied Crane.

'How'd you get on?'

'Oh, I kissed her and she told me everything.'

Nelson looked over his glasses, unsure whether he was being goosed or not. 'Really?'

'What do you think?'

One of the town's many cats wrapped its tail around Crane's

leg, the bells on its collar tinkling. He dropped it a piece of gristle.

'I guess not. I'm in no hurry. None of us is going anywhere.'

Crane looked out at the water streaming down the street and the coolies battling their way through the downpour. He watched an imperious Naxi woman, her signature blue and white apron already sodden, stride unbowed through the swirling rainwater. 'I am. Calcutta, remember?'

'Yeah, yeah. It's taken care of. You're scheduled for Dum-Dum again.'

The chicken arrived and Nelson examined it carefully, making sure it was the genuine article and not heavily disguised pigeon, paddy rat or large frog, before he cut it up.

'Maybe not,' said Crane.

'Meaning?'

'I'm not doing it, Nelson.'

'C'mon. She's a pretty gal—'

'I'm not doing it. Period. I'm not being your gigolo.'

'I got you the low route.'

'I'll take my chances.'

'Well, there is the little matter of the circumstances of you leaving the Tigers. Desertion. Cowardice in the face of the enemy . . .'

It was all the charges he'd been threatened with, although none had been brought in the end. Nelson liked to take credit for that. 'Yah-dee, yah-dee. Go ahead. I used to be scared of all that crap. Now, I think you'd just all look stupid. And you'd have to prove I was under US military jurisdiction at the time.' Crane cut himself another piece of meat. 'Look, I like Laura. It's not exactly, what do you call it, an onerous task. But I ain't screwin' her to order. Even if she was that sort of girl. Which she's not.'

The other man considered this for a moment. 'No. I guess you're right. So how do you feel about being a platonic friend?'

Crane chewed for a second. 'I'd probably feel great if I knew what it meant.'

'A non-sexual friendship. Shoulder to lean on. Friendly face. Man who can get nylons and chocolate. Nothing you wouldn't do anyway.'

'And if she should let slip something of value . . .' Crane waved an arm in the air.

'Of value to Uncle Sam, remember.'

Crane considered for a moment. 'Maybe. There's another condition.'

Nelson shook his head in frustration. 'Not Kitten again. I looked for her, Crane. Every goddam place. I saw her when I delivered the letter, remember? A good-looking woman. But . . .' He looked down at the table, not wanting to catch Crane's eye as he said his next piece. 'You know the majority of people tried to make it across the hills into India after the Japs invaded? On the map, it looks like nothing, but on the ground, Jeez, it's rough. They reckon twenty thousand died trying to cross into India. Twenty thousand. Soon after the refugees started on the trails, the rains came, flooding the rivers, sweeping away the bridges and rope crossings. With the rain came mosquitoes, and ten days later, the first malarial cases.'

'You think I don't know all that?'

'I'm just sayin' . . . nobody took down the names of those people who died on the trail or were swept away trying to swim the rivers. Nobody buried them. Hell, I looked everywhere last time you asked, Lee.'

Crane stood up and threw some change down. 'Look again, Hyram. Look again.'

Nineteen

The next hop back from Calcutta was one of those days on The Hump that made Crane think he had the best job in the whole CBI theatre. They took off from Dum-Dum, heading north-west into the smudge of a rising sun, the inky-blue world of sabre-toothed mountains and dark, forbidding jungle growing lighter by the second.

When they reached cruising altitude, the Himalayas on their left were on fire; to their right, the tangle of green, now tinged with orange, stretched to the horizon. Immediately below them were the thinner, mixed deciduous forests of the Lower Himalayas. The only sign of life was a cloud of dust they spotted. Cowboy reckoned it was elephants on a river bank, but it could just as easily have been vehicles of some description, such as the Japanese mobile anti-aircraft units, so Crane let *Myra* drift to the north, well out of range, just in case. He breathed easy when no black roses – the shell bursts from ack-ack – appeared in the sky.

Behind them, apart from Pickle at the radio, there was only cargo. No marines, no passengers, just music for the PX, beer, a couple of 55-gallon fuel drums, prophylactics, candy and lots of mail. The air was unnaturally still, *Myra Belle* sang sweetly and the nav beacons stayed where they were meant to be. After a course correction, the early-morning rays formed a spiked crown around the black lump known as Sunrise Point, telling them they were heading just right.

On a lustrous day like this, when the mountains looked less like rows of dangerously serrated teeth, and more like patterns a kid had made in whipped cream, Crane and Cowboy loved the Sperry autopilot. Sometimes, with a high, bright sun streaming into the cockpit, one of them would hunker down and doze off.

Then, Crane would allow himself to drift back to Toungoo, imagining a hot, steamy afternoon, stroking Kitten's skin, kissing the sweat that ran onto her shoulders, basking in the afterglow of the lovemaking that followed tiffin. It made waking up kind of hard.

China came into view without incident, gradually becoming more verdant and welcoming as the rocky plateau gave way to geometrical rice terraces and then paddy fields. As they flew over the Middle Kingdom's hills, Crane could see the disfiguring marks of concrete, housings for the steel hawsers that were still strung high across the valley to thwart dive bombers or ground-strafers. They passed to the south of the old AVG dispersal base west of Yunnanyi, a neglected scratch on the surface of the earth.

'How come you got fuel stashed down there?' asked Cowboy.

'I did some horse-trading with Mason. Before you transferred in.'

'Ah.' Mason was a famous Mr Fix-it who could get anything. If you signed a chit for Mason, you better read it carefully. So if you burned up thirty gallons hopping a P-40 from Kunming to Yunnanyi, Mason would often put you down for sixty. The spare thirty would end up being sold to the Chinese, or to an Air Transport pilot hedging his bets.

'You sure it's still OK? Neglected gas has a way of, y'know, evaporating down there.'

'I'm not that dumb. I buried it.'

173

As they came near the main Yunnanyi airstrip, Crane could see a group of US planes practising their dogfights, P-51 Mustangs against the older P-40s. It seemed like they only had each other to fight these days. It was a while since Crane had seen serious incursions by Japanese planes this far east. Those early waves of bombers and the escorting Nates and Hayabusas seemed like a long time ago.

One fighter skidded in front of them, 100 knots faster than *Myra*, tucked into their path, waggled its wings and rolled away. *Myra* bounced over the disturbed air in its wake. Crane watched the P-40 level out, struggle back up to their altitude and fall in alongside. It took some time: they never had fixed that climb-rate problem, even in the later models. He looked across and saw Gospel, grinning like an idiot and offering the thumbs-up. There was something odd about the fighter, and it took a second for Crane to realise what it was. He raised Gospel on the radio.

'What the hell are those tubes under the wings?'

'Top secret, Lee. Just gives us our own personal Fourth of July.'

'Rockets?'

'Can't say, Lee.'

'How are you, Gospel? Still giving civilians free flying lessons?'

'Who said they're free?'

Crane shook his head at the idea of Elsa and Gospel, the tiger cat and the Bible boy. 'Yeah, well, don't you eat all those candy bars at once.'

He heard laughter returned in his ears, and Gospel dived away once, down towards the Mustangs; Crane felt a little flash of regret that he couldn't follow him. *Myra Belle* just whispered on, eating up the miles of the air corridor, doing her unsung bit.

He let Cowboy take her into Kunming, a flawless approach through the mountains and over the plateau's watery veins.

As they taxied to a halt on the cinder, Crane felt his good mood evaporate like gasoline on hot concrete when he saw Hyram Nelson standing in the shadows of the hangars, staring his way.

'Cowboy, can you do the paperwork?'

Cowboy looked down and saw him too. 'Sure. That your new best friend?'

'He's nobody's best friend but his own. But he's the one keeping us on the south route.'

'Well, he's my new best friend then.'

The props had barely stopped before several eager figures – cooks, supply clerks, entertainment officers and Staff Sergeants – rushed forward, keen to claim their share of the bounty. Marshall, the Senior Stores Sergeant, sprinted to head them off, while the coolies who would unload looked on with bemused detachment. This was one of the many danger times, when goods mysteriously vanished into the black economy.

'And shoot anyone who comes on board before we get signed off by Marshall,' Crane added.

'Be my pleasure.'

Nelson led Crane over to the chow shack and uttered some pleasantries about the flight while Crane had his drink, then they walked away and stood next to a P-40 Tomahawk, an older model, that was being cannibalised for spares. With a shock, Crane realised it was *Bacon*. The writing and logo under the cockpit had faded and were almost illegible. There were nine little Japanese planes marked on it. There had only been four and a pig when he'd walked away from her for the last time.

She looked forlorn now. The engine cowlings were open, part of the manifold was undone, the carburettors had gone, wiring looms spilled out of several of the access hatches, and hydraulic fluid dripped from half a dozen places. The Perspex of the cockpit was cracked and milky-white. She was clapped-out.

A C-46 kicked up dust as she bumped towards the far end of

the strip. Crane could tell from the way she bounced that she was virtually empty, probably a few passengers the only manifest. It should be a high, fast flight. He mentally wished them Godspeed.

'Your fat pal Gilbert has been taking the Michelin a lot of late.'

The Michelin was the train that used to run direct from Kunming to Hanoi. Now it stopped at the border where, incredibly, a Japanese crew took over and ran it down into Indo-China. Even in the midst of a particularly brutal war, it seemed, accommodations could be made for commerce.

'Maybe he's after their sugar.'

There was a brisk demand among coffee drinkers for white sugar, like the Japanese used, rather than the local brown variety, which seemed to ferment in a heartbeat.

'Perhaps. Or maybe he's trading something else.'

'You don't think he's working for the Japs?'

Nelson shook his head. 'The question is – is he working for the Brits or himself?'

'Or both.'

'Yeah. How are you doing with the McGill woman?'

Crane shrugged. 'Do you mean – am I in her pants yet?'

Nelson smirked. 'I thought you said she wasn't—'

'She's not. And I'm nowhere,' Crane said truthfully. 'I've seen her a couple of times since the picnic. I said she was a nice girl.'

Nelson offered Crane a Lucky Strike but he refused. Nelson lit up. 'There's a party tonight. Up at the Dragon House.'

'You know I'm not welcome up there,' Crane said.

'There's a party tonight,' Nelson repeated, 'and I hear that the McGill woman will be attending. Now, I don't have to tell you about the Dragon parties.'

'No.'

'So, if she ends up with some Ivy League Colonel . . .'

'Who you can't lean on.'

'Yeah. Who I can't lean on. Look, that whole AVG thing, what you did. It was a long time ago.'

'Yeah, but word gets around.'

'I think you flatter yourself.'

Crane laughed. 'You know, pilots pretty much depend on their reputation.' Chennault had let it be known that Crane had flown off to see his girlfriend, rather than help his pals defend the Blenheims in the air raid. Told like that, it did sound like dereliction of duty. Perhaps it had been. 'And mine's pretty crap at the villa.'

'Well, maybe so. But I can always get ATC to review your file. Have you grounded. Even flying The Hump is better than not flying at all. You'll be at the party.'

It wasn't a question, and Crane wanted to get away for a shower and something to eat from the Dai shack. Maybe it was bluff, but he knew Nelson had enough strings to open a marionette theatre. So he just said: 'I'll be at the party.'

Twenty

That evening the clouds scudded in, bringing thick, cold fog with them. The weather boys predicted it would be one of those two-day sock-ins, when you might as well stay put, unless you really wanted to kiss a mountain with the nose of your plane.

The news that flying was suspended meant that almost everyone wanted to crash the party up at the villa. Crane was glad. It was unlikely he'd be noticed. Although there was room in the ATC *basho* most stopovers, Crane stayed in Windsor Castle because he got a room of his own: cot bed, chest of drawers, hanging space. It was small but comfortable. Crane had lit the mosquito coils and changed into his best khakis when there was a knock on the door. It was Gilbert, a gin and tonic in each hand. 'Drink, Captain Crane?'

'Make it Lee. Is that gin?'

'Real London gin, not the filth they'll be plying up there.' He nodded at the source of the music and voices that were being blown down the hill and through the valley by the fetid wind.

'Thanks.' Crane accepted the drink, which came without ice and with lime instead of lemon, and took a sip. It really did need that ice. 'You going?'

Gilbert squeezed his bulk into the room. 'May I?' Crane nodded and he lowered himself onto the folding wooden chair that looked tiny beneath his bulk. 'Do I look like a man who enjoys parties? Oh, don't bother answering. You know my father was this big. Mother a tiny thing. Tiny. Don't know what to do about it. Don't eat, can't function. Do eat, stay big.'

Crane checked his tie in the mirror and ran a brush over his hair. 'I've seen bigger men than you who dance real good, Walter.'

'Well, I'm afraid I resemble more those elephant shows the timber-wallahs used to put on in Burma. You're going up, I assume?'

'Yeah. Cowboy is giving me a ride.'

'Laura's there. With Elsa.'

'Right.'

'Crane, are you dallying with that girl?'

He let his jaw drop as if the thought had never occurred to him. 'Elsa?'

Gilbert's mouth set firm at the joke and his eyes narrowed in the puffy face.

'I'm not dallying, as you put it,' Crane said immediately.

'I promised her sister Diana I'd look after her. I mean, I've asked around and, to be frank, opinion about you seems a little divided.'

Crane took some more of the warm drink. 'You know, sometimes I can't make my mind up about myself either.'

'An agitator and a coward.'

Whoever had briefed Gilbert knew how to put the worst possible spin on the story. Crane looked at his watch. 'Look, I have to get going. Cowboy'll be here soon. I can assure you—'

'Listen, people say pretty hurtful things about me too. Doesn't mean they are true. You think I don't realise what they say about me back in Calcutta and London? A rum cove, I'll bet. Not at all clubbable. A bit shifty, and not quite, well, English. Doesn't even like cricket. But, you see, they tolerate me for the moment because I get results—' His mouth snapped shut. He stared into his drink

179

as he swirled it. 'Let's not pretend that we aren't involved in a different kind of dance, you and Nelson and me. I think I know what you are up to. If I am right, and you hurt that girl, I'll . . .'

The overloaded chair chose that moment to collapse under him with a loud crack, pitching Gilbert and his gin onto the floor with a thump that shook the framework of the entire building. He let loose a string of curses with a force and invention that Crane had only ever previously heard from mechanics who had just spannered their hand.

Crane stepped across to help him, but Gilbert batted him away and struggled to his feet, his face red, his chest heaving. He stood up and looked down at the splintered framework. 'Well, you'll end up looking like that chair. You know Sergeant Russell is ill?'

Sergeant Percy Russell was a kind of housemother to the Brits. 'No.'

'Couple of bomber pilots got him plastered last night on their damned moonshine. Doc says he will be able to walk again in a day or two. If he's lucky.'

'And you think this was deliberate?'

Gilbert didn't reply, but he fished into his voluminous trouser pockets and brought out something. 'Hold out your hand.'

Crane did so, and Gilbert dropped a silver cylinder into it. 'You know what to do?'

Crane considered for a moment. His popularity rating, already at rock bottom, was probably about to plunge further. 'Yeah. I know what to do.'

Cowboy drove Crane in the Willys Jeep he had bought off some pilots from Kweilin who were shipping out of China for the last time. Whether it was actually theirs to sell was a moot point, but nobody had come looking for it, and while they were flying, he rented it out at five bucks a day plus gas.

'I called in at the ATC office,' said Cowboy. 'Two lifts before next weekend, and then we've got those marine boys running down to Chungking. After that, *Myra*'s starboard needs an overhaul.'

'Do it at Dum-Dum,' said Crane. 'Not here. Guys are more used to C-47s there.'

'There was also a message from Nelson.'

'Yeah?'

'It said: he checked again. No record of subject in our files, or at the Office of Refugees or the Red Cross. He drew a blank.'

'Right.'

'Still lookin' for Kitten, Lee?'

'Still lookin'.'

'She might be . . . You know. They had it rough.'

'I know. Just like to find out f'sure.'

'Right.'

Cowboy rounded a corner and dropped a gear, the tyres slithering on the loose stones. They passed people trudging up towards the villa, bottles of locally brewed 'country spirit' in hand. A couple of the fitter rickshaw drivers were pulling clients up, their spindly legs pumping hard.

'Ever thought about what we do when this is over? One day they'll get that damned Ledo Road built and The Hump will close for good.'

'Amen to that,' said Crane.

'And we'll be out of a job.'

'Always be a job for good pilots, Cowboy. You should get yourself into the left-hand seat. You need to move on.'

'Yeah, that's what I was thinkin'.'

He slewed the Jeep to a halt behind a dozen other vehicles, some military, others commandeered civilian. Crane was about to get out when Cowboy said, 'Lee, here, put this on.'

He handed a bottle across to him. Crane unscrewed it and sniffed and he was back two years. 'I'll be damned.'

'You smelled it before?'

'Toungoo. This is Elsa's bug juice.' He slapped some onto his neck and the backs of his hands. 'Where'd you get this?'

Cowboy unlatched the Jeep's bonnet and swiftly removed the rotor arm. Those who could hot-wire a car didn't care whose transport they took after a party. 'Gospel. I think you were right about the flying lessons. She's paying him, but not in sexual favours. He gets all the bug repellent he can use.'

They were still laughing when they entered the garden, made it past the two burly guys who were meant to vet guests by bribing them with one of their two bottles of Canadian Club, and were pitched into a tight-packed mêleé of bodies. The sun was sliding behind the hill, the shadows lengthening, and the voices around them were already thick and slurred.

Chinese waiters in ill-fitting off-white jackets were handing out trays of cocktails, which they both refused. Crane found them a couple of tumblers and Cowboy slopped out the whisky, before sliding the bottle back under his jacket. *'Kan bei.'*

Like Windsor Castle, Dragon House was an amalgam of swooping art-deco lines dotted with Chinese flourishes, such as a green-tiled pagoda roof. It sat at the centre of a large walled garden, strung with coloured lights, Chinese lanterns and canvas awnings for the party. A band played jazz on a small open-air stage, and a dance floor had been created using the crates from spare aircraft parts.

'Hiya, guys.' It was Gospel, a smile lighting up his face. 'Lee, you should know. The Old Man is coming, so they say.'

Cowboy raised an eyebrow, as if questioning whether they should stay. 'It was a long time ago,' said Crane.

Gospel forgot that in a second. 'I've got to dance with Elsa. She owes me three – for the flying lessons. You know, I don't think she's wearing any underwear. Have you tried these cock-tails? They're great. I saw Robertson doing the rhumba – man, can he move. There's food inside, but it's going fast.'

Crane tried to unravel this car wreck of images from each other, but failed. 'Last time I saw you at one of these things you drank water,' said Crane.

'I have seen the light!' the other pilot bellowed, and swayed off after a waiter.

'I think he's seen the dark,' said Crane. 'Or at least, he will by tomorrow if he hits any more of that hooch.'

Cowboy went off in search of the food and Crane eased his way through people, swatting away the clouds of moths that were gathering at each lantern. The band, three local musicians and a trumpet player from the 23rd, were belting out their own slightly arrhythmic version of hot jazz, and he could see Elsa's head rocking back and forward somewhere in the crowded dance area. He couldn't locate Laura, though.

A phalanx of Chinese girls, mostly in Western clothes, walked past him, making for the house. They disappeared inside, clearly with their mind on something other than dancing. Crane looked around and did a rough headcount. As in the clubs of Calcutta, men outnumbered women, although here it was by around five to one. There were some Anglo-Indian girls, plus nurses, FANYs, the latter mostly Brits but with the odd Aussie or Kiwi, and a few US PX workers, but many of them were either spoken for or wary about entanglements with pilots.

Chennault had realised that sexual release was in as short supply as fuel, spares and ammunition, and he had turned a blind eye to a brothel that had operated just off-airstrip. Once he'd rejoined the USAAF, they'd made him close it down.

A rocket whooshed off from one of the first-floor balconies and, illuminated in its glare, he briefly saw Laura's face, and that of the pilot standing too close to her. What was his name? Mike Kennedy, that was it, a 23rd Fighter Group ace, who had come to China after the days of the AVG. It still rankled that those guys called themselves the Flying Tigers when, in fact, the genuine article had been disbanded in 1942.

He'd heard something about Kennedy coming down near the Burmese border after engine failure and making his way back thanks to the network of observers that Chennault had installed, passed from one to another like a parcel. Crane followed the Chinese girls inside, Nelson's words about letting another man muscle in on Laura still fresh in his ears.

Walking through jungle, paddy fields and across rock-strewn hills isn't great on the feet, and Kennedy still had a pronounced limp that necessitated the use of a walking stick. When Crane found the balcony where the group was enthusiastically sending off rockets, Laura was pressed with her back to the wall, and the crippled pilot was shielding her from the streams of sparks that the crude projectiles showered over the spectators. Or, at least, that was his excuse.

'Laura.'

Her head flicked around and she smiled at him. Her eyes were bright, but Crane wasn't sure whether that was excitement or booze. She wore a bright dress, local material cut in a Western style. 'Lee! I hoped you'd be here. This is—'

'Mike Kennedy,' the pilot interrupted, holding out his hand.

Crane took it. 'Lee Crane.'

There was a heartbeat of awkwardness. Both knew there was going to be a skirmish and Crane led with the most underhand blow he could think of to a man with a walking stick. 'Laura promised me a dance.'

Kennedy shuffled, lost for a suitable parry.

'I did,' she said, the question mark almost undetectable.

'Particularly if they played this tune.' Whatever it is, he wanted to add.

'We were just going to get a drink and maybe something to eat,' protested Kennedy.

It was too little, too late and Crane's arm was already sliding through Laura's. 'I'll bring her back,' Crane lied behind his grin. 'Count on me.'

'Did you drink the cocktails?' asked Crane as they squeezed downstairs, picking their way between the bodies. From somewhere in one of the bedrooms he could hear a gramophone playing, and the sound of laughter. He figured a second party was going on there, for the Chinese girls were nowhere to be seen.

'Walter gave me some real gin before I left. It kept me going.'

Crane spotted Cowboy talking to a nurse, and pushed through to him, cajoling a top-up from the rapidly diminishing supplies of the Canadian Club. He couldn't help but notice the nurse had a rather generous measure.

'Here,' he said to Laura.

'I don't really like whisky.'

'Try it.'

She took a sip and pulled a face. 'Horrible. About that dance . . .'

'You may have noticed, I didn't do much dancing in Calcutta.'

'But you can dance,' she said, as if it was inconceivable that anyone shouldn't foxtrot or waltz.

'Everything I do kinda comes out as a two-step,' he admitted. 'Virginia-style.'

'Oh, come on.' She grabbed his arm and tugged. Crane looked around for somewhere to park his drink, but knowing it wouldn't last five seconds he knocked it back in a single throat-burning gulp.

They managed three turns around the floor, each progressively better. The hit of whisky was making Crane surprisingly loose-limbed, and he was picking a decent path between the other dancers, he thought, when he felt the tap on his shoulder. 'Excuse me,' said a soft, Southern-inflected voice

'Beat it,' he said as he turned, then felt the colour drain from his face.

'You think I can show you how it's done?'

Crane stepped back, releasing Laura but reluctant to take his hands from her waist, his face from her hair. 'Lee?' she asked.

'Right. Laura McGill,' he said, his lips dry, the words barely passing his throat, 'may I introduce General Claire Chennault, late of the Flying Tigers.'

Twenty-One

By now, Chennault was well past fifty, although nobody knew for sure the exact figure. Old Leatherface still had a swaggering, dangerous air about him that women liked and men admired. He might be twice as old as most of his command, but it was Chennault who had the reputation as Kunming's premier cocksman.

Crane walked off the dance floor, found Cowboy and hustled the last finger of whisky from him. The nurse had disappeared.

'Throwing up,' said Cowboy ruefully. 'She mixed the whisky with a cocktail. Next thing I know, her stomach is turning over like a Pratt and Whitney. Jesus, is that the Old Man with your girl?'

'She's not my girl.'

'Not now she ain't,' said Cowboy ruefully. 'He's doing it because it's you.'

'I know. You got the time?'

Cowboy looked at his watch and Crane followed suit. They both had three minutes to midnight. From his pocket Crane retrieved the cylinder that Gilbert had dropped into his hand.

'What's that?'

'In the absence of Sergeant Russell, I have the panic button.'

Cowboy laughed, but when he saw the expression on Crane's face, his smile faded. 'You're not . . . you'll get lynched.'

'I'll take my chances. You think of another way to break up Chennault and Laura?'

'You could shoot him.'

'Ha-ha.'

And then, as the music stopped, Laura was pushing her way through, walking towards him, leaving a puzzled-looking Chennault on the dance floor. The bodies closed again and Crane lost sight of him.

'He can dance, I will give him that,' she said breathlessly, her hand on her breastbone.

'Not many girls get away with just one turn round the floor.'

'He's a little fast for me,' she said with a grin. She took the whisky from Crane and grimaced as she sipped. 'No, it's no better the second time. How many drinks before you like the taste?'

'Oh, you just gotta work at it.'

She pointed at his hand. 'What on earth is that?'

'A whistle,' said Crane.

'I can see that. What's it for?'

'There's a little party game, invented by you Brits,' explained Cowboy. 'At midnight, that baby gets blown, you girls head for the cars and you beg, steal or borrow a lift. Anyone left up here after ten minutes is . . .'

'Fair game,' completed Crane.

'Goodness.'

'I promised Walter,' he said. 'That I'd do the honours.'

Crane had just raised the whistle to his lips when the bottle hit him, high on the forehead with a dull thud. He staggered back, the whistle hitting the floor and rolling away. His vision filled with flashes of light and he could feel something warm running down his face. A group of revellers pressed against him, and there was the slap of flesh on flesh and then the harder crunch of bone on bone. Someone screamed.

Crane, still swaying, managed to get an arm out to a pillar to steady himself, shaking his head, trying to clear it. One eye swam back into focus, but there was blood flowing into the other.

Cowboy was standing over three prostrate bodies, his fists still clenched, facing off a fourth attacker, who had a bottle in his hand.

'You planning on doing anything with that?' he asked the guy between clenched teeth.

His opponent was not yet twenty, but he was bred big and beefy, with a square face and a barrel chest that stretched his shirt. Cowboy was dancing on the balls of his feet, his spurs clinking as he did so. Crane pushed himself upright and took a step forward, feeling the world lurch.

'My fight, Cowboy.'

The young guy laughed. Cowboy yelped as someone grabbed him from behind, and he started to twist and kick. The beefy one with the bottle moved towards Crane, who raised his fists in-effectually.

The whistle was shrill and loud and it made them all stop dead. There was a second blast, even more urgent. Crane looked around and saw Laura on her knees, the silver tube in her mouth, blowing for all she was worth.

There was sudden movement from all corners of the house and the crash of overturned furniture as couples untwined, women made their farewells and guys tried to persuade them to stay. The confrontation melted away, even those Cowboy had downed leaping to their feet to try and prevent the exodus, the fight temporarily forgotten. Crane wiped the blood from his eye and crossed to Laura, gently taking the whistle from her lips and helping her up.

'You can stop now.'

There was shock in her eyes as she saw his face. 'Oh, look at you.'

'Nothing,' he said. He touched the cut and winced.

'Come here, party pooper.' It was Elsa, resplendent in a

violently purple dress, who wiped away at the wound with her handkerchief. 'That was a dumb thing to do.'

'Which part?'

'Doing the Brits' dirty work for them. And not ducking fast enough. It needs a stitch or two. I think we're out of here anyway.'

As they left, Crane noticed Chennault near the gate, drink in hand, talking to one of his officers' wives. The Old Man looked up, glared darkly at him. 'Still putting your women over the welfare of the men, I see, Crane.'

Crane was in the mood to make something of it, but Cowboy put a hand on his shoulder. 'Come on, Lee. Forget it. Let's get your head seen to.'

'Good idea,' said Chennault as Crane left. 'But a couple of years too late.'

'I disobeyed orders, I answered back and by my actions I encouraged a lot of pilots to resign,' Crane told Laura. 'In the end, only about six pilots transferred across from the Tigers to the regular Air Force. That's why the Old Man dislikes me so much. Always said that if I hadn't opened my big mouth, more of the guys would have stayed on. Wanted to have me court-martialled, but of course the Flying Tigers weren't part of the USAAF at the time, so it wasn't clear what he could do. I did hear tell he could get the Chinese to do it, but they would have shot me. Extreme, even for Chennault.'

It was close to 2 a.m. now. Elsa had once more used her nursing skills to patch him up. After his head wound had been dressed, he and Laura had adjourned back to Sandringham, where Crane had tracked down the remains of some *bei kan jui*, the white rice brandy which, while not as lethal as the local gin, had to be treated with respect.

They were standing on one of the stone bridges that arced across the canals, both smoking pungent local cigarettes, listening to the creak of the moored sampans downstream, the occasional raised voice from within, and the chirp of crickets.

'Don't get me wrong. I think Chennault was – is – a tactical genius. What he taught me kept me alive. What he did with the Tigers was remarkable. But somehow, he belly-flopped right at the end. Blinded by the General's stars, I guess. He should have fought harder for us.'

'You said you'd tell me about Toungoo,' Laura said as she reached for the bottle that stood on the wall between them. She sloshed a half-inch into the tumbler.

'I did, didn't I?'

Crane poured the last of the bottle into his own glass and sniffed, enjoying the sting of the alcohol on his eyes. He explained about the attempts to blackmail and threaten them back into the USAAF and the flight to Toungoo. And what he found there. 'I changed my mind about Snelling that day.'

'What would you have done if you had found her – Kitten?'

He watched a moth the size of his hand loom out of the darkness and disappear on silent wings. 'You can carry a passenger in the baggage compartment of a Tomahawk. It's not a nice ride, but it's better than . . . you know.'

She placed a hand on Crane's. 'I'm sorry. Was she someone special?'

'Yes, she was pretty special,' he said.

Laura laid her head on his shoulder and Crane thought this would be the time to make a pass, if he were so inclined. He could hear Nelson's voice yapping in his ear: *Why not? You like her, don't you?* For sure. *So what's the problem?*

The problem was, Crane couldn't get the image from his mind of the scene awaiting him at Kunming after he had returned from his attempt to rescue Kitten. The mission had been a fiasco. Two Tigers had been lost, and most of the Blenheims. One of the bombers had limped back, only to pile into the rocks at the end of the strip. When Crane climbed out of the P-40, the trapped pilot was burning to death inside. Sometimes he could still smell that spectral odour, the stench of incinerating gas and oil not quite masking that of crisping flesh.

Crane threw the last few drops of the brandy into the canal and walked Laura back home, the tender moment gone, his face hot at the memory of Kitten, wondering for the thousandth time what exactly had happened to her at Toungoo.

Part Four

Myra Belle Starr

Twenty-Two

Singapore, 1948

'Thing is, Lee, I know where she is,' said Cowboy. 'I know what happened after Toungoo. I can give Kitten back to you.'

Around us the go-down night market had grown noisy, so I didn't have to lower my voice when I spoke. 'You bastard,' I said slowly to Cowboy. 'How long have you known?'

'What happened to Kitten? Not long. A couple of weeks, that's all.'

I signalled for another beer, although I really just wanted to get up and walk away, to get on a Pan Am or BOAC flight out of there, out of Asia for ever. It is what I should have done back in 1945. Instead I said: 'You're not going to tell me, are you? Whether she is dead or alive?'

'Only on the point of parting,' he said amicably. 'You help us . . .'

'There are a thousand pilots to choose from in Indo-China. Some of them even a little bent. So I heard.' I accepted the beer and took a pull without wiping it this time. I felt like living dangerously.

Cowboy took off his hat and ran a hand through his hair before replacing it. The hawker smoke was thickening and I could feel the oil burning my lungs. 'I flew with you over the worst terrain in the world, Lee. We go back out there, I want you next to me. As co-pilot.'

I laughed at this. 'You can want all you like, buddy. I am not flying The Hump again. And if I was, I'm not sitting in the right-hand seat. Too old for that.'

'We ain't flying The Hump. No need. We reckon we fly north, then west, then east again. We retrace our steps back into Indo-China.'

I tossed the bottle from hand to hand, trying to think fast, but my brain kept zinging back to one thought: *He knows what happened to Kitten.* In the end I asked: 'Where is the gold, Cowboy?'

'Well now, if I tell you that, what's to stop you taking the new *Myra Belle* north y'self?'

I stood up, knocking over the beer as I did so. 'Fuck you.'

Elsa also started to rise, but I pushed her back down, more roughly than I intended, but the regret didn't last long. I could feel my face burning, the old anger flooding back. I'd been restrained, I'd been polite and it wasn't the right thing to do. Cowboy reached across for me and I scooped the Tiger by the neck and rapped it hard across his knuckles. I hoped that was his gun hand.

The twittering conversation around us died. All I could hear was my breathing, hard and raspy. I pointed a finger at Cowboy. 'Don't come to me with your old friend's act, then tell me you don't trust me. I'm not the one who ratted on his pal.' I spun round and cleaved the air with my lethal finger in Elsa's direction.

She didn't duck and the words jammed in my throat, so I walked off through the market, oblivious to the protests of the soup-drinkers I barged past. Elsa and Cowboy didn't follow, and I didn't get a bullet in my back. I didn't find out what happened to Kitten, though, either.

They knew we'd meet again, one way or another.

When I got to Changi airport the next day, Tommy Kwik, Indo-Air's line chief, had jacked up *Myra* using the big cradle rig, which minimised pressure on the wings, and was supervising the mechanics who were loosening the wheel-bolts. Henri was standing off to one side, a Coke in his hand. He saw me and produced a second bottle, which he threw over to me. I flipped the top with the opener on my knife and joined him.

'Tyres will be here by midday,' he said.

'You sure?'

He squinted at me. 'Sure I'm sure. Why not?'

'I think the tyres were dependent on me playing ball on something.'

'Ah. And let me guess – you're not.'

'I'm not. No.'

'Well, we'll have to take the old tyres off anyway, so I'll let them carry on.'

I looked at my plane with fresh eyes. *Myra Belle Starr II* was nowhere near as banged-about as her predecessor, but she was still looking like she lived too fast and too hard. Which she did – it wasn't just women who aged faster out in the tropical sun. The weather, the cinder airstrips, the rudimentary maintenance, all took their toll.

'She's quite a woman, your friend.'

'Yeah. Punches me in public, gets me beaten up in Chinatown and then slashes my tyres.'

'She got you beaten up?' There wasn't much surprise in his voice.

'A guess. I think that was a bungled snatch – she wanted to have a little chat from a position of strength. You and Bill nixed

that one. In a fit of pique she got Cowboy to do the Goodriches,'
I nodded at where they were rolling the port wheel towards the
tyre irons.

'What do they want you to do?' he asked.

'Go back in time.'

'Is it to do with this Kitten?' By now Henri knew an outline
of the story.

I shrugged. 'That's one part of it. Cowboy claims he knows
where she is. He could be lying.'

'Can you take that chance?'

'There's something else . . .' The rest of my words were drowned
out by a plane on its final approach. The C-54 that came in to
land was painted matt grey, and had no markings apart from its
international identification numbers. I held a hand up as Henri
started to press me for more information. I didn't like the look of
that plane. Only one outfit was happy not to advertise its pres-
ence.

The aircraft taxied to a halt and the rear door opened. As the
short ladder came down, if I'd been able to bet a hundred bucks
on who was going to emerge, I would've laid it down in a flash.
He had a smart cream suit on, a straw fedora, and held an attaché
case in his hand.

It was no good me ducking out. He knew I was here. I finished
my Coke and went across to meet Hyram Nelson, late of the OSS
and now, no doubt, a valued member of its recent successor, the
CIA.

'I hear you been hanging around with old friends.'

There had been few formalities. A quick handshake, and Nelson
had taken me across to Joe's chow shack. Joe had a repertoire that
involved scrambled eggs and not much more, but they were damned
good scrambled eggs and Nelson ordered a mess of them. He
spoke while he shovelled them into his mouth.

'You always did make mistakes about who my friends are.'

He stabbed at me with his fork. 'You were bullshittin' me. I always knew that. The bullion is still out there, isn't it?'

'I never bullshitted you, Nelson. Look, I was as shocked to see them—'

'It's ours, Crane. The US Government's. We need it. You guys think the war is over. It was never over – not out here. Ask the Brits up the road.' He indicated Malaya with the fork. 'Ask the French in Hanoi, ask Chiang Kai-Shek.'

'Is that where you've been?'

'Saigon,' he said. 'In an advisory capacity.'

'Remaking the world in our own image?'

'No, I think you're mixing us up with the other guys. The Reds. Ask Stalin what kind of world he would like, or Mao.'

'You asked the locals?'

Nelson laughed. 'Out of your depth, Crane. Stick to flying clapped-out old warhorses.'

'Talking of which, that outfit you came in on . . .'

'What about it?'

'Not much in the way of logos. Funny, I get reports of grey planes from all over, all those places you mentioned and more. Bringing men, machines . . .' I paused. 'Guns. Drugs.'

He pushed the empty plate away across the table. 'Don't lecture me, Crane. My organisation is still fighting for this peace. The war isn't over yet. Next to go will be Malaya. Look what's happening in Berlin. The Russians are trying to squeeze us out.'

'I was meant—'

'I know.' I didn't ask how he knew I had a job offer from Germany. The same way he knew Elsa and Cowboy were in town. He was a spy. It is their job to know such things. 'And if I were you, I'd go.'

'Just a few technical problems to sort out first.'

'I'm going to find those two jokers.'

'Elsa and Cowboy? And do what?'

'Cigarette?' I shook my head. 'Officially, well, there's not much I can do that won't take years. Even getting a warrant in this town would mean court-time. Unofficially, though, I can do what I like. This is our backyard now, or soon will be.'

'Why are you telling me this?'

'Because I like you, Crane. Because you did your bit figuring out what the Fat Man was up to. I need the truth about what happened after Elsa and Cowboy left you.'

'It's old news, Nelson. Your war might not be over. Mine is.'

Nelson took a long drag on his cigarette, then let the smoke stream up towards the dirty bamboo fan that was turning above our heads. Joe came and collected his empty plate, and I indicated I'd have a refill of coffee. 'I can stop you flying in Berlin.'

'I'm sure you can.'

'It's a US operation. In fact, I can stop you flying anywhere. Remember that.'

There was movement in the doorway and I squashed a mosquito that was trying to creep up across the table-top with a slap that made Nelson jump. I saw the silhouette of Cowboy's hat, but it was a fleeting glimpse. He would know Hyram could only be trouble, so would make himself very scarce. And as I needed to talk to him once more before Hyram took him down, I wasn't about to turn him in. 'Ever had dengue fever?' I asked.

He nodded. 'Who hasn't out here?'

I examined the splat of organic matter on my palm and wiped it off. 'Well, we're getting Singapore Haemorrhagic Fever now from the day-biters. It's what you get when you are immune to ordinary dengue. It's like its ugly brother. Oh, and it can be fatal.'

'Thanks for the warning,' he said.

'Look, Nelson, I don't know what idiot scheme those two have dreamed up to go gold-prospecting, but my guess is it's all too late to go back to China. And there's the little problem of the CCP and the Nationalists slugging it out over there.'

'I believe you. I just want you to tell me what happened that day.'

'I already told you.'

'No, I want to know the exact details. There were a few vague points, as I recall.'

I drank my fresh coffee: it tasted unusually bitter. 'I only know up until a certain point. Anything else would be speculation. Only the people on the plane can tell you what really happened.'

'Correction. Only the people who were on that plane who are still alive can tell me what happened.'

'Meaning?'

'The marines, Lee. You ever think about what those two did to the marines?' From inside his pocket he took out photographs of two smart young men with almost shaven heads smiling at the camera. Patterson and Sorkin.

He produced a reporter's notebook and a freshly sharpened pencil. 'Can't say this will stand up in a court of law, but I would like you to consider yourself under oath.'

Despite the humidity, I felt a cold chill run through me. I knew what he was here for now. He was trying to build up a case to charge Elsa and Cowboy with the homicide of these two kids, four years after the event.

He was poised to write. 'Now, take me back, Lee. Take me back to the day they screwed you. That's an order from your Government.'

Twenty-Three

Calcutta, 1944

Crane knew something was up with Laura as soon as she stepped out of the car that had pulled up alongside *Myra*. Even in the unforgiving glare of Dum-Dum's sodium lights, her face was exceptionally pale and drawn, the eyes circled with red. She seemed unsteady, and even forgot the precious valise for a moment, reaching back inside the staff car to get it. She barely acknowledged either Cowboy or Crane, and even the two tight-assed marines, Patterson and Sorkin, stood aside as she walked straight to the access door of the plane.

It couldn't be nerves, he figured, because this wasn't the same Laura he had flown that first time. This was her seventh return trip over The Hump; she was almost a vet, tougher and more resilient. Over the past few months he had watched her change; whatever she did with Gilbert on the trips on the Michelin and flights to Chungking had given her a confidence and ease with the locals that he envied.

As with many Americans, for him China was something that mostly happened on the other side of the windshield, while Laura had taken the first steps towards becoming what the British called on OCH – an Old China Hand. Physically, too, she had changed. The soft-focus prettiness she had arrived with was giving way to a brittle beauty. In fact, she was beginning to look like her older sister, Diana.

Crane handed the manifesto back to Cowboy and walked across to where Captain Snelling was slamming the door of the car. 'What's up?'

Snelling shrugged. 'Nothing, Crane.'

'You're an hour late.' Crane checked his watch. He had cut short a beer and steak at Firpo's to be here at the appointed hour, and he knew Snelling was a stickler for timekeeping, too. 'No, closer to two hours. Those marines were about to make us take off at gunpoint. I had to invent a tech problem to shut them up. Why is she upset, Snelling?'

Behind him, the moon was clear and large. It was true they were taking off late, but Crane didn't mind. The weather had improved nicely, and reports were good. He was looking forward to seeing the mess of the rockpile in a clear dawn light.

'Look, I can't really tell you.'

'Snelling.' Crane grabbed his arm. 'The US Government entrusts me with a million dollars in gold every couple of months, and you can't tell me why one of your people has been bawling her eyes out?'

He licked his lips, his eyes as apprehensive as if he were about to divulge the date for the invasion of Europe. 'It's her sister. She's been posted missing.'

'Diana?' Crane used the name to let Snelling know that he was pretty familiar with the McGill family tree. 'Diana is in London.'

'Nominally, yes.'

Crane took off his cap and scratched his head. His hair was sticky with sweat. It was the beginning of the long, airless run-up to the monsoon. He moved Snelling away from the car, towards the dark cargo hangars, where Sepoy guards moved through the blackness, alert for the thieves who had taken to busting through the perimeter fences. 'So where has she gone missing?'

'France. She went there to check on the other end of the, um, operation.'

'Occupied France?'

'There's no other kind these days, old boy,' said Snelling with a grim smile.

'Laura should go back home,' said Crane.

'Yes, perhaps she should.'

'So why is she on my plane? She should start heading west.'

'She has a delivery to make to Gilbert.'

'I can do that for her.'

Snelling shook his head. 'She won't allow that. I offered, but no dice.'

As Crane turned to go, it was Snelling's turn to grab his arm. 'Listen, it's none of my business, Crane, but about you and Laura—'

'What?' Crane snapped.

'I want to know what your intentions are.'

Crane laughed in his face. 'Sorry, I missed the part where you turn out to be her dad.'

'I hear you have a close relationship with Nelson.'

'Yeah. We're engaged.'

'If you are in any way manipulating Laura . . .'

'Look, Gilbert gave me that speech nine months ago. I like her. We have fun together. End of story.' It was true. Nine months and a few chaste kisses, some heart-to-hearts and precious little information for the OSS. She was no blabbermouth, that was for sure.

'What's in the damn bag,' Crane finally asked, 'that is so important?'

Snelling smiled. 'I'll tell you something: even I don't know.'

'Bullshit,' blurted Crane, loud enough for the marines to hear.

'I know what it says on the paperwork back in London.'

'But you aren't going to tell me.'

'Bombsights. High precision ground graticules for bombsights.'

Crane began to walk back to *Myra*. Cowboy was in the cockpit, running the checks. Crane flicked on his flashlight to perform one last visual check. As he examined the undersurface of the wings, he turned to Snelling, who was climbing into the staff car.

'Hey!' Crane yelled. 'Bombsights? That makes no sense at all.'

There was another smirk from Snelling. 'It rarely does, old boy.'

Myra was in good form, thought Crane. They made the initial altitude easily enough, and the moon stayed bright, washing the world with its white light. Below them, the jungle seemed to glow a luminous emerald, and the snow on the distant mountains shone silver, so bright it almost hurt his eyes.

He let Cowboy have the controls and went back to see his three passengers, Laura and the two marines.

'Hi, guys,' he said to Patterson and Sorkin. They merely grunted. 'We've got another climb in about twenty minutes just to clear one of the high ridges. You're going to need oxygen. You know the drill, right?'

They nodded. Both had done this guard duty before. Crane glanced back at the cargo. How come they physically had to take this stuff across, when the rest of the world used promissory notes, bankers' drafts and manifestos? It seemed archaic to him, but maybe people who demanded gold liked to be able to see, feel and smell it.

Laura was sitting on the opposite side from the guards, closer to the rear of the plane. He knelt down in front of her; she looked up as he touched her knee. 'Snelling told me about Diana.' She turned away for a second, tears brimming. 'You know what happened?' he went on.

She shook her head. 'No. I'm not even meant to know that

she's not reported in. It's only because she was working for Walter that we found out.'

'So, you're thinking the worst.'

'It should have been me, Lee. I was meant to do her job, but no, I wanted to come out here and see the world. I sulked and stamped my foot until she let me.'

'You were meant to go to France?' he asked, unable to keep the incredulity from his voice.

'No. I don't know what all that was about. It was a London-based job. But she should have been here, out of harm's way.'

Crane touched her fingers, shocked at how cold they were. He rubbed her hand between his. 'I'm glad you're here.'

'I should go home.'

'That was my first reaction too, but Laura, think about it. You can't go looking for her. What good would that do?'

'I'll deliver this,' she indicated the valise, 'then come back across to Calcutta with you. Snelling will make the arrangements to get me back. I'm owed leave. I want to be with our mother.'

Crane nodded. 'OK. We have to go to Chungking with this gold after Kunming. My guess is, we won't be flying back until tomorrow.'

She sniffed loudly, then extracted a handkerchief and blew her nose. 'You'll be in Chungking tonight?'

He shook his head. 'No. I'll bring *Myra* back tonight. Probably only flying eggs in for the PX. I'll be in Kunming by this evening.'

She lowered her voice to a half-whisper, half-croak. 'Lee?'

'Yes?'

'Will you stay with me tonight?'

He wanted to ask exactly what she meant, just so he under-stood her properly, but this wasn't the time to insist on chapter and verse and IOUs. 'Sure,' he said softly. He was sincere when he added: 'Whatever you want.'

*

Even the low route had its barriers. You didn't have to hop through valleys at 21,000 feet on a regular basis, but the Crawshaw Ridge tested an unpressurised C-47.

Crawshaw Ridge, also known as Sunrise Point by The Hump pilots, wasn't a single ridge, but a trio of sharp-edged sisters that ran south from the main mountain ranges, cutting into the jungle. Coming from the west, you knew you were heading correctly when the first shafts of the new day shone around a tall, jagged outcrop of rock sitting on the tallest of the three. It also told you it was time to gain some height. The middle sister, the one with Sunrise Point on it, was the real barrier, nudging 19,000 feet. True, you could fly around Sunrise by heading south, deep into Burma, but they rarely had enough fuel for that. Not fully loaded, as they were that night.

However, *Myra* took the ridges in her stride. Crane de-iced twice, but there wasn't the build-up he'd have experienced further north. She rode through the inevitable puckers in the atmosphere, juddering as if she were bumping over cobbles, and Sunrise Point's rocky protuberance slid below them just to port. The cockpit began to glow with the orange of the dawn slashing at the eastern sky ahead.

'Pickle?'

'Skip.'

'They'll be able to ease off on the oxygen in five.'

'Sure.'

'How are they?'

'Sleeping like babies.'

Yup, *Myra* was doing all right. A good flight feels right from the get-go. Odd, that. Things that start badly rarely get any better. It was part of the reason that pilots were so fussy about pre-take-off checks. Start well, end well.

Crane recalibrated for the beacons. There was a new one at Pyongii, built on a plateau, which served as a northern marker for the low route, a southerly one for the high. It was clear and strong and Crane was grateful for it. He'd heard it had cost the lives of a dozen men in construction, including one C-46 crew who'd bellied into the strip that had been cut into the mountainside. It would probably save more than that in the long run. It was just one of those checks and balances of war, he guessed.

He glanced over to his right where his peripheral vision had picked up lights. They disappeared when he stared into the night for them. It was probably the glow of Myitkyina, one of the northernmost towns in Burma, which sat on the broad Irrawaddy. He heard Pickle talking to a plane heading their way. Weather good, its flight engineer was saying, no stacking over Kunming.

'OK?' he asked Cowboy, who had been unnaturally quiet so far. His co-pilot just nodded.

Below, the jungle was giving way to mixed forest. Ahead was the long stretch of barren rocks, and then the rice terraces and paddy fields and the rolling hills would start, and they'd be as good as home. Just those Kunming mountains to thread between.

'How many flights we done, Lee?'

Crane shrugged.

'A hundred and ten,' said Cowboy. 'That's me. I guess you're more, eh?'

Crane nodded. He didn't like to talk about it. Paying too close attention to the count was bad luck. His eye caught a glint, possibly of sun on metal or Plexiglas, some way to the south and squinted. The trouble with this low route, as he'd told Nelson, was that Japanese fighters came up looking for stray transports to drop. He scanned the sky, but could see nothing. The early sun playing tricks? Could be.

'Thing is, Lee, I think my luck is running out.'

'Shut up, Cowboy,' he said irritably.

'Just feel it in my bones.'

Crane watched him scratch a bedbug bite on the back of his

hand. He'd never sensed this fatalistic mood in him before. 'Maybe it's time for a furlough, eh?' Crane said. 'Take a break somewhere quiet.'

'Yeah. I was thinking that. Hawaii maybe.'

Crane laughed. 'They won't fly you to Hawaii.'

'No. No, they won't.'

Crane felt the barrel of the gun on the side of his neck. Cowboy reached over and took Crane's .45, dropped the magazine, put it in his jacket pocket and pushed the empty pistol back into the shoulder holster. The pressure on Crane's neck eased. He turned and saw Pickle in the doorway. The flight engineer smiled apologetically.

'What the hell are you two doing?' asked Crane.

Cowboy sighed. 'We wondered whether you'd be with us or against us?'

'The gold?' Crane asked as understanding came. They were over the jagged, barren section of the Himalayan/Tibetan plateau now, and dawn was rushing into full daylight. He lowered his voice. 'You've got two armed guards back there . . .'

'Sorry, Skip. That wasn't just oxygen in the tanks this time,' said Pickle.

Myra gave a little shudder of apprehension. Crane knew how she felt. 'How long you been dreaming this up?'

'Every time we packed that stuff on board,' said Cowboy. 'You've been so busy with little Miss Prissy back there. Hey,' he said suddenly, as if it had just occurred to him. 'We can see what's in the bag.'

'Are you crazy? Count me out,' said Crane. 'Just go back to as you were, and we'll forget about this.'

'Oh, come on. Nelson would want to know what's in there, wouldn't he?'

Crane ran his eyes over the gauges, checking airspeed and pressures. Everything seemed fine. He'd been wrong about the flight, though. This was anything but good. This was insane. 'Cowboy,

209

I don't know how you think you are going to get away with this. They'll throw everything after you.'

'Just keep your hands where I can see them.'

Cowboy flicked off the autopilot and began to take *Myra* down. Crane could see the end of the rockpile, its brown and beige giving way to the green that marked the beginning of what he thought of as China proper.

'A million dollars, Lee. Four ways if you come in.'

Four? He only made three, even with himself. He hoped someone else was doing the math.

'They'll come for you, Cowboy.'

'Yeah? How many planes never arrive after a flight over The Hump?'

'In bad weather.'

'There'll be a Mayday,' Pickle said.

'With a false position, no doubt,' added Crane, without mentioning that there was a loose end to consider, one who knew the truth: namely, himself. He didn't want to follow that to its logical conclusion. 'There is nowhere in China you can go, you know. You've got Americans, Nationalists, Chinese bandits, Communists and, oh yes, the Japanese. You can't go shunting a plane full of gold round this sky.'

Cowboy nodded as he levelled her off at 10,000 feet. 'We realise that. Which is why we're going back over The Hump.'

Twenty-Four

As the plane rumbled on towards Kunming, Crane used the smelling salts from the first-aid kit on Laura. She awoke with a start, her eyes stinging, and began to cough the crap from her lungs. He had a bag ready in case she threw up. Pickle had forced more 'oxygen' into the marines, who were still out.

'What is in that shit?' demanded Crane.

'It's safe,' insisted Pickle. 'I tried it on myself.'

'Lee? I . . . oh.' She reached up to her temple.

'Causes a doozy of a headache, though,' Pickle added ruefully.

A streak of anger flashed through Crane and he jumped up.

Pickle whipped his pistol around. 'Unclench your fists, Skip. Won't do you any good.'

'Lee, what's going on?' Laura asked, frightened by the sight of the gun.

He looked down at her and touched her hair. 'We'll be OK. I'll go and talk some sense into Cowboy.'

He walked back to the cockpit, now hot and airless from the full glare of a risen sun and worked his way back into his seat. 'You thought this through, Cowboy?'

'Every night for a year, Lee.'

'So what if I say no? What if I say you'll have to kill me?'

211

Cowboy shot him a look that made him shudder. 'Don't make me think about that, buddy.'

Myra bumped through the wash of the other plane as it came across their nose. It disappeared from view, and Crane stared at the roof as if he had X-ray vision, until the P-40 Kittyhawk, with prominent rocket tubes, appeared in the side window.

Crane peered out at the newcomer, saw the pilot raise a thumb. 'Gospel? My, you have been busy. How did you convert him?'

'Oh, we all share the same religion deep down. Gold is a spiritual thing,' laughed Cowboy. 'Just one letter away from God. Come on, Lee. How is this different from the little deals you did with Mason?'

'Deal,' said Crane. 'One deal for some fuel. It's hardly taking Fort Knox.'

'Nor is this. Drop in the ocean, buddy. Anyway, who is going to blame us? You know where this money goes? You think it goes to the war effort? Come on, China is the most corrupt country on God's earth, and that is sayin' plenty. This will probably buy Mrs Chiang some new wardrobe, a young lover, I dunno. But it isn't going to help us win the war.'

Crane knew it was no good arguing. Cowboy had already made up his mind. 'Not directly, perhaps. But it's going to take some good pilots out of it.'

'Who?'

'You and me. One way or another, we're going to be lost to the CBI effort. Aren't we?'

'Me, for sure, Lee. I'm out.'

The two planes carried on eating up the miles towards Kunming. There were perhaps 200 to go now, and never had the earth looked more welcoming. Crane wanted to be down on it, in one piece. With Laura.

He looked at the Kittyhawk again, its tiger face seeming to leer at him. Cute no longer, it was a hungry, carnivorous grin. Or perhaps that was just the pilot. He'd mostly lost contact with Gospel when he'd gone into the 23rd and Crane had switched to transport. He'd assumed he'd stayed the same God-fearing straight arrow. Then he remembered him at the party all those months ago, the last time he'd really spoken to him. He claimed he'd seen the light then. Was it Cowboy's light – the soft glint of gold bars – he had been talking about?

'Is Gospel here to shoot us down? With you on board?'

'It's a contingency plan. We got chutes. One option is for us to jump, shoot you down, get the gold later.'

Crane shook his head. 'No. You'd be searching dozens of square miles to get every last bar.'

Cowboy leaned across and spoke quietly. 'I don't want anyone to get shot, Lee. Help me out here, and no matter what happens, you and the girl can walk away.'

'And the marines? Patterson and Sorkin? What about them?'

'I'll worry about them later.'

'You know you haven't got enough fuel to get back to Calcutta.'

'We're not going to Calcutta.'

'Then where?'

He hesitated. 'Backra.'

Backra was a smallish strip south of Chabua, used mostly by the Indians. The only way to access that was over the high route. 'You certainly ain't got gas enough for that.'

'No. We're going to Yunnanyi dispersal, Lee. I'm gonna buy some fuel off you.' He checked the heading and banked *Myra*, who responded as willingly as always, even though she was being deceived. I could hear Kunming tower in my ears, faint but audible. This was the home run, and we were about to turn our back on it.

In retrospect it wasn't the best place to build airstrips. Yunnanyi dispersal was situated in a wide, flat valley between two lines of hills, at an elevation of around 3000 feet. The field's runway was the usual strip of crushed stone, although now the surface was dimpled with depressions where the packing beneath had collapsed or been washed away. The trouble was the way the rainfall on the nearby hills tended to coalesce into flash floods, which scoured at the strip on a daily basis in winter.

Still, back in 1941, when it was thrown together, any dispersal strip was better than none. Now, with Japanese bombing raids rare, it was hardly used and tricky to land on.

For the moment though, *Myra* coped. Cowboy brought her in over the rusty cables of the anti-bombing wires strung between the hills, and Crane gritted his teeth as her weight took her through the top layer of gravel, churning up the fist-sized rocks underneath and flinging them against the fuselage. It was easy to lose a tyre on the stones, and he was relieved when she finally slithered to a halt.

Cowboy cut the engines and Crane watched the propellers solidify out of the spinning discs. Crane liked *Myra*. She was a good plane and he took in what might be the last breath of her cockpit's crude aroma and went aft.

Pickle kept a gun on Crane as he unclipped a still-woozy Laura and pulled her to her feet. She held back for a moment, grabbed the case and went with him.

As they stepped out into the brightness of day he could see the P-40 circling, scouting the strip, the buzzing of its engine and the tick-ticking of the C-47's engines the only sounds.

Crane examined the area. There used to be locals camped out in lean-tos back in the days of emergency dispersals, but they had disappeared. There was a row of huts used for spares, but the doors had been torn off and the insides were stripped clean.

'Looks like we're out of luck,' Crane said loudly. 'Someone got here before us. Fuel's gone.'

Cowboy, gun in hand, heard this as he jumped to the ground. 'Yeah? I got a better memory than that, Lee. You said you buried the fuel – not put it in some huts for any passing jock to take.'

'Did I?'

They both watched the Kittyhawk come over at around eighty feet, its wings waggling.

'Is he trying to attract attention,' Crane asked, 'or is he going to land?'

'The fuel, Lee.'

Crane didn't like the hungry way Cowboy was looking at Laura when he said it. She was weak and vulnerable as it was, her legs shaky, her pallor sickly. Crane knew how they could make him talk, and he didn't want to go down that route.

'It's over there,' he said, pointing behind him. 'In a cave in the hills. The entrance is disguised. You can roll the drums down real easy.'

'We, you mean. Come on.' His brow creased. 'It's been standing a while, Lee. You got muslin?'

Stored fuel was filtered into the tanks through wide-weave fabric to catch any large particular contaminants that might block the carburettor meshes. It was standard procedure, because metal tended to flake off from the inside of the drums. Crane nodded, and made to follow when he realised the P-40 was finally coming in, at too steep an angle and too fast. It hit the stones with a teeth-jarring crack. Crane half-expected to see the landing-gear struts pop through the top of the wing, but the tough old bird bounced, the engine whining, hit again, sending a wingtip dangerously close to the ground, and then finally grabbed the earth and clung there. A lesser plane might have come apart, but not the P-40. The engine cut and the canopy slid back and Gospel climbed out.

Crane wanted to give him a roasting over that junk landing, but he couldn't. As the pilot approached, removing helmet and goggles and releasing a cascade of hair, Crane realised it wasn't Gospel who had clumsily piloted the P-40 in.

It was Elsa.

Twenty-Five

They were all exhausted by the time *Myra Belle* was fully charged with fuel once more. Crane's eyes stung from petrol fumes, and his clothes were sodden with sweat. Laura was sheltering in the shade of one of the strip's few spindly trees; Elsa was watching her with one of the marines' carbines held loosely.

'Comin' with us, Lee?' Cowboy asked once more.

'Wastin' your time,' said Elsa. 'I told you – I know people. Lee Crane is the kind of guy who flies back to Toungoo to pick up a woman who put out for him once.'

Crane kicked at one of the empty drums, watched it roll away, the metal booming as it went, skidding off the stones and into the long, spiky grass. 'That wasn't why,' he said, 'and you know it. You shouldn't have left her.'

'You weren't there, Crane,' she said. 'I liked her. It wasn't my fault she didn't get on the train, so don't start preachin' at me. I got enough of that from Gospel.'

'You try and recruit him to this?'

She raised an eyebrow, suggesting that was a ridiculous question. No, poor old Gospel was just a means to an end. 'Hey, Crane. Wanna see what's in the bag?' She pointed to Laura's valise.

'No.' Laura grabbed it and held it to her chest.

Simultaneously Elsa and Crane stepped forward, but Cowboy held onto Crane's arm.

Elsa raised the carbine and pointed it at her. 'Don't you join him in the Stupid Club.'

Laura clutched it tighter and hissed, 'You should be ashamed of yourself, Elsa Cross.'

The laugh rang off the hills. 'Should be, but I'm not. I'm past all that, darlin'. Come on, let's see.'

'No.'

Elsa prodded the other woman hard with the barrel of the carbine, a nasty jab to the cheek which drew both blood and a scream. Crane shrugged off Cowboy and took three steps forward.

'Lee!' the voice barked from behind.

Crane slowed and turned. Cowboy was standing with his pistol levelled at his head. 'Easy now.'

Crane raised his hands in submission and walked on unthreatening tiptoe until he was at Laura's side. Elsa backed away from him, kicking the valise as she went. He knelt down and cradled Laura's head. 'You OK?'

Her cheek had swollen to a lump, and the skin was broken, but he reckoned it was nothing too serious. It would be ugly-looking for a few days, though.

'I think we got company!' It was Pickle, on one of *Myra*'s wings, a pair of binoculars clamped against his eyes. Crane squinted into the distance, where he saw the faintest plume of smoke spiralling from the dried-out fields.

'I guess that was you,' Crane to Elsa. 'Buzzing around like a homeless bee and attracting attention. Gospel never get round to teaching you a decent landing?'

She made a face at him, reached down and tried to yank the bag apart. The lock held firm.

'It's a truck,' confirmed Pickle. 'Maybe twenty minutes away.'

'What kind of truck?' demanded Cowboy.

'Whatever it is,' Crane said slowly, 'it's the wrong kind.'

The crack of the carbine made him jump, but it was Elsa mutilating the valise. She fired off two more rounds in quick succession, knelt down and wrestled the two halves apart. Laura gasped in dismay, but Crane put his arms round her shoulders. 'Doesn't matter now.'

Elsa began to laugh.

'My God, we thought *we* were working the system.' She stared at Laura in disbelief. 'Little Miss Goody-Goody there.' She put her hand in, pulled something out and tossed it to Crane. He watched it glint in the sunlight as it spun through the air, a burst of blues and greens, and then he caught it.

'Watches?' he said to Laura.

'Not just any old watches, darlin',' said Elsa, standing. '*Swiss* watches. Rolexes, no less. Diamond-encrusted ones. The man has been smuggling trinkets.'

Crane said: 'Did you know?'

Laura inclined her head. Yes.

'Well,' said Elsa, 'now you have your answer for Nelson – after all this time. Don't even have to carry on screwing her.'

Pickle said: 'We ought to get going.' The smoke had thickened into a distinct white column of dust now, rising into the sky.

'What do you mean?' asked Laura, half of Crane and half of Elsa.

'Oh, didn't he tell you? Crane here has been told to hang around you so he could get into your pants. And that way, get into your bag.' How could she know that? He hadn't even told Cowboy. Unless Nelson spilled it to her. And why would he do such a thing? 'The OSS know most of what Gilbert is up to. But these bags from London intrigued them.'

If she expected hysterics, she was disappointed. Laura shrugged. Whatever the truth, it was nothing compared to a missing sister and the stolen valise.

'Laura, I'll explain later.'

'You don't have to.' It was hard to read anything into her tone.

'I'd like to.' He dropped his voice to a whisper. 'But now they have to make their minds up.'

She turned to him. Her left eye was closing from the swelling. 'Make their minds up about what?'

'Whether to kill us.'

There was a hurried conference between the three of them, and Cowboy came over with a canteen. Crane and Laura were sitting under the spindly tree, grabbing the shade. Crane took the container and a slug of water from it and passed it to Laura, who took the canvas sack without a word. She looked absolutely crestfallen, although whether it was due to her missing sister, Crane's treachery or the loss of the bag's contents – Elsa had taken the watches and the bag of De Beers diamonds she had found stitched into the lining – he couldn't tell. She sipped at the water. 'Thanks.'

'OK?'

She nodded.

'We're in trouble, then?'

He could hear the truck clearly now, its gears grinding on the long climb up towards the airstrip. 'I guess.'

Cowboy stood in front of him, hands on hips. Crane shaded his eyes so he could read the man's face easier. 'Well?'

'I want you to come with us. She can come too.' He nodded towards Laura. 'I don't know who's in that truck, but you're right. Out here, it's never the right kind of folk.'

'I can't come with you, Cowboy,' Crane said. He watched Elsa walk across to the P-40 and rummage in the luggage compartment. She eventually emerged with a small knapsack. She was travelling light. Mind you, thought Crane, you have a million dollars in bullion, you can shop as you go.

'I'm sorry about that, Lee.'

219

'Yeah. I know.'

To Crane's surprise, Cowboy turned and headed for *Myra*. Crane had fully expected to be shot where he sat.

'Cowboy,' he called out.

The other man glanced over his shoulder. Crane held up his empty Colt. 'I need a fighting chance.'

Cowboy pulled out the pistol's magazine and examined it, pondering what to do. Eventually he tossed it high in the air, across to the far side of the strip, where it disappeared into the coarse grass. 'Won't take you long to find it.'

'Thanks.'

He put the empty .45 on the ground at his feet.

'You aren't planning on coming after us in that, are you, Lee?' He nodded to the Kittyhawk. 'Do I have to put a bullet through its block?'

Crane shook his head. They both knew it was his only way out ahead of whoever was in the truck. 'No, I'm not coming after you,' he promised.

His old co-pilot nodded. 'I wish you was up there with me, Lee.' He turned and trotted back to the plane.

'Cowboy?'

'Yeah?'

'Good luck,' shouted Crane. 'You'll need it.'

'You too, partner. You too.'

Crane turned to Laura. 'Cover your eyes.'

There was the familiar whine before the port engine kicked into life, followed by the starboard, and a cloud of grit enveloped them as the C-47 lurched forward and turned, ready for take-off. It sat there for the best part of two minutes before Cowboy opened the throttles and *Myra* rolled forward, gathering speed, whipping up a white storm of dust and debris. She finally clawed into the sky and banked away, the light reflecting on her pockmarked skin. Crane whispered goodbye to her, as if he had just lost a lover.

Two women in one day, in fact. Not bad, even by his standards.

'Will they make it?' Laura asked.

'He's a good pilot. But if there's weather, four hands are better than two.'

She thought about this for a moment. Clearly the marines were no use, but there was more than one pair of hands on board. 'He's got Elsa. And Pickle.'

Crane indicated the Kittyhawk. 'You saw her land that thing. No feel for it, even after all this time. I know it looks easy, but not everyone can do it. And Pickle is a radio man, not a flyer.'

Laura looked up at the blue sky, at the few wisps of high cloud. 'Weather appears good, though.'

'You can never tell,' Crane said. 'If I could, I'd become a Met man and charge the Air Force a fortune.'

The truck was loud now, hauling itself up the last section of the track. Crane jogged across the strip and found the Colt's magazine on the rocks between a couple of grass hillocks. It was scratched, but intact. He returned to the tree, just as the truck's radiator appeared over the ridge. He put the gun on the ground and shuffled over to sit on it.

'What are you waiting for? Shouldn't we get on the plane?'

Crane watched the vehicle. It was not one he recognised, a Chinese or Soviet copy of the US's Dodge trucks, only smaller. There were two men in the cab, four in the rear, their faces shrouded by kerchiefs to keep out the dust.

'I just need to know one thing: time or altitude.'

'What?'

The truck stopped between them and the P-40 and all six men jumped out. They were dressed in grubby blue peasant garb, over-laid with various military webbing and makeshift gunbelts. Not Kuominting. Maybe CCP, the Commies. Crane stayed very still. They were all young, none yet twenty, he reckoned. All were armed with rifles, and several had heavy revolvers shoved into

221

their belts. Their leader was on the far right. Crane could tell by the way the others' eyes kept darting to him, to take their lead from him. He held a PPS-40 submachine gun with a drum magazine. This was not good.

Tu fei, he decided. *Dacoits*, as they said in Burma. Bandits.

Crane put his hands on his head in a submissive gesture and said, '*Ni hao*,' hello in Mandarin, but the leader remained impassive. That was his Chinese pretty much exhausted. Most communication with natives was either through one of the 'pointy talkie' picture books issued by the Army or pidgin, but he had a feeling this wasn't the time or place to try either.

A couple of the men jabbered something in a dialect Crane didn't know but the leader silenced them with a shake of his head.

'Laura,' he said quietly. 'If I start firing, run over to those boulders behind me.'

'I don't think that will do me much good.'

'Do you have a better idea?'

'Yes.'

She reached across into his jacket and took out the Rolex watch Elsa had left behind and, before he could stop her, had advanced on the men. She was bowing deeply and holding up the watch, so the jewels sparked as they caught the light. He saw the leader's eyes narrow. She said something Crane couldn't catch and the leader seemed taken aback.

'Laura.'

'Shut up,' she hissed over her shoulder. 'I'm telling him it's for his favourite mistress.'

The leader took the watch and examined it. He nodded his pleasure, then indicated his men.

'Oh dear,' said Laura.

'What?'

'They all seem to have a mistress.'

'OK, walk back here. Slowly. Don't turn and show your back.'

Laura retraced her steps and Crane asked: 'What are they speaking?'

'It's called *fangu*, one of the dialects from the villages down on the Burmese border.'

'How do you know that?'

There was an irritated urgency to her voice. 'Through Walter. It's what the watches are for. We bribe the local warlords to look after British interests. Money is good, gold better, but Walter found you can't beat a Rolex watch. Or diamonds. It's how he runs his trading network.'

'That's why you take the Michelin to the border?'

Before she could answer, the leader shouted something to them. Crane could guess what it was. The crude submachine gun was pointed at them. A Colt .45 was going to be no kind of reply.

'Tell them,' he said from the corner of his mouth, 'that the rest of the watches are in the plane.'

'What rest?'

'Just tell them.'

'Lee—'

'Please. Tell them the other Rolexes are in the plane. But don't show them. Let them look for themselves.'

'Why?'

'I'm just gambling that my knowledge of human nature is up to scratch,' he said. 'Is your *fangu* up to that?'

Laura set her mouth and nodded. He looked into her eyes for signs of fear, but there were none. 'I'll try.'

She walked back towards the line of men and pointed to the parked P-40, sitting beyond the truck. The leader made a gesture and one of the younger men grabbed Laura.

Crane resisted the urge to shoot him. Not yet. The young guy, his gun levelled at Crane's stomach inviting him to do something about it, held onto Laura while the remaining five trudged towards the Kittyhawk, laughing among themselves.

The leader clambered up onto the wing and peered inside the cockpit. He began to yank at the various straps and levers, tossing out anything that wasn't screwed down for the rest of his team to look at. Crane watched two of them pulling at the parachute, arguing over the silken booty. The leader shouted something at the guard, who barked into Laura's ear.

'What?' shouted Crane.

'They want to know where they are.'

Shit, thought Crane. Maybe I'm wrong. 'Tell them they're in the luggage compartment.'

'I don't know *fangu* for luggage compartment.'

There probably isn't *fangu* for luggage compartment, he thought. 'Well, do you know the *fangu* for go and fuck yourselves?'

The leader couldn't possibly have understood, but something in Crane's tone made him snap his head around. He pulled back the bolt on the submachine gun and jumped from the wing. From where Crane was sitting, it looked as if he had stepped on a mine, for the moment his feet hit the ground, that was when the P-40 exploded into a red and black fireball.

Laura reacted faster than he imagined possible. She stomped down on her guard's foot, the old technique of scraping down the shin and putting all the weight onto the instep. He screamed in agony. Then she stepped away from him, giving Crane a clear sighting. Even as the smoke and flame from a second, bigger explosion billowed towards him, Crane raised the Colt and shot the man three times, just before they were all thrown to the ground by the punch of the shockwave.

Time, then, he thought as the rocks and stones rained down on him.

Twenty-Six

Singapore, 1948

Nelson stopped writing and let out a sigh. 'Yeah, you know we traced the watches all the way back, eventually? Seems they told everyone involved they were bombsights made in Switzerland, destined for crack RAF bomber teams. They smuggled them out through France, across to London and then out to Calcutta and over The Hump. When we found out, we couldn't believe it. All those lives at risk for watches. You know he also used the information he picked up to play the markets? If there is a big Japanese push coming, the Chinese dollar falls. Walter buys, and then plants rumours of a counter-attack. He sells when the dollar goes back up. That's what they were doing in Kunming. Buying stock tips.'

I ignored the caffeine jitters I was getting and ordered a fresh coffee from Joe. 'Jesus. And I thought the Chinese were devious.'

'So, the plane – Elsa's P-40. You told me back then it had totalled on landing,' Nelson said. 'That's not quite the whole story, is it?'

I shook my head. 'I think she'd instructed Cowboy to kill us. He couldn't, or wouldn't, do it. But she'd already anticipated that. I knew she'd have wired the plane to explode. Look, she couldn't be sure we wouldn't jump to Yunnanyi main field and get a whole

225

squadron after them. It was the logical thing to do. What I couldn't figure was whether she'd do altitude or time as the trigger. I figured altitude was too tricky.'

'But you thought she'd know how to make a bomb?'

I accepted my coffee from Joe. 'Everyone in a position of responsibility at Toungoo knew how to make a crude bomb. It was part of the evac plan – deny the Japanese everything. She had primed the hospital to blow, remember?'

'So, then?'

'I took the truck, which wasn't too damaged, and drove southeast. Dumped it and walked into a village where I knew there was an advanced-warning station. By the time I got back to Kunming, the Japanese invasion was in full swing and nobody gave me a second glance. You were at Chungking. Chennault was at Kweilin. I got Laura back out to Calcutta on a C-46 before you guys could grab her. You know the rest.'

He pointed the business end of the pencil at me. 'You don't.'

'Meaning?'

'We found the marines, or what was left of them, about six weeks ago. An MIA team located them in the foothills. They were ID'd by dental records and what was left of their clothing. You know, there were those who thought the pair of them were in on it, that they had jumped aboard and the whole gas-in-the-oxygen thing was a stunt to fool you.'

'You didn't buy it?'

He shook his head. 'Thing is, we found the bodies, but no sign of parachutes. Not a single line.'

I knew the answer to the question, but asked it anyway. 'So you think what happened, exactly?'

'That your friends got into trouble and tossed them out over the Himalayas to save weight.'

'Yeah.' I drank some of the bitter coffee. 'That could have been my fault.'

I took a deep breath. This part wasn't easy to face up to, which was why I had never told another living soul.

'The fuel dump at the main Yunnanyi airstrip used to flood. A lot. I knew the gas I had bought from Mason might be contaminated, but I helped pour it into *Myra* just the same.'

'Weren't the drums rusty?'

'Mason had put it in new drums. After I bought it, I heard he'd pulled a similar stunt on another crew. Thing was, I never had time to go and check. I figured I'd just separate it when the time came.'

He nodded. 'What would water in the fuel do?'

'If they were lucky, foul the engine before they got too high. It'd pop and kick and they'd know something was wrong.'

'And if not?'

'Ice in the carbs. Big time.'

'And . . . ?'

I didn't want to spell it out. I didn't want to think of the panic as Cowboy tried the carb heaters, altered the mixture, anything to keep the engines going. Then the horrible noise as they spluttered and died. All I said was: 'And you don't want ice in your carbs over the Himalayas.'

'Didn't Cowboy suspect?'

I shrugged. 'Cowboy wasn't that good at thinking things through. Besides, he hadn't been a Tiger. Hadn't flown Yunnanyi, so didn't know about the water problems. He realised there might be particulates, so we filtered it. Filtering doesn't do zip to water contamination.'

He considered this for a moment before he said: 'So all this time, you thought they'd crashed?'

'When I never heard anything, it crossed my mind more than once. I thought they were dead, yeah. That I'd murdered them all. Well, maybe murder is too strong. Been responsible for their deaths. But I couldn't be certain of that until I saw Elsa at Raffles. So then I knew at least one of them had survived.'

'And how did that make you feel?'

I shrugged. 'I'd wanted to fuck them up, not kill them. I always thought that once he realised about the gas, Cowboy would turn around and land somewhere in China. I would have. Any other pilot would have. But I hadn't considered that they might try and save weight by ditching Patterson and Sorkin. Hadn't banked on how gold can cloud your judgement, I guess.' I thought of Chennault's old lecture: greed can make you careless, blinkered and prone to mistakes.

'What happened about the girl? Laura?'

'I promised not to tell you about the watches or diamonds until she had had a chance to warn Walter that the game was up, and for him to cover his tracks. I also said I'd get her back to Calcutta and homeward-bound before any OSS complaint about the Brits treading on our toes could get to her.'

'Which you did.'

'Yup. *Ichi-go* helped.' This was 'Number One' – the big Japanese push of 1944, when their troops crossed the Yellow River to the north and poured out of Hankow to the south. It was the biggest land offensive of their war, and part of its objective was to overwhelm US air bases, removing American aerial superiority. To add to the confusion, the weather turned bad, hampering ground-attack missions. It was an Asian Battle of the Bulge, but one with much more likelihood of success. Kweilin fell, and then Liuchow, cutting China in half with hardly a defensive shot fired. In the chaos of such an unexpected lightning strike, one purloined and missing C-47 over The Hump was a minor sideshow, even if it did have a million bucks on board.

With the Japanese on the doorstep, that seemed like small change. The OSS rapidly switched from politicking to running guerrilla resistance. Nelson became a liaison for Major Frank Gleason's OSS team, which was the only Allied unit slowing the Japanese 11th Army, mostly by blowing bridges, mining roads and razing towns.

At the same time, I got moved from The Hump to supply drops for the ground troops, including the Marauders and the OSS teams. There never was a formal enquiry of any kind. I guessed Nelson was about to start a belated one.

'You seen Laura since?' he asked.

I shook my head and felt an old hollowness in my heart I thought I'd filled in some time back. 'No. We parted on good terms, but, well, somehow the revelation that I was working for you rather dampened her passion for me.' And in the aftermath, we never got a chance to talk it through, but I didn't tell him that. 'Strange, huh?'

'Yeah.'

'It was Elsa who told her about our deal.'

'Really?'

I put a sugar in my coffee and stirred it hard while I asked the next question. 'How did she know about me and Laura?'

Nelson looked puzzled. 'Who?'

'Elsa. How did she know that I was hanging around Laura for you, to begin with at least?' It was an answer I'd wanted ever since that day.

'Maybe Cowboy told her.'

'I never laid it out for Cowboy. So how did Elsa know for sure?'

Nelson got to his feet and pushed his chair back. 'I have a better question for you. We know that Elsa and Cowboy survived. What happened to Pickle, eh? Ever think on that? Did he go out over the mountains, too?'

I stood up as well and reached across and grabbed the lapel of his nice cream suit. 'You told Elsa about us because—'

He tried to pull away, but I had him pretty tight. When he spoke, the words came from a face distorted by hatred. 'Because she was one of ours. At least I thought she was. Elsa was OSS, but it turns out Elsa was mainly working for Elsa.'

Elsa was a rogue agent? No, there was something else in there as well, an undertow that was strictly personal. 'Were you lovers?'

He mumbled something I didn't catch and finally got my hand off his suit.

'Were you?'

He put his notebook and pencil away. This was all off the record. 'Yes. For a while.' The hurt and self-pity shocked me. This was Hyram Nelson, after all, not an eighteen-year-old kid who'd been dumped by his prom date. Or maybe we men were all that at heart. 'Turns out she was everyone's lover. I bet you even fucked her.'

I hit him, pretty hard I think, and he sprawled down over the benches, scattering the condiments. Two mechanics came in at that moment and watched him struggle to his feet, holding his chin. Joe, the café owner, hovered, unsure of what to do, wringing his hands on a dirty cloth, his face as pained as if he himself had taken the hit.

Luckily for Nelson the bench was between us, and I couldn't get to him for a second pop. 'No, I didn't, Hyram. Even I had more sense than that, but you didn't. Did she get wind of *Ichi-go*? Did she know that there was so much chaos coming, people would forget about one stinking consignment of gold? Did she sucker you, too, Hyram?'

He shook his head to try and clear it. 'You're out of line, Crane. And way off-beam. None of us knew about *Ichi-go*.' But the shakiness in his voice suggested otherwise. You didn't have to know the specifics to realise something big was brewing. Or was timing the heist with *Ichi-go* just dumb luck?

'You better stick around,' he barked. 'There's a lot more to be said about this.'

I was tempted to remind him that I was a civilian and out of his reach, but I wasn't so sure that was entirely true. The freshly minted CIA had long arms in South-East Asia, even then. In the end, all I said was: 'Get the hell outta here.'

For once, he did as he was told.

Twenty-Seven

The C-47 tyres came into Changi early afternoon, a couple of hours after my one-sided fight with Nelson. I was surprised by this, but Henri had just shrugged. 'It was a deal with Mr Kip, not your friends. He is keen to break into aviation chandlery. Hey, he doesn't want to start by pissing around Indo-Air.'

Why not? I thought. Everybody else does. But I said nothing. What I needed was a drink, but I also needed to make sure my plane was looked after, so I sat there seething while they put *Myra* back together.

When the last hub-nut had been tightened and torqued, Henri came over. His face was streaked with rubber, cut by rivulets of sweat. 'You want a beer?'

'You read my mind.'

'No,' said Henri. 'I can see it in your eyes.'

The thing about a place like the Tashi is that you can leave it for a day, a week, a month – even, I suspect, a decade – and when you come back, the same people will be at the bar telling the same stories. I swear I heard someone mention Lanzarote when we walked in. The place was busier than last time. There were even some women, although they looked to me like off-duty taxi-girls

231

whose meters could be flagged up at any moment, but nobody seemed to mind.

Henri and I found a corner and I ordered two Tigers and told the table boy to keep them coming. My partner went for twelve-year-old Scotch, a double. I was glad he was paying.

'Quite a forty-eight hours, eh?'

'The kind I can live without,' I replied and gulped back the first beer.

'You going to tell me?'

'I wish I'd had your war,' I said gloomily.

'Mine? Mine was no great shakes. My country had been invaded, I became a pilot, I didn't kill enough Germans. When I got back home, I found the place I had left was no longer there.'

'Spoken like a true Tashi regular.' I raised the second bottle in salute. '*Kan bei.*'

'You be careful, my friend. I'd keep that cynicism in check. When you get back to America, it might not be there. It's been a long time. When I . . .'

'Go on.'

He pursed his lips, remembering the days after the fighting was over. 'I didn't want medals, you know? Or, what do you call them, tickertape parades? I just wanted to slot back in. But when people found out what I had done in the war, flying for the British and the Free French, first Hurricanes, then Lysanders, you know they turned away. No mention of "well done" or "thank you". They were just . . . embarrassed.'

'Because they hadn't done much? Or were they ashamed of something they had done?'

'I don't know, Lee. I am not talking about collaborators here, I am speaking about ordinary French men and women. I know what they went through. Staying alive was enough. Staying French was a bonus. But there was this desire to forget it – pretend it never happened. And people like me, we were a reminder.' It was

his turn to take a hit of alcohol. He pursed his lips in apprecia-
tion. Then: 'You going to tell me while you can still speak about
what happened today?'

So I lined up the third Tiger, determined to slow down now
my stomach was warm, and outlined the story for the second time
that day. I watched his eyes grow wide.

'Jesus,' he said, when I'd finished. 'A million dollars?'

'And change.'

'Well, it would be worth pulling a stunt like that for a million
bucks, no?'

I shook my head. 'No, it didn't work out.'

'Only because of the fuel.' Only because of me, he meant. I
knew Henri wasn't quite as fastidious about cargo manifests as me.
There were rumours that some of his rice sacks contained moving
parts – like guns. I would imagine his head might be turned by
the gold. I was beginning to think it was me who was the odd one
out in that respect.

'No wonder you were shocked to see Elsa.' He considered further for a moment. 'No wonder she slugged you.'

'Yeah.' Cowboy would have figured out eventually why the plane
was misbehaving. He might not be the brightest fly-boy in the
world, but he'd have put it together and told Elsa what he suspected. They would have spent the intervening years cursing me.

'Listen, be very cautious.' He spread his hands out at his sides,
like scales. 'You have Nelson on one side, Elsa and Cowboy on
the other.' He clapped quickly, his hands a blur, as he were
squashing a fly. 'Don't be caught in the middle.'

'Cowboy and Elsa won't bother me.'

'No?'

'Why should they?'

'Because you are bound up in this gold, Lee. You are the reason
it failed first time. If they fix you . . .' He let that fade away.

'Thanks for the warning. I'll watch my back.'

233

'You still have a gun in your room?'

'Yes.'

'Good. Sleep with it under your pillow eh, promise? OK.' He signalled for another Scotch. 'So this Laura, did you ever . . . ?' He winked.

'That's a very French question.'

He laughed. 'It's a very male question.'

'No. I didn't.'

'Aaahh.' He sounded disappointed in me. 'Why not?'

'I was hung up on Kitten. By the time it seemed right, well, the moment passed.'

'And now? She is married?'

'I don't know. I sent letters, but . . . I don't know where she is. She went to find her sister, to discover what happened to her. She wanted to know the truth.'

'Like you and Kitten?'

'I guess.'

'That's the other option they could be counting on, of course.'

I took a long pull on the beer. 'What?'

'Cowboy and Elsa don't have to come looking for you. Sooner or later, you'll go to them and ask about Kitten.'

I nodded, sensing the truth of what he had said.

The banging on the door woke me at around two in the morning. It inveigled its way into my dream, where I was flying *Myra* and the gold over the Himalayas. Cowboy had spiked my tanks, and the banging was the port engine misfiring as the carbs iced up.

I awoke, sticky and breathless, and shouted something with my over-thick tongue. How many Tigers had I had? Too many, was all I knew. I slid out of bed, found a pair of trousers and hopped over to the door. I swung it open. It was Mr Kip, our new tyre supplier, and he had a gun in his hand.

Lots of strange explanations for this played through my head, such as he wanted his tyres back, or Henri had stiffed him on the deal, but he just indicated I should back up and sit on the bed.

I'd promised Henri I would sleep with the pistol under my pillow. Now I regretted forgetting the pledge in my alcoholic stupor. I sat, and finished fastening my pants. Mr Kip flicked on the bedside lamp and turned off the overhead light, so we were all dark and cosy. He fetched a pillow and squashed it over the barrel of the gun, as a kind of feathery silencer. Then he sat on the room's only chair, against the wall, the now invisible weapon pointed at me.

I tried to keep my voice steady, to mask the apprehension that was spreading through me, numbing my limbs. 'What gives, Mr Kip?'

He hardly acknowledged I'd spoken, until he put a finger to his lips and made a soft hissing sound, which I guessed meant: be quiet.

We sat.

My mind ran through speed and trajectories, and told me, not unreasonably, that I was hungover and slow and that Mr Kip could put two bullets in my stomach before I was fully on my feet. So we sat some more and we waited.

The phone was louder than I remembered, its shrill bell making me jump. Mr Kip didn't move a muscle, so I knew he'd been expecting this. On the third ring he inclined his head to indicate it was for me.

'Crane,' I said, as if it were just another day at the office.

'Lee.'

'Cowboy. Is this your singing telegram I got in the room here?'

He laughed. 'Mr Kip is there to stop you doing anything stupid while I tell you what's what.'

I blew out my cheeks and let the air bleed into the room. I didn't like the sound of this one bit. 'I thought we were done, Cowboy.'

235

'You remember Pickle, don't you?'

'Yeah.'

'He decided he'd go back and get the gold himself about two years ago. Cut Elsa and me out. Got himself a couple of hotdogs in Bangkok, and a little Lockheed Super Electra twin.'

'And?'

'He was shot down by the Air Division.' This was USAAF planes and crew, helping the Nationalists. 'They thought he was a Commie up to no good in their airspace.'

'I don't—'

'Amateurs, Lee. Pickle chose a couple of amateurs. They took the wrong routing, too near the AD base at Kunming. We won't make the same mistake.'

I looked at Mr Kip's unblinking eyes, trying to read them. They were blank. 'Cowboy, I've already given you my answer.'

'Your friend, Hyram Nelson, was shot tonight.'

'What?'

'Twice. In the head.'

'You killed him?'

'No. Not me. You.' I heard a quiver of satisfaction as he said: 'You killed him, Lee.'

Twenty-Eight

I stood up, keeping the phone clamped to my ear, and I was aware of Mr Kip shifting his position to cover me. 'Cowboy, I have a tongue coated with an inch of fur that can prove where I was.'

'Well, how come he was killed with your gun?'

I instinctively looked down at the floor where I kept my .45. Mr Kip helpfully kicked back the rug for me. I knelt, slowly, so as not to make him jumpy, and lifted the board. The oiled cloth was still there, and a spare box of slugs, but the pistol had gone.

I should have mourned Hyram Nelson, I knew. He might have been an underhand spook, but then that was his job. He didn't deserve to die. He certainly didn't deserve to die just so he could be used as a piece in some fucked-up chessgame. However, spitting blood and venom would have done me no favours at that moment, so I said: 'Very good, Cowboy. Nicely done. But I still have an alibi.'

'I would say he died in the last hour, Lee. Where've you been? In bed alone? And the fingerprints . . . they're all yours, my friend.'

'What are you driving at here? Just cut the crap.'

'There is a Police Inspector called Holland who will be on his way over to see you from the Tanjong Pagar police station. He is going to screw your life up real bad, Lee. Real bad. And that's before the CIA come down on your ass. You'll lose your plane, your liberty, everything while this drags through the courts.'

'How's your hand, Cowboy?'

'That's not what this is about, Lee. My hand is fine. Mr Kip has a car outside. *Myra Belle* is fuelled and ready to go. You can be out of here in no time, and the gun will disappear from the evidence lockers. Inspector Holland will find better things to occupy his time than a missing pilot.'

I didn't say anything, my brain was turning over too fast.

'Don't forget, Lee, a lot of people saw you hit Nelson, will testify that you two argued. It's a shaved deck, Buddy.'

'You shaved it.'

'You'll still get a share of the money, Lee. No question about that. But otherwise, in a couple of hours you'll be on your way to Changi, and it'll be to the prison, not the airfield. You in or out?'

I could smell the stench of Elsa all over this, could imagine the smile of those scarlet lips as she laid it out for Cowboy. I also couldn't think of a way out. I said something, but it came out dry and crackly, like autumn leaves being trodden on.

'What?'

'I'm in,' I said, my voice heavy with reluctance and regret. 'But you'll have to give me Kitten.'

'Not till we're airborne.'

'Cowboy—'

'You ever seen the inside of Changi, Lee?'

'When we're airborne?'

'Promise.'

For what that's worth, I almost said.

Dawn came as a grey wraith, sneaking in under the clouds that threatened more rain. Elsa and Cowboy were already there when Mr Kip dropped me off at the field, both pacing nervously, as if I had kept them waiting for an important meeting. Cowboy had a bandaged hand and was dressed in flying jacket and jeans, but with fine leather mosquito boots rather than the usual Western version on his feet and a forage cap on his head. Elsa had on a light safari-style suit with trousers, the jacket belted tight at the waist. I'd say she looked like a million dollars if I didn't know what a million dollars looked like. And how much it weighed.

With them were two Chinese guys I had never seen before. Both were squat and strong, and no introductions were made, except that they worked for Mr Kip. I could guess what they were there for: muscle. However, they were no ignorant peons. The clothes were good and they had proper haircuts, not the massacre the street barbers like to execute. The hair was combed and oiled flat, as was the fashion that year in Singapore. I looked at Yin and Yang once more and decided, good barbering or no, I didn't like the odds of them ever seeing Singapore again.

I had to accept that Elsa had won; I didn't want to be caught up in the machinery of the city-state's legal system. This was a time when civil liberties took a back seat to fighting Communism and subversion. You could lose years of your life while they decided whose side you were on.

Still, nobody said I had to be happy about being outflanked, or about knowing what they had done to Nelson, so I was sullen and grouchy and I barked a lot at anyone who came near. They could force me to go along, but they couldn't make me enjoy myself. I insisted on a visual of *Myra*, even though Cowboy told me he'd done it. I ignored him and fetched a flashlight and made a great show of looking into every crevice and dark corner. Actually, it wasn't all for effect. The local birds could build themselves a very comfortable nest while you took a coffee break in Indo-China: you don't want to try taking off with a bunch of twigs hidden in your flaps.

'Lee,' said Cowboy, 'we're gonna be on the plane too, y'know? Why would we have pulled any stunts?'

'I don't care about your ass,' I said with some truth. 'I care about mine.'

'We need to get going. I'm going to start inside. Look, Lee—'

I knew some kind of explanation, or excuse, for what they had done was on its way so I cut him short. 'Don't go sitting in my seat, Cowboy, or I might get really pissed. You know what I'm sayin'?' He hesitated and then nodded. 'Good. Where are we filed for?'

'Vientiane.'

I resisted laughing in his face. That would simply be to cover our tracks. 'Where are we actually going?'

'Hanoi.'

I shrugged as if it were all the same to me, and turned to hide my smirk. So now I knew one thing: wherever we were heading, it wasn't Vientiane or Hanoi.

It wasn't that there had been violent unrest in both cities, even though that was true. But Hanoi and Vientiane had groups of Americans who were ostensibly searching for missing POWs and MIAs, who all used those unmarked grey planes a lot. They sometimes 'advised' the French on any problems they had with insurgents. I was pretty certain Elsa didn't want to tangle with Nelson's employers, because I was sure that's who they were. No, Cowboy had been trying to throw me, and anyone else who was listening, off the scent.

I finished the external and went inside the plane. Elsa was strapping herself into the engineer/radio operator's seat, Yin and Yang were making sure the fuel canisters that were our main cargo were properly secured. I checked their work and nodded my approval.

'Where's Henri?' I snapped.

'He went off into town,' replied Elsa.

I didn't like that; it didn't sound like Henri – not unless they'd slipped him a few hundred bucks to make himself scarce. Henri was not averse to a bribe. But then again, it seemed neither of us were these days. At least my motive wasn't anything as crude as money – it was my freedom and the promise of knowing what became of Kitten that bought me.

In the cockpit Cowboy handed me the checklist. 'Just like old times, Lee.' I threw him a withering look, but he stayed remarkably unwithered. 'Except for this,' he went on. 'What is it?' He indicated a red light on the control panel which was winking at him.

'Progress, Cowboy. Fuselage door open warning light,' I lied. I reached over and flicked it off. 'Just a little extra you get on the later models.'

'And you fixed a mirror?' He pointed at the glass-disc-on-stalk bolted on my side of the cockpit.

'Yeah. This is the mark seven, I reckon. The secret is to make the mounting post flexible. That way, it blurs the image a mite, but it stays on in rough weather. Course, I can only see my side of things.'

'She's a nice crate,' he said, patting the column before him.

'How long since you flew one?'

'Don't worry about me. It's like riding a bike – it'll all come flooding back.'

'Where are we really going, Cowboy?'

'Lashio.'

'Oh, great.' Since the assassination of General Aung Lee, Burma had been what the State Department described as 'turbulent'. It always had been. The General, now a posthumous hero of independence, had first fought on the Japanese side, before switching to the Allied cause either because it was clear they were going to win, or when he became disgusted and disillusioned at the way the Japanese treated the Burmese. Take your pick.

I didn't pretend to understand the politics: all I knew was that the Karen and Kachin hilltribes who had supported, and often fought with, the guerrillas of Merrill's Marauders and Wingate's Chindits, and who had worked with the OSS's Detachment 101 to rescue downed Hump pilots, were being brutalised by the new regime. *Thanks for the help, guys*, the West seemed to have said, *but you're on your own now.*

On the other hand, these were inter-tribal animosities that stretched back centuries. This was just the latest phase; with a history of vicious slaughter on all sides, it was a fraught business.

'All the real shit is going down in Mandalay and on the Siam border,' said Cowboy. Karen insurgents were in control of much of Mandalay. 'We're not even going into Lashio itself – we're going to use the strip south of Bhamo.'

'Bhamo?' The town, which sat on the Irrawaddy, had been a forward Japanese port and fighter base. From there, they had harassed us on the Kunming run with the Nakajima Ki-43s, 'Oscars' of the 64th Sentai. Cowboy and I had been lucky, we'd never really run into them. We knew guys who had.

'The Bhamo strip is also about sixteen hundred miles away from here,' I told Cowboy. 'I only get thirteen, maybe even twelve out of this *Myra*. And that's sucking in air.'

'We fly five hundred, refuel in Bangkok, file a new flight plan to somewhere, but head on up to Burma. There's plenty of gas at Bhamo.' He indicated the cargo area with his thumb. 'Plus, I have enough gas back there to get us out of China.'

'With two tons of gold on board?'

'Yeah. And this time, I know it's good gas.'

'They found the two marines you turfed out, Cowboy.'

His face looked pained, as if the memory hurt. For a second, he was my old co-pilot, the one before the twisted alchemy of gold fever started working on him.

'It's why Nelson came looking,' I said.

'We had to do it, Lee. Had to do it,' he said quietly, but I don't think even he believed it.

'It's why they'll come after us. Especially now Nelson is dead. Changing flight plans won't throw them for long.'

'I know,' he agreed, 'but we don't need long.'

He began to recite the checklist that would take us to starting the engines and leaving Singapore. Never mind Yin and Yang, I thought. What odds did I get on ever seeing the place again?

We had barely taken off and set a course north before I said, 'We had a deal, Cowboy.'

'So we did.'

'Tell me where she is, or we turn right around.'

His look dared me to try, but his face softened. *Myra* began to climb towards the fading stars. 'You sure you want to know?'

'Tell me.'

'You should have given her up a long time ago, Lee. She froze you, trapped you like a fly in some of that prehistoric tree sap.'

'I want to know. Are you going to tell me where she is?'

'And we'll still have a deal? You're with us to the end?'

'Yes.'

'No matter what?'

I snapped at him. 'Cowboy, you know me by now. I give you my word. Is she alive?'

He hesitated before he replied. 'Yes.'

I felt relief flood through me for a blissful moment before the other concerns kicked in. I'd met a lot of people who had survived the Occupation and its work camps. Not all of them were whole any longer. 'Where? And how is she?'

'She's alive, Lee. But . . . y'know, I wouldn't get your hopes up. They had it rough in Burma. Indians especially. Anglo-Indians . . .'

I knew all that and I snarled at him, *'Have you seen her?'*

'No, Lee. But I know where she is.'

'Tell me.'

He did. I knew Kranji, of course I did. Everyone knew it. Kranji was the biggest war cemetery in Singapore.

Twenty-Nine

Why, I wondered, were the most troubled parts of the globe often the most beautiful? We had passed over the dusty, cactus-covered plateau at the centre of the country and now, for the first time in four years, I was looking down on the gorgeous hills of the vast Burmese jungle, its tree canopy steaming in the last of the day's heat. It had been a long, punishing day for both us and *Myra Belle*. I'd pushed her pretty hard, cruising at 130 knots, putting her through a fast turn-around at Bangkok. She'd been in the air for the best part of ten hours, and we still had an hour to go.

'Bhamo have lights these days?' I asked, as the bottom half of the sun's disc kissed the hills to our port.

'Yes. All checked. If it's dark, you do one circuit of the field. They'll get you lights.'

'It's still operational?' The jungle in the past couple of years had reclaimed many old wartime strips.

Cowboy smirked. 'For one week only, at a town near you.'

I didn't rise to the bait, didn't ask who he had as a ground agent up there near the Chinese border. I'd find out soon enough.

'How was India during partition?' he went on. 'I heard you did some flying over there.'

'Hairy,' I said dismissively. I didn't want to go near there, just in case. 'You're going to have to tell me where the gold is sooner or later as I need to know what sort of conditions I'll have to land in.'

'Tell him now.'

I turned around. It was Elsa, with coffee. For a sulky moment I thought about refusing the drink, but the only one who would suffer then would be me. I took it. As the sun fell further, we looked down at a series of magnificent valleys, darkening wrinkles in the jungle floor, where spumes of water plunged over steep sides and disappeared into clouds of spray. To our east, a vast quicksilver river curved through the forest, the wakes from the traffic on it just visible to the naked eye.

'So?' I asked. 'Where is it?'

Cowboy sipped his drink. 'The so-called fuel we put in the tanks got us as we were coming over Sunrise. The carbs on both engines iced and started spitting like shit. Christ, we lost so much altitude in a minute, I didn't think we were going to clear it at all.'

I looked at Elsa. There was fear, or the recollection of fear, on her face.

'So we knew we had to ditch the gold. No way I could clear twenty-two thousand feet, the height of the next set of mountains. We put down at the Pyongii beacon.'

My mind flashed to the site, a narrow shelf sitting on a mountainside, with very little room to manoeuvre. No wonder he was holding back. It was a hell of a fly-in. One gust, one correction taken wrong and you got flipped into the cliff-face. I said: 'And you unloaded the gold, using the marines as grunts. My guess is that Elsa talked them round – made them see sense.'

'You wouldn't believe what a powerful motivator gold is,' he replied. I was beginning to appreciate it, though. 'You know how long it took to unload?'

'I can imagine. You'd have to overnight there.'

'Yeah. We dragged it as far as we could into the undergrowth on the maintenance level and covered it up.'

I couldn't quite believe what I was hearing. 'You didn't bury it?'

'Didn't have time.'

'So you've got to hope nobody else has found it,' I said, irritated. 'They sent maintenance crew in there at least every six months.'

'Who'd get in and out as fast as they could. You know that. That beacon had maybe three visits before The Hump shut down. It's still there, all right.'

I looked at Elsa. 'You could've blown a hole in the ground. I hear you are pretty good with explosives.'

There was not a flicker of emotion, just a thin smile, flashed on for a second. Blowing up the Kittyhawk, with or without me in it, was just expediency.

'So we all got to take one bar each, that was the deal,' continued Cowboy. 'Keep us going till we could get back. I got her off the strip, over The Hump into India, although it was touch and go, man. A coupla times I thought we were dead.'

'The marines are,' I said pointedly. 'You decided to take their bars off them.' I wasn't asking questions now, I could guess how it went.

'It wasn't just a case of the money,' said Cowboy defensively. 'It was the weight.'

'You could have tossed the gold overboard first. You tried that, I guess?'

Elsa laughed and slapped a hand on his shoulder. 'Same old Lee Crane.'

She went back to her seat and I stared at Cowboy, but he wouldn't catch my eye. The plane droned on over the darkening canopy below, and I suddenly felt very lonely and far from home.

*

Night came around us quickly, and my sense of isolation increased. The jungle green faded to featureless black, with no lights visible, and there were certainly no functioning radio beacons, not that I could find. There were stars, though, bright and true, and there was Cowboy to navigate by them, and after thirty minutes of slicing through the night I saw a welcome luminescence on the horizon.

'Lashio,' Cowboy said, with the confidence of a man who knew it was there all along.

I wondered what it looked like now, if trains still ran to it, if convoys of scruffy trucks still trundled through it, picking their noisy way between the bullock-carts, heading for the mountains and the Burma Road; or whether, with other, less arduous routes into China now open, it had fallen back into a provincial torpor. If the latter were the case, I knew the tortuous path to China that had cost so many lives would be disappearing rapidly, washed away in some places by monsoon rains, swamped by *belokar* – thick, fast-growing secondary jungle – in others.

Cowboy gave me a new heading for Bhamo and I swung to it, passing Lashio over to port, losing altitude as we went. I dipped a wing to get a better look at the town. The main road was marked by strings of electric street-lights, their glare as always softened by the smoke from wood-stoked mud ovens, the shanties around the core lit by kerosene lamps, a chaotic corona of tiny dancing pinpricks. It looked attractive from up above, but I knew it was deceptive. Life was tough down there.

Then I remembered it was no bed of roses for me. Ahead of us, a few minutes' flying time away, were invisible mountains, and beyond them, China, a pot of gold . . . and a civil war.

Thirty

The airport at Bhamo was to the east of town, on the opposite side of the settlement to the glistening belt of the Irrawaddy. There were lights at the strip, as Cowboy had promised, but they were burning oil drums, and we had to do two passes while they were fired up. I watched the flames flicker on the second pass, trying to judge an approach that wouldn't leave us sliced and diced between the trees I could make out as dark columns at the end of the runway.

The sight of flames on an aerodrome brought back the memory of that burning Blenheim. I never flew a Tiger again after my jaunt to Toungoo. I was pretty sure that Chennault's petty-minded memo that went out in the next few days was really for my benefit:

> *Please issue instructions to CNAC and Pan American not to employ former AVG personnel. Many AVG men quitting hope to take better-pay jobs with these companies. Also issue orders that US Army air transport may not carry AVG personnel except by written order.*

Which was when Hyram Nelson came in and offered to scoop up any damning reports and get me on ATC, flying in the new special 'S' section he was setting up, the outfit that one day would become known as Air America and fly all over South-East Asia in unmarked planes. Back in the war, though, it involved no more than doing the odd favour for the OSS, that was all, and at the end of the conflict he promised my record would read like Audie Murphy's. Actually, it wasn't quite as glittering, but he'd come good on that promise.

'That's as bright as she is going to get, Lee,' said Cowboy, as I pulled *Myra* out of the turn and over where the outer marker should have been. 'Shall we take her in or do you want to waste some more gas?'

'Gear down,' I said, and a few seconds later *Myra* gave a little wobble as her wheels left their housings. I set the cowls to 'trail' and she began to buffet. We were going in.

It wasn't my best landing, and when I left *Myra*, my back jarred and my teeth still chattering, I realised why. At some point the old stone runway had been asphalted, but it was rippled and cracked by roots and thousands of tiny stems poking through the black surface. It had maybe a year, two at most, left before it was useless.

A couple of locals chocked the wheels and began jabbering at me. I raised a hand to silence them and gave them some dollars.

'Get some kit,' said Cowboy behind me. 'We're staying the night.'

'Fine by me.' I had no desire to try and land at Pyongii beacon in darkness. I had no desire to land at Pyongii period, but if we were going to do it, I wanted to do it with the sun up.

I looked around at the field, wondering where we would bed down. It was still illuminated by the dying orange glow from the drums. The air was wet and hard to pull into the lungs, and the smoke from the makeshift landing-lights stung my eyes. Already I could hear the buzz of bugs in my ear, feel the first sweat-hungry flies landing on my neck.

Many of Bhamo's buildings had fallen into disrepair – the bamboo hangars that the Japanese had thrown up had rotted to almost nothing – but electricity blazed from one steel Quonset hut across the apron from where I was standing. Someone was framed in the doorway, just a silhouette, but I knew who it was by how little of the internal light was managing to get past him. The impressive bulk of Walter Gilbert would be unmistakable anywhere.

Inside the hut, Gilbert had laid out the equipment for us: a roller ramp, to assist with pushing heavy boxes uphill into the cargo hold of a C-47, grappling hooks, ladders, a winch, block and tackles and two-wheeled trolleys, of the kind luggage porters use. Everything you needed, in fact, to shift a weighty cargo quickly, plus several new, unopened cans of paint, and spray guns.

At one end of the hut, a couple of stocky black-haired locals, Kachin tribespeople by the look of their green-and-black plaid sarongs, cooked over a pair of gas rings. The food smelled good. Next to them, three overworked fans blew cool air around the room.

The cooks talked softly to each other in *Jingpaw*, laughing now and then. The Kachin were the first people to really strike back at the invading Japanese: they kept score by collecting their ears, leaving the owner with a neatly cut throat. As the Japanese believe they are lifted up to heaven by their lobes, this was a particularly apposite touch. Along with the British Chindits, the Kachin finally made the invaders afraid of the jungle they thought they had mastered.

'How are you, Captain?' Gilbert asked, mopping his face with a handkerchief. He was perspiring freely, and his shirt was mottled with sweat stains.

'Surprised to see you here.'

He nodded, as if he was taken aback to have fallen among such company too. Elsa and Cowboy barged past us and sat at the long table. 'Can I get a coffee?' barked Elsa.

Gilbert spoke a few phrases in *Jingpaw*, and the natives furnished all of us with a strong, black hit of caffeine. 'Lovely chaps, these Kachin,' he said. 'Bloody shame the way they have been abandoned.'

'What gives, Walter? You weren't in on this the first time. I never had you figured for a common thief.'

'No, I should hope not. But things change. You know how much Operation Remorse made for the British Government?'

I shook my head. 'A couple of million?'

'With the currency deals, the diamonds, the watches, I estimate . . .' he took a gulp of coffee, but I knew he was really pausing for effect '. . . seventy-seven million.'

I laughed. I repeated the figure, and it still sounded ridiculous. 'You're kiddin' me?'

'I paid for the whole of the clandestine operations in the Far East, and probably beyond.'

'So why are you here for a cut of a measly million?'

'Closer to two these days, if you market it properly.'

I nodded. His being there made more sense now. 'That's your job.'

He grinned. 'You know what the SOE once described me as in a secret memo? "A thug with good commercial contacts".' He indicated Elsa, who was huddled with Cowboy, talking in low whispers. 'I think that's their opinion, too.'

'What are you going to do with the money you make?'

'Oh, start again. I made seventy-seven million once, I can do it again. And help these people.' He meant the Kachins, I realised, not his partners in crime. 'Been treated appallingly, you know.'

'That's not your speciality, Walter – charity. What is it? Oil, rubber?' A little light went on in my head. There was another Burma-Indo-China commodity he could market. 'You going to become a drug lord, Walter?'

He ducked the question. 'You know what they offered me when

it was all over? A bloody knighthood. Sir Walter Gilbert. At seventy-seven million, must be the most expensive knighthood ever. I told them where they could stick it. We'd fought a war to get rid of such tripe, so I thought. Created a world fit for heroes.'

'Have you heard from Laura?' I asked.

'No. A few letters a couple of years back. Still obsessed with her sister.'

'She ever find out what happened to Diana?'

'Lasshofer. A concentration camp in Alsace. She was . . . Well, you can guess.'

I nodded.

'But when Laura last wrote to me, she was convinced Diana had been betrayed, and she was trying to track down the man responsible. She believed him to be in Berlin.'

'Berlin?' My senses tingled at the thought of seeing Laura again. It had taken me a long time to sort out my feelings towards the two women who dominated my war – not counting Elsa, that is – honed during the many routine hours in the cockpit. Maybe, in Berlin, I would get a chance to give my side of it all to Laura. By then I might have laid the ghost of Kitten to rest once and for all. 'She's in Berlin?'

'Yes. And she asked about you, you know.'

'Me?' I said, trying to hide my pleasure.

'I think she was rather smitten, truth be told. Just wasn't the right time or place. Thought you Americans were not entirely trustworthy.'

'I wonder where she got that idea.'

'Yes, I wonder,' he said absentmindedly. 'Plus, of course, you never stopped going on about that other woman. Doesn't do much for the old love-life, that sort of thing.'

'Tell me about it.'

I walked over to the table, where Cowboy looked up and said: 'Sit down.'

I did so, and pre-empted his briefing by asking: 'Why all the paint? What we going in as?'

'A Civil Air Transport plane.' CAT was Chennault's transport airline, which mostly worked for the Nationalists and the US government. 'We'll put the logo on the tail, the tiger on the nose, an ID on the side.'

'Why?'

'Remember what I said about Pickle? Shot down by Air Defence out of Kunming. Now we aren't going near there, but if we hit a patrol . . . they aren't going to touch a CAT plane with a glitchy radio.'

He hoped. Patrols could be jumpy and trigger-happy, was what I remembered. 'You got a pencil and paper?' Cowboy pulled them from his jacket pocket and handed them over to me. 'What about Commie air defence?' I asked as I scribbled.

Walter's voice came from behind me. 'There is no CCP air force to speak of. Everything that came on the market, Chennault bought up for CAT. They are still waiting for the Soviets to give them aircraft. Stalin is urging Mao to form a coalition government to stop the war. He is holding back the planes as a carrot.'

'And so if we have to do an emergency landing on some unfamiliar strip, we'll look like friends?'

'Right,' agreed Cowboy. 'We'll mostly be overflying Nationalist territory anyway.'

I drew myself a little sketch of what I remembered about our ultimate destination. 'How long is the Pyongii strip, Cowboy?'

'Funny enough, I never measured it, Lee.'

A thick rice pancake and a bowl of meat stew with vegetables was placed before me by the Kachin cooks and my stomach spasmed in anticipation. 'Guess,' I urged him.

'Three thousand feet.'

'Elevation?'

'A shade over eight thousand.'

253

I scribbled some more and threw him the figures. 'All that gold, six people on board – one of them worth two . . .' I indicated Gilbert '. . . minimum two-seven needed to get her in the air. That's a tight call. I'd like it to be longer.'

'Maybe it's grown while we were away,' smirked Cowboy.

'I will not be going,' said Gilbert, 'don't worry, Captain. My job is to be waiting at the other end for you to get back in one piece.'

'Where's the other end, Walter?'

'Macau.'

It figured. It was a gambling and gangster town, a good place to sell gold of unknown origin. There was only one problem I could think of. 'Macau doesn't have an airport.'

'That's why Walter is in on the deal,' said Elsa. 'Borders are his forte.'

'You are going to land on Nationalist soil and cross into Portuguese territory?' I queried. 'You know, forgive me, but this isn't a cargo you slip into your back pocket while you go through customs.'

Walter shrugged his huge shoulders. 'A thug with good commercial connections, remember?'

'You leave all that to us,' said Cowboy. 'And I've taken off on that strip, with a couple of stuttering engines, Lee, thanks to you. I know it can be done.'

I stood and grabbed my bowl of chow. 'I'm going to sleep in *Myra*.'

We often bedded down in our planes in the old ATC days, just in case someone came a-looting. Cowboy looked doubtful about me being allowed outside with a fully-fuelled C-47.

'You'd hear her starting up if I tried to run, a good five minutes before I could even taxi.' A cold Gooney Bird was not a plane to use if you were in a hurry, not unless you wanted to ruin the bearings on the prop shafts or the ends on the power plant: they liked to wake up nice and gentle. 'If you don't trust me,' I said, 'disable her.'

'I have,' he said ruefully, patting his jacket pocket to let me know he had some vital fuse or relay in there. 'It'll be hot in there. Don't dehydrate. I need you fit.'

Walter pointed to the pile of equipment. 'There is some *leng kai shui* over there.' Boiled, cooled water.

I thanked him, fetched a canteen of it, and headed outside to take my chances with different kinds of bugs from the ones in the Quonset hut.

I heard the noise outside the plane just as I was laying out my sleeping bag, my head a Wurlitzer from the mass of possibilities that presented themselves. I crept over to the door, which was partly open to let some air in, and pulled away the gauze I'd rigged up as a mosquito and midge net. Outside was illuminated only by stars, moonlight and a few feeble embers of the smudge fires. There was enough light for me to make out Elsa, though.

'You're not asleep,' she said.

'No. Stay there. I'll come down. It's an oven in here.'

I slithered down the short ladder into air like warm milk. It wasn't much cooler outside, but I had good reason to keep her away from *Myra*'s interior.

'Lee . . . I'm, uh, you know.'

'Sorry? It's real easy to say. *Sorry.*'

'I'm sorry it turned out like this. Pulling the stunt with Nelson and all.'

'Stunt? Blackmail and murder is what it's called.'

She gave a shrug. 'You want a cigarette?'

I took one as a bug deterrent, and also because it gave me something to do with my hands that wasn't slapping her face. After she had lit me, I asked: 'Did you have to kill him?'

'Nelson? We'd been posted.'

Posted was CIA-speak for wanted dead or alive. 'How do you know?'

'I still have some friends left in South-East Asia. Anyway, he's probably really pissed off, but he's not dead.'

I let that sink in. 'You bluffed me?' Now I knew why Cowboy had smirked when I talked about it.

'Afraid so. Mr Kip has him under wraps on Pulau Blakang Mati until this is all over.' This was an island just off the tip of Singapore, covered in old British fortifications.

I succeeded in not exploding at the news, but it was a close-run thing. 'You must have gone soft, Elsa.'

'That's what I thought. Old softie Elsa.' There was steel in the voice as she said it, suggesting I shouldn't push the theory.

'Or do you draw the line at murdering old lovers?'

She ignored the jibe. 'It just seemed as easy to hold him as kill him.'

'Have you been planning on going back to get it all along?'

She nodded. 'Ever since we left it there.'

'Why now? What have you been doing?'

'Cowboy and I tried a few things. Like forgetting all about it. After some business in Ceylon and Tasmania, we had a small stake in a casino in Macau, which is where we ran into Walter again. That's when we started to think we might really have a shot at getting the gold.' She took a long drag of the cigarette, weighing up her next words. 'You know, back at Yunannyi, I never really thought you'd get on the Shark when I planted the charge. Not the way I'd flown it in. You'd be too cautious. I wanted to disable the plane, not kill you.' I didn't answer – there was no way I could tell the truth of that. She lowered her voice further. 'Lee, Cowboy and I, we're not really together any more. Not in that way.'

I was aware of how close she'd moved. It wasn't just the night that was hot. I took a small step away. I had a feeling she'd been sent out to bring me onside under something other than duress.

I might be dumb falling for the Nelson murder scam, but I wasn't yet certifiable. 'So what's Mr Kip in all this?'

She let out a sigh mixed with the smoke. 'Mr Kip? He's an investor. That's all.'

'I think you're all crazy. In fact, I'd count me in on that. We're all crazy. But now I know Hyram is alive, what's to stop me . . . ?' I made the sign of taking off into the wide blue yonder.

Her voice was ripe with irritation. This wasn't going in the direction she wanted at all. 'That can be changed. One telex to Mr Kip—'

'You can only pull that bluff once, Elsa.' I looked around. 'And I don't see any Western Union office.'

'It's not a bluff this time. He told you about Kitten?'

I nodded. 'You can't use that a second time either. You are running out of weaknesses to exploit, Elsa.'

'I know what you think of me, Crane. I know what all you flyers thought. You see the big lips, the big tits and you think, Oh, she's that kind of gal. Even Nelson thought that: the CIA wanted to use me as their tame whore. And guess what? I got fed up with having to make my way with my ass. It's gonna sag one of these days, and you same guys'll be goin': "Jeez, I remember when it was like a couple of bowling balls in a bag." So all I wanted was something to cushion that blow.'

It was quite a speech for Elsa, and for once I think she was telling the truth. She saw the money as a key to a new life, the fresh start that she deserved. People always assume that's what an excess of cash will give them. Trouble is, the old life is never easy to shake off.

'I think you'll find you never get a soft landing on stolen gold, Elsa,' I said. I stubbed out my cigarette and went back to the plane, unaware of just how much I'd hit the gilded nail on the head.

Thirty-One

Yin, Yang and the Kachins prepped *Myra* at first light. They sprayed out the Indo-Air name and logo, and set about turning my C-47 into a CAT plane. I sat in the shade with Walter, but we weren't the only audience. A few stragglers had turned up out of the jungle to watch the show. The women, some of them bare-breasted, others with intricate jerkins made of coin-sized metal discs, all with thick pig-tails, squatted over makeshift cooking fires, the pots of aluminium clearly recycled aircraft parts. The scrawny men were smoking through long pipes made from joined-together beer cans. All wore the standard sandals carved from truck tyres that had been lost on the Burma Road.

'I think they're hoping for a crash on take-off,' I said to Walter. 'More booty.'

'No, to them we're just the equivalent of a Punch and Judy show,' he said dismissively. 'Something to pass the time.'

'They kidnapped Nelson, you know. They say he's all right, but . . .'

'You don't believe them?'

'Well, as far as trustworthy goes, I give them neck and neck with Tojo. Slightly behind Goebbels, perhaps.'

'Too bad about Hyram – if he is dead.'

'Too bad? Is that all you have to say?'

Walter raised an eyebrow, and wiped his forehead with the handkerchief that could have doubled as a parachute for a normal-sized guy. 'We were never quite on the same side, Hyram and I. Before he left to go and play jungle soldier, he damaged my operation quite severely, once you told him about the watches.'

'I had to eventually. I didn't do it right away.'

'For Laura's sake,' he said correctly. 'Afterwards, we had to be more circumspect. I reckon we might have made it to a hundred million, without him and his OSS chums forever claiming China was theirs. The arrogance!' He shook his head. 'We should all just go home and leave these people alone.'

By 'we' I knew he meant the French, British, US and Dutch Governments, but I said: 'Then why don't we?'

He looked at me for a moment before he said: 'After you.'

I checked the weather and then I checked it some more, listening to every station on air, tuning into Kunming and Lashio and troubled Mandalay. They were all unanimous: it was a beautiful day for flying.

We took off early afternoon, the paint still wet, and the whole plane stinking of cellulose and turpentine. *Myra* managed to get off the bumpy asphalt OK, but she was slow into the climb. As well as three passengers in Elsa, Yin and Yang, we had a lot of fuel on board, because she needed plenty. *Myra* burned about 95 gallons an hour when cruising, plus 2 gallons of oil. She did a lot more gas when she was taking off, and when she was climbing, so there was enough liquid dynamite sloshing around inside her to turn us into a very pretty firework for our rag-tag audience.

I took everything nice and slow, not using full power or manifold pressure on take-off, making sure the turns were soft and gentle. Our passengers must have thought it was a magic-carpet ride.

259

As soon as we had enough altitude, we could see the old Burma Road beyond Lashio, its scar carved deep into the endless hog-backs of the mountains, a series of hairpins that switchbacked upon themselves, over and over, looking as if a child had scribbled them in a fit of pique. Here and there were the dust-tracks of trucks still using sections of it, moving teak from the forests. Further north we would be able to see where the Ledo Road, one of the great, if futile, engineering feats of the war, intercepted the original routing. Disease, mishaps and the Japanese meant an American soldier died for every one of its 1100 miles, yet it was finished just as the war moved to its endgame. A gallant waste – the sort of thing the Brits normally do so well, but this time it was Uncle Sam's folly.

'Crossing gone there,' said Cowboy, pointing to a twisted steel Bailey bridge that ended halfway across a gorge, an apparently placid river flowing beneath it. That same river that probably puffed itself up to an angry torrent and swept away the span in the spring melt.

'When you lit out on us I did some drops in this part of the world. Pigs mostly,' I said.

'What kind of pigs?' he asked.

'The live kind.'

He snorted. 'You dropped live pigs?'

'With parachutes on static lines. The idea was, two sides of bacon falling from the sky can cause a lot of damage, to people and property. We had to let them down slow.'

'So pigs really did fly. What happened if the 'chute didn't open?'

I winked at Cowboy. 'I heard tell it was a real tender piece of ham.'

We both laughed and for a second there we were back in our old partnership, us against the mountains and nothing else. It was just a fleeting moment, quickly replaced by the cold, gnawing feeling I'd had inside all night.

We were more or less following the Burma-China border, just to the east of the tumbling Nmai River. To our starboard, way out of sight, at the far side of the jungle and the distant fields of bamboo and rice that we could glimpse on the horizon, was Kunming and its US-controlled fighters.

I reckoned that's where we would go on the return trip. That was where Gilbert would wait for us, to sweet-talk the locals with one of his get-rich-quick schemes. And from there? A long leg to Macau or Hong Kong or Canton or, possibly, Formosa, where the lust for gold was feverish. A long leg, but not hard. They wouldn't be needing me by then.

Ahead were the endless rows of mountain peaks, their sparkling glaciers the source of the Nmai. I couldn't lie, I was grateful we weren't heading too deep into there. The beacon was in one of the Himalayan valleys in the Kumon range to the north-west of us, just beyond the Sunrise Point ridges, where the ground was covered in thorn forest and dense thickets of tall grass, rather than snow at this time of year.

'How long to load the gold?' I asked Cowboy.

'A few hours.'

'So we'll be spending the night there.'

'We'll take off at sun-up.'

I nodded, hoping I'd be alive to see that dawn. And Kitten, no matter what state she was in.

The world looked gorgeous and unsullied. We were too high to see the settlements that we knew were down there, or the smoke from their fires. It all looked pristine and pure, the way it must have looked thousands of years ago.

'What do you make of that?' Cowboy pointed to the clouds, building tall and bulbous – above 25,000 feet, for sure – well over to my right. They were a shimmering white, streaked with a more threatening black.

'I reckon we stay out of their way.'

'Let's hope they don't come lookin', eh? Sunrise Point ahead.'

I looked at the first of the three knife-blades running across my field of vision. The initial ridge reached up its razor edge to 15,000 feet, the second peaked at 19,000, the third a whisker below 14,000. Then we were home and dry. The sky was a reassuring deep blue, apart from that troubling spot to starboard. We put the masks in position and switched on our oxygen.

The first bounce caught me unawares and smacked my teeth together. I tightened my buckles. 'Make sure they are strapped in, back there. I have the aircraft.'

He nodded. 'You have the aircraft.'

'And they'll need oxygen.'

Cowboy was gone for a couple of minutes, by which time *Myra* was vibrating in my arms as she passed through the haze layer. 'She OK?'

I took this as a personal affront. 'She'll hold together. She's as good as the first *Myra Belle*.'

True to my word, she took the ripples in her stride, see-sawing and yawing a few dozen feet at a time, but nothing an old hand would call turbulence. I had never liked Sunrise Point. The three sisters, unlike other peaks, seemed to shrug off the snow, remaining dark and featureless, black-hearted and unforgiving. I could feel *Myra* strain as I pulled the nose up for the central ridge, her props slashing at the thin air, trying to find grip.

Cowboy and I both breathed out as the jagged edge slid 300 feet beneath our belly, and I could let her rest a little. I eased the nose down a few degrees and asked him to check our bearing and heading.

'You got a big drop into the valley after the third—'

'I know.'

'We should come in virtually over the beacon.'

'You want to check again?'

He cranked the receiver, but shook his head. 'No signal. She's dead.'

When we finally found her, we knew why. The Pyongii beacon and station had been built on three levels. At the top of a sawn-off peak, in an area the size of a small baseball field, was where they had constructed the tower. That metal spire was now bent double, thrashed into submission by the Siberian storms that scoured down the Kumon range from the north. Nobody came to repair it, of course. The Hump wasn't needed any more, there were safer routings to fly, more modern planes to stay well above these treacherous wrinkles in the earth's skin.

Some way below that, down stairs that had been hand-carved by coolies, was the landing field, a wide ledge that had been sliced in the side of the mountain by ice, wind and water. The coolies had simply regraded it and compacted the earth and stones to make the strip. Below that, in the sheltered area where the twisted clumps of coarse vegetation began, was the camp, used by the maintenance crews. That was where the gold was.

I did a fly-by, as usual, with the plane dipped at a 30-degree angle to give us a good view. I didn't have to say anything to Cowboy as we passed the crude strip. He saw it too, and he groaned. Nature hadn't quite finished sculpting the ledge. There had been a rockfall, a big one. What had once been a three-thousand-feet length of runway had shrunk to less than two. That was technically below what we needed to take off but, just as importantly, it was far too short for a heavy C-47 to land safely.

We were screwed.

Thirty-Two

I was aware of Elsa in the cockpit, breathing down our necks, but I was in no mood to acknowledge her.

'Nearest put-down strip?' I asked Cowboy.

As we came around he looked at the rubble-strewn landing field once more, grimaced, then looked down at the chart on his knee. 'I guess we fly back as far as—'

Elsa let out a roar of disbelief. 'What is the matter with you? Fly back?'

'Show her,' I said.

'See the rockfall?' he said. 'There. It's come from the plateau above. It's knocked maybe a thousand feet off the runway. A C-47 needs a minimum of two thousand four hundred to land at sea-level. More up here.'

'I can show you the tables if you want.' I reached for the Stableford charts, named after the RAF pilot who devised the tables for plotting landing and take-off distances of C-47s and DC-3s. They wouldn't make happy reading, but she cut me short anyway.

'Shit, don't bother. And once we are down, we can't get off?'

'I can get a Gooney up in under two-five,' I said, 'but not one stuffed to the gunwales with gold at eight thousand feet above sea-level.'

She barked at her partner. 'Is he telling the truth?'

'Yeah,' replied Cowboy tersely. 'He is.'

I turned. 'Is this where you pull a gun on me and order me to try and land?'

She shrugged and smiled one of the old Elsa grins. 'Would it do any good?'

'No.' But I had looked down at our fuel reserves. Struggling back over the Sunrise Point was going to empty those tanks damned fast. It meant we probably wouldn't make any kind of strip. We'd be crash-landing in the jungle or the rockpile, neither of which was an attractive proposition. Not that my next suggestion was a day at Virginia Beach.

I looked at Cowboy: 'You ever done a genuine full-flap three-point in one of these?'

'I hear it can't be done.'

'You heard wrong.'

'They crack at the door. Snap it in two.'

I nodded. The fuselage where they cut the entrance was indeed the weakest part of most C-47s. They'd strengthened some models with steel bands, but not *Myra*. She was a delicate flower.

'What's a three-point?' asked Elsa.

It was Cowboy's turn to explain while I made sure we didn't hit the mountain. I could feel a cross-wind tugging at us, which I didn't like. 'On a normal C-47 landing you come down on the two big wheels, run along the ground, let the tail drop, brake, taxi to a halt,' he explained. 'With a three-point you bring her in so that all three tyres, two main wheels and tail-wheel, touch down at once. Then you slam on the anchors and hope you don't tip over.'

'You don't,' I corrected, 'just slam on the anchors. Or you'll be trying to burrow your way to the centre of the earth. That's when you need to hold your nerve.'

There were plenty of old Hump pilots who claimed they always did three-points, but it was possible to perform something that looked like one to the casual observer, when in fact the tail-wheel stayed just off the ground for most of the run, which meant a lot less stress on the plane. The real thing, a flat-out stall, banging down onto three wheels, was rare.

Elsa's voice took on a subtle hint of panic. 'Can you do this, Lee?'

'Truth?'

'Well, it's a good time for it,' she snapped.

'I don't know. Not in that length.'

'For fuck's sake, Crane.'

'But I know a man who does. Cowboy, you have the aircraft.'

His eyes narrowed but he just said: 'I have the aircraft.'

Elsa watched me suspiciously as I undid my straps and went aft to fetch Henri.

Thirty-Three

Henri was in the hidey-hole we had built when we were trying to get Muslims and Hindus on the right side of the divide as India convulsed itself into two separate nations. I'd known as soon as I had seen that red light on the dash: it warned us we had baggage in there. I had gone back and asked what the hell he was doing. 'Watching my back,' was what he claimed. He hadn't mentioned some kind of reward for that. He didn't have to.

The hidey-hole wasn't a big space and it was hot and noisy, but I'd fed and watered him at Bhamo, so he was in reasonably fine shape when he unfolded himself from the smuggler's compartment.

'Jesus,' he muttered as he staggered on rubber legs. 'We're still in the air. I thought I said to let me out when we'd landed?'

He went to reach for the pistol that he had brought but I grabbed his wrist to stop him. 'You won't need that. We got bigger problems.'

He stuck out his lower lip and followed me through the cargo area, past a bemused Yin and Yang, and into the cockpit. Cowboy looked up and laughed. 'The light on the dash?'

I nodded. 'Yeah. It's not a door-open warning. It's a stowaway-on-board warning. So I knew we had a guest back there.'

'You think I would let my friend fly off with two blackmailing

267

villains? Hello, Elsa. Hello, Cowboy. Quite a view,' said Henri. He watched the plane slide over the greenery of the valley and then rise up to begin a circle over the damaged airstrip. I quickly filled him in on the problem. He stroked his stubble as I talked, occasionally asking questions about *Myra* and the strip.

'It's possible but for one thing,' he said finally.

'What?' asked Elsa. 'I'm getting dizzy going round in circles up here.'

'What's my share of the gold if I do this?'

Not hide just to watch my back, then.

He settled on a hundred thousand dollars, which Cowboy told me was the same share as mine. As we had never discussed my cut this time around – I was pretty sure equal shares was off the table – it was possible he'd divided mine in half and given it to Henri. I didn't really care. It was all funny money anyway. Funny that any of us thought we'd live to spend it.

'You sure he's that good?' Cowboy asked me.

Henri snorted and I said: 'I'm sure he's that good. Sorry, ninety-nine per cent of the time, I'd have you up there. This is the one time I want someone who flies on pure instinct.' Also, I couldn't have left Henri where he was hiding. The original plan, worked out once I discovered him, was for us to play the Henri card when we were on the ground but, given the location of the smuggler's space, a three-point could have broken his back.

'Does he know C-47s?'

'Get up,' yelled Henri, 'and shut up! Let me earn my money.'

Cowboy reluctantly vacated his seat for me and I indicated Henri should sit in the co-pilot's seat. He hesitated, and for a moment I thought he was going to insist on senior position, but he quickly climbed in and adjusted his straps.

'I want two dry runs over the strip at fifty feet,' he grunted. 'Less if we can do it.'

Cowboy strapped himself into the radio operator's chair, where he could keep an eye on us. Elsa went back to sit with Yin and Yang.

We brought *Myra* round and lined her up for the dummy approach. Shadows were beginning to fall across the surface of the shrunken landing area from the larger boulders. The sun was sliding from the sky. We had to do this quickly.

'Gear down.'

I did as I was told. 'There's a side wind,' I told him.

'I know, I can feel it.' He dipped the wing towards the gusts. To our left, the cliff that led up to the useless beacon seemed very close. I could see the desperate plants growing in its crevices quite clearly. Henri adjusted the trim, brought the throttles back, let her come in at a shallow angle, falling towards the rubble-strewn strip, closer and closer, until I was sure I would hear the wheels catch the earth, but then he powered up and I helped him pull the nose up and bank away from the cliff.

'We have to drop just the other side of the rockfall, as soon as we can, or it isn't going to work. It'll give us maximum length.'

'As long as you don't catch the tail-wheel on the rocks,' added Cowboy. Henri ignored him. We were coming around again. My mouth was dry and my hands were wet. I tried to wipe them as surreptitiously as I could.

Henri noticed and winked. 'Ah, shit, Lee. Let's just do it,' he said.

We turned once more, lining up for strip along the length of the valley, praying we could ask this one favour of *Myra*. Just this once, girl. Won't ask again. Well, apart from take-off.

I let Henri do most of the work. I had more hours on C-47s by far; but he had the luck of the devil, or that of someone on first-name terms with him.

I didn't breathe as he let the airspeed drop and adjusted the angle of descent. The ground began to rush towards us, and I swear the wingtip was brushing the cliff.

'Full flaps,' he shouted and he got them. *Myra* started to vibrate. We were at 100 knots. Too fast. I said so. He told me to shut up.

'Watch the ASI.'

I had done nothing but watch the Air Speed Indicator. Suddenly it jerked down, stopping at just above 70 knots, a whisker above stall speed.

The chaotic field of boulders, rocks and scree disappeared from view as the C-47's nose rose and the tail dipped. Now we could see only sky, with no idea of where the ground was. Just instinct.

I risked a glance at Henri. His eyes were closed and his lips were moving. I looked away just as the plane smacked into the ground and sent my head jerking forward. It sounded like every rivet and bolt popped and there was the terrible creaking sound of distressed alloy.

Henri hit the brakes and *Myra*'s metal skin began to shriek in protest. There was a loud bang as something broke loose in the cargo area. Stones drummed onto the plane's belly skin as the wheels dug into the earth. She swung widely and I made to compensate, but Henri, his eyes now wide open, said: 'I've got it.'

Then she was slowing, still bumping, the world through the screen blurred, but she was losing speed too slowly. I slid open the side window and looked out into the grit storm, and I could see the drop-off, mere yards ahead. 'Shit, we're going ov—'

Henri kicked hard on the rudder, and *Myra* spun herself around, still travelling towards the edge of the cliff, but sideways now until, with a sickening tilt, she lifted clear of the ground. The port wing swung up into the sky, held for a few seconds and then *Myra* crashed back down with a spine-jolting thud.

Henri looked at me and wiggled his fingers, as if he had just played a piano concerto. 'It's all in the touch,' he said.

As I stepped down from the plane, I felt the first chill of a high-altitude night. Distant animal cries reached us, of alarm or courtship, I couldn't tell. A buzzard circled high in the fading light, mocking our puny attempts at heavier-than-air flight.

Above us was the beacon; below, the base camp for maintenance crews; and below that, thick vegetation that tumbled down the hillsides to the slither of a river far, far beneath us.

I kicked at some of the larger rocks that dotted the ash-dry surface of the strip and walked back to examine how we'd done. *Myra*'s progress was marked by thick gouges in the soil, and by the dust that still hung in the air. She'd stopped about 30 feet from a precipice. I didn't want to look over and see how big the drop was. We'd done it. Or, rather, Henri had done it. Getting off, even fully loaded with booty, should be a walk in the park in comparison.

The others came out and joined me in checking just how fortunate we'd been. Cowboy offered me some gum, and I folded a stick into my still-parched mouth. 'Glad you brought him along.'

'Worth a hundred thou?' I asked.

'Every cent.'

'What now?'

'We have some lights, we have some tackle. The gold is down there.' He pointed to the camping area on the level below. 'We'll work through the night in shifts so we can catch the dawn.'

He wasn't referring to any kind of sightseeing, I knew. At altitude, it was better to take off in the morning, in cool air, around about sunrise if possible, when you had light but not heat. If it was a bright, hot day, the sun could make the atmosphere at 8000 feet the equivalent to that of 10,000 or 11,000 feet by midday – thin and unreliable, with minimal lift for an overloaded C-47.

He watched Elsa and Yin and Yang head for the steps down to the camp area. 'You guys wanna come and see?' she yelled. Henri nodded and followed.

'I'd better get some flashlights,' Cowboy said, turning for the plane. 'Before it gets dark and we all start breaking our necks in our eagerness to see some gold.'

We walked down the crudely chopped stairway towards the lower level, flashlights under our arms, navigating by the last of the daylight. I didn't want to use the torch batteries until we were forced to. 'You carried the gold down here?' I said, as my foot sank into rotten wood and I staggered.

'No. We tossed it over the edge and stood well back. Those cases were pretty tough – designed to withstand a crash or a car-wreck, I guess. Then we dragged them into the brush.'

I heard another animal cry and stopped. It seemed to hang in the air, like a warning.

'Monkey of some kind,' Cowboy said. 'Or a *wah-wah.*' It was the local name for a gibbon. 'Maybe a bear. Perhaps a mountain lion.'

'Regular Tarzan of the Jungle you turned out to be,' I sneered. 'So, tell me: whose idea was it to sucker me with the pistol and Nelson thing? Making out like you'd shot him with it.'

'I said you'd never fall for it.'

'Thanks.'

'Elsa said you thought she was capable of anything.'

'She's not far wrong.'

'No, but you are. About her.'

I let that go. He wouldn't believe she'd been hitting on me the previous night, even if I told him. I wasn't sure exactly what she had been suggesting myself. 'Listen, one other thing. What did you do with *Myra Belle* the first?'

'Oh, she was pretty beat-up by the time I got her back. I pan-caked her in a field outside Moran. She was probably cut up for cooking pots within twenty-four hours. It was *Ichi-go,* remember; everyone had a rocket up their ass, thinking the Japs were going to roll right over us and come into India. Fields were being evacuated left right and centre, planes turning up in unexpected places. Nobody cared about us and a sick Gooney Bird.'

I stopped. The vegetation was thick below us. I could hear Elsa and the others moving around in the undergrowth, but couldn't see them. We would need to machete some of the thorn bushes and rattan creepers out of the way. 'Why did you do it, Cowboy?'

He looked away and shook his head. 'I asked myself that. We just wanted a share of what everybody else was getting. Everyone was skimmin', every skyrat was getting rich except us, just because you didn't want no part of anything. Booze, girls, everything I suggested to give us a little extra, you vetoed.'

'Right. Of course. It was my fault.'

I carried on down, the harsh sound of his breathing in my ear as he followed, a dislodged stream of rock and soil trickling before us. We were going to need that winch: there was no way of carrying almost two tons of gold up this slope. Eventually, just as the spindly trunks swallowed us and I switched on my flashlight to cut through the gloom, I gave him the benefit of my wisdom. 'Money is like sex, Cowboy. You always think everyone else is getting more than you. It ain't necessarily so, buddy. Ain't necessarily so.'

At the bottom of the steps there was a small clearing which contained evidence of previous human activity – C-ration containers, cigarette packets, the tattered remains of a bivouac, an eviscerated sleeping bag, rotted to mulch, but nothing that had been used for many years.

'Elsa!' yelled Cowboy.

'Over here,' came the reply.

Back in 1944 they had made a kind of cairn of stones and branches to cover the bullion. Much of that had been blown away, but the dull steel boxes, dented and creased from their fall, were still there. Elsa had ducked into the tangled undergrowth and opened one of them. My torchbeam made the gold within flash; the dancing light seeking to dazzle and entice. To me it looked dangerous and corrupting, the metallic equivalent of a painted lady, the bright plumage hiding the disease within.

Still, nobody spoke while we all contemplated life with a million – or, if what Gilbert said was true – two million dollars.

'I suggest we get the hoist set up while the rest of us begin dragging it over to the bottom of the cliff,' said Elsa eventually. 'Then we can use the trolleys to wheel it to the plane.'

'I want either Henri or me on board at all times,' I said, 'supervising where the stuff is placed and how it is secured. The centre of gravity will be all-important.' Henri nodded his agreement. 'I also think we should clear some of this undergrowth away before we start dragging the boxes or our faces'll get cut to pieces. There's some *parangs* in the plane that'll do the job.' The Malayan jungle knives were small, but effective if used properly.

'Agreed,' said Elsa. 'And I want you,' she pointed at me, then Henri, 'and you, to get some sleep at some point. You have to get us out of here, remember.'

I didn't need telling twice. I knew that I was running on low reserves. Even the news about Kitten hadn't jolted me the way I was expecting. My emotional batteries were drained. I'd red-lined it the past few days, and unless I got a couple of hours' shut-eye, I wouldn't be capable of the physical effort of flying *Myra* off the rockface.

With the chirping of insects loud in my ears, I trudged back up the steps to fetch the knives, ropes and more torches, and to rig up lights around the plane. It was going to be a long night. I was both looking forward to this coming sunrise, and dreading it. After all, it might be my last.

I got to snatch some sleep around 3 a.m. I hunkered down on the far side of the strip, at the base of the cliff where the steps began that led up to the snapped beacon tower. I found a patch of wiry moss, and although the ground still felt hard and cold, it was well away from the lights and noise of the loading. I had a US Navy-issue sleeping bag and leather gloves, and I reckon I managed two hours before the damp of morning set me shivering and I awoke.

Standing up, I shook some warmth into my muscles and bones. There was no sound from the plane, but far below, the animals were up and about, calling each other in strange squawks and yab-berings. I swatted ineffectually at a battalion of hungry midges who thought I looked like breakfast. Clearly, they hadn't read the memo that said they weren't supposed to operate at that eleva-tion.

I zipped up my jacket to my neck and walked stiffly across to descend to the next level. A soft mist had occupied the valley. Parakeets appeared to be skating over it as they flitted from one branch to the next. Once more I had that feeling I was looking down on something primeval. The forest looked beautiful. It always did until you had to walk through it and found the leeches, ticks and biting ants. Or they found you.

I poked my head inside the door of *Myra*. There was a large stack of loot, still in the bent steel boxes, all lashed down as securely as they could be. There appeared to be more of it than I remem-bered from four years back; or perhaps it was just because there was less runway than I liked for such a big load.

Climbing inside, I realised I had better be prepared for what-ever the day had to throw at me. I checked the hidey-hole. The pistol was gone.

After visiting *Myra*'s cockpit and giving her one of my peptalks, I carried on down to the next level, where I could smell coffee. Henri and the others were brewing up in the clearing we had made with the *parangs*. The last few boxes of gold were still there in the undergrowth, awaiting their turn at being hauled up and stowed.

Elsa looked pretty beat, her skin ghostly white. I guessed she hadn't slept. Yin and Yang were some way distant, talking to each other in low voices, eating sticky rice from hollow bamboo tubes. Cowboy was heating the coffee on a small stove. 'Want some?'

I nodded, beating my arms around me to thrash out the damp.

'You get any sleep?' Henri asked.

'Yeah. You?'

'An hour.' I noticed he had the missing pistol in his belt.

'You got the Stableford figures?'

He handed me a scrap of paper while I took the coffee with my other hand and hunkered down onto my haunches. I read the numbers and looked at him.

'Yup,' he confirmed.

'What?' asked Elsa irritably. 'Share it with us, please do.'

I handed it to Cowboy, who also quickly digested what it meant. 'We are already overloaded for the take-off.'

She glanced back at the unstowed boxes, doing calculations of her own. It was in units of hundreds of thousands of dollars. 'We can't be.'

'The figures don't lie,' I said. 'And I want to get off in one piece.'

'He's got a date,' said Cowboy, and I shot him a look. I was in no mood to have my obsessions ridiculed, not when theirs had got us stuck out here. But he'd reminded me about Kitten and I made an effort to put her in a safe little compartment in the back of my mind. I couldn't afford distractions now.

'It's no big deal if it's a million seven or a million nine, is it?' I asked. I could see from the look on her face she suspected a trick. 'Go ahead and ask Cowboy. It's all about altitude, power, weight, cargo, number of people. It's simple math.'

There was a silence, broken only by the rustle of primates in the tree-tops in the forest below us, and their occasional screeches to each other.

276

'Well, we can do something about one of those factors,' she said at last.

We all knew she meant Yin and Yang. Together they must have been worth a box or two.

'It's not that simple,' said Henri.

Something in his voice made me look back to where Yin and Yang were standing. Now, instead of rice tubes, they both held compact MAS-38 submachine guns, of the type used by the French throughout Indo-China. They came with low-powered cartridges, which meant, unlike many SMGs, they were extremely easy to use accurately. If you knew what you were doing.

'Ladies and gentlemen,' said Henri, 'allow me to introduce Mr Kip's associates, Mr Liang and Mr Qu.'

'Everyone stay very still,' said Qu in a perfect, but strangely accented English we hadn't heard before.

Henri stood, believing this didn't refer to him. Of course, he would have arranged all this with them before he stowed away. The negotiations with Elsa and Cowboy for a hundred thou had been just play-acting. He was banking on taking considerably more than that out.

Henri looked appalled as Liang pulled back the bolt on the MAS and swung it towards him. 'That means you too. If you would take the pistol from your belt—'

'Guys, guys. Come on.'

'Do as he says.' Qu began to circle round, aiming to get himself between us and the remaining gold. The barrel of the gun didn't leave Henri, who lifted the Browning pistol out with his thumb and forefinger and flung it down. He looked as if he had just got a mouthful of rancid snail.

'Mr Kip was well aware of what you planned to do with us,' said Liang to Elsa. 'Just a couple of disposable Chinkies, eh?'

'You're Force 136 Invisibles, aren't you?' I said.

Qu laughed. 'Very good.'

My thighs were beginning to ache. I shuffled so I was sitting properly, but with an exaggerated slowness. I could see confusion on Elsa's face and enlightened her as best I could. 'Invisibles were foreign national Chinese who could be trained and infiltrated into the country. Unlike the Big Noses, they would blend in. A lot of Canadians were used, right?'

'Correct,' said Liang.

'And some went native and stayed on, kicking around the East, fallen between two cultures, looking for the main chance. You knew who they were all along, didn't you?' I said to Henri.

'Well, Mr Kip explained the situation while we were talking tyres. We're OK, you and me. They still need us to fly *Myra* out,' Henri said. 'This wasn't a double-cross against you, Lee. Your guns, please?'

'I don't have a gun,' I reminded him, unzipping my jacket a ways. 'I'm the abductee, remember?'

He nodded and turned to Cowboy and Elsa. Henri reckoned Elsa didn't pack her own hardware and concentrated his pistol on Cowboy, who extracted his weapon and threw it down. Cowboy then spat on the floor, about as eloquent as he was going to get. 'So what now?'

'You two lost,' said Henri to them. 'Again. You might be able to walk out of this valley. It's more than the chance you gave to the marines.' He said it as if he actually cared about Patterson and Sorkin, but he wouldn't catch my eye as he spoke

Qu glanced over his shoulder, as if he were making sure the money was still there. 'Actually, it isn't quite that simple,' Qu said, echoing Henri's line. 'Liang here is type-certified on C-47s. We really don't need two pilots.'

'In fact, if push comes to shove, we don't need either of you,' added Liang.

'You think you're good enough?' sneered Henri, realising what they were saying. 'You think you don't need a couple of good pilots. Being certified is one thing . . .'

'Having the moxie to get off a cliff-face, that's another,' completed Cowboy.

'I think we need to talk this through,' I said. Elsa laughed and nobody else seemed to think that was a good idea either. 'Henri?'

He shrugged. 'I'm in.' He turned to the invisibles. 'But we can do this without the guns, guys.'

'Do we look that stupid?' asked Liang.

Henri actually sniggered, which was more brave than I'd be with an MAS pointing at me. 'Who do you think supplied Mr Kip with your guns? Who do you think would be mad enough to give you fully functioning weapons?'

It took a second for it to sink in. Qu frowned, turned to the jungle and squeezed the trigger. Henri sounded so confident, we were all surprised when the weapon kicked up in his hands and the leaves of the nearest plants exploded into dust.

The shock and the noise were all I needed to yank the flare gun that I had lifted from *Myra*'s cockpit out of my jacket. I scrabbled backward like a cockroach, arms held out straight, and pulled the lever with all my might. And missed.

I should have aimed for the body, not the head, but perhaps part of me didn't want to go into the human cannonball business. The propellant made a whooshing sound as it discharged and the white-hot ball of flame streaked towards Liang's head. He moved to one side just in time, but it must have brushed him, because a halo of flame arced around his head. His hair was on fire.

Henri had already made it to his pistol, but Qu was too well-trained to be distracted by the screams from his partner. He let off a burst that threw up dust around Henri's legs. The Frenchman, though, was a better shot than me and Qu, and his rounds went straight into his target's neck.

The next shots came from Cowboy and, mercifully, the

screaming stopped as Liang hit the ground with a thud. The smell, though, had only just begun to attack our nostrils. I tried not to retch. Instead, I took off my jacket and threw it over his upper body to douse the flames. One thing was for sure, I'd never use oil on my hair again.

'Looks like we got room for our extra box of gold,' Henri said softly. His eyes were creased with pain and I could see the glint of tears on his cheeks. He was hurt.

Despite the flowers of white light that streaked my vision every time I blinked, I managed to get the second flare cartridge into the gun, burning my fingers as I did so, and aimed it at Cowboy, who was standing over Henri. I knew what he was thinking. 'Don't,' I warned him. 'You shoot him, you lose us one of our aces.'

'He's a double-crossing—' he began.

'Yeah. It's hardly an exclusive club round here, is it, partner? We need him, Cowboy.'

Henri was looking at his legs. Judging by the spray of blood across his trousers, one of them had a hole in it. Maybe more. He grimaced as a wave of pain washed over him. I knew we had stuff for that in *Myra*, as long as we could stop him bleeding to death.

'Elsa can fix you up,' I said. 'She's had enough practice on me.'

I looked at her and she nodded wearily. She spoke through her hand, trying to block the stench of blood and singed hair. 'Let's get the fuck out of here.'

Thirty-Four

We warmed up a refuelled *Myra* just after the sun had cleared the mountains and burned off the mist, hoping we'd be heading off into air that was still thick and fresh. I had Cowboy in the right-hand seat, with Henri banished to the flight-engineer's slot. He was the luckiest man out of all of us. He had three big gouges in his left leg, one close to his knee, but an intact patella, femur, tibia and fibula and a whole bunch of major blood vessels. It was going to hurt like hell, but he could walk – or limp – and in a few weeks all he'd have were some deep battle scars. It was possible that the bullet that bounced off his knee might give him a little reminder of this day every time he stomped down on his left foot too hard, but that would be a very small price to pay. I made sure Elsa gave him enough dope from the medical kit to numb the pain, but not enough to deaden him completely. We still might need him sharp: I hadn't been bullshitting about that.

Elsa and Cowboy were quiet, taciturn even, shaken by the near-miss with the Invisibles, no doubt, maybe worrying about what lay ahead. I had my own reasons to be extra downcast, though. The previous night, I had found the telltale wrinkles of disaster around the fuselage, near the door. I had looked again in the morning light, and they were still there. The three-point had bent

Myra in the middle. Structurally, the plane was fatally compromised. I was as certain as I could be that she had this one final flight in her, but that was all. The next landing would be it. Whether I came back to these mountains or not, this was *Myra*'s swan song. It was a one-way ticket to the scrapheap now.

All I ask of you, I said to her when nobody was listening, *is just one last go at Sunrise, just once more over that damned ridge. Then we can all go home.*

I gave Myra all the juice I dared, taking her all the way up to War Emergency Power levels, the kind of effort that a C-47 can sustain for no more than a couple of minutes. But this was no time for kid gloves.

She trundled over the stones, slowly at first, picking up speed in far too leisurely a manner. Cowboy and I could both feel the cargo holding us back, and pushed the throttles forward. The chaotic mess of the rockfall rushed towards us, just waiting to sheer off the undercarriage and chew up the props. You can get a C-47 off at minimum airspeed, but usually it stalls and crashes. And we were barely at that minimum.

The rubble was getting closer. 'Lee—'

'Pull with me.'

We heaved together, and *Myra* lifted her skirts and skimmed the boulders. As she left the ground I felt her slow, the controls turning to mush in my hands. I dipped her to port and let her fall over the cliff towards the tangled forest below, giving her all the time she needed to collect her thoughts. *Come on, baby,* I said. Below, the tiny thread of a river was growing into a thick ribbon.

Navy pilots do it all the time, I reminded myself – let the plane drop just after take-off from a carrier, a heart-stopping moment for onlookers but not the pilots, who know she'll respond if they don't panic.

So don't panic, I reminded myself, as *Myra* ignored my gentle coaxings.

The trick is not to do anything too hard or too fast. I tried to suppress the anxiety boiling up inside me. It wouldn't help. She'd come good.

Oblivious to my prayers and my borderline despair, *Myra*'s props carried on thrashing air over the wings, finally giving us lift. The ASI crept up and she handed me control. I pulled her away from the valley and up into the clear sky, watching as the river grew small once more.

I tried to ignore the unfamiliar judders through my arms. Cowboy didn't. 'She all right?' he asked once he dared breathe again.

I nodded and concentrated on getting us through the first thermals of the day and clawing enough altitude to start on Sunrise Point.

After a few minutes, I felt Henri's hand on my shoulder. 'Lee, I'm sorry.'

I shucked it off. 'Don't be. We all do what we think we have to do.'

'All except you, eh, Lee?'

I scowled at him. I'm no angel. I'd like a million dollars or two, but somehow, I never got over the feeling that unearned money has a way of biting your ass. Not that the gold in the back was exactly unearned. Someone deserved it, after all that effort. And how many lives? Patterson and Sorkin, the marines, and Qu and Liang, the Invisibles. Four, that I knew of, five if Mr Kip decided Nelson should go. Pickle, of course, and his crew. I didn't want to add my name to the tally, that was for sure.

Perhaps it was partly my fault, opening my big mouth. I shouldn't have told Cowboy how much the gold was worth in the first place. A million dollars and you can start thinking about your crappy little airline taking on Pan Am.

'Make some coffee, Henri.' I turned to Cowboy. 'I'm going back to check the lashings. You have the aircraft.'

'I have the aircraft,' he replied.

On my way aft I sat next to Elsa. She looked wan all right; I didn't even get the killer smile, and she'd neglected to refresh her lipstick. 'Well, you did it,' I said.

'It's not over yet,' she replied. 'We have to hope Walter Gilbert can work his magic.'

'Where's our stopover – the genuine one? Kunming?'

'Too busy. Too many Americans, too many spooks. We're refuelling at Mengzi. Gilbert has some of his old warlords there, probably still with their Rolexes on. The Commies haven't made any inroads thereabouts. Cowboy will give you the headings once we are over Sunrise.'

'Still ultimately aiming for Macau?'

'Still Macau.'

I went to the cargo and made a great show of checking the web strappings, but in reality I was watching the line around the fuselage at the doorway. Perhaps it was my imagination, but I thought I could see a snaking in the tail as she rode the bumps. I could certainly hear tiny squeaks of stressed aluminium. In one way, it was nice to know Henri wasn't quite as good as he thought he was. On the other hand, I could think of better ways of finding out.

Back at the controls, I took *Myra* up very, very slowly, ostensibly to conserve fuel. I also scanned for weather with an apprehension that gnawed at my stomach. We'd got in without hitting any. Getting out, in this region, without a little rollercoaster action, was almost too much to hope for.

The C-47, in my opinion one of the finest aircraft ever built, can take a hell of a lot of punishment, but there comes a stage where you are asking too much of any plane. If we were to hit a storm, or even bad clear air turbulence, we would have reached that point with *Myra*.

Our luck held, though, and the hard edges of Sunrise Point slid beneath us without incident. Ahead, in an empty sky, populated only by high, lonely wisps of white, were the giant boulders and lower peaks of the last section of the rockpile, and then the rice terraces and hills that would take us past Kunming to refuel at the little base at Mengzi. Then, theoretically, we could hop on to somewhere near the coast. Except Mengzi might be our final destination when *Myra* fell apart on landing. Elsa was right, it wasn't over yet.

I started the descent from 19,000 feet, wincing as a jetstream buffeted us, relieved as we came through it into relative stillness. Cowboy was lost in his own thoughts, and didn't pick up on any tension I was showing.

Henri finally gave me a coffee and we watched China get nearer in the screen. I was letting *Myra* fall down well below 10,000 feet now, so we could all breathe easy. I knew Henri wanted to talk, to break the ice that had formed between us, but I didn't. Not yet. He could explain what had happened back there when we were at a bar, drinking champagne, paying with the proceeds of the cargo.

I shook my head in irritation at the fantasy. The virus of gold fever was beginning to infect even me now.

'How's the leg?' I asked Henri.

'Throbbing.'

'Be thankful you've still got something to throb with.'

I turned to say something to Cowboy when I saw the speck beyond him, closing fast. 'Shit,' I breathed.

He spun his head and said something similar. There was a sleek single-engined plane heading straight for us. I shouted to Henri: 'Get on the radio. See if they are trying to raise us.'

'Americans?'

'Almost certainly. If anyone asks, we are a China Air Transport flight on a mercy mission, remember. With smallpox vaccine from Calcutta.'

The plane flashed over us, high, and I tried to see what make and model it was. It looked worryingly unfamiliar.

'Nothing,' said Henri. 'Not in English.'

'Who is he talking to?' I asked.

'A controller, I think. I don't speak Chinese, remember?'

No, we killed both of the guys we had who did, I thought. I looked behind us, using the big mirror mounted on the fuselage next to me, but all I could see was *Myra*'s tailfin, and beyond that, empty sky.

I looked to my left and the fighter hove into view, close enough for me to see the pilot sitting in his cockpit, which was oddly positioned way back towards the tailplane. Certainly he was close enough for us to see the big red star painted on the side. It was a CCP – Communist – plane, without a doubt. And, I seemed to recall, we'd gone and repainted *Myra* as a Nationalist running-dog lackey.

'What kind of plane is that?' I asked.

'Mig-3, I think,' said Cowboy.

'Fast?'

'Yes. Well, faster than us.'

'Most things are. Well-armed?'

The plane continued to keep pace with us, the pilot looking on impassively.

'I guess. It's not state-of-the-art, though. The Mig is pretty old. Not a Lavochkin.'

We were clutching at straws; that plane would be every bit as good as, say, a P-40. Every bit as deadly, too.

'You said there was no CCP air force,' Henri snapped, his voice full of frustration. 'The fat man told you.'

'You're lookin' at someone's CCP air force,' I said.

'The Commies aren't this far south,' said Cowboy. 'They haven't crossed the Yangtze.'

'Not on the ground.'

I was still losing altitude, but the Mig was locked in place, framed in the side-window, shadowing my every move. Then, without warning, he waggled his wings. I waggled mine back, in a friendly kind of way. He waggled once more. I knew what it meant. *Follow me.*

I kept staring as he made a thumbs-down gesture and waggled once more. I did the same, but my thumb was pointed up.

'What's going on?' yelled Elsa.

'Just playing dumb,' I shouted back. It comes naturally these days, I thought.

The Mig dipped its port wing and peeled off, diving out of sight.

'He must be low on fuel this far from home,' said Cowboy. 'It's a bluff.'

'He had drop tanks,' I replied.

I felt the rounds hit *Myra* before I heard them, the plane twitching as its skin was punctured by high-velocity shells, and there was the crackle of shorting electrical cables. I pushed the nose forward as fast as I dared and started to roll, but *Myra* was no Tomahawk; she was big and lumbering and it was agonisingly slow.

More bullets hit her, and the screen split and the cockpit filled with red mist. I could taste and smell metal and smoke. I kept her rolling, waiting for the tail to fall off, but she stayed in one piece. Elsa screamed.

I couldn't see forward, there were streaks of blood crawling horizontally across my vision. I levelled out and dared to look at Cowboy. He was slumped against his harness in the seat, the back of his skull mostly gone and what was left unbearably grisly. I tried to wipe his blood and brains off the Plexiglas, but it just smeared.

'Here.'

It was Elsa, her forehead discoloured by a fresh bruise. She had removed her jacket. I took it and scraped away what I could of the gore. I tried to ignore her sobbing. Even hard-nosed bitches have to love someone, I guess. 'Get strapped in again,' I snapped at her. 'He'll be coming back round.'

The Mig reappeared like a bad dream, in the opposite window, beyond Cowboy. I was sure he could see what he had done to my co-pilot. The wings wobbled once more. The thumb went down: *follow me*.

We'd been holed, but both engines were still turning, and the controls felt light and responsive. Cowboy might have been the only vital thing he had hit. Another wobble of the wings, and he managed to convey impatience.

I recognised where we were. Close to Yunnanyi. Did he really want me to go down there? Maybe he was thinking of forcing me down to the old dispersal trip, where all this trouble with gold began. That would be ironic. We'd have come full circle. Well, not Cowboy. It was over for him. He, too, had flown his last. I found an old protective mechanism kicking in, the one we used in the AVG and the ATC. Time to wipe Cowboy off the slate and think about saving the living.

'Lee?' It was Henri. I looked at him and he had blood on his arm. 'It's nothing, but she's got a few new ventilation holes in her.'

'She's still flying.'

'I think we'd better go down,' he said.

'Do you? You might be right.' I looked over at our escort and gave a thumbs-up.

Henri clearly expected a fight from me, because he said: 'What are you doing?'

'Hold on and watch.'

The Mig snapped away again, to line up for another run, and I pushed the stick forward on *Myra*. She arced towards the earth, engines screaming, the extra weight of the gold pushing her down fast. I heard a tearing sound from the rear and ignored it. The controls grew light, then heavy once more as she began to vibrate. I kept my eyes off the ASI. I knew at what point she was meant to come apart; best I didn't tell *Myra*. I was pinned back in the seat, and Henri was trying to tell me something. I looked into the rear-view mirror. It was vibrating, but I could just make out the black spot that was our pursuer in it.

I caught *Myra* and brought her back up, fighting her reluctance, easing her out of the headlong rush earthward, and began to weave. He wasn't going to have us easy.

The ground was huge in the windshield now, filling it, and still I took her from side to side in large irregular arcs, all the time keeping my eye on the gash that was the Yunnanyi Valley below. I saw something spark on one of my props. He was firing again.

'Lee—'

I stood her on the right wing and banked her down towards the valley. In the mirror I saw him lock onto my tailplane. The altimeter showed 5000 feet, but the plateau here was at 3000, so we only had 2000 feet before we kissed the earth. I started to pull back, to cut the dive. She didn't respond.

She'd hit a control surface.

'Henri, help me.'

He unbuckled himself and came forward, dragging his bad leg. There was no time to shift Cowboy, so he leaned over and grabbed the column and heaved for all he was worth: 3500 feet and falling. I wiped the sweat from my eyes with my jacket sleeve. We were beneath the ridges of the surrounding hills; we'd be in the valley proper soon. And in the river, if I couldn't get her up.

She started to level, the nose coming up, the tail dropping. I let her dip below the level of the valley sides, and began running above the muddy river. I glimpsed frightened sampan crews staring up as we thundered over their heads.

The controls freed with a groan. Something had unbent itself and the stick was responsive once more.

He was still behind us, though. I saw flashes of light dancing along his wing edges as he fired, felt the impact once more. Yunnanyi and its airfield was a couple of miles ahead. If we made it there, he was finished. But then again, so would we be once we had landed. It would be hard to explain, this cocktail of dead bodies, bullet-holes and gold.

'I'm going to let her drop some more.'

'You're already shaving the trees,' protested Henri. The sound of the engines thrumming off the valley below must have been tremendous as we fell to around 120 feet. I stayed level and true, unable to weave, a sitting duck. I then scanned the valley walls ahead and saw what I was looking for, the ugly grey scars of human activity.

'I have to lose another fifty,' I said.

Henri's voice had lost his firmness. It had just dawned on him what I was doing. 'Lee, pull up.'

I pushed down, just in time.

I saw the cable snap over our head, missing the tailfin by inches. The high-pitched singing as it vibrated in our propwash briefly filled the cockpit and was gone.

I watched in the mirror as the platted metal rope snagged his prop, shearing it off, the disc spinning crazily away. The Mig appeared to hang in the air for a second, before it flipped topsy-turvy and plummeted downwards, spiralling as it went. I tried not to think of the pilot, pinned in by the G-forces, too low to make a parachute jump anyway.

We didn't see the explosion; we were busy forcing *Myra* upward to clear any remaining wire hawsers strung across the valley. They'd been put in back in 1941 as a deterrent to Japanese dive-bombers. And to any Commies who might try and shoot down *Myra*, I added to myself.

Thirty-Five

I circled the rope of black smoke that billowed up from the river bank, hoping the crash hadn't killed any innocent bystanders down there. Henri unstrapped Cowboy and moved him aft. Despite the fresh air streaming through it, the cockpit smelled strongly of his blood, so I tried to breathe through my mouth. That just meant I could taste it, dull and rusty.

Henri thumped down next to me.

'You have the aircraft,' I said.

'I have the aircraft. What's my heading?'

'Just circle to gain us some altitude, and make sure his chums don't find us.'

'Chums?' he asked.

'He'll have friends,' I confirmed, 'who'll come looking for us. They may have us on some kind of portable radar as I speak. He was talking to a controller, remember?'

'Lee?'

'Yes?'

'You have a six-inch gash back there in the fuselage. I think it's growing.'

'Yeah.'

'Was that me?'

I wasn't in a sparing-his-feelings mood. 'Yeah. That was you.'

In the cargo area, Elsa was kneeling over Cowboy's body, stroking his damaged face with its dense spider-web of dark, congealing blood. It would have been a tender and touching moment with anybody else. I couldn't help thinking that sooner or later she'd realise his death meant double share for her. I was going to have to tell her it was a double share of nothing.

First I looked at the slash in the roof. It was a foot long now, and icy air was streaming through it. The fuselage was squeaking real good, too.

I returned to Elsa and forced her to sit up, so I had her full attention. 'That Mig knew we were coming.'

'What?'

'It was waiting for us. I would reckon it was one of several patrolling the main corridors out towards Kunming airspace looking for a C-47 in CAT colours.'

'But why?'

'Walter. I never figured him for a ten per cent man. Not when he could get fifty or more.'

'Walter wouldn't do that.' But her wide eyes told me she wasn't so sure.

'He's done a deal with the Communists. Get us to land or shoot us down, all the same to him. The gold would be recoverable. My guess is he'll cop for fifty per cent. A cool million.'

'Walter? Are you certain?'

'Yes.' I wasn't, but it had the ring of the kind of twisted truth I was getting used to. Even if the Mig was just a lone patrol plane that got lucky – and then unlucky – I was going to play this hand for all it was worth while she was off-balance.

'So he's not waiting for us at Mengzi?'

'I would guess not. We're fucked, Elsa.'

She blinked long and hard, trying to accept that things had turned out bad again. 'What are we going to do?'

'The only thing we can do right now. We're going back over The Hump.' It was then I realised I'd lied to my plane. I had asked her to do one more crossing over the Crawshaw Ridge and Sunrise Point. Now I was going to ask her to do it for one last time again. '*Myra*'s wounded pretty bad, but she should hold. We've got enough fuel to make one of the Assam airfields. Just.'

'Why not go on East?'

'I don't want to land back in Burma, or anywhere in China – not if I am right about Walter. Once he knows we're through, there's no telling what he might do. We can make it to India, Elsa.'

'OK.'

I stood up and gave her the really bad news. 'But only if we dump the gold.'

Thirty-Six

Myra Belle Starr was whistling, a mournful, unsettling sound as the Himalayan air forced its way through the bullet-holes in her fuselage and screen. Still, she gave me 19,000 feet without much of a grumble so I left Henri at the controls and went aft. Elsa and I turfed Cowboy out together, just as we flew over Sunrise Point for the final time. I watched him fall into the valley between ridge one and ridge two, his arms and legs spreadeagled, as if his 'chute was going to open any minute. But, of course, there was no 'chute. The Hump had claimed about 3,000 lives during the CBI campaign. Now it had one late addition.

I checked *Myra*'s condition, running my hand along the jagged line where the icy air was blasting its way in. The fuselage rip was continuing to grow. Back in harness, I realised I was getting a pressure drop on one engine, and I could hear sounds and feel vibrations I didn't like to hear from a powerplant. Something in the port Pratt & Whitney must have taken a hit. I just hoped it wasn't terminal, or at least, not yet.

Elsa understood that the weight of the gold wasn't helping our ability to climb to and clear the high passes. In fact, it would kill us if we didn't get rid of it. The strain on *Myra* was just too much. Henri and I took turns to assist Elsa with throwing the bars out, helping ourselves to gulps of oxygen from the cylinder every few minutes. We worked in silence, each accepting it was better to be alive than rich.

As we came to the last of the boxes, I said, 'One bar each, as before, and two for luck.'

'Luck?'

'For the customs and cops at Chabua. Just in case.'

She laid out five heavy gold ingots on the floor, then tipped the last of her expensive dreams out into the sky. I held on tight in the doorway and watched the ruinous bars tumble into the icy air, the sun glinting on them as they fell, but they quickly disappeared from view.

I slammed the door shut and went back to examine the wound in our skin. It was holding, but I could see the tail section was flapping now. I touched *Myra*'s wound and apologised for all the requests, but asked her to please hold together. If she did, I promised there would never be another *Myra Belle Starr*. She would be the last one, the best one.

She did as she was asked.

Chabua was used only by the British tea companies at that stage, and it was easy to declare an emergency and land. We didn't need to bribe anyone; in fact, the Europeans seemed glad of the company and the tall tale of being jumped by Commie fighters on a routine cargo mission. Henri's bullet wounds made the saga even racier.

After we had secured the plane, and the company doctor had redressed Henri's leg and pumped him full of painkillers and antibiotics, we were taken by the manager to drink at the local planters' club. Henri protested, but I let Elsa keep the extra two bars. I figured she was the one who wanted it the most and who had lost the most. I was too dog-tired to hate her or blame her. I simply wanted her out of my life.

I last saw her talking an impressionable young trainee from the London Tea Exchange into giving her a bed for the night and getting her a ride, or a flight, out the very next day. He seemed happy enough to oblige and I didn't have the heart to disillusion him.

Poor broken-backed *Myra* I would sell to one of the scrap merchants at Dum-Dum. They'd come up and strip her for spares and burn her fuselage into chunks of aluminum. I wouldn't get much. There were lots of surplus planes in India. When nobody was looking, I stroked her one last time. There were few aircraft that had done – that could have done – what she just did. I patted her goodbye and slouched away, feeling mean and ungrateful about what the future held for her.

After we had got rid of the manager and were on our third warm gin and tonic, I asked Henri: 'How much did you save?'

His eyebrows shot up. 'What do you mean?'

I looked into his drug-widened pupils. 'When you were in charge of loading. How much did you put in the hidey-hole?'

He thought about denying it, but after a while he shrugged. 'No more than ten bars,' he said with a grin.

'Felt more like twenty. I had to retrim the plane after we dumped the last of the gold. It felt like there was still something substantial back there.' I was fishing, I could tell no such thing, but he wasn't to know that.

'Of course. Can't fool you, Lee.'

I laughed. I wouldn't have gone that far. 'How are you going to get it out of here?'

'I'll get them to telex me for a Cessna or something similar.' Henri patted his pocket. 'I brought enough dollars to smooth any request.' He took a large gulp of his drink. 'I suppose half of that gold is yours.'

Part of me wanted to say, 'No, forget it.' But I had lost a plane, and an old friend, and felt like I deserved something. 'Wire me my share when you have sold the stuff.'

'I will, Lee. For sure.' I think I believed him. 'Where shall I send it?'

I finished my drink and thought of Laura McGill for what seemed the first time in an age but was, in fact, only twenty-four hours – when Walter had told me where she was these days.

'Berlin,' I said.

Thirty-Seven

I had one last stop in South-East Asia before heading for Europe. At Dum-Dum, I talked my way onto the jump seat of a commercial flight back to Singapore, hired a car and driver at the airport and drove north. Kranji Cemetery is around twenty kilometres outside downtown Singapore. It was about as far north as you can go without hitting Malaya and all its troubles. I parked the car and walked up the grassy slope towards the main memorial.

I passed row after row of tombstones, 4500 of them, the grass and shrubs around each obsessively neat, as if to compensate for the squalor in which the residents died. I stopped and looked back over to the Johor Strait, where the Japanese had crossed, bluffing their way to victory. I guessed we shouldn't be too hard on those who had surrendered to a force that were outnumbered, had no water and only dwindling supplies of ammunition. Who could have predicted that Changi or the death railway would result from the capitulation?

A sudden voice made me jump. 'Hey, mate. You mind doing me a favour?' The speaker was whippet thin and tanned, his body wiry under the ill-fitting suit, his neck lost in the collar of the white shirt. He didn't look like he was used to such formal attire.

'What can I do for you?'

'Take a picture of me with my brother.'

I looked around for a second before I realised he was pointing to one of the burial plots. 'Sure.'

I took the Ilford camera from him and he limped over and slowly knelt next to the tablet of stone, his knees cracking as he did so. He couldn't be more than thirty, but he moved like an old man. 'His name was Billy. They call him William here, but we always called him Billy.'

I read the inscription. *Cpl. William Sexton, Signals 8th Australian Division – buried somewhere near this spot* was the best it could offer.

'You Canadian?' he asked me.

'American.'

'You got someone in here?' There was confusion in his voice. Indians, Chinese, Malays, Australians, Canadians, British and others were at the fall. There were no US units.

I shook my head, feeling like I didn't belong there. 'I hope not. I mean, no, I don't think so. You're Australian?'

'Yup.'

'Were you here too?'

'No. Kokoda.' I knew that was the bloody battle for Papua New Guinea and Port Moresby. He'd been a jungle fighter.

'Billy was in the camp near here. That's how it became a burial ground, but they didn't always mark the graves properly. So when it became official after the war, they only knew approximately where he lay.'

I snapped the picture, did a second for luck and handed the camera back.

'Thanks, mate,' he said.

'I'm sorry,' I found myself saying.

'Why?'

I wasn't sure, but I said, 'Because they don't know where he is exactly.'

'Ah, no worries.' He pointed up the hill. 'It could be worse.' He held out his hand. 'George Sexton.'

'Lee Crane.'

I left him with Billy and carried on up the slope until I reached the memorial, which looked like an aeroplane wing supported by thirteen walls, each of which had row after row of names inscribed on it. On the low, curved stone panel in front of the monument was written these words:

1939–1945

ON THE WALLS OF THIS MEMORIAL ARE RECORDED THE NAMES OF TWENTY-FOUR THOUSAND SOLDIERS AND AIRMEN OF MANY RACES UNITED IN SERVICE TO THE BRITISH CROWN WHO GAVE THEIR LIVES IN MALAYA AND NEIGHBOURING LANDS AND SEAS AND IN THE AIR OVER SOUTHERN AND EASTERN ASIA AND THE PACIFIC BUT TO WHOM THE FORTUNE OF WAR DENIED THE CUSTOMARY RITES ACCORDED TO THEIR COMRADES IN DEATH.

THEY DIED FOR ALL FREE MEN.

Twenty-four thousand, who had no known grave. That's what George had meant. At least he knew roughly where his brother was. For a moment I felt like inscribing Cowboy's name on there, but I didn't. In the end, he had forfeited the right to be in such company.

I moved to the left of the memorial and towards the red-roofed house just outside the cemetery grounds. I slipped through the gate in the fence and into the garden of the bungalow, which was shaded by a lone Casuarina. The verandah was well kept, with pots of hibiscus and bougainvillaea climbing the walls, the paint was fresh, and the wind-chimes made a comforting tinkle in the breeze.

A small plaque identified the house as belonging to the War Graves Service, and the person who lived here as the head gardener at Kranji.

The Englishman who opened the door was about my age, I guessed, but I recognised from the pallor of his loose skin, and the look in his eyes, what he had been through. The Japanese camps left marks for all to see.

'Yes?' he asked. 'Can I help you?'

'I'm sorry to bother you. I'm looking for information about a woman called Kitten Mahindra.'

The peal of laughter from the hallway behind him iced my heart and I became a young, confused boy catapulted into the world of men once more.

'My goodness, I haven't heard that name in such a long time,' said a woman's voice, and she appeared at her husband's shoulder, a pair of glasses on her nose, peering over them at me, trying to place me.

'Lee Crane,' I prompted.

'Lee?' Her face broke into a blazing smile. 'Lee Crane! Bert, put the kettle on. Lee, come in, come in.'

She didn't tell me what happened after she failed to catch the last train out to Lashio. I didn't have to ask. Like her husband, she bore the scars of incarceration, the thin-skinned angularity that years of starvation and deprivation leave you with. It was hard to see in her the ebullient, exotic lover I had taken. Or rather, had taken me. Maybe she couldn't see the young hotshot pilot I had been in the beaten-up figure before her either. But she was in one piece and she could still smile as though she meant it. It was a result, of sorts.

We had tea, biscuits, homemade cake, and I learned more about Bert's war, spent surviving the death railway, than I did about Kitten's – or Christine Talbot as she was now. Cowboy had told me he had accidentally discovered that she was alive, working at the cemetery with her husband. She'd been there all the time I was booting across South-East Asia.

After thirty minutes, Bert left us to say our goodbyes on the doorstep, and when she touched my face I jumped at a flash-memory of other caresses.

'Why did you come, Lee?' she asked.

'I came to make sure you were all right. I came looking for you at Toungoo, you know. I always felt bad about everyone pulling out without you. You should have been on that train.'

'Perhaps. But I wasn't. Lots of people weren't, Lee. There was no train big enough to take us all. I gave my ticket to Sandra. You remember the girl? She deserved her chance. I'm all right, Lee. It'll never be as it was for me or Bert. That's why we are together. We understand each other. You'll find that a lot.'

'I always worried about what had happened to you. Couldn't shake it. I spent a long time asking about Kitten Mahindra.'

'Thank you. But it was the wrong name. Kitten never survived Burma.'

'I suppose.'

'Is there someone else, now?'

'No. Not really. There was a girl . . .'

I told her about Laura and she smiled as I stumbled over the story, unsure of my feelings, both then and now.

'You should have forgotten me. I got in the way, didn't I?'

'No. That's not true—'

'It is. You were always the worrying kind of boy, Lee. When I first met you, I thought you weren't really cut out to be a Flying Tiger. I thought you might not get out of China alive.'

'Is that why you . . . ?' I tried to think of a polite word for what we did on those few precious afternoons.

She put a finger to my lips. 'No, that was because Kitten wanted to.' She winked. 'And Kitten is still glad she did.'

My mouth was dry; I couldn't speak. I managed a weak smile.

'Don't worry. There's nothing else for you to say.' Kitten kissed me on the cheek and told me to go now. I'd done what I had to do, and I had a life to get on with, a woman to find and settle down with. Maybe even Laura, who knew? But, she stressed, my future wasn't in Singapore. Just my past. And it was time to leave that behind.

So I turned and walked back towards the cemetery and the car, my eyes hot with tears, my soul lighter than it had been in a long time.

Glossary

ATC   Air Transport Command. Originally set up to deliver aircraft from the United States to wartime Britain, on 20 June 1942 the Ferrying Command became the Air Transport Command with world-wide responsibility for transporting planes, personnel, material and mail, and for maintaining air-route facilities outside of the USA.

AVG   American Volunteer Group aka the Flying Tigers. Claire Chennault retired from the USAAF as a Major in 1937; he went to China as a flight instructor, but quickly became aviation advisor to Chiang Kai-Shek, with the rank of Colonel. After intensive lobbying in the US during 1941, he was allowed to recruit a group of paid volunteers (mercenaries, in effect) who would assist China in its fight against Japan. The legendary Flying Tigers existed for only eight months – December 1941 to July 1942; during that time, they were credited with 230 air-to-air victories, not counting planes destroyed on the ground. There were around eighty pilots; sixty-seven of them received one or more of the $500 bonus payments for shooting down enemy planes. Eighteen were aces (five or more kills). In that time, twenty-one of the US pilots were lost, although a great many of those deaths were due to accidents and forced landings. On 4 July 1942 the group was rolled into the USAAF's 23rd Fighter Group: the time for privateers was over. Chennault was promoted to General. See *www.danford.net* for more details.

CAMCO — Central Aircraft Manufacturing Company. The umbrella outfit created to supply men and machines to China. Also responsible for salaries and combat bonuses.

CAT — Civil Air Transport, Chennault's airline, was a postwar operation that flew men and equipment for the Nationalists during the Chinese revolution, and later for the CIA in Indo-China.

CNAC — China and the Curtiss-Wright Corporation formed the China National Aviation Corporation (CNAC) in 1929. It became part of ATC operations during the airlift over The Hump, and ceased to exist in 1949.

FANY — First Aid Nursing Yeomanry. A volunteer force that can trace its lineage back to 1907. Members served in World War One as ambulance drivers and field hospital staff; during World War Two they supplied the organisational backbone of

Britain's clandestine operations. More than 600 women worked for SOE in the Far East, as cipher clerks, signallers and fingerprint experts. See *www.64-baker-street.org* for a comprehensive account of FANY's wartime activities.

GOONEY BIRD Nickname for the C-47, the military version of the DC-3, also known by the British as the Dakota.

THE HUMP When Japanese troops invaded Burma they destroyed the road that carried supplies to Chiang Kai-Shek's Nationalist armies (and the AVG). The only way to keep China in the war was to bring supplies by air over the Himalayas from India. There were two routes – the high one from Assam, which took in mountains of up to 24,000 feet – and the low route from Calcutta and Chittagong, which went across Burma and the foothills of the Himalayas, past Japanese fighter bases. After a stuttering start, eventually the airlift was moving a staggering 34,000 tonnes of goods a month. It proved to the USA and Britain that they could later pull the same trick in Berlin.

OSS Office of Strategic Services. Forerunner of the CIA.

SOE Special Operations Executive, the British sabotage and subversion organisation. Its India Mission was known initially by the clumsy acronym GSI (k); the later name of Force 136 has been used throughout.

Acknowledgements

This book was inspired by conversations with Lorna MacAlister and John Debenham–Taylor, both of whom served with SOE in the Far East.

On one occasion, I asked John if he had ever heard of a shady operation called Remorse, which was run out of Kunming. He replied that he not only had heard of it, he knew the two sisters who helped run it, one of whom was Lorna. We met and she told me about socialising with the Flying Tigers, although when she was there this would have been the 23rd Fighter Group, not the original AVG.

The Last Sunrise is not intended as an accurate history of the American Volunteer Group. I have avoided using as characters some of the genuine legendary pilots, such as Greg Boyington, R.T. Smith or Tex Hill; time has been compressed or stretched in places; the Blenheim mission to Chiang Mai was mooted but never actually took place, although the pilot rebellion did. However, the general arc of the Flying Tigers' remarkable story is true. For any and every aspect of the AVG, I would point you at Daniel Ford's book *Flying Tigers* (Smithsonian History of Aviation Series). It is not only a definitive history, it is an unflinching portrait of Claire Chennault, who really was a tactical genius, even if he did know how to bear a grudge and seemed to have mishandled the induction of his men into the USAAF.

Daniel Ford also runs an excellent website, *www.danford.net*, which will answer any questions you have. In addition, he wrote the introduction to the reissue of Olga Greenlaw's *The Lady and the Tigers*, a fascinating first-hand contemporary account of the Flying Tigers. Olga kick-started the idea of Elsa, but not much more: no resemblance whatsoever in their characters is intended.

Sharks Over China by Carl Molesworth (Castle) and *Into the Teeth of the Tiger* by Donald Lopez (Smithsonian) were also very helpful. I also used incidents from the following sources: John Toland, *Flying Tigers*; Robert Lee Scott Jr, *Flying Tiger: Chennault of China*, *God is My Co-Pilot*, and *The Day I Owned the Sky*; Erik Shilling, *Destiny: A Flying Tiger's Rendezvous With Fate*; Frank S. Losonsky, *Flying Tiger: A Crew Chief's Story: The War Diary of an AVG Crew Chief*. There is also much useful information on *www.flyingtigersavg.com*.

For The Hump, I relied heavily on *Flying The Hump* by Otha C. Spencer (Texas A&M University Press), *Born To Fly The Hump* by Dr Carl Grey Constein (1st Books) and *CBI Hump Pilot* by Thomas E. Herrod (through *www.cbihumppilot.com*). All contain incredible stories of endurance and luck (both good and bad) and make you realise what unsung heroes the crews were.

Gold for Chiang Kai-Shek really was transported over The Hump, as were millions of Chinese dollars printed in India; pilots did dream about hijacking the bullion, girls were flown in, live pigs parachuted to troops, whisky pilfered, planes flipped upside down in storms of unbelievable ferocity.

I have downplayed slightly the risk to the pilots from Japanese planes during fine weather: at one point, the Japanese claimed fourteen transports in one day. I have also played very fast and loose with the geography of The Hump, especially Crane's low routing, which would normally have taken him south of Myitkyina, whereas he goes north here. Please do not try to navigate the Himalayas using this book.

I am also grateful to the many DC-3/C-47 pilots who replied to my e-mail enquiries, especially Roland Rogers in California, who also shared his memories of being an Iowa farm-boy, which influenced Crane's background. Ex-RAF and SAA pilot Brian Stableford in South Africa gave me the charts of take-offs and landing distances he had compiled for the DC-3.

Both men kindly read early versions of the book. Any mistakes and exaggerations are, of course, mine alone. C-47s, for instance, rarely had any kind of rearview mirrors. There are also ongoing arguments about the advisability of three-point landings. I have gone with conventional thought, which is that you risk damaging the plane if you try it. The steel hawsers across the valleys were genuine, although only a few rotting anchor-points remain.

The S section of ATC is a fiction, although civilian pilots were employed by the outfit, often drafted in from commercial airlines when they were short. The order asking airlines not to hire ex-AVG men from Chennault is verbatim. For an excellent overview of the situation in China-Burma-India, I thoroughly recommend *The Burma Road* by Donovan Webster (Farrar, Strauss and Giroux), a first-class piece of work.

SOE in the Far East by Charles Cruickshank has details of the use of Chinese-Canadians and the Burma hilltribes, and of the real Operation Remorse, run by one Walter Fletcher, a naturalised Austrian. He really did make £77m (equivalent to at least £2bn today) profit from trading currency and commodities, including diamonds and Swiss watches, and was knighted for his efforts; but again, the real man bears no resemblance, except a physical one, to my invented Walter Gilbert. Remorse was a wonderful success; little surprise that the OSS really were very curious about what was going on and tried to infiltrate the operation. The SOE did describe Fletcher as 'a thug with good commercial contacts'. The accounts, and monthly reports of Operation Remorse are available at the National Archives in Kew, London.

The story of the brawl at the club with the Major and the embroidered knickers in Calcutta was adapted from a tale told to me by Lucy Moore, author of *Maharanis: The Lives and Times of Three Indian Princesses* (Viking), which has many such bizarre and magical moments. I borrowed the name Kitten Mahindra (although the surname is actually Mohendra) from an Indian Princess whom the British journalist and broadcaster Alan Wicker once interviewed. Again, no similarity is intended.

My thanks go to Andrew Chapman and Veronica Huntington for their help with all my travel arrangements; to Tony Champion of the *Magic of the Orient* travel company for advice, and to Yi Ping of Kunming (not to be confused with the dissident Chinese writer and poet) for the descriptions and photographs of the prewar and wartime town. Don't go looking for the city as it was. It is now the regional capital, full of modern buildings, many constructed for a huge Expo, with McDonald's and other familiar chains. Kunming's lake is heavily polluted and silted, all the forests have gone and a controversial plan to dam the Tiger Leaping Gorge will flood some of the stunningly beautiful countryside and displace 100,000 locals. However, there is still much to recommend it and the Yunnan Province as a whole, not least the people and the food.

For Singapore I have to thank Elisha, my guide, also Wai Lin Haythornthwaite, Lee Choon Noi, Giles Tay, Annie Tan, Sandra Leong and the Singapore Tourist Board. I am also grateful to Mr Nedumaran, Curator at The Battle Box, Fort Canning, for his background to the fall of the city. Kranji War Memorial is just as described here and I did meet George there, looking for his brother, but I have changed his name. Special thanks to Loi Zhi Wei for taking me there.

Once again I am indebted to David Miller, Susan d'Arcy, Christine Walker and especially to my editor Martin Fletcher who put me back on track when the various strands of the plot threatened to form a Gordian knot.

Finally, I am very grateful to Lorna MacAlister who shared her experiences of Kunming (including the whistle-blowing end to the parties with the Flying Tigers at their villa), Calcutta and The Hump. Needless to say, she was never involved in a gold-stealing plot in any way. She did get to wear a nice Rolex, though.

Robert Ryan
London